$\frac{5}{8}$°

THE
WORLD
AS IT
IS

OTHER FICTION BY NORMA KLEIN

Novels

Give Me One Good Reason
Coming to Life
Sunshine
Girls Turn Wives
Domestic Arrangements
Wives and Other Women
The Swap
Lovers
American Dreams

Short Stories

Love and Other Euphemisms
Sextet in A Minor

NORMA
KLEIN

THE
WORLD
AS IT
IS

E. P. DUTTON   NEW YORK

PUBLISHER'S NOTE: This novel is a work of fiction.
Names, characters, places, and incidents either are
the product of the author's imagination or are used
fictitiously, and any resemblance to actual persons,
living or dead, events, or locales is entirely coincidental.

Published in the United States by E. P. Dutton,
a division of NAL Penguin Inc.,
2 Park Avenue, New York, N.Y. 10016

Published simultaneously in Canada
by Fitzhenry and Whiteside, Limited, Toronto.

Library of Congress Cataloging-in-Publication Data

Klein, Norma, 1938-
The world as it is / Norma Klein.—1st ed.
p.   cm.
ISBN 0-525-24719-X
I. Title.
PS3561.L35W6   1989   88-22767
813'.54—dc19   CIP

Designed by REM Studio

1 3 5 7 9 10 8 6 4 2

First Edition

To John and Judith Saly

CONTENTS

PART ONE

Side Effects   3
Out of Love   38
Leo the Lion   74

PART TWO

Ward Eight   113
Missing Links   143
A World of Fears   177

PART THREE

Seventh Heaven   215
The Way Out Discovered   237
Do Sharks Ever Sleep?   262

PART FOUR

Tying the Knot   289
Sheltered Lives   300
Socks   311

"Good cheer and mournfulness over lives other than our own, even wholly invented lives—no, especially wholly invented lives—deprive the world as it is of some of the greed it needs to continue to be itself. Sabotage and subversion, then, are this book's objectives. Go, my book, and help destroy the world as it is."

Russell Banks,
CONTINENTAL DRIFT

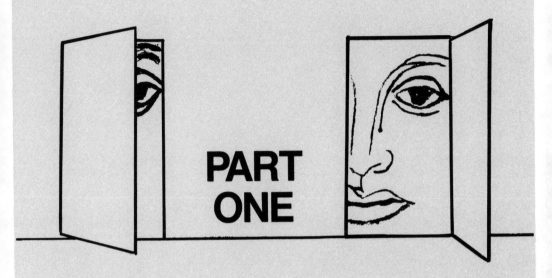

PART
ONE

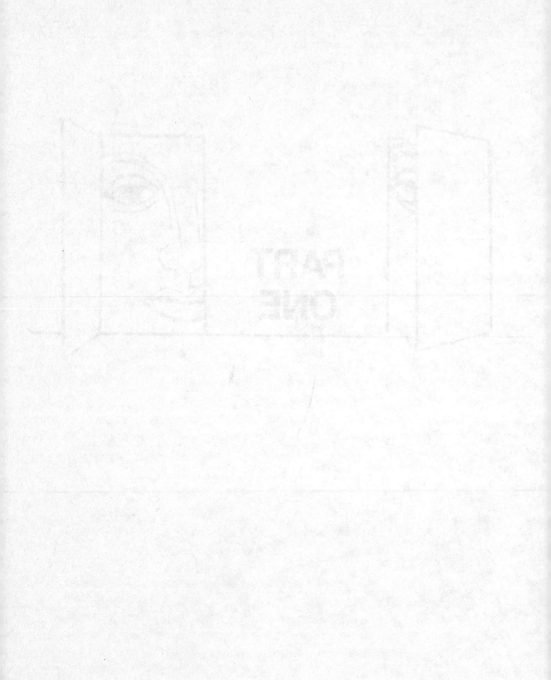

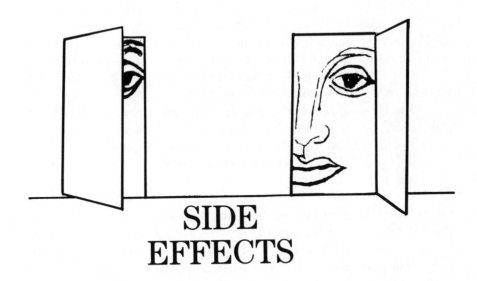

SIDE
EFFECTS

"Congratulations."

Stern started. It took him a moment to make sense of Jonah Welch's remark. Welch was always horsing around in a way that glided effortlessly from good natured joshing to outright needling. Could he have found out already? Hesitating, Stern smiled tightly, waiting for a follow-up.

Welch, one of the third-year residents, was beneath Stern in the hierarchy at the Lionel Nash Institute for Mental Health, but he had a brashness that made that often seem irrelevant. " 'Sydney Sutton to wed Stuart Stern, Psychiatrist,' " he quoted from memory. "Sounds like a tongue twister. My wife says that she'll know the *Times* is liberated when they have a photo of just a man with the heading, 'Dr. So and So Becomes Groom.' " He chuckled. "A harpist, huh? Sounds appealing. Does she strum softly while you're going over casework? Waist-length blonde hair? Blue eyes? Gotta be."

"You've met her," Stern said, immensely, insanely relieved. The wedding announcement had appeared over the weekend. The crisis with his two patients, Blades and Quinones, had been on his mind all weekend long, circumventing any other thoughts, pleasant or unpleasant. "At the Christmas party. You even talked with her."

"Did I?" Welch looked mockingly taken aback. "I forgot a blonde with waist-length hair? Unlike me."

"She wears it up. And if you read the fine print, that's not her profession. She was trained as a harpist, but she's an administrator now, at the Belzone School of Music in Philadelphia."

"So, you'll have a commuter marriage?" Welch pursued. "Sounds tricky."

"We both have excellent jobs . . . Maybe if at some time in the future something opens up here in Manhattan for Sydney or in Philadelphia for me, we'll think of that." He was aware of somehow trying to keep Welch at bay, as though he were an avid dog trying to sniff out scandal, something suspicious, even in the innocuous wedding announcement.

"Listen, I think it sounds great," Welch went on. "I'd love a wife in Philly—San Francisco, even. The day-in day-out thing can get mighty tiring, as you've no doubt heard."

"I've heard," Stern said curtly. What he knew, as did most members of the faculty, was that Welch had occasional flings with the new female nurses. None lasted long enough to keep track of. Stern prided himself on the fact that no one, as far as he was aware, knew about himself and Roxanne. She worked on another unit. They scrupulously were never seen together.

There was always a sense of most of the faculty being, on some level, out for blood, waiting for a colleague to fall, to make some crucial mistake in judgment that could be used to damage his professional career. But sexual peccadillos were accepted, could even add status. Entering the meeting room, Stern glanced across at the table where the associate director of Nash, Milton Grieff, was talking with the director, Mortimer Szell. Grieff had been Stern's training analyst years earlier, his mentor, friend, father surrogate. They had been on the phone all weekend about how to handle the impending crisis. "I'll get you out of it," Grieff reported. "No sweat." When Stern started his analysis, Grieff's only son had just been killed in a motorcycle accident, literally the week before. "I guess you're my son, now," Grieff had said. "Perfect timing." Stern had been taken aback. He knew Grieff was known for his unorthodox variations on

the Freudian method. He had written a well-known and often attacked book on what he called the technique of "sharing." His
contention was that, skillfully used, with calculated effect, the analyst should reveal personal details from his own life in order to bring
out hidden feelings on the part of the patient. You were no less of
an authority figure for seeming to, as he put it in his typically earthy
mode, "let your pants down." The trick was to do it with discretion,
with calculation.

But Stern was never sure, in fact, how much calculation there
was in Grieff's outbursts. He had begun his analysis talking about
his painful relationship with his own father, trying to explain, justify,
possibly understand. "Forget it," Grieff cut in. "It won't work. The
old guy's not alive anymore. Maybe he hated you, had contempt for
you, beat up on you. Who knows why? He had his own problems,
his own sense of failure to deal with. Let it go. You find the father
you want, you make him your father. You let poor old Sollie boy off
the hook." This sounded appealingly easy: no need ever to deal with
oedipal problems, just whisk them out the door or under the rug,
then start afresh. From what Stern heard, Grieff's son, Owen, had
been a troublemaker, on drugs, rebellious, had, despite the fact that
Grieff acquired custody of him after his divorce, run away to live
with his mother. Ironically or maybe not so ironically, he'd sounded
not very different from Stern himself in high school before he pulled
himself together and decided, as Grieff put it, "to make a mensch
of yourself."

Most of their sessions were spent on Stern's problems, either
with his patients or with his own life. But sometimes Grieff would
let out a deep sigh and say, "Kiddo, this is baby stuff. These aren't
problems. These are—what can I say?—you don't even know yet.
Let me tell you. The waves are just up to your big toes, your ankles,
maybe." Then he would spend thirty minutes going on about his
own failed marriage, what a cold, spoiled bitch his Danish wife had
been, what a relief it was that her drinking problem had been severe
enough for Grieff to get custody. Stern was in his early thirties
then—he'd made a detour after college into neurobiological research and hadn't entered medical school until he was twenty-nine.
When he complained about his sex life, the poor quality of women
who seemed available, Grieff would guffaw. "Look, what're you
going to do? Move to the moon? That's what there is. What you see
is what you get. Pick someone who doesn't deball you before you
sit down for the first course and you're ahead of the game." He was

wary of Roxanne from the first session in which Stern described her. "Psychiatric nurses are the pits. Those Jewish girls who wanted to be doctors and didn't make it, seeing shrinks since they were born—forget that. You want peace and quiet. Marry a deaf mute. Seriously."

When Stern met Sydney through mutual friends and she went through several months of holding him at bay sexually, surprisingly Grieff was approving. "You've got the real stuff. She's playing you. Let her. Play her back. You've got her, just reel her in slowly. Fuck the foxy one if you're going crazy. It's a perfect combo." Stern finally did become sexually involved with Sydney. She allowed him to undress, admire, and "take" her (the event had that quality, down to the slow, careful way she released her long hair, held in place by tortoiseshell combs.) Grieff was delighted. He was even delighted at her lack of orgasms, at the fact that she had once, with gentle plaintiveness, said that sex often seemed to her like "hard physical labor." "Perfect!" Grieff yelled. "You hit the jackpot. When it happens, she'll adore you. When it doesn't, she'll blame herself. The hot numbers drive you nuts, tear you apart. They're insatiable, a menace. Frankly—this is my own theory, but it's true—I think Freud gave up sex at forty because he was fucked to the teeth by his sister-in-law and he pooped out. Figured sublimation was worth the whole bean bag."

As opposed to his analyst, Stern's real father, a harrassed, obsessive man, failing in one small business after another, had seemed caught in an emotional treadmill Stern could never understand. At home he was silent, brooding, checking his frequently sky-rocketing blood pressure. His occasional outbursts of violent rage terrified Stern. His mother's way of dealing with them was to hide, to be as innocuous and submissive as possible. She tried to train Stern in this method: don't talk back, don't get him upset, keep away from him. Sometimes it seemed to work. Other times their feigned nonchalance appeared to provoke him either to verbal abuse or, occasionally, physical violence. When the latter occurred, Stern's mother would shield him. "Kill *me,* kill *me,*" she would shriek. "Don't touch *him!*"

The morning after, everyone tiptoed around, ashamed. There were no apologies, no explanations. "He can't help it," his mother would say. "It's his blood pressure. It's driving him crazy." No matter how bad things were, she always contrasted what was to some ultimate series of disasters: "At least we're still alive." "Thank

God he hasn't lost all our money." "He never *really* tries to hurt us."

Maybe that was why Grieff's earthy, expansiveness appealed to Stern. Even Grieff's looks—his pockmarked, fleshy nose, double chin, rumpled suits, cigarette ash dusting his trousers—seemed to say: Here I am, like it or lump it. Now the analysis was over, though Stern went back at times if a crisis arose. Once ensconced in his job at Nash, which had been acquired with Grieff's influence, they had mainly consulted over management problems, patients. It wasn't until the past weekend that anything had arisen that seemed a serious threat to Stern's career.

There was no way this could be taken lightly. Stern had prescribed a perfectly routine drug, Thorazine, for two patients, a Puerto Rican woman who was a dressmaker and a black man who had once been a legal aide, but was disintegrating due to alcoholism. The past weekend the temperature rose to over ninety, the air-conditioning system failed to function (this was not infrequent), and it turned out that a possible, though rare, side effect of Thorazine in excessive heat was death: hyperpyrexia. By Sunday morning Blades was in a coma—by mid-afternoon he was dead. Quinones had rallied; it was still not clear whether there would be brain damage.

Grieff loved crises, he fed off them. The more dangerous, the more exciting. He had gotten himself out of impossible situations. Once when a group of residents had demanded his resignation, he had managed to turn the case completely around and make it seem like a personal triumph. "I'm a magician," he would smile wryly, "what can I tell you?"

Stern sat down, crossing his legs stiffly. His hands were icy. Normally they would have started the meeting, discussing new admissions, any unusual events on the ward over the weekend. Instead Grieff looked up and said, "Any of you heard about Blades?"

Of the twenty-five people in the room—doctors, residents, nurses—only five raised their hands. "Okay. Well, here's the story. I want all of us to be clear about what happened because there's a chance the press may come sniffing around and we need to have our facts clear. As we know, they love scandal. Blades had an impaired liver due to drinking. He was on a standard dose of Thorazine, one hundred milligrams a day. Due to unforeseen circumstances, the drug may have reacted unfortunately with the abnormally high temperatures we experienced over the weekend. To be brief, he lost consciousness and died."

Sharon Wishnick raised her hand. A tiny woman in her thirties with fluffy blonde hair and a squeaky voice, she was head of outpatient services. "Who was the attending physician?"

"Dr. Stern . . . But, as I say, the doses used on Blades were routine. We're using them all over the hospital, all the time."

"Is it described in the literature as being inadvisable to use doses like that under these circumstances?" Dr. Wishnick persisted.

Grieff leaned forward. "The circumstances? It's April. How many times a year or even a decade do we get two ninety degree days in April? No one could have foreseen it."

Bernard Menschel, the director of couples therapy, stood up. "But by Saturday it was clear we were in the middle of a freak heat wave, it was on every radio and TV weather program. Didn't Dr. Stern think to reduce or even stop the dose?"

"Dr. Stern was not in attendance on Saturday. I believe he tried to call in and was unsuccessful in reaching Nurse Kefaldis." That, as he had announced on the phone, was part of Grieff's game plan. If it got serious, if the blame started to descend on Stern, it was to be shifted to the attending nurse who had a reputation for being a little spacey; she was a cocaine addict. The fact was, Stern had never tried to call her, but there would be no proof of that, other than her word.

Menschel continued. "As I heard it, *two* patients were affected. Is that correct?"

"It's partially correct. Ms. Quinones had a bad patch over the weekend but appears to be a great deal better."

Menschel squinted, his nose sniffing a bad odor. "And she was on the same pill, same dosage?"

"I believe she was." Grief looked over at Stern. "A lower dose, wasn't it?"

It was the same dose, 400 milligrams, but Stern, who prayed he could alter his records, said, "Yes."

Menschel was short, no taller than Grieff, but wiry and intent, almost bald. "What are we to say when the press comes around, if they do? Do we tell them what we know? That there's been a possible case of malpractice or do we close ranks? I'm not quite clear what you're forcing on us, Dr. Grieff."

"Forcing?" Grieff looked taken aback. "I wasn't aware any forcing was going on. Is that the way everyone here sees it?" He looked around the room.

Sharon Wishnick cleared her throat. "We just want to know

what happened, and why." She cast a sympathetic glance at Stern. "Something like this could happen to any of us. We want to know how to deal with it."

"Something like what, Dr. Wishnick?" Menschel said. "Not bothering to read the fine print on the medicine we prescribe? Playing with patients' lives?"

She flushed. "We're all human," she said nervously. "It could happen to any of us."

"It could not!" Menschel shouted. "I don't know about Blades's family, but frankly, as it's been described, this man was murdered, under our auspices. If this isn't malpractice, what the fuck is?"

Stern's insides were tightly coiled. His toes were clenched inside his shoes. Luckily, Menschel's tirade was directed at Grieff, who merely smiled. "Why don't we let lawyers attend to their business while we attend to ours? At the moment there is no malpractice threat. I think Dr. Wishnick's point is well taken. Before we go throwing stones, let's examine our own consciences and realize that very few of us, even you, Dr. Menschel, have time to read about every possible side effect, when the chances of some of these ever taking place are, quite literally, one in a million. If we did, we might be experts on side effects, while our patients languished."

Menschel snorted. "They'd rather languish than die, I would imagine."

"The cause of death is no single thing, Dr. Menschel," Grieff said curtly. "The weather, the state of Mr. Blades's liver . . . But as I say, we, Dr. Szell and myself, are concerned first and foremost with keeping the staff here appraised of all developments, but we also have a clinic to run, new patients to admit, and so forth. Accusations serve no purpose. We are here as a medical team, a hopefully smooth-working unit. Dr. Stern's presence among us has added greatly to the prestige Nash enjoys. His integrity is proven by the fact that the moment he was aware anything was amiss, he contacted me and wanted precisely the full discussion which is now taking place."

Stern saw Menschel glance his way with an expression of barely disguised cynicism. Sharks circling. *Protect me. Get me out of this. I need my career. I can't handle something like this, not now, not when things seemed to be going so well.*

The rest of the meeting was about other matters. Stern tried, with only partial success, to subdue his terror. He had seen other residents, even associates, made scapegoats for troubles at the institute. One doctor was always easy to sacrifice if a body was needed. It wasn't clear yet that one would be, and Grieff's backup plan of shifting blame onto Nurse Kefaldis could work in that event. Stern had two fears, the greater being for his job and, even more important, his ultimate professional reputation. Some doctors had left Nash scarred for life, unable to get staff positions anywhere, lacking any future referrals from colleagues. The other, lesser, but still keen fear was Sydney. She would only find out about this if it got into the *Times.* She loathed scandal.

Stern had two patients scheduled after the meeting. Luckily, Grieff had taught him a technique for what he called "the monster days." Say nothing except to repeat, about every five to ten minutes, exactly what the patient had said in the form of a question. "Sure, one way it's passing the buck, but another way it's Talmudic, you're turning them back on themselves. And it gives you time to collect yourself, which you need. Who's to know?"

The first patient, Luise Browner, was a nurse at the institute. She had a lower rank than Roxanne; they weren't friends. Still, the fact that both of them had suffered breakdowns in the past made Stern profoundly uneasy. On the other hand, Luise was due to be dismissed as a patient from Nash the following week. It wouldn't be difficult to ease his way through the session without really giving what she said much attention.

His mind was still at the meeting, seeing Menschel's contemptuous face, Szell's steely reserve, Grieff's impish game playing. Luise's voice was like static on a radio. He heard words, phrases, but took nothing in, until she said, "God, it got me so spooked! Because she's been fine for exactly five years, the exact time *I've* been fine. And when I heard she took an overdose, I thought—shit. It can happen again. You fight it off, you get over it and whammo—again!"

" 'It' can happen again?" Stern repeated, shaken. He had not seen Roxanne for a month but, at their last meeting, she had seemed fine, resigned to their mutual decision to see less of each other.

She sucked in her breath. "You think you've got it together and then you flip. I know you don't believe in this spiritual stuff, but Roxy has the same birthday I do. April eighteenth. We're both Aries. And she grew up in Scarsdale, just like I did. A few years ago when I cut my hair she even cut hers in the same style, just by a coincidence. She used to wear it long, down to her waist, just like

I did, and then one day I figured what the hell, I'll take the plunge, and I had it cut. I go in and there's Roxy, and her hair's the same length. After she'd worn it to her waist all her life, since second grade!"

Stern remembered that day, his own shock. He loved Roxanne's beautiful long auburn hair, which seemed to shift from dark brown to red to almost black, depending on the light. She had strangely pale skin for a brunette and the sight of her long hair against her skin, twining across her breasts, was achingly beautiful. He never knew if she'd cut her hair to punish him; it was a month after he'd met Sydney. She claimed no, just felt it was time for a change. "You see all of my actions as connected to you," she had said playfully. "Can't I be a free agent, ever?"

"You're concerned because she's in danger?" he said carefully, finding it hard to breathe.

"No, she's okay," Luise said. She was in her thirties, like Roxanne, still wore her brown hair short, but had a boyish rather than sensual appeal. "I knew she was having problems. Maybe I should have said something, but who to?"

"To me?" Stern suggested.

Luise glanced at him, then away. *She doesn't know,* Stern thought. "I didn't want to hack over more depressing stuff, you know what I mean? And I figured she might come out of it. She's real moody."

"You identified with that?"

"Yeah, well not so much with her character, but with the fact that she's a nurse, she knows all this stuff, bookwise, and yet what good did it do her? Plus, man trouble. She's beautiful, better looking than me, and what does it get her? She gets shat on just like I do. She's a feminist, and who does she pick to fall in love with? Some schmuck!"

It could be she did know and was toying with him. Stern remembered one of Grieff's maxims: *If you're not feeling paranoid, it's because you're not looking behind you.* Roxanne had always said she would die rather than tell anyone at Nash about their relationship. But here she had risked death, so perhaps that wouldn't seem to matter anymore. She had seen the wedding announcement. It had to be that. The timing was too perfect. "You feel most men are trouble?" he asked.

Luise frowned. "I don't know what I believe . . . But, like I say, Roxy evidently loved this guy, maybe against her will, against her better judgment. It was a long-term thing, not just a fly-by-night. He strung her along. But what gets me is she *knew,* she *knew* that's what he was doing, but she didn't have the guts to get out. She waited for him to shaft her . . . Why? Why do women *always* do that?''

"How did he 'shaft' her, as you so gracefully put it?" Stern asked. His heart was thumping in a loud, pounding rhythm which forced him to open his mouth to breathe evenly.

"I guess he deserted her for some other woman." Luise looked at him. "He was playing the two of them all along, and when the time came, he ditched Roxy."

Stern looked out the window, at the beautiful spring day, the blue sky. "Of course, you don't know the actual circumstances. Perhaps she was more ambivalent about him than she let on."

When he turned back to look at Luise, she was staring at the portrait over his bookshelf. Roxanne had painted it; her hobby was portrait painting. It showed him sitting at his desk, staring straight at the viewer. She hadn't signed it. If anyone asked, he always said it was painted by a college roommate to whom he'd given the apocryphal name, Dion Curry.

"I hope so," she said. "She seemed real upset to me."

"But her fate needn't be yours necessarily," Stern said, trying to preserve a façade of calm.

She gazed at him. "I think it will."

Stern stood up. "Well, this appears to be it . . . You'll have an appointment with Dr. Wishnick to set up your out-patient threatment?"

Luise gleefully snapped up that mistake. *"Threat*ment? Is that what it is? More of what I've gotten in here? More threats?"

Let it slide by. He held out his hand to shake hers, but she had turned and left the room.

Mentally Stern slept through his next session. Wolcott Fish, the head of a rope factory in upstate New York, had been fine for ten years on lithium. Last month he'd gone off it and, in the week since he'd been at Nash, had been high as a kite. At times it was hard to understand him, not because what he was saying made no sense, but because he talked a mile a minute, swallowing words, exclaiming so loudly and frequently that it had the effect of a monotone. He barely required a response, though usually Stern tried to cut in to organize the material. This time he just let him babble on uninterrupted, relieved at the break. Psychotics or neurotics undergoing a psychotic break were sometimes easier to handle than less disturbed neurotics like Luise who could have an uncanny perceptiveness. Stern still was not positive she didn't know he was the man with whom Roxanne had been involved.

Finally, mercifully, it was lunchtime. He strolled down the hall to his office. On the way a young Eurasian nurse, Yvonne Chen, passed by with a tray of medications, and smiled at him. "I was so pleased to hear of your engagement, Dr. Stern," she said in what seemed like a genuinely pleased voice. "When will the wedding be?"

For a moment his mind went blank. *Just say anything. It doesn't matter.* "September," he stammered.

"That's when my wedding was," she said. "It's a lovely month, especially for a honeymoon. Not so hot." She had a lovely smile, entrancing, not openly seductive, but feminine. "Yes, I'm . . . I'm looking forward to it."

"Your wife-to-be is a musician?"

"Well, she . . . Yes. Not a doctor, not a nurse." *Why did he say that?*

Yvonne looked understanding. "My husband is in construction. He says, 'We need separate worlds.' "

"Exactly." Separate worlds. Philadelphia. Sydney's crisp efficiency at her work, her modulated, soft-spoken family—none of whom had ever been in therapy—her living room with its blue and white English plates, rosewood table. She actually had a hope chest, something he'd only read about in English novels, a large wooden one filled with family lace tablecloths, hand-embroidered napkins. There was a silver pattern that had been in the family for generations; everyone used it. Only her younger brother, who was in training for the foreign service, was probably about to marry a woman who, to the family's horror, preferred stainless steel and even used paper plates for dinner parties. Breck's baby shampoo for Sydney's hair, washed twice a week, dried carefully, so unlike Roxanne's thick, tangled curly mass, which at times could look like a three-dimensional sculpture. Sydney's eyebrows were almost invisible, pale lines which she only darkened for social occasions. In profile, bent over her work, she resembled a Flemish drawing: long, perfectly formed nose, severe mouth, pale, thoughtful eyes.

He ordered a sandwich and a Coke from the institute cafeteria, then locked his office door and took out a joint from a supply he kept in his bottom drawer. He indulged in cocaine socially, never with Sydney, but found it made his responses too erratic at work. Today, of all days, that was the last thing he needed. Luckily, now that he was older, grass worked much faster and more potently for him. Either it really was stronger or his responses had been heightened by less frequent use. He didn't like to smoke in his office for fear the smell might be noticed, but today the weather was still warm; he opened the window and carefully blew the smoke out as he exhaled. In fifteen minutes, by the time there was a knock on the door to indicate his lunch had arrived, he was floating, perfectly spaced out, still able to think and function with that wonderful sense that it was all happening somewhere far away, to someone he barely knew.

The last time Roxanne had made a suicide attempt, Grieff, with whom he was still in analysis, had told him to use it as an excuse to break off the relationship. "She's fucking you over, Bonzo. Look, I wrote a book on this. *Suicide as Manipulation.* Didn't you read it? I got on the 'Today' show. She's killing you—you're the target. Do you want to get in bed with a killer?"

"She loves me," Stern had stammered. "She did it out of love. She's jealous of Sydney. She found her photo and a letter. She's afraid she's losing me."

"Sure she is. She's no dumbo. She's not like you. Of course she's losing you! Here I've been yakking my head off for five years and some of it has started to sink in. You're listening to me, for a change. Finally she got the point." He pointed to his head. "Drop her. Do yourself a favor. Life at Nash has enough *tsuris.* Don't toss your balls into the washing machine."

It seemed to Stern he *had* tried to break it off then. He had been frank with Roxanne once she recovered. He told her he could never marry her, that there was a chance he might marry Sydney. That wasn't equivocating. Nothing was definite. He still couldn't quite imagine a life with Sydney, and she, which was one of her appeals, had had no desire, at thirty, to rush into marriage; she saw nothing wrong with a five-year period of thinking it over. "So, what do you need *me* for?" Roxanne had asked desperately. "What's the point in going on?"

He could have said, "Sex," but it would not have been accurate. He felt he couldn't live without Roxanne's volatile intensity. Sex was just the metaphor; it went beyond that. He wanted to have his cake and eat it too—or eat two cakes, maybe. Greed. Snow White and Rose Red. Many men needed those two extremes. Surely, as an unmarried man, he was entitled.

If he had listened to Grieff, he wouldn't be here, thinking these thoughts. Maybe at some subliminal level the overdose for Blades and Quinones had been tied in. *Maybe I knew Roxanne would try it. I know she reads the* Times. *Am I trying to do myself in, play games with my career and my life, get so close to the edge there's a real chance I'll fall off?* That was what Roxanne had been doing all her life. She understood his self-destructiveness because in that regard she was his twin, the deadly kindred spirit you pray to meet and dread to meet, the one who understands everything without needing to ask. He had fled from that closeness dozens of times in the decade since he'd met her and then had been drawn back, just as he'd fled drugs after they'd almost gotten him pitched from medical school, but remained always aware of their appeal, always knew exactly who on the staff had the same problem, could see it miles away. Grieff was a successful version of that person; he had a high tolerance for vodka, but an even higher tolerance for danger and playing with dynamite. Stern saw himself in the middle, struggling with it, and Roxanne as the failure, throwing her life away.

He could pick up the phone and call information, find out what ward she was on, find out what her condition was. *Why? Luise said she was okay. Cut the cord.* Sitting there he imagined her finally succeeding at suicide, no longer a part of his life. The thought horrified him. He leapt to his feet. This was the flip side to grass. It distanced you, but it also brought thoughts like these to the fore. How would he get through the day?

The persona technique. Another of Grieff's specialties. On bad days pick someone on the staff who you know for a fact admires you unequivocally and force yourself to act as though you were that person. Stern picked Yvonne. In her eyes he was an authority figure, but a kindly and thoughtful one, who always remembered to ask about her husband who recently had dialysis for a kidney condition. She knew nothing of Roxanne, his weakness for drugs, his overly close relationship with Grieff. *Until six today you will act as though you are that person: the good doctor.*

By six Quinones was not only out of danger, but seemed to be responding normally to questions. Grieff, who said he would meet

Stern at his house for an emergency session, suggested he look in on her. She was lying in bed, her eyes dilated, but blurry.

"I gather you've had quite an ordeal, Mrs. Quinones?"

"I fainted . . . I couldn't breathe." It was evidently still hard for her to speak.

"You've pulled through, that's the main thing. All your vital signs seem excellent. How's your appetite?"

She shrugged.

"Eat a little, for me. We'll have you up and around in no time."

Mrs. Quinones smiled faintly and nodded.

Stern sighed. He turned to go down the hall and out the door, when suddenly someone grabbed his arm. It was Leroy Demos, a Sixties radical, a patient who had been at Nash eighteen months, bearded, whimsical with large light green, startling eyes. "Hey, Doc, who died? Did someone die?"

Stern recoiled, terrified. He had been physically attacked several times by patients and it always unnerved him. "I'm on my way out," he stammered.

"Hey, man, someone died. Did you hear? They're killing off the patients. Blades, he kicked off. Quinones almost kicked off. What do you think?"

"Please," Stern said. "Discuss this with your doctor. I have an appointment."

But Demos barred his way. "Who's next, huh? How does it go? Is it alphabetical? Ethnic groups first? Blades was black, Quinones is Puerto Rican. Thank God I'm pure Irish. You go for the Jews next, right? Or no, most of you are Jews. Who's next? Lemme in on it." He was doing a kind of dance in front of Stern, hopping back and forth, his eyes weirdly bright.

Stern signaled to Nurse Kefaldis who was sitting in her office, writing. She came rushing out. Almost six feet tall, angular, with long apelike arms, two years ago she had had a brush with cancer and had bought a wig to conceal her temporary lack of hair. Although she was fine now, she had kept the wig, a bright orange cap of curls, totally unlike her grey-brown natural hair, which used to hang limply to her shoulders. "I'm having some problems here," Stern said. "I have to go. Please call someone if you need help."

Demos backed off. "Hey, Doc, no sweat . . . You're clean, you're swell. I love you. You know that? I really do."

"Does he need a shot?" Kefaldis asked. Her eyes had the vacant look they got when she'd taken cocaine before reporting to work.

"Whatever." Stern rushed past the two of them and made it to the exit.

Grieff's office was in Manhattan, forty minutes from Nash on a quiet street in the East Seventies.

"So!" Grieff was leaning straight back in his recliner, almost horizontal, smoking one of the cigars he allowed himself at the end of the day. "The *Times* is in on it. They're sending someone around tomorrow. But no problem. Blades has no living relatives in this country—he's Jamaican. And Quinones lives with her eighty-year-old mother who doesn't know from shit. So you're covered. Just doctor your charts; cut the dosage. If Kefaldis questions it, just insist. She knows she's zonked half the time. She won't squeal."

Stern stared at him, still shaken by the way Demos had charged at him. "I pray you're right," he said. "Everything could go down the tubes for me otherwise. I've been petrified."

Grieff grinned; his childlike smile seemed to stretch his mouth almost ear to ear, like a Sesame Street puppet. "Relax. I saved your life, Bonzo. How do you like that? Am I there for you or not?"

Stern just nodded. Suddenly the day had caught up with him, not by degrees, but in one fell swoop. He felt himself disintegrating.

Grieff was staring at him. "Hey, hey, what's up, kid? Tell Daddy. That was a beautiful wedding announcement, by the way. I meant to mention it, but with all this megillah, I didn't have time. A beauty."

Stern looked at the rug. "It's about that," he said.

"How? What gives?"

Wanting to get it over with quickly, Stern said, "Roxanne made another suicide attempt. Luise Browner, one of my patients who used to work on Roxanne's ward, told me today. She even knew the cause—man trouble, a guy who Roxanne told her was stringing her along. A schmuck," he finished painfully.

"Is she dead or alive?"

"Alive . . . I gathered the overdose wasn't that serious."

"So, what's your problem? That she blabbed? That it'll get back to someone who could hurt you? You know, kiddo, as I recall, five years ago I told you drop her—she'll get you into trouble, she's out for blood. Did you listen, huh? Did you?"

Stern cleared his throat. "Could you open the window? The smoke is getting to me."

Grieff shot him an amused glance, but lumbered out of the

chair and with an ironical gesture threw the window open. "Who else did she tell it was you?"

"She didn't tell anyone. Even Luise only knew it was a man, didn't even know it was a doctor. No, it's not that."

Grieff exhaled some cigar smoke, turning with exaggerated courtesy to the open window. "What, then?"

"She must have seen the wedding announcement. That's what triggered it."

"Sure, stands to reason. What'd you expect?"

"But I . . . I'd told her, I didn't give the date, but I'd told her it was going to happen." His eyes fixed on Grieff's glass of straight vodka, tempted by the effect he knew it would have. He hated scotch and gin; only vodka worked, apart from grass.

Grieff smiled. "She didn't believe you. Why should she? For five years, it's back, forth, love you, love you not. She thought she had a chance. She knows you. She knows you're self-destructive. Look, kid, I thought she had a chance myself, and it scared me shitless. It was a flip of the coin, but you flipped right. Common sense came to the rescue, amazingly."

Despite the open window, Stern had the feeling there was not enough air in the room. There seemed to be a stench, either from Grieff or his furniture. He started breathing shallowly through his nose. "I . . . I don't know if I can give her up," he gasped.

"Who? Which one?"

"Roxanne. When I heard about her, I . . . I almost fainted. What if she had died? What if I had caused her death?"

Grieff looked pained. "Bonzo, sweetie, who causes whose death? Who? No one! If she wants to die, one day she'll die. We all make it sooner or later. Some sooner, some later." He pointed to his cigar and the vodka glass. "This'll get me eventually, but so? Hey, by the way, you look like you could use a drink. Name your poison."

"I smoked some grass at lunch," Stern said. "I don't want this to be a habit again."

"Why not? How else do you think anyone at *Nash* manages to function? Wishbone pops Valium like there's no tomorrow; Szell claims he needs morphine for his chest contractions. Show me a shrink who can get through a day without artificial stimulants, and I'll show you someone who died and they didn't have time to bury."

Suddenly Stern leapt to his feet. "I'm terrified!" he cried.

"What of? Your job? You're safe as roses. I told you. What's wrong with you? Get a hearing aid."

Stern started pacing up and down the floor. "I'm afraid Roxanne will die, that they'll let her out and she'll make another attempt."

"And?"

"How can I stand by and let that happen? I've loved her for five years! Doesn't she deserve more than that?"

"No!" Grieff shouted. "She deserves nothing. She deserves what she has—a safe bed in a decent hospital and probably a decent job when she recovers. Who says she needs to feed off a good Jewish doctor? Is she a man-eating plant? Are you plant food?"

"She loved me!" Stern shouted, trembling. "A thousand times more than Sydney ever will, or ever can."

"Please. Spare me. Love? You call that love? That woman *savaged* you. Life with her would've been hell on earth. *You* know that. Come on. Is everything I've said for fifteen years going straight out the window? If that's love, I'm a twelve-armed octopus. You had a good thing in bed. She knew how to turn you on. Call a fucking spade a spade. Love!" He snorted derisively.

Stern tried to calm down. "It was more than that. You're oversimplifying, maybe to make me feel better. I'd rather you didn't."

Grieff's cigar had burned down to almost the end, but he pointed to it. "Look, I love cigars, okay? Am I going to marry one? I love vodka. Do I drink like a fish from morning till night? No! Restraint, common sense. We all have drives. Deny them and we die. Whoever said a word about monogamy? From what you've said about the Philadelphia filly, she won't care, won't even notice. Once a month will exhaust her. You have nurses on this unit alone that'll last you till you're sixty. By then, who knows? You may figure, why bother?"

"I can't live like that," Stern said. "I want to decide once and for all. I *want* to give Roxanne up, for her sake as well as mine. I had to sit on myself all day. I wanted *desperately* to go and see her. It was all I could think about."

"Why today?"

Stern was puzzled. "What do you mean, 'why today?' I just found out about her attempt today."

"Sure, but how about the tiny obscure matter of your job being in serious danger? How come it's then, exactly when you should be focusing all your energies on how to get through this, that you want to jeopardize everything to run to the bedside of a suicidal ex-girlfriend?"

Stern sat down. He was breathing more easily. "You think it was self-destructive?" He half smiled.

Grieff looked at him as if to say: What else?

"But what if it weren't for all this? What if this clears up? Can I go see her then?"

"Bonzo, you're a big boy. Sure you can go. You can also put your head in a meat grinder or expose yourself on rounds tomorrow. If you want to act stupid, world-class stupid, your possibilities are infinite."

Stern closed his eyes. He remained silent for a long time. "Your advice, then, is ignore the whole thing permanently? Even if, say, she were to call me—"

"Change your number. Get an unlisted one."

"What if she comes to my office? Throws a scene?"

"You never saw her before. Call Kefaldis and have her booted. Have her fired. You want me to have her fired? Say it and it's as good as done."

"No."

"Transferred? Another job, just as good, somewhere else? The suicide attempt is a perfect excuse."

Stern recoiled. "No, that's pointlessly cruel."

"Just a suggestion." Grieff's expression consummated irony.

"What if she comes to my apartment? Starts coming on to me?"

"Stuart, I have a big surprise for you. Hold on to your hat. There are other women to fuck! There are other women who are great in bed! Some can be bought, but many can be had for the asking. It's a buyer's market, sweetie. Wake up. A Jewish doctor, married, not married, who cares? Wonderful sex, but without all this *tsuris,* all this suicide stuff. A lot of them are like men. It's just fun and games for them. Should I introduce you? Do you need help to get going?"

"I'm getting married," Stern said. "I can't . . . I have to at least try."

"Super, give it your best shot. And who knows, you could end up in the *Guinness Book of World Records* as the only monogamous shrink in the whole sordid history of Nash. They'll bronze your pecker."

Suddenly Stern felt relaxed. It had worked again. Grieff had pulled him out of it. He would handle it all: the job crisis, Roxanne, Sydney. Standing up, he grabbed Grieff's hand. "I can't thank you enough," he said. "Somehow you give me perspective. You see me for what I am, but you never give up on me."

"You're my son," Grieff said simply. "I'll never give up on you."

At home Stern heated up a casserole he had prepared earlier in the week, a sausage and sauerkraut combination with a handful of caraway seeds tossed in. He decided a beer—pilsner, his favorite—would suffice. It was eight. At nine every evening, Sydney called. He would spend the next hour getting in the mood for her call. Earlier in the day he had debated sharing with her what was happening, in case it came to her attention. But now that possibility seemed remote and he felt certain he could handle it if it did arise. *Roxanne.* He saw her lying in the hospital bed, felt the sharpness and tang of her bitterness and despair—as though it were a perfume someone had inadvertently spilled on the floor, or formaldehyde. Yes, he had had glances, gestures from other women, remarks. But despite everything Grieff had said, he knew it wasn't just sex that bonded them. It was also the understanding she had of every sick or insane impulse that had ever troubled him from earliest childhood to the present moment, the uncanny way she had experienced almost identical moments, which she told him about before he told her. He had not wanted or expected to meet with this in another human being: it unnerved him. It even made both of them laugh; they both loathed people who fell for "psychic garbage," as Roxanne put it. *But she would know you too well. You would never escape.* Whereas Sydney would never know him, never come close. *Think of the peacefulness of that.* Roxanne claimed he compartmentalized his emotions: If only he could! But they were entangled, horribly entangled. If he never saw Roxanne again, they would remain entangled in his soul to his dying day.

And he knew deep down that a part of him wanted nothing more than to go tomorrow and see Roxanne, just to flout Grieff's advice, to escape from his clutches. Yes, he was the "good father," he had literally and figuratively saved Stern's life, but at times Stern wanted to kill him, had fantasized that Grieff's death would free him, would make *him* finally the father, not the son. *Just have a son. But with Sydney.* She was terrified of the idea of childbirth, but she wanted a child. She was still using her diaphragm. *Convince her. Deep down she must want to be a mother. But I'll be here in New York and she'll be in Philadelphia . . . Get another job. Break all the ties: Grieff, Roxanne. A really new start.*

But it would be almost impossible to get an equally good job elsewhere. Were it not for Grieff, he would never have made it into Nash. He was hanging on by his toes as it was.

When the phone rang, he answered, trying to sound carefree, "Hi, sweetheart."

She laughed. "What if it hadn't been me? Do you always answer the phone that way?"

"I knew it had to be you."

"Am I that predictable?"

"Only in important things . . . So, how're things on the home front?"

Sydney let out a soft exclamation. "Super! Mommy is crazy about the announcement. And she thinks that photo of me is wonderful. *I* think I look like a total sourpuss."

In the hysteria of the day, Stern had forgotten, and still forgot, what Sydney looked like in the photo. "You looked radiant."

"I guess . . . Well, anyway, we're official. No escape now." She laughed.

"Who wants to escape?"

"No, it's true. I said I didn't want to marry until I was thirty-five, and I'll be thirty-five in June. And I always said I wanted a successful career going, and I have one. And I always thought, get to know him—whoever 'he' is—really, *really* well before you decide, and I did . . . So I've done everything I said I would."

Did she feel she knew him? "I've never had such defined goals," Stern said. "I never expected to meet anyone like you. I didn't know women like you existed."

"Well, you led a sheltered life," Sydney said, seemingly without irony. She paused. "But, you know, I was thinking. Jane was saying the other day how she now feels she and Peter married too young and how they should have, well, had other experiences, because now they'll never know, and I think it's good we both have, that we can truly value what we're getting because we know what's out there."

What she meant was that she'd become engaged in college, very briefly, to a son of her parents' best friends, then had had a decade of "dating" which meant, as best he knew, going to concerts, museums, some light necking. When they met, she was twenty-nine and, she'd said, a virgin. Stern never saw cause to disbelieve this; she acted like one still, after six years. As for her knowledge of his private life, it was hazy. All she knew of Roxanne was that once he had had an affair with a psychiatric nurse who was demanding and overly intense.

"I've had an incredibly brutish day," he found himself saying.

"Have you? Poor darling. Anything special?"

"Oh, just routine, really . . . I'll tell you on the weekend. It'll have blown over by then."

"It's amazing how you keep your cool, dealing with all those insane people. It would drive me bananas in a second."

"It gets to me," he said evasively.

"I love you," Sydney whispered. "Sweet dreams."

"Love you too." This was their bedtime ritual; she insisted on it and became miffed if he deviated. But he found it charming, like the fact that she had, in her apartment, the dollhouse her grandfather had built for her and admitted to sitting in front of it occasionally and moving the tiny figures around, "just thinking silly thoughts."

When he arrived at Nash the next morning, Nurse Kefaldis said, "There's a reporter here from *The New York Times,* Dr. Stern. She wants to see you. I told her you had a very busy schedule." She looked as though she regarded this as a special honor. Thank God she was that spaced out.

The reporter was a young woman in her late twenties with very short curly dark hair and wire-rimmed glasses, dressed in jeans and a man's shirt. Stern was immediately relieved. She had to be new on the job. Therefore they didn't consider this very important, might not even run the story. He had an appointment with a patient, but rescheduled it for later in the afternoon. Better get this over with while his mood was still calm. He ushered her into his office. "What can I do for you, Miss . . . ?"

"Helen Pearce. Just a few questions, really. Do you mind if I tape this?"

"Go right ahead."

Stern watched as she pressed the record button. Then she looked up with a serious, intent expression. "Dr. Stern, I understand that a patient in your care, a Manuel Blades, died here over the weekend. Is that true?"

"Yes, it is."

"What was the cause of death?"

"Well, as you may know, Nash is renowned for our carefully administered drug program. There are patients here who, however, do not follow these programs as diagnosed."

"Could you elaborate on that?"

"Yes, gladly . . . It's important to give the body a chance to build up a tolerance to certain drugs. That's why we often start on a low dosage and gradually build up, to determine what a particular patient's tolerance is. Now, technically, the nurses observe the patients taking their medication, but with a group as large as this, that's not always feasible."

"What are you implying about Mr. Blades, Dr. Stern?" Helen Pearce asked. There was an avid gleam in her eye. Maybe she suspected something, but Stern felt secure.

"That he may not have been taking his medication or failing to take it. That could explain his reacting so violently to what was a standard dose."

"What dose was he taking?"

"One hundred milligrams."

Helen Pearce gazed at him with her unreadable but bright-eyed look. "Is there a record of that?"

"Yes, I have a record at home and would be glad to send it to you."

"You don't keep records at the hospital?"

"Sometimes. But usually Nurse Kefaldis just copies my instructions on to her own sheets and follows them."

Helen Pearce licked her lips. "I've spoken to Ms. Kefaldis, Dr. Stern. She stated that the dosage you recommended was four hundred milligrams."

Stern tried to look shocked. "Really?"

"You seem surprised. Why is that?"

Stern hesitated. "Well, there have been instances—How shall I put this? The nursing staff at Nash is unequalled anywhere in the country, some might say anywhere in the world. But they are also, sadly, overworked. There is no one at Nash in whom I have greater faith than Nurse Kefaldis, but instances have been known where mistakes have been made."

Helen Pearce's head was cocked slightly to the side. "If this is so, what you're saying means that Ms. Kefaldis could—inadvertently, as you put it—have been responsible for Mr. Blades's death?"

"Not at all," Stern said. "I would never make such an accusation. All I am saying is that we, and this includes the nursing staff, are human. Mistakes, due to the incredible pressures we are under, have been known to occur."

"Mistakes leading to death?"

Stern smiled. "I believe we're diverging here. I am not suggesting Mr. Blades's death was due to a possible increase in his dosage by Nurse Kefaldis. He had an impaired liver due to a lifelong history of alcoholism. There is, unfortunately, a possibility which does occur of patients getting access to alcohol on the floor. It's illegal, naturally, but it happens."

Helen Pearce looked down at her notes. "How about the weather? I've been studying the leaflet that comes with Thorazine and it states that there can be a fatal response if the temperature is over eighty degrees."

Stern nodded. "Correct. You've done your homework, I see. Well, we were all, naturally, not expecting a ninety-degree heat wave in April. And usually the air conditioning functions perfectly. I think what you're seeing, Miss Pearce, is a combination of highly unusual—one might almost say freakishly unusual—circumstances. That a patient should die as a result of these is a tragedy for us all."

For a second Helen Pearce looked around the room, as though there might be some concealed evidence she had overlooked on the walls. "Is that it, then?"

"Pardon me?"

"Will there be no further investigation to prevent such a 'highly freakishly unusual combination of circumstances' from recurring?"

"Such an investigation is already underway," Stern said. "Dr. Grieff and myself have been devoting ourselves full-time, to the extent our other professional duties allow, to that very end." He looked directly at her.

With a quick deft gesture she pressed the off button. "Thank you, Dr. Stern."

Stern tried to smile. He got to his feet. "Not at all. And if I can be of any further help, if any other questions should occur to you, please feel free to call me at any time." He gave her his card with his direct office line.

As the door closed behind her, he felt a peculiar elation. Could he have handled it better? No. He had learned from the master, Grieff. And yes, unfortunately it was a high, that closeness to danger, the necessity of thinking on one's feet. Perhaps it was why acrobats preferred doing their acts without a net.

The phone rang. Stern picked it up. "Stuart?" It was Roxanne. Her soft, hesitant voice. He said nothing, too shaken to speak.

"I wasn't going to call you," she went on, seeming to know he was there. "But today, just by chance, I was leafing through the Sunday *Times* and I saw your wedding announcement." She laughed. "It's so ironical. I hadn't seen it. I took the overdose Saturday. I just wanted you to know that. Don't feel guilty. It wasn't the announcement."

What was it then? Tell me. How are you? But Stern still said nothing.

"I'll be okay. It was a lot of things. I just wanted you to know . . . I hope you'll be very happy." Quietly she replaced the receiver.

Instantly Stern had a feeling he had described often to Grieff. It was as though a large winged creature had flown in the window and settled on his back, its talons clutching his shoulders. When Grieff pressed him, he found it hard to describe. No, he didn't hallucinate, he didn't see anything fly in the window. But he felt a pressure on his back and shoulders and a sense that something was pressing him down, trying to force him flat on his face. Sometimes he could feel sweat break out from the effort it took to keep erect.

What if her call had come when the *Times* reporter had been present? Even so, her voice was too soft to be heard. Helen Pearce could not have heard it. But what would he have done? What if, right in the middle of the taped interview, he had had this attack? *Maybe I'm having a delayed reaction to the interview* . . . She had taken the overdose Saturday. Could he believe that? It could be checked, but even so the Sunday *Times* could be bought Saturday afternoon. Why would she lie, then? *To get you off the hook?*

I hope you'll be very happy? . . . Was that possible? Maybe women could love that way, altruistically, beyond a sense of self. Maybe Roxanne truly wanted his happiness, truly believed in the possibility of it—in a way even he could not?

Why hadn't he said anything? He was too terrified, too surprised. He had imagined calling her, calling to check on her, but not her calling him. *Call her back. That isn't a way to end it, saying nothing, denying her existence.* Stern took the phone off the hook, but sat there, just holding the receiver. *Figure out what you want. The wedding announcement was an end, an end to her hopes, an end to the possibility of the relationship continuing. . . . Why? Sydney will be in Philadelphia. You should see Roxanne as often as you like and no one would know. . . . But I want a family, a normal life, to the extent I'm capable of it. . . . Then drop Roxy, drop her!* He had a flash image of himself as a giant bird dropping her, her body falling endlessly into space, like a stewardess he'd once read about who had been sucked out of an emergency door on an airplane.

Stern went to the window. Outside a group of patients were being led to occupational therapy. He saw the building Roxanne worked in. Her voice, that insidious, quiet voice that burrowed into his consciousness. Grieff never understood that. He had never let a woman have that access to his inner self. He was too guarded.

If I married her, I could save her, give her that sense of security she's never felt . . . Break it off with Sydney. She'd find someone else easily. He allowed himself the indulgence of fantasizing an appearance on Roxanne's ward, falling to his knees, begging her . . . *No! God, are you crazy?*

Eleven o'clock. Time for staff meeting. Stern pulled himself together. He still felt that aching soreness on his back, but so what? Half the people he knew had back trouble. The human back was designed poorly. And physical pain could be a relief. It gave you something to concentrate on. Boldly, he walked into the meeting room and sat down next to the man he was most afraid of, Menschel, who barely noticed his appearance. It was curious, his fear of Menschel, who was far below him in status. Why not fear Szell? Most people did—his German stiffness, inapproachability, coldness. But Menschel had that eager, idealistic look. Nothing would deter him, neither fear of being fired nor fear of being publicly humiliated. He had a shining shield of virtue that protected him.

Szell conducted the meeting. He went over some matters concerning a few new patients. There was crossfire between Maxwell Chaskes and Philip Ivey, two residents, about an incident involving Leroy Demos. Chaskes was his doctor and had requested Demos be put in solitary for the day. Ivey ran the therapy group he was in and felt that that would be a mistake. "He's been making progress, finally. Now he's being made to feel an outcast again. We tried that. It didn't work. I should have been consulted."

Chaskes was six feet two, a bald, beefy man whose hands looked like baseball mitts. "Demos was hysterical. He attacked Nurse Kefaldis . . . Isn't that so?"

Nurse Kefaldis smiled. "Oh, as attacks go, it was minor. You see

Dr. Stern was on his way out and Mr. Demos was running after him. He seemed agitated and Dr. Stern suggested I give him something to quiet him."

Ivey looked at Stern. "There's a lot of unrest among the patients about Blades's death, a lot of fear. I think we can't brush this under the rug. We have to deal with it. It may be exaggerated, even paranoid, but it's there."

Stern hesitated. Before he could reply, Grieff said, "Exactly what do you feel is being brushed under the rug, Dr. Ivey? A full investigation is under way. But Mr. Demos has had several bursts of anger at other patients as well as staff. The Blades incident may have touched it off, but it certainly isn't its underlying cause."

"He's been set back," Ivey said. His freckled face was pink and shiny; he was wearing his habitual red bow tie.

"That's unfortunate," Grieff said dismissively. He looked around the room. "Any other reactions?"

Sharon Wishnick raised her hand. "I had a long talk with Mr. Demos this morning. He's much calmer. I think he just needs extra attention, a sense that we're all concerned for him. Perhaps he could switch to my group therapy session. We only have a few patients now."

The strange thing about Sharon Wishnick was the contrast between her manner and her dress. Her manner was prim; she often pressed her lips together in a quick, nervous gesture. She always wore grey or navy suits, but with them she wore white blouses, sometimes embroidered with lace, that were just barely, but definitely, see-through. She was married to a man who ran an antique jewelry store on Fifth Avenue. Stern had once bought Sydney a birthday present there: a Victorian brooch with a small amethyst. He didn't listen to the to and fro between Wishnick and the others. Instead he found himself thinking of this contrast in women, how even in their public persona, they revealed their private persona. Which was the real Sharon Wishnick? Did she really have, as Grieff supposed, a deep need to be savagely violated by one of her patients or did she have a perfectly satisfactory sex life with her husband? Or both?

Roxanne claimed a lot of the nurses joked about the male patients, whom they would make it with under other circumstances, that some even sought out patients after their dismissals and propositioned them. "Did you ever?" he had asked. "Have the thought, or actually do it?" "Do it," she had smiled, "I only had the thought."

Roxanne had her own version of the Sharon Wishnick syndrome. She had beautiful breasts, but always wore loose-fitting high-necked blouses and long dark skirts, with boots in winter. But she wore her hair loose, which was unusual for a professional woman at Nash. She was always flipping it back and then it would fall forward again, concealing one of her eyebrows. *Now you see me, now you don't . . . "I hope you'll be very happy."*

How about Sydney? Yes, she too had a version of the syndrome, hers being that at home she often walked around in the nude, said she felt totally at ease that way, didn't mind being stared at, but was also seemingly unaware of this being provocative. She claimed that her apartment and Stern's were overheated and that when alone she worked that way, naked, at her desk. "It's not a sexual thing," she insisted, and kidded him about overdoing his emphasis on the id. "The id will out," as Grieff said. In bed all that naturalness vanished: she was the Victorian maiden on her wedding night, married off to a bearded man three times her age. Grieff insisted that was an act, designed to turn Stern on. Stern felt it was real; it didn't turn him on. He almost always was mentally making love to Roxanne while in bed with Sydney.

Would that always be true? Say he never saw Roxanne again? Would he for the next thirty years make love to her in his head? Sydney's parents had been married even longer than that. In fact, they'd just had a huge fiftieth wedding celebration. Mrs. Sutton had Sydney's fair coloring, and her petite figure; she had worn to the party her original wedding gown, which still fit. Sydney's lanky, Yale-educated father looked awkward but pleased, drank too much champagne, started making unnecessary toasts. Roxanne's parents had split up when she was four, she'd been sent to boarding school at five, came back when her mother remarried, was sent away again when that marriage broke up. "I never knew security," she said. "That's why I can identify with the patients."

Sydney claimed her parents were repressed, that their happiness was to some extent a masquerade. Stern knew that, but even as a partial act it seemed so humane, so dignified, so civilized when he compared it to the rampant warfare between his own parents—the sight of his father actually pulling his mother's hair out by the roots, the wakeful nights he had spent thinking his father might burst into the room and murder him in his sleep.

After the meeting Stern started to leave, when Nurse Kefaldis crossed the room to speak to him. "Dr. Stern?"

"Yes?"

"That reporter, that Miss Pearce?"

"Yes?"

This was the way Kefaldis spoke, in little bursts of words. "She said you had prescribed an overdose, I mean a dose for Mr. Blades of one hundred milligrams. That's not what I have written in my notes. You can come see them. Would you like—"

"There may have been some confusion about that," Stern interrupted. "Miss Pearce didn't seem aware of how we work out the dosages, the gradual increases and so on. I tried to explain it to her . . . I told her how much we all value you."

"Yes?" Kefaldis blushed.

"There is nothing to worry about," Stern said. "Put it out of your mind."

Kefaldis beamed. "Thank you, Dr. Stern. I thought it must be a mistake."

Stern's next patient was at one-thirty, in an hour. Would he have time to drive to the small restaurant down the hill? He decided to chance it and got there in seven minutes. There was a very short line. As he took a place in it, he saw to his dismay that Sharon Wishnick was standing in front of him. She turned and smiled. "Oh, hi."

"I just have time for a quick bite," he mumbled. "My next patient's at one-thirty."

"Me too." As she said this, the hostess, assuming they were a couple, led them to a table for two. Shit. Should he make some excuse? But they were already sitting down. With her ice water Sharon gulped down two Valium. "Are you all right?" she said. "It's been such a hectic time for all of us. You look a little—Would you care for one or two of these? Or do you have your own?"

"I'm fine," Stern said, looking down at the menu. He would have sold his soul for a joint, but once a day was too much. His rule was every other day, even at times of greatest stress. Valium did nothing for him.

Sharon was gazing at the menu. She looked up with her pale myopic blue eyes. "I think I'll have a cheeseburger, french fries, and a chocolate milk shake," she said. "I always get so ravenous after staff meetings!" She said this with her usual ingenuous smile. Meaning she felt like eating all of the staff? "That's how I got through med school—Valium and chocolate milk shakes. It's such a soothing combination."

Stern eyed the salads. At five feet seven he had to constantly restrain his appetite. He prided himself on having shed the pudgy physical self of his childhood. Now stocky, bearded, he knew he was attractive to certain women, despite his lack of height.

When he glanced up, having made his choice, Sharon was still looking at him with that pensive look.

"Could I ask you a personal question?"

God, what next? "Certainly."

"Well, what I really want to know is, do you think I'm being paranoid thinking that Dr. Chaskes was attacking me in the meeting?"

Stern tried to remember. He had started tuning out at about that time. "His manner is always—"

"No, but that's it. Do you think his manner was any different toward me than toward any of the other doctors? I know I can be hypersensitive." Her lips parted; she looked on the verge of tears.

"He's a fool," Stern said, both wanting to comfort her, and because he felt it was true.

Sharon's eyes glistened. "I know Mr. Demos is his patient. I wasn't trying, as he put it, to 'poach' on his patients. I have a very full work load, *too* full . . . But poor Mr. Demos was so low. I saw him lying on the couch in the living room, curled up in a fetal position, and I wanted to cry! So I rearranged one of my patients and I took Mr. Demos into my office and I just held him in my arms for almost an hour." She smiled. "It was just what he needed! They need nurturing, not all this abstract jargon about neurosis. These people are *hurting*—they've been rejected all their lives. I didn't dare tell Dr. Chaskes that was what I did. He would have a fit. But don't you think it's true?"

"That we all need nurturing?" Stern said, having a flash image of Sharon Wishnick naked from the waist up pressing Demos against her breasts.

"Yes, to be held, to be physically held. We're not just mental beings." Her voice was still trembling.

"I think that's true," Stern equivocated. "Yes, physical things are important. And women often—"

"It's our nature!" she cried excitedly. "It's what we're good at. Why not use it to help patients? Why deny it and try to become male clones?"

"Exactly." Stern looked around nervously for the waitress who, luckily, was approaching. They gave their orders. After a moment, at a loss, he asked, "Do you have children? I'm sorry, I can't remember."

Her mouth turned downward. "No, it's been a terrible disappointment to Harvey and myself. We've tried everything—in vitro, artificial insemination." She sucked in her breath. "But just last month I was thinking, perhaps I've been selfish. Maybe if I had children I wouldn't have as much love to give to my patients. So it could be a blessing in disguise."

Stern thought of Sydney and her terrors of children and childbirth. "It must be sad for your husband," he said.

"Do you not have them also?" she asked. "I mean, have you and your wife tried, or have you—"

"Actually, I'm not married," Stern said. "That is, I'm engaged, I'm going to be married in a few months, but I haven't yet made the leap, as it were."

Sharon looked surprised. "Really? How funny. I was sure you were. I've seen you often with that lovely woman, your fiancée, I'm not sure what her name is. She has such beautiful long dark hair."

Stern froze. Seen you so often? How? They had been so careful. "Oh no," he said quickly. "I think you must mean Ms. Arlen. She's just a friend, a very good friend, but no . . . My fiancée is named Sydney Sutton. She lives in Philadelphia."

It was hard to tell if Sharon Wishnick's expression was one of disbelief or just surprise. "Is she a psychiatrist too?"

"Oh no," Stern said heartily. "She's . . . well, she's director of a well-known music school, and she is also a harpist."

Sharon frowned. "What *is* a harpist exactly?"

Was she joking? "Someone who plays the harp," Stern said.

"Oh, of course. I don't know why, but I was thinking—harpy, or . . . That's good, I think. That's like *my* marriage. I mean, being married to someone outside the profession. I come home so full of everything that's gone on here and it's restful to hear about Harvey's problems, which are so different. He's a jeweler."

The waitress set down their platters. Sharon poured catsup and relish on her cheeseburger and chomped into it, then took a deep slurp of her milk shake. There was something delightful about her. Stern imagined her in knee socks in high school, a plaid skirt held by a safety pin, a white blouse with a round collar. "Yes, I know," he said. "About your husband, I mean. I once bought my fiancée a brooch in his store. It was lovely—white gold with an amethyst."

"I love Victorian jewelry," Sharon said. "One can tell you're the kind of man who would pick just the right presents. And that's rare. But, not to harp on this"—she laughed—"oh, I didn't mean to pun, but do you and your fiancée want children? Please don't answer if you feel it's too personal."

Stern picked at his chef's salad. "We would. That is, I definitely would, and Sydney . . . Well, of course right now she's in Philadelphia and I'm here, so it might be difficult."

Sharon was devouring everything on her plate with an avidity that was almost comical, given that she was relatively slender. "Does she have fears though, is what I mean? Fears of childbirth?"

"Well, yes, she does, actually," Stern said.

Sharon sighed. "I do too. I just do, and Harvey thinks it's so silly. But then he's a man, so what does he know, really? He says things like he thinks a lot of men would actually like to have the experience of being pregnant and giving birth. But I think they just want the idealized version of it. They don't really want to lug something around in their wombs for nine months. That is, assuming they *had* wombs, even . . . And I'm not sure. I know Dr. Ivey wrote a paper on it—womb envy. But do you think it's so very common? I mean, do you ever have those fantasies, of wanting to be pregnant?"

Stern saw himself waddling across the institute grounds in a maternity suit. He suddenly saw the whole male faculty pregnant, complaining about aching breasts or back pains. "I don't really think so," he said. "It could be denial, of course."

"Well, but that's exactly how *I* feel about penis envy," Sharon said. "My analyst was Dr. Parker-Lloyd, have you heard of him? He just insisted until he was blue in the face, literally *blue,* that penis envy was a real thing, that women really wanted this object hanging there just to . . . I don't know what, twirl around or hold or whatever. And I kept saying it has nothing to do with that! It's all about male privileges. I mean, my goodness, one doesn't have to be a feminist to see that!"

Stern had never heard her so voluble. At staff meetings she was so timorous. "I suppose we all envy what we *see* as the perogatives of the opposite sex. Men would like the freedom not to work, to lie around reading novels and munching on candy bars—"

"But women don't live like that anymore!" Sharon exploded. "Are you joking?" There was a faint trace of chocolate on her upper lip.

"I think some women, my fiancée's mother, for instance, do lead what one would call lives of leisure, shopping, et cetera."

Sharon had cleaned her plate down to the last pickle chip, which she now popped into her mouth. "Those women, to the extent they exist, are miserable," she asserted.

"I admit, I don't know any women like that," Stern retreated. "I mean of our generation."

"And if you did, they would bore you senseless," she informed him. "You wanted a modern, liberated woman because you're a modern, liberated man."

Roxanne thought Sydney's career was a "pseudo career," exactly the kind Stern would never be jealous of because it involved little intellectual endeavor, that he had picked her partly because she was "soothing," rather than challenging. "We ought to get back," he said.

"Could I ask you just one more thing?" Sharon asked. "It's connected, in a way. Do you think men and women can really be friends? I mean, without sex intruding in any way?"

Stern hesitated. "Look at us. We've been having this discussion. We—"

"But we're not intimate friends," she insisted. "I mean . . . like, say, you and your friend, Ms. Arlen. Do you really, I mean, do you feel you can talk to her? Just the way you would with a man? Can you say anything?"

"I don't say everything to men." He looked away. Suddenly he found himself saying, "It's a little painful, discussing this, because, actually, I just found out yesterday that over the weekend Ms. Arlen made a suicide attempt."

"Did you know she was going to?"

"No, I—"

"Not even that she was thinking along those lines? Not even that she was depressed?"

The pleasure of confiding in women was often strong, if they had a sympathetic manner, but he usually tried to avoid it with colleagues. Why in God's name was he doing it now? "She's had a difficult life," he stammered. "A lot of—"

"Is she married?"

"No."

"Does she have a boyfriend?"

Stern's heart was thumping. "She . . . sees men."

"But no special man?"

"Well, yes, I think there was someone special, but he . . . wasn't available."

"Married?"

"The equivalent. Please don't mention this, but he works at Nash actually."

Sharon's face grew somber. "I wonder if it's Dr. Chaskes. I know he's unfaithful to his wife. He told me. He boasted!"

"This man isn't married."

"Do you know who it is?"

Stern cleared his throat. "I'm not at liberty to say."

They stood up and moved to the cashier. "Those men should be hung!" Sharon said vehemently. "Those men who torment women, who play around with their lives—they should be hung! And a doctor! A psychiatrist!"

"But surely not everyone has such perfect control over their life," he said. "Even psychiatrists."

She looked at him angrily. "Then what is it all about? Our training? Our supposedly trying to help others? Is it all a sham?" Her lips were pursed.

"Maybe it *is* partly a sham," Stern said.

"That's appallingly cynical," she said. "I hope that isn't your true feeling. Or are you trying to bait me, like Dr. Chaskes?"

They walked out into the cool, mild April day. Stern cleared his throat. He could not afford to alienate her, either by being foolishly confiding or trying too abruptly to distance himself. "I'm sorry," he said. "I've just been upset. This business with Blades. I've never lost a patient before, and now Ms. Arlen . . ."

Suddenly Sharon reached out and hugged him. He felt her warm full breasts, her light, lemon-scented cologne. "You'll be fine," she said. "Don't worry. We're all behind you."

"Thank you," he said, relieved.

He drove back to the institute. More than anything, he would have liked it to be Friday, to be driving away from the institute, not toward it, to be on the highway going to Philadelphia. Maybe he would stop in at Wishnick's store and buy Sydney a spontaneous present, in honor of the engagement announcement appearing in the *Times*. Shower her with presents! . . . *Those men should be hung!* Grieff: *You could end up in the* Guinness Book of World Records *as the only monogamous shrink in the whole sordid history of Nash.*

Stern got through the afternoon. He saw his patients, sat in on another meeting, and finally, exhausted, retreated to his office at five to gather up some papers. Grieff peeked in the door, then closed it behind him with a mischievous smile. "How's it going, kiddo?"

"Fine," Stern said, pretending to be preoccupied.

"No anxiety attacks? No urges to spill the beans?"

"It's all under control," Stern said, wanting more than anything for Grieff to depart.

"I checked on your girlfriend, by the way, just because I thought you'd want to know. She's fine."

Without stopping to think, Stern said, "Yes, I know."

Grieff raised his eyebrows. "How?"

"She called me." Because Grieff was remaining, just staring at him, he went on. "To tell me it hadn't been because of the announcement in the *Times.* Ironical, but she took the overdose Saturday, before it appeared."

"You can get the Sunday *Times* on Saturday," he said.

Playing games with Grieff was impossible. He was faster than light at this. "She wanted to let me off the hook," Stern said. "She said she hoped I'd be very happy."

Grieff burst out laughing. "God, that woman should be giving a course somewhere. She's a master, a grand master . . . And you actually—well, tell me, *did* you fall for it or not?"

Stern knew he owed his life to this man and yet he would have given anything to throw him out the window, out of his life. "I'm not as cynical as you," he said, pretending to gather his papers together.

The grin that spread over Grieff's face was like a child's. "No? You could have fooled me. But maybe you're right. So, what now? You rush to her bedside? Flowers? Candy?"

"She said nothing about wanting to see me."

Grieff was practically sitting on top of the desk. "You've told me a lot about what *she* said. What'd *you* say?"

"Nothing."

"Huh. Well, I take it back then. Good for you. She threw you a line and you didn't bite? Maybe you *have* learned something in fifteen years. But tell me—why *didn't* you say anything?"

"I didn't think it was necessary. I happen to believe her story, but I think she really just wanted me not to feel guilty. And I don't."

"*Mazel tov!*" Grieff backed away, tipping an imaginary hat. "See you tomorrow, then."

Alone in the room, Stern sat at his desk. He was drenched in perspiration. There was a knock at the door. "Yes?"

It was Nurse Kefaldis. "I just wondered . . . did you want to check my records, Dr. Stern? You said before—"

"No!" Stern yelled, his voice trembling. "I said it was all right. Please! Leave me alone."

Kefaldis straightened up. "Well," she said. "I'd like to see *your* records, if you can remember to bring them in. I don't think you did write down one hundred milligrams. My eyesight is twenty-twenty." She smiled derisively. "But what good would that do? You'd doctor the records, right? All of you are the same. What a bunch. You can't tell the doctors from the patients half the time around here."

It was time to get out of here. If he saw one more person, he might, just possibly, leap at his throat. Briskly, Stern exited and went down the stairs to the ground floor. When he reached the door, he stood there, hesitating. Unfortunately, he knew where he was going.

He was going to see Roxanne.

OUT
OF LOVE

"So the reason you never signed any official agreement was that she was your sister?" Alix asked. Although like most lawyers she always used a tape recorder, she also jotted down notes from time to time.

"She's my twin," Bernice Daley exclaimed. "You don't understand. Ever since we were born, we've been as close as *that!* She brought the palms of both hands together. In a way, genetically, we're the same person. So, how could I expect she'd turn against me?"

Alix cleared her throat. "That was part of your motivation, then, in seeking her as a surrogate mother for your child—that not only would the resulting baby contain your husband's genes, but, in effect, your own as well?"

"Of course!" Bernice Daley was tiny, five feet tall at most, with tinted blond hair and long pink nails with which she picked up objects as though her fingers were a pair of tweezers. Now, with that same gesture, she plucked a cigarette from a pack lying on the cocktail table. "This is one way Barbie and I *aren't* alike," she said. "We both started smoking at sixteen, but when she married Joe, she stopped. He was an athlete. He thinks it's a filthy habit. I think that's one of the things he holds against me. See, my theory is that it was *him* who turned Barbie against me, who made her change her mind. I don't think she wants another baby at all. A year ago she was even talking about having her tubes tied!"

Alix leaned forward. "Would there be any evidence for that? Did she ever go to her doctor and consult him about it?"

Bernice shrugged. "Gee, I don't know. I don't think so. Because then—and this is what I mean about Barbie, about the way she can be influenced so easily by those around her—I said maybe she should think it over, after all she's just thirty-four and something could happen to Joe. I was reading an article about it in Ann Landers just the other day. This woman had her tubes tied, then her husband died and she married again and she wanted another baby and she couldn't have one. That's what I told Barbie. You never know. Sure, Joe's in perfect health, but those people can be struck down too. This woman in my office who never smoked a cigarette in her *life* got lung cancer! Things like that. You just don't know."

"Right," Alix said, flinching. This had been happening ever since Gerald's death a month earlier. Some remark—usually concerning illness, death, sudden unexpected events—and her chest would constrict. She was thin, had low blood pressure—was it some vicarious connection to Gerald, since he had died after a severe heart attack? Usually she managed to mask her reaction to the pain by turning away, pretending to do something, but Bernice Daley must have seen her uneasiness. "Are you okay? Is the cigarette smoke bothering you?"

Alix was dizzy, the room was moving slightly, but she said quietly, "No, I'm fine. It's just—a friend of mine died like that, suddenly, a month ago, so I know what you're talking about." This was totally unlike her. Neither in her professional or personal life, had she ever been given to quick confessions or personal remarks. But lately she had found herself saying things like this more often.

Bernice beamed. "You know, I'm *so* glad that your firm sent a woman. I mean, I don't know if you're the only woman they have, but I figure in a case like this, a woman understands, she can empathize. Do you have children?"

"No," Alix murmured. The room was still swaying.

"How come?" asked Bernice. Then she stopped, clapping her hand over her mouth. "Oh, that's nosey. Don't tell me."

"My job keeps me very busy," Alix said. "I've just been made a partner recently and I suppose I feel I have to give it my all."

Bernice put down her cigarette in a green malachite ashtray shaped like a turtle. "But, see, that's okay for you, you're a career woman. I don't mean to be insulting, I just figure from everything— from the way you dress, from your being with this big Wall Street firm, from everything—that that's what you *are*. But I'm not! I work, I have this job . . . But it's not, like, a career. I'm not *living* for this job. And you want to know the irony? When Barbie and I graduated college, *she* was the one who wanted a career. In fashion. *She* was the one who said she wasn't even sure she wanted children, *ever!* Then, of course, she met Joe and whammo, in three years she had two of them. But I was the one, even way back then, who said, 'No, all I want is a man to love and a house to take care of and some terrific kids.' That was all I wanted." She looked wistfully ingenuous, younger than thirty-four, despite her makeup.

Alix was feeling calmer. Ten years earlier she had given up smoking, but occasionally seeing someone smoke brought on an urge that was almost visceral. "And you say it was your sister who brought up the idea of acting as a surrogate mother for your child? She was the one, not you?"

"Right! Gosh, I would never—It took Barbie months to get back in shape after Susie, and she used to complain—back pains, varicose veins—she has a great figure, but she said she *hated* being pregnant, so I'd never have suggested it just because I wouldn't have imagined she'd want to go through the whole thing another time."

The room they were sitting in, the living room, was small, with dark tweed furniture. At one end was a dining alcove with a multicolored lamp suspended above it. Bernice was wearing a pantsuit in pale lime green and high-heeled beige sandals. Alix wondered if this was how she dressed for her job, as a secretary in her husband's construction firm. "Did you say yes right away, when your sister mentioned the possibility? How long did it take between the time she proposed she would do it and the time you and your husband . . ."

Bernice licked her lips. The pink of her lipstick had tinted the end of her cigarette. She smoked daintily, holding the cigarette away from her. "Well, it was on a Friday. I know that because Friday's the day I always go over to Barbie's. It's the day I don't work and the cleaning lady comes in. And of course I rushed home and told Ted that night. He was the one who said—now this is interesting, because he's not that psychologically minded, but he said, 'Are you sure she won't change her mind? Why would she want to go through another pregnancy?' And you know what *I* said?"

Alix shook her head.

"*I* said—boy, this will sound really naïve, but it's what I felt—I said, 'Out of love.' I figured Barbie loved me *that* much. I knew she wouldn't go around just doing this for anyone else. Like, once she was swimming too far out at the beach. I don't know if she was drowning exactly, but she was yelling and we were on this kind of deserted beach and I'm a terrible swimmer, but I swam in to get her. I didn't even think!"

"So, at bottom," Alix said, "why *do* you think your sister changed her mind?"

Bernice leaned forward, she lowered her voice. "You want to know what I *really* think?" she asked. "I think it's because she knew it would be a boy. She has two girls and I think deep deep down Joe always wanted a boy. Only maybe his sperm didn't make boys, and Ted's did. Who can predict? I think the minute she had that test and they knew it would be a boy, that's when she had her change of heart."

"Was it then that she started seeming hesitant?" Alix asked. The tape had run out; she decided to rely just on notes.

"Kind of," Bernice frowned. "I was so naïve, like I said, that I didn't pick up on it. Now, looking back, she'd make remarks, but I wouldn't take in their real meaning."

"Remarks like what?"

"Oh, like how excited Ted must be at having a son. I just thought, she's happy for Ted. I didn't think that what she was really saying was Joe wanted a son."

"What if the test had shown the baby was going to be a girl? Do you think she would have stuck to her part of the bargain?"

Bernice shrugged. "How do I know? Yeah, I think so. I mean, Miss . . . Zimmer?"

"Yes?"

"My sister isn't a mean person. I say that even now. This isn't like her. I think if it had been going to be a girl and Ken hadn't started in on her, she would've done what she said she was going to do."

Suddenly Alix was exhausted. It was growing dark. She had to go back to the office. "Why don't we stop here?" she said. "I'll try to speak to the doctor you mentioned, the one to whom your sister may have mentioned wanting to have her tubes tied."

"Okay," Bernice said brightly. She popped up from the couch and started walking with Alix to the door. "There's one other thing," she said.

"Yes?"

"I don't know if it's relevant or not."

"Why don't you tell me and I can decide?"

"It's about Barbie's marriage."

"What about her marriage?" Oh God, she was so tired; a headache was pounding at her skull.

Bernice was looking at a painting on the wall of two cows grazing under a tree. "Well, I promised Barbie I'd never tell anyone about this, but, maybe, like you say, it's relevant . . . Once—this was after Kelly was born, but *before* Susie was born—Barbie had this . . . she was, like, seeing, this other man. She was, like—"

"Having sex with him?"

"Right. And what I'm saying—this is something Barbie actually told me at the time—was she never really did know whose kid Susie was. I mean, she could have been either man's kid."

Alix sighed. "Do you know this man's name?"

"She used to call him George."

"Was his real name George?"

"No."

"Do you have any letters from your sister describing this affair?"

Bernice laughed. "Barbie *never* writes letters! Ever! To anyone. Ask my mother. Even when we were at summer camp and they made you, she never did."

"So, you have no evidence?"

"Yeah, but don't you think it's relevant to the case? I mean, if only one of her kids is really hers, maybe she figured . . . Or maybe another way of looking at it is, if Joe knew, maybe he'd feel differently about Barbie, because right now he worships the ground she walks on based on what is *not* true—that she never would look cross-eyed at another guy. That's how she acts in public." Bernice rolled her eyes knowingly.

"Mrs. Daley," Alix said, "the only things that will help us are pieces of evidence, nothing else. We can't stand up in court and talk about rumors or gossip or things that might have happened. Do you understand that?"

Bernice looked hurt. She pressed one long pink nail to her cheek. "This *isn't* something that 'might have happened,' " she said indignantly. "It *did* happen. She told me."

"But you must have it either in writing or on tape—or you must have the man's name. Otherwise it could be invented."

"Is that what you think, that I'm inventing it?" She looked tearful.

"No, of course not. But in court everything we bring up has to be documented. That's the way a trial works."

Bernice sighed. "She never would tell me his real name. Maybe she was afraid. You know . . ."

Alix tried to pull herself together. "Look, I think we have plenty to work with. Don't worry. I'll be in touch." She closed the door behind her.

The subway was two blocks away. It was a good neighborhood, Park Slope, but Alix felt uneasy. She saw a man loitering on the corner and quickened her step. She had been afraid of the dark as a child and, even though she now went out at night frequently, at certain times the fear returned.

In the subway Alix sat stiffly, wanting to close her eyes, but afraid she might doze off and miss her stop. The train stopped at Astor Place. That was where Gerald had lived, across from an Italian bakery. When he separated from his wife, he had given her the beautiful nine-room apartment on Central Park West; his own apartment was only two small rooms, unusual for a man in his position, a senior partner of a large Wall Street law firm. Alix had thought it strange, when she first came to work there, that he was not divorced but had been separated for ten years. "There was no one I wanted to marry," was all he would say. "It didn't seem necessary." He admitted that he felt it gave his children cause to believe that one day he and his wife might get back together, but that was all that seemed to bother him.

His wife's name was Daphne. She had been beautiful when he had met her thirty years earlier, he said, very pale and blond, willowy. Her hands were so beautiful that she was a model for hand cream and nail polish commercials. For years she had earned an excellent living, for years more than Gerald had earned as a beginning lawyer. Then gradually the jobs had begun tapering off, she had started drinking, had become something of a recluse. "But she was always a wonderful mother,'' Gerald would say. He seemed to believe that the way other people believed the world was round. Because he was unusually aware about most other things, Alix came to accept this as one of those myths one needs to survive. Lord knows her own life was full of them. Inwardly she felt both pity and slight contempt for Daphne Lehman, clinging to her children, hardly leaving the house, bloated from drink. Maybe in some way she had seen Daphne as some kind of rival. But why? Why not, if she was going to be jealous, focus on Giselle Fleming, the woman Gerald had started an affair with before his marriage broke up, whom he had gone on vacations with until his death, after the affair was over—platonic vacations, he had assured her. Giselle was a legal secretary for a firm two floors below theirs. Maybe originally she had been a Daphne substitute: She, too, was blonde, slender, retiring, nervous. *I had contempt for her, too, of a different kind. I saw myself as the ideal, the woman he'd been waiting for all his life. He said that.* Another myth?

Daphne Lehman lived five blocks away from the apartment in which Alix had lived with her husband Luke for the past twelve years. Probably she shopped at the same markets, maybe they had passed each other on the street. But it wasn't until Gerald's death that Alix found herself becoming obsessed with her, even walking past the building in which Daphne lived on her way home, although it took her out of her way. Would she even recognize her? The only photo Gerald kept was from years ago when she had been beautiful, blooming: she was in a sailboat, laughing, her hair blowing in the wind. And what if Alix saw her? Would she go over, start a conversation? What about?

I want to talk to someone who loved him, who maybe still does. Gerald always pooh-poohed Alix's theory that Daphne still loved him, because she'd kicked him out, had summarily ended the marriage when she found out about Giselle. "She was hoping you'd come back," Alix would say. "Deep down I bet she still thinks of that every day." He would smile sadly. "It's a lovely, romantic notion. It's just not true. She hates me. You've never been in that kind of marriage so you don't understand."

That always irritated Alix, but it was true. She and her husband were given to silences, weekends where neither spoke or where one took long walks and the other read. They had such a large apartment, each with their own study, that they could almost have gotten divorced and not have noticed. "You have no fear of his finding out about us?" Gerald would ask. "He doesn't know what firm I work for, he doesn't know I've given up eating red meat, he doesn't know who I am!" Alix would reply. "It sounds terribly eerie," Gerald would say. "I don't know marriages like that. I know screaming and scenes, ultimatums." "This is death by suffocation," Alix explained wryly. "The air keeps getting thinner and one day you realize you're turning blue, that there's no more air."

Her husband in some ways, except for the scenes, sounded like a male version of Daphne, and perhaps she had sought, as Gerald had, what beauty and blondness and non-Jewishness seemed to symbolize: calmness, stability, scrupulous obedience to forms and rules. Luke, her husband, had been on the ice hockey team at Bowdoin, but he had excelled in other sports as well. His family was reasonably wealthy, enough so that, especially combined with Alix's income, they could live well in New York, even with his small salary as a curator of Oriental prints at the Brooklyn Museum. He never spoke of his job. He had been at the museum since they had graduated college and had gotten some small raises. When friends suggested he could change jobs to improve his status, he always said he was perfectly content with the way things are. "I'm not ambitious," he would say in a way that seemed to regard ambition as something slightly unseemly. "Life is a garden, not a ladder." Alix wondered if it was being from a wealthy family or being gentile that allowed him that graceful diffidence which had seemed so appealing to her after growing up in a New York world of Russian-born striving Jews, moving from neighborhood to neighborhood until you had finally arrived. Though she was of the second generation, some of it remained in her, enough so that she still worked overtime, still felt she had to prove herself, knew she would always feel that—no matter what she earned, no matter how seemingly secure her professional identity was.

Gerald had shared that feeling. In some sense, it could have been said that his dedication had gotten him to where he had been professionally, but it went beyond that. It had been as much a contributing factor to the breakup of his marriage as his timorous affair with Giselle. Probably it had helped cause his first heart attack, the one that had taken place before Alix met him. Certainly it had led to the second, which killed him. The week before he died, he had said to her, "I felt a pain as I bent over this evening, but I know if I go to the doctor, he'll put me in the hospital. I just can't, not now. I have too much work." Every day she replayed that conversation in her mind a dozen times. Instead of saying, as she had, "Well, take it easy a little, at least," she should have said, "Go to the doctor right away. Don't be silly! What is more important, your health or some foolish case?" She hadn't said that because he disliked references to his health. "I'll live as long as I can and then I'll stop living," he would say. When the idea came up of her leaving Luke, he would always say with a pained expression, "But what if something happens to me? It's too risky." They had circled around that question for five years. Ironically it wasn't until the final six months before he died that Alix had decided she should break up her marriage. Even after reaching the decision, though, she had put off doing anything about it. Was she glad now? Gerald would have been. He saw her marriage as giving her a kind of security. But it was an eerie security. Everything was fixed in place, but also curiously floating, like some precisely painted surrealist painting in which all the objects are not where they should be, like their incredibly neat apartment in which one room contained only Luke's harpsichord, the one he had made from a kit the summer after they married, a reclining chair, a stereo and a lamp. Luke only played the harpsichord about once a month, but he enjoyed reading sheet music and sitting in that room, "the music room," and listening to recordings on his stereo.

Despite her intention, Alix fell asleep on the subway—not a deep sleep, but she dozed off in brief fitful moments, came to with a start, fell back again. Snatches of dreams began, were cut short, came on again, like a movie projector run at the wrong speed. In one she saw Bernice Daley's sister, Barbie, and her boyfriend, George. They were sitting on a park bench, but both of them looked like dolls. Barbie looked exactly like Bernice; she wore the same lime green pantsuit, the same spike heels. She was telling her boyfriend she was pregnant, then suddenly she was pregnant, she started giving birth . . . Alix jolted awake. It was her stop. She staggered out of the train groggily.

This was the way she slept at night lately, even though their apartment was on the seventeenth floor and completely quiet. She would wake up after fifteen minutes of sleep in that same jerky way and sit bolt upright, amazed, upon looking at the digital clock, that so little time had passed. All the usual remedies—warm milk, a glass of brandy, reading something soothing, seemed ineffective. Clearly she had lost the resiliency she had had in college where, after a few hours sleep, she could function perfectly, even feel a kind of triumphant high after being up all night studying. Now it was causing her to become distracted during the day, to miss parts of conversations, to be forced to pretend. It seemed to her so far she was doing a good job of pretending, but in court, obviously, it would never work. The Daley case wouldn't come to trial for several months. By then what? *You'll be fine. It's a reaction. This has to be common. Someone you loved died.*

She had come through so many deaths in the past decade, seemingly unscathed, that it surprised her that Gerald's death was taking this kind of toll. First, her father had died when she was just out of college; from emphysema—he smoked three packs a day. Then, five years ago, her sister, Pamela, who was married and lived in Colorado on a ranch had fallen from a horse, although she was an expert rider, and had gone straight into a coma from which she had never recovered. Two months later, their mother developed cancer, a long, drawn-out illness with remissions. Finally, last year, she, too, had slipped away. It reminded Alix of a drawing of a family where, every year or so, a large hand reaches down and erases one of the figures. Of her immediate family, the family she'd grown up in, she was the only one left. Maybe what was happening now was her reaction to all of this, buried too long.

The office was quiet. She passed Gerald's former office, glanced into it quickly—*why, were you expecting to see him?*—and went into her own. All she had to do was gather up some papers and leave, but, sitting down in the chair behind her desk, she closed her eyes and dozed off again. This time she dreamt of herself, Daphne and Giselle. They were all, seemingly, living together in the same apartment, Gerald's old apartment, which she had never seen. He had said one of the rooms had nothing in it but a pool table. Daphne and Giselle were playing pool; they both seemed to be very good and they wanted her to play also. They were urging her, but there seemed to be some kind of mocking complicity between them, as though they knew she would do badly, as though their motive was somehow to expose her, to humiliate her. She excused herself, saying she needed to go to the bathroom, intending to leave, but she couldn't find her way out. There were too many doors . . .

"Can I give you a lift?" It was Silas Foss, one of the other senior partners, the only one who had been there longer than Gerald. Alix's chair was turned toward the window, away from the door. He must not have known she was asleep. "That would be wonderful," she said. "It's been such a long day." Silas was tall, and angular, so much taller than Gerald who was only five feet six, that together they were like Mutt and Jeff. In some ways he reminded her of Luke's father. He had that same detachment, but also a glint of quickness as though nothing escaped him. Alix had never been sure who at the firm knew about herself and Gerald. At times they laughed, thinking they had everyone fooled. Other times Alix was sure everyone knew. Didn't people always know? But Silas Foss was the kind of man who could know or not know and totally not care. The ways of the world, whether it was his clients, his colleagues, or his family, seemed to happen on some plane far beneath him.

Alix slid into the seat of Silas's car and pulled the seat belt around her. "I had another talk with Bernice Daley today," she said.

"Oh, how's that going? I meant to ask."

"She's a little rambling. I'm going to follow up a few leads, but it's pretty irritating so far."

"I think the issue of being deserted by her own twin sister will appeal, though," Foss said.

"Definitely." She glanced at him. He was in his sixties, he had to be. He had been a lawyer almost forty years. Didn't it get to him? Didn't he ever feel crazed with boredom or an impulse to get out, to lead some other life? Gerald claimed no, that without his job Silas would cease to exist, would literally crumble. She yawned, and then covered her mouth.

"You've been looking very tired lately," Foss said.

She shrugged. "A little. Nothing very—"

"I think we've all been affected by Gerald's death," he said. "I find myself thinking about it frequently during the day. He was the only one from the old era, so to speak, the only, well, friend I had . . . Perhaps friend is too strong a word, but someone with whom I felt an unspoken rapport."

Did that mean he knew? That he connected her fatigue with Gerald's death? If "friend" was too strong a word for him to use, then Alix doubted he would ever go further than he had in indicating what he knew or didn't know. "Yes," she said, trying to keep her voice steady. "He was a very . . . unique person."

"It was a pity about his marriage," Foss said.

That was such a general remark that Alix just said, "Yes."

"I knew Daphne in the early days, before she started . . . deteriorating. Christine and I saw them quite often, actually. It was before we moved out of the city. She was an extraordinarily beautiful woman, very ethereal. One wanted to protect her. But evidently one couldn't. I'm sure no one tried harder than Gerald did."

Alix kept trying to read between the lines of the conversation. One always had to do that with Foss since he said nothing directly apart from matters relating to work. Was he saying he was surprised that after a woman like Daphne—did he know about Giselle?— Gerald would pick someone like Alix with her small dark eyes and beaky nose? In fact, over the years she had "come to terms" with her looks. Enough men—not droves, but a few—had fallen for her that she could look in the mirror and not cringe. She had the kind of thin, high-cheekboned face that everyone said—and so far this seemed true—would improve with age, to the extent that was possible. Her thick dark hair was pulled up behind an ear on one side, cascading loosely to her shoulders on the other. Sometimes she wore a single earring on the ear that showed, but more often not. When she smiled, her face took on a slightly sardonic expression, her eyes gleaming mischievously. This was added to by her heavy straight eyebrows which tilted upward at the ends. "Devilish," Gerald used to say, "as though you want to kick loose the traces." She was tall and had always verged on being too thin; when anxious, she found it difficult to eat. At thirty-six, she dressed carefully, allowing herself eccentric touches—bright scarves, strange jewelry—but making sure that the total effect was subdued.

"I'm sure no one tried harder than Gerald did." How could Silas be sure? Men were so quick to bond with each other, especially on matters concerning women. She understood Gerald's point of view but in a corner of her mind had some kind of compassion for the betrayed, destroyed Daphne. Not so much an identification—as in, it could be me—but a connection. Her mother had had a breakdown when Alix was growing up. She saw the possibility of that in many seemingly stable women, the ones whose eyes darted too quickly from person to person, whose speech was too rapid, too disconnected. They might never fall over the edge, but the edge was always there in their minds.

Alix became aware that she had said nothing for a long time. "I never met Gerald's wife," she said. "I gather they never formally divorced." She was glad to hear that innocuous sentence emerge from her lips.

"He said it was for the children. But I don't believe he ever met anyone he wanted to marry . . . anyone who was available."

Alix glanced at him. His eyes were on the road. "Yes, well, it's probably difficult," she said vaguely. He must know; didn't that remark make that clear?

"Perhaps if he had had that—a stable, warm, caring family situation—things might have been different," Foss said.

"But his health—"

"Even there . . . It makes a big difference, I can assure you."

Suddenly Alix realized they were near Gerald's former apartment. "Could you let me out here?" she said. "I just need to stop off for some groceries on the way home. Thanks so much."

"Take care of yourself," Foss said gently, as she stumbled out of the car.

It was too exhausting, trying to figure out meanings. Or maybe she was just too tired. She replayed their conversation in her head. What had the last part meant? Was it an accusation? She had thought that also, since Gerald's death. If they had been married, if she had made the break years ago, instead of just endlessly toying with the idea, maybe she would have insisted he work less hard, would have insisted he go to the hospital right away the day he felt that pain in his chest. "Second-guessing is a waste of time," was one of Gerald's favorite sayings. She knew, had he been alive, or had he died and yet been able to hear her thoughts, he would have leaned over, smiled, and said, "Stop!"

Stop! She was right in front of the building, a medium-sized apartment house on Seventy-sixth Street. There was a doorman, but he was frequently not on duty; you could buzz yourself in, if someone answered the door. Alix looked at the names, came to Lehman, then impulsively pressed the button. "Yes?" came a soft voice. "Who is it?"

Alix fled.

What are you doing? You don't have to do it this way. You can just call her, say you're a friend. This is absurd. Call her on the phone. She might like someone to talk to. But wouldn't she guess? *No, why should she? You're a colleague, nothing suspicious about that. And not his type, not his physical type or even his emotional type.* Normally Alix talked quickly, assertively, held vehement opinions. "I don't belong in the ballet lineup," she used to say, meaning not only that he picked ethereal blondes, but their names. "You should have looked for an Odile next."

They had finished dinner. Luke never brought work home at night. On nights he wasn't reading music scores, he liked to lie down and just play records, drinking red wine. "Why don't you listen to some music with me?" he said.

"I have work," Alix said. She always did, but it was also an excuse.

"You look so tired. Perhaps you're overdoing."

"I haven't been sleeping well," she admitted.

"I know. I hear you get up at night."

She waited for him to say, "Is anything special bothering you?" but he didn't. He never asked that kind of question, perhaps not even in his mind. Sometimes she told him about her work. He always listened attentively, but never asked questions. *"Life is a garden."* But weren't there different kinds of gardens? Not that she would ever know, but she often wondered what his was like. Wouldn't it be claustrophobic? She imagined it as the secret garden of the book she had read in childhood, a high stone wall, overgrown with vines. And her ladder was a tall, thin one that went straight up into a bare blue sky, never ending, nothing at the end of it, but since you would never reach the top that wouldn't matter. A ladder that wobbled in the wind so that you had to grip the edges tightly in order not to fall off.

"I've been thinking of Pam lately," she said which was half true since she had started thinking constantly of everyone she had loved who had died. "I got a letter from Michael that he's remarrying. He even asked if I wanted to fly out for the wedding, if we wanted to."

"Do you?" Luke was deferential; they were her relatives, if only by proxy. Pamela's daughter, Laurel, was nineteen, a student at Wesleyan, her son, fourteen. They were both healthy, outdoor types, like their father. Alix had never really seen Pamela that way, despite her passion for horses and her love of the West. It always seemed unnatural, a fad, something that would one day run its course. She wondered about Pam's marriage. They had never talked about that. Both of them had married handsome, non-Jewish men who were good at traditionally American things. Michael owned a ranch, looked like a stouter, greyer version of the Marlboro man. Alix never could think of what to say to him. And Pam had never been able to think of what to say to Luke.

"I don't have time, really," Alix said. "But also . . . I don't know. I want to keep in touch with the children, but to see him with another wife—"

"I'm amazed he would remarry so quickly," Luke said.

"It's been five years," Alix reminded him.

"Amazed that he would remarry at all," he went on. "I don't understand that kind of thing."

What did he mean? Surely he understood why men remarried! "You wouldn't remarry if I died?" she said, trying to joke.

"Of course not," he said. He looked puzzled. "How could I?"

"People do," she said lamely.

"People!" That was part of the garden thing. Outside it were people who did outrageous, incomprehensible things, people like Bernice Daley and her twin sister. Alix saw people like that every day and was fascinated by them, sometimes repelled. But she still somehow loved Luke's sweeping all that aside. She could imagine him, now that he had presented the image, as a celibate widower with his Scarlatti and his Persian prints, long walks in the park, maybe an occasional ski weekend. She had grown up awkward at all sports. It amazed her that people could ice skate with their ankles not flattened to the ice, that they could remember the rules in tennis, that they could be interested in climbing on a large unstable object like a horse, literally—as had proved true with Pam—taking their life in their hands. Sports seemed dangerous and incomprehensible to her, but when she saw Luke engaged in any of them, when she had first seen him ski, for instance, she had been entranced by his physical grace, the way his body seemed an integral part of him, moved so instinctively, so smoothly. He, on the other hand, couldn't comprehend what she meant when she said that she didn't know how to stop when she was skiing. "What do you mean, not know how?" he asked. "You do it the way I've told you." When she cited dangers, people crashing into trees, falling from horses, he said, "People get knifed on the subway or mugged walking down the streets in New York, but you say you're never afraid there."

In a small way Luke had been a sports star at Bowdoin. They had met when Alix put up a sign offering tutoring in math, a required subject that he found as incomprehensible as she found sports. Rather than being insulted by her total unawareness of his stardom, of his many varsity jackets, he found it charming. "You didn't know we had a football team?" he asked, thinking she was joking or pulling his leg. Once they began going out together, she started going to games. She brought a book—Willa Cather, she remembered—and read it while the players charged up and down the field. When the crowd got to their feet and roared, she stood up, her hand in the book to make sure she wouldn't lose her place. When the crowd sat down again, she sat down again. At the end of the game, she asked someone who had won. Even then, despite his physical beauty and skill at sports, Luke seemed curiously uninterested in sex. They made love—they had both been "broken in" by other people—and it was good. Alix had learned to have orgasms quickly enough so that never became a problem. Sex was exciting, but when it was over she got almost more pleasure watching him sleep, looking at his lanky, lean body. Even the fact that he never really lost that detachment during sex was intriguing to her. She had never known detached people, not in that way. It seemed to imply not indifference, but an acceptance of things so deep that there was no need for surface hysterics or carrying on, moaning and groaning, throwing things.

When her mother met Luke for the first time, she took her aside afterward and said, half playfully, "Darling, he's too handsome. Women will be after him all his life. Be careful." "It doesn't bother me," Alix replied blithely. This was true. She knew she was brainy and bespectacled—this was before she got used to wearing contacts and discovered her own way of dressing—but she always felt, as she felt now, that she had Luke's undivided attention. He would even show her the notes he got from groupies with a kind of mild amazement. "Would you ever have thought there were so many crazy girls out there?" he would say, shaking his head, perplexed. Alix didn't regard them as crazy at all; they were just nervy, wanting what they imagined as "a piece of the action." If they had ever seen her, she knew they would have regarded her as no challenge at all. They would have been wrong.

In the twelve years they'd been married, their sex life had hardly changed. It had never been intense, exhausting, staying up all night unable to keep their hands off each other, exploring every position. It was a more stately, graceful act—silent, mutually enjoyable, never a source of despair or humiliation, never especially exhilarating. A thing people did, a thing Alix enjoyed. But she could easily imagine, now that he had provided the image, Luke as a widower, deftly avoiding all the widows and divorcées who would strew themselves in his path like those groupies of old, stepping over them, possibly not even seeing them.

She had known Gerald four years before they went to bed together, and until then, had never given him a thought sexually. He was two inches shorter than she was, chubby, constantly struggling to give up food and drink, a smoker, like her father—though unlike her father, he succeeded in stopping after his heart attack. She found him funny; he laughed her into bed which, he said later, had always been his technique with women. Amazing that people could laugh and even talk in bed! Looking at Gerald asleep, she would feel the opposite of what she felt with Luke. How peculiar it was that she could get so much pleasure with someone who was physically out of shape, had a potbelly, was funny-looking, so totally not her type. She tried to see it as a father-figure thing, since he was twelve years older, but if so, he was certainly the antithesis of her actual father who had been conventional, reticent, hard working, and slight in build. A religious Jew, at least as far as obeying the forms went.

Luke retreated into the music room. Alix took her work into her study. I'll lie down for just a minute, she thought, and then look at the Bernice Daley notes. Stretching out on the couch, she pulled an afghan over herself, keeping the desk light on. She was exhausted, but also afraid of falling asleep, both because of those odd dreams she'd been having and because if she really fell asleep so early—it was only nine-thirty—she might wake up at four or five. Pam used to get up that early to tend the horses; she said it was her favorite time of day. Alix closed her eyes. The image that came before her was Pam galloping over the field in the back of their house. She was going toward the tree where she would be killed, she was galloping toward it, and Alix was there, but not there, was invisible, couldn't stop her. I don't want to watch it happening, she thought. The galloping just went on, as though the horse wasn't really moving and the goal would never be reached. Behind the house Michael was marrying his new bride. For them it had already happened years ago. Alix, who was also a part of the wedding ceremony, stood there holding a bouquet of flowers, but heard the galloping sounds that no one else heard. Finally she yelled, "Stop!" If they didn't stop, Pam was doomed, she would have to die . . .

"Alix, darling . . ." It was Luke, bending over her.

She sat up, petrified.

"What's wrong?"

"It was Pam, she was—I can't describe it, she was about to die again."

He sat beside her. "Maybe getting that letter from Michael . . . Do you feel he's betraying her?"

"How can I?" Alix said. "It's been five years . . . It's just, I don't know, so many people dying! Everyone seems to be dying!"

He reached for her hand. "But we have each other."

Did he mean that at all ambiguously? Had he known about

Gerald? She could imagine him not knowing, or knowing and accepting, or half knowing and choosing not to know the part that would cause him discomfort or pain. "What do you mean, 'we have each other'?" she asked, still groggy. The room was dim, the only illumination from the desk lamp.

He looked puzzled. "Just that. Here we are, the two of us, our lives are linked. That's all I meant."

The two of us.

When they were first married, they had discussed having children, and had decided to put it off until they were thirty. At thirty, and then at thirty-five, they discussed it again, but it seemed to Alix each time it came up subsequently, it became more theoretical. She didn't feel a sense of what she had read about so often, the biological clock. If anything, she was relieved it existed, that she was already approaching a time when it might be physically dangerous for her to be pregnant. If Pamela's children had lived close by, she felt she would have enjoyed being an aunt. She felt she had an auntlike look and had even asked Luke jocularly why there was no female form of the word "avuncular." Auntlike. On certain days, with her felt hats and silver-handled umbrellas and dark boots, she thought she looked exactly like someone's aunt.

Children seemed frightening to her, not just because they were loud and unpredictable, but because her own mother had seemed so thrown by the experience, had seemed so much an example of how it didn't come naturally. When Pam had her babies, their mother had looked at them in complete amazement, "as though she'd never had one, had never even *seen* one," Pam had said to Alix. "She was afraid to hold Laurel, afraid she'd drop her!" Somehow that seemed not as peculiar to Alix as it had to Pam who, as with riding horses, had an ease about babies and childbirth that amazed Alix, in the same way that Luke's proficiency at skiing and swimming did. "Women are born knowing how," Pam used to insist. "Then what happened to Mother?" Alix would ask. Pam would just shrug.

Maybe if she and Luke had had children, their lives would seem more solidly linked now. Instead the link Alix saw in her mind was like a fine gold chain, so fine it was like threads or hairs woven together. "I feel so shaky," she whispered. She saw she was actually trembling. "Could you hold me?"

"Of course." They sat there, entwined. After a moment, he said, "Do you think you should see a doctor, perhaps?"

"About the sleeping?"

"And these dreams you say you have—thinking about death all the time."

"What can doctors say? They can't bring people back from the dead."

He hesitated. "They could bring you back."

Alix drew back. "What do you mean?" She felt frightened.

"Well, just make you more the way you were before. That's all I meant."

She frowned. "How was I before? Was I different? I thought I've always been like this."

"You've always been a little like this, but I think now maybe it's getting out of hand. I don't know. How do *you* feel?"

Alix thought of Silas Foss saying, "Take care of yourself." She saw her hand reaching out impulsively to press Daphne Lehman's buzzer and then fleeing. "Let me think," she said. She tried hard to gather herself together. "I think it's that I never reacted to those deaths when they happened, Pam's especially, but everyone's . . . and now it's all piled up."

Luke was sitting slightly hunched forward, his fingertips touching. "And then your boss, Gerald Lehman. *His* death was so sudden."

Instead of recoiling, Alix cried eagerly, "Yes! Because, you see, up till now it was just family, and that made it seem as though it might never stop, a widening circle."

"He was like a mentor to you," Luke added.

"Yes, the way Professor Barnes was to you. And a mentor is like a father." Suddenly Alix felt almost hysterically relieved. "It's all tangled together . . . What if *you* die too?"

He laughed. "I'm in perfect health."

"So was Pam."

"I'm very careful when I ski, I don't take unnecessary risks."

"Do you think *she* did? Do you think that's why she died?"

Luke drew back at the intensity of her voice. "We'll never know. No one was there when it happened."

In her mind Alix saw Gerald reach over, feel the pain, and decide to ignore it. *"The doctor would put me in the hospital and I don't have time."*

"I've disappointed everyone," Alix said. "That's part of it. I let everyone down. I never wrote to Pam, we really almost lost touch—"

"She never wrote you."

"Yes, but I set the tone. And my father. I despised him, really, in a lot of ways. He seemed so held in, so unreal. But maybe there was something behind that which I never bothered finding out about. And my mother. And you—"

Luke put his arm around her again. "There's nothing to be guilty about in relation to me . . . or to any of these people. Darling, let it go. Don't try to figure it out. Let it all slide away."

"Yes." She let him fix her a drink of hot milk with brandy and sugar and sipped it thoughtfully in bed. *Let it all slide away.* There were two worlds: Luke's garden, his quiet self-enclosed garden with stone walls and the vines, and everything outside—where people fell, vanished, were killed, engulfed. *Stay in the garden. Believe it exists, because if you don't it won't be there.*

It seemed to her a coincidence. When she was going down for lunch the next day, intending to have a quick bite, Alix saw Giselle Fleming in the elevator. They smiled at each other. Smoking was forbidden in the elevator, but Alix saw how Giselle's hands were already clutched around her leather cigarette case. Gerald had claimed it was seeing how desperate cigarettes could make you, living with Giselle, that made him stop.

They walked toward the door of the building together, almost in step. Suddenly Alix said, "Do you have a date? I don't have much time, but I've heard there's a nice new Italian place around the corner."

Giselle, who was already smoking, looked delighted. "Yes, yes. I've been there." She had an incipient stammer. She never quite repeated words, but she hesitated or seemed about to trip over certain words which gave her speech a halting, uncertain quality.

Walking to the restaurant, Alix felt excited. *This was just what I wanted. Someone who loved him. We don't have to talk about him. Just what I wanted.*

Giselle was almost anorectically thin. She wore a gold chain around her neck that had a tiny stone set in it, and because of the angularity of her collarbones the stone sank into her flesh as though it were embedded there. Gerald had claimed she was very bright, but insecure, that he had encouraged her to go back to school, to try out for a more satisfying or challenging job, but that she always blanked out at job interviews, became so anxious she could hardly speak.

"How have things been?" Giselle asked. "Any interesting cases?"

Gerald had sworn Giselle knew nothing about them, had boyfriends, but would be jealous if she knew. "Well, I have an interesting one about a surrogate mother," Alix said. "Her twin sister offered to bear a child for her since she had two of her own already, but then changed her mind."

"I think that whole thing is so sick," Giselle said, wrinkling her nose. She had tilted, slightly Oriental grey eyes with long, thin, dark lashes. "I think it should be forbidden."

"You feel it's unfair to the surrogate mother?" Alix asked, surprise at her vehemence.

"Of course! I had a child once in college and I had to give her up for adoption and I think of her every day of my life! Every day!" Giselle grabbed her water and drank some. "You never get over it. It's inside. It's visceral."

"I've never had a child," Alix said.

Giselle looked surprised. "I thought you did. I thought you had two."

"No."

"But you're married?"

"Yes." Alix looked at her, frowning.

"Maybe I got you mixed up with someone else," Giselle said enigmatically, with a half smile.

"Someone else from the office?" For some reason her heart was pounding.

Giselle still had that half smile. "There was a woman at the office whom Gerald Lehman saw, or at least I believe he might have been in love with . . ."

Alix said nothing, paralyzed with fear. "I never heard any rumors about him," she said.

"Did you know about me?" Giselle asked, mischievously.

"In connection with Mr. Lehman?"

"Yes . . . that we'd been lovers for five years?"

Alix looked at the stone in Giselle's necklace. "All I knew, really, was that he was separated from his wife, but had never gotten a divorce."

"We lived together for five years," Giselle said, lifting her head proudly. "That's the longest I've ever lived with anyone."

"Were you still living together when he died?" Alix asked. *I was crazy to ask her to lunch. Why did I do it?*

"No. But we went on vacations together."

"Then you were still in love, but couldn't . . . live together?"

"We weren't in love, but we loved each other." Giselle crunched on a breadstick. "I sometimes felt he might have been in love with someone, but he always denied it. He said it was a figment of my imagination."

The waiter had brought their wine. Alix sipped deeply from her glass. "What made you think that?"

"When you live with someone that long, you get to know a lot about them, from what they don't say as much as from what they say. He never wanted to sleep with me when we went on vacations together. Not that I—I was going with him for that reason. But we always slept in separate beds."

Alix had always wondered about that, though it fitted Gerald's description exactly. "Well, it shows you, that there was something between you other than sex, that he would still want to go on vacations with you even after . . ." The sentence seemed to meander, unable to complete itself.

Giselle flushed. "Of course there was more than just sex!" She looked down at her plate, seeming hurt. "Why did you say you thought it was just sex?"

At that moment the waiter came. They ordered silently and tensely.

"I—I don't think I said I thought there was nothing between you but sex," Alix stammered. "People don't live together that long unless there's more than that."

Giselle's grey eyes were accusing. "How do you know how long we lived together? I thought you said you knew nothing about it!"

"You told me . . . Just a few minutes ago. You said it was five years."

Giselle was silent. "Yes," she said. She looked right at Alix and smiled with the half smile that now seemed overtly malicious. "To what do you attribute *your* happy marriage?" she asked.

"Did I—did I say I was happily married?" Alix asked evasively.

"Aren't you?"

Alix looked around the room. She had a sense that some trap was being laid, which she would fall into. "I *think* I am," she said slowly. "Of course all marriages have certain . . . Nothing is perfect."

Instead of replying, Giselle sat there, staring at her.

Alix felt unnerved. "Gerald was, in a sense, my mentor," she rushed on, "and his death has affected me a great deal. I don't seem to be able to—I've had a lot of trouble concentrating. My husband thinks I should see a doctor. Or perhaps take a leave of absence from work."

"Maybe you should," Giselle said. "Some people end up having breakdowns if they let things go too far. My mother did."

"Mine did too," Alix said. Suddenly she felt a tremendous closeness to Giselle. "Do you have a boyfriend now? Anyone special?"

"No one special," Giselle said. "I don't know. I don't think my specialty is men. Though they're always attracted to me for my looks. And they like my being insecure. Gerald loved that. They *love* my being an underachiever." She laughed. "Did you know that? Some men find that terribly appealing."

"I *do* know that," Alix said, hating her.

"Gerald could have had his choice, but he said all those women he worked with, all those women lawyers were just castrating cold bitches. He said he wouldn't have gone near them with a ten-foot pole. They were just clones of men." She paused. "But, of course, there are exceptions."

Their food had arrived. Alix had forgotten what she ordered, some kind of fish. She couldn't even remember ordering. *She knows and she hates me.* Alix picked up her knife and fork. "Gerald's wife was an underachiever also," she said. "That must have been his type."

"Are you implying I'm like his wife?"

"How could I? I never met her . . . And I don't really know what you're like."

Giselle's expression softened. "I just find everything very difficult actually. That's why I stay in this job—because it's so undemanding. I find many things incomprehensible and frightening. Men, sex, life . . ."

Am I like her or the opposite? If someone were looking down on us, what would he think? What would he say? "Did Gerald's death affect you very much?" she asked tentatively.

"I don't think about it." Giselle brought a piece of pasta delicately to her lips. "I don't believe in dwelling on things like that. I didn't even go to his funeral."

"Why was that?"

Giselle leaned forward, her voice very soft, intimate. "I knew *she* would be there, and that I would recognize her somehow. I knew she'd be there, crying, making a scene. Women like that always do, carrying on. And it would be so false!"

Giselle's face seemed to expand and contract. The familiar constriction tightened in Alix's chest; the room swayed. *You set this up yourself; therefore you can get out of it.* She found herself unable to speak.

"Did *you* go to the funeral?" Giselle asked.

Alix nodded.

"And did you cry? Do you cry at funerals?"

Alix shook her head. But at the same moment tears started falling down her cheeks, onto her plate. "I never cry," she whispered. It was unclear to her how long they sat there like that, Alix weeping silently, Giselle either eating or staring at her, but saying nothing. "I just can't go on," she said finally. "I don't know. It's too difficult."

"Do you want to go home? Should I call you a cab?"

"Everyone I know is dying," Alix said, looking at her plate, her voice unsteady. "The only one left is my husband. First my father, then my mother, then my sister, then Gerald."

Giselle still had that curious air of aloofness. "Who do you think will be next?"

"I don't know." She had stopped trying to eat, she felt as if everything had collapsed.

"Gerald had been ill," Giselle said, as though explaining. "He'd had a very severe heart attack. His health was impaired. Which is why I feel possibly that woman was responsible for his death. They say sexual excitement is very bad if your heart is weak. That's why I never approached him when we went on vacations. But some women are selfish, insatiable. Even if they're married, even if they have someone else—"

"Stop it!" Alix screamed. "Stop!"

The waiter rushed over. He bent solicitously over her. "Are you all right?"

"She needs to go home," Giselle said. "She's sick."

Alix was confused about what happened next. Giselle seemed to disappear and she found herself in a cab, evidently going home. "Did I give you the address?" she asked the driver.

"Yes, ma'am," he said.

What happened? I have to try and recreate it. I saw Giselle in the elevator. She was holding her pack of cigarettes because smoking isn't allowed in the elevator. We started walking out together . . . But then Alix saw the restaurant, Giselle's mocking smile, the smoke drifting in front of her face. She was talking, but Alix couldn't remember anything she had said. *Did we talk or did I just sit down and then feel dizzy? Or did I tell her everything about Gerald? And now will she go back and tell everyone at the firm?* Alix pressed her hand to her forehead. She tried hard to remember the scene in the restaurant, but it had vanished except for visual images, like the platter of fish being set down in front of her, the necklace Giselle had been wearing with the embedded stone.

When she got home, Alix called the office. She spoke to the receptionist. "Is Silas in?" she asked. "This is Alix Zimmer."

"He's in a meeting right now."

"Could you let him know that I wasn't feeling well? I went home."

"Yes, he knows," the receptionist said.

How did he know? Perhaps Giselle had left word. *Should I call her and find out what she said? Will she tell the truth? No, don't call. I can speak to Silas tomorrow. Or call him at home tonight. It doesn't matter.*

Alix wandered around the apartment. *It really is sick in a way— such a large apartment for a couple without children. There are so many families without homes and here we are with our music room and our two studies . . . I could get pregnant. It's not too late, really. I could have two children, even! We could put the crib in the room with the harpsichord and later, perhaps, move the harpsichord into the living room.* Alix got excited, thinking about it, and even dragged the harpsichord into the living room to see how it would look placed near the window. Then she went inside and fell into a deep dreamless sleep.

When Luke returned, he said, "Alix? Are you all right? They called me at work."

She sat up in bed, clutching the blankets. "Who called you? Why did they call you? I was just feeling dizzy. I've been working so hard."

He sat down on the bed beside her. "They seemed concerned about you."

"Was it a woman? Did a woman call you? Someone named Giselle?"

"No, it was Mr. Foss."

Alix was silent.

"Who is Giselle?" Luke asked.

Alix wasn't sure if she should even mention Giselle. If she did, he could call her and then he might find out everything—if, in fact, she had told Giselle everything. She still couldn't remember the conversation at lunch. "Just someone I know from work." Suddenly she smiled. "Did you see the harpsichord?" she asked.

"No, where is it?"

Alix got out of bed. In her stocking feet she padded into the living room and showed him where she had put it, near the window, brushing up against the large plant they kept there. "How do you like it?"

"Well, I do, but . . . Why move it? It was fine where it was."

She smiled shyly. "I was just thinking. If we did have a child, we could use the music room for the baby's things. I wanted to see if the harpsichord would look good in the living room."

Luke puzzled. "Do you want to have a child? I thought we'd decided—"

"Yes, I do," Alix said. Her face felt flushed. "Maybe two, even. We have all this room. We're both earning good salaries. We could even have a live-in nurse, if we wanted. What do you think?"

Luke looked uncertain; he was frowning. "I thought we had decided against it," he said. "Your work is so pressured. You said it would be too much."

"That was before," Alix said. "I could get another job, a less pressured job. Otherwise we could just become automatons, not really alive. That's what I'm afraid is happening right now. We're already a little like that. We need a link, the way you said last night. We—"

He grabbed her hands. "Slow down. You're talking so fast."

"Am I?"

"Let's have a little supper," he said. "We can talk about it over supper."

He made supper, some fish and spinach with a salad on the side. He opened a bottle of wine, lit the dark red candles. "I had fish at lunch, I think," Alix said. Her excitement was dying down. He had seemed so unresponsive about the idea of having a child. "Do you not want a child?" she asked plaintively.

"Yes, eventually," Luke said. "I think it's a fine idea. But now, I think you need to rest, to get back in shape. It would be a big undertaking, I'm not saying dangerous, but you *are* thirty-six and—"

"But that's why we mustn't lose time!" Alix said. "We've waited too long already. We mustn't wait. I thought we could make love tonight. It could happen tonight!"

Luke was looking off into space. "It's too sudden," he said slowly.

"We've talked about it for years. How is it sudden?"

He reached over and placed his hand over hers. "Why don't we just take things one day at a time?"

"What does that mean?" Alix looked at him suspiciously.

He was talking very carefully, very precisely, but that was the way he talked. "I want you to get back in shape, feel relaxed, and then we can talk about it."

"Tell me one thing," Alix said.

"Yes?"

"Do you want me to be the mother of your children?"

"Of course I do. It's only a matter of whether we want children. We've been so happy alone together, just the two of us." His blue eyes looked at her with concern.

"Have we?"

"Yes, I think so . . . Don't you?"

Alix found she couldn't eat. She sipped at her wine. "I've been happy," she repeated. "Things can never be perfect—"

"Of course not."

There was a silence.

She looked at him carefully. He looked almost ridiculously handsome, his hair barely grey at all, his grey jacket so soft and beautifully cut. "Don't women ever approach you at work, though?" she asked.

"You mean—in what way?"

"Sexually? Don't they ever come on to you?"

"Not that I've noticed."

"That's strange," Alix said thoughtfully.

"Why strange? They see I'm not available." He touched his thin gold wedding ring.

"Everyone wears rings," Alix said with a dismissive gesture. "That doesn't mean anything."

"Of course it does," Luke said. "How can you say that? It shows the world one is married, that the kind of behavior you're talking about would be unacceptable."

She was picking at her fish, pulling off the bones. "It's not like that where I work. Everyone is available . . ."

He smiled. "Even Silas Foss?"

"Probably even him." She looked around the room. He had drawn the ivory drapes; he thought it looked softer that way. "I guess I wanted a commitment from you, about the child. It means a lot to me. I feel you're retreating."

Luke stood up from his chair. "Darling, you have it. We will have a child. Just not this very instant."

She reached up and stroked his hand. "But can we make love? It seems like it's been so long . . ." She couldn't remember how long it had been.

"Of course." He walked with her into the bedroom and they took their clothes off. Alix was undressed first and watched him from the back, the lean, exquisite line of his body. They made love quickly and in silence, as always. She didn't think of Gerald. All she had was a sense of him hovering at the periphery of her consciousness. When she came, she saw herself jumping from an open window into a landscape filled with snow. The snow was so thick it seemed to buoy her up, as though she were flying.

"I wish we could make love every day," she said into the dark silence.

"No one does at our age, when they've been married as long as we have." But she felt his voice was more intimate than it had been during dinner when he had seemed so remote.

"I suppose," Alix said. She wanted him to say that this night, anyway, they would make love all night, but he seemed to be drifting off. *It's warm here. I'm safe. No one is dying, no one is dead.*

When she woke up in the middle of the night and went to the window, it was snowing. How odd for April. Then she remembered snowstorms around Easter. It's rare, but it happens. She thought of the fantasy she'd had of flying out the window, into the thick, whirling snow. *But I don't really want to do that. I'd rather be inside where it's warm and safe.* She tried to remember if she had cried at Pam's funeral. *I don't think I did because I didn't want to upset Mother. Michael was crying, and the children . . .*

It was four in the morning. *The main thing is to go to work and to go on as though nothing has happened. Because nothing has happened. I only missed half a day of work. And if I did behave strangely, no one at work saw me. The only one in the restaurant was Giselle.* Was that true? Again she put the scene of the lunch in front of her as though it were a photo, and tried to look around the edges. There must have been other people in the restaurant. It was very crowded. Anyway, why does that matter? *"I never cry at funerals." "They love my being an underachiever." "Some men find that terribly appealing." "Sexual excitement is*

*very bad if your heart is weak." "But some women are selfish, insatiable."
"Even if they're married, even if they have someone else." "Cold, castrating
bitches . . ."*

Who had been saying those things? Alix wondered if she had
overheard a conversation at the next table. Sometimes she liked to
eavesdrop. It might have been two women, talking about a man,
someone they had both slept with. One heard of that. She had read
an article on it recently. Man-sharing. And wasn't it supposedly a
common male fantasy—two women at the same time?

She went back to bed and fell back to sleep with greater ease
than usual. In fact, she didn't awaken until later when Luke was
bending over her. "Darling?"

"Umm?" She was so sleepy, as though she were drugged.

"I have to leave for work now. It's past eight-thirty. Will you be
all right?"

"Of course." She wasn't sure what he meant.

"The weather's terrible out. Why don't you stay home? It's
Friday, near the weekend." He already had his coat and fur hat on,
his sheepskin gloves.

"Yes," Alix said, yawning. "That's a good idea."

After he left, she lay in bed sleepily for another hour, enjoying
the warmth of the bed in contrast to the cold air in the bedroom.
They always kept the window partially ajar, even when it was very
cold out. When she finally got up, she put on a robe and went into
the kitchen where the coffee was on. She sat down at her desk, with
her coffee, and began going through the mail that was in the "personal" section. *I've fallen so far behind. There's so much I need to do.* She
came upon the wedding invitation from Michael: "Michael Ames
requests the pleasure of your company at his wedding to Stacey
King on April 4th at four P.M." It was an engraved card with the
address of the home where he had lived with Pam. It was a ranch,
but the house was separate. *Why there? Wasn't it tasteless, rude, to get
married in the home of your dead wife? But he's not religious so where else could
it be? It's still his home. Luke says he won't remarry if I die. But Michael has
children; he wants someone to help raise them. Maybe Stacey King has children
of her own. No, probably she was younger, in her late twenties, skinny,
tawny-haired. How did Laurel and Dalton feel? I hope they hate her. They
have to; she's an impostor, taking over Pam's life, her husband, her children.*

*No, Michael has a right to a new life. Most men remarry. Luke says he
wouldn't, but of course he would.* Michael was rugged, macho in a way

that had always slightly revolted Alix. He actually chewed tobacco and spat it out, like a baseball player. His legs looked bowed, from riding all day. It seemed to her he didn't shave often enough or at least he had a grizzled look, bushy grey hair, squinty eyes that were shrewd, appraising with women, as though they were cattle he was trying to decide whether to buy. Alix saw Luke and Michael as the two trajectories away from her father. *Pam and I both wanted something totally different, someone who fit into American life in that way Jews never seem to.* They had both, in a sense, married foreigners.

The snow was tapering off. Alix thought of how lovely it had been in the middle of the night when it had whirled around, seeming not just to fall, but to swirl in all directions like a paperweight shaken violently. Then it had seemed mysterious and wild; now it was just snow falling silently. *I could go to the wedding. If there's a plane to Denver, I could be there by four, even earlier.* Suddenly she knew that was exactly what she would do. Luke wouldn't want to go especially, but she would go as an act of forgiveness, to show Michael she accepted his decision. First she called the travel agent and booked a flight. One was leaving in two hours which would arrive at two, Colorado time. She made a reservation at a local hotel she and Luke had stayed at once. Then she called Luke at work. His secretary answered. "He's in a meeting."

"Could you just tell him—this is his wife—that I'm flying to Denver for my brother-in-law's wedding. He knows about it. I'll call him tonight."

"I'll tell him," the secretary said. "Have a good trip."

"Thanks."

Alix showered, dressed, packed. She felt buoyant, excited. *Maybe all I needed was a change of scene, some travel. I should do this more. We both should.* Earlier in their marriage they would go to London for a week just to see plays, a different one every night. *We should do that again, make our lives more exciting, take control of them. Even if I get pregnant, we can still . . . But that's not definite. We'll have to see.*

Her mood of elation lasted until she was actually on the airplane. Then, looking out the window, she had a slight pang of anxiety. She didn't think it was about flying. *Perhaps this is a mistake. I should have gone with Luke. It will be awkward. I'll be the only one from Pam's family. They won't want me there . . . But he sent you the invitation. It said RSVP. But I didn't have time . . .*

She thought of the dress she'd packed, a lovely black chiffon dress with a full skirt. To wear with it, she'd bought a beautiful opal necklace and earrings that dangled just below her ear. Was black morbid for a wedding? No, she recalled reading an article somewhere that said it was now acceptable. It was a flattering color, after all. She had always been told she looked good in black. Gerald had liked her black underwear. "Your skin is so white."

The thought of Gerald disquieted her further because it brought back the lunch with Giselle the day before. She was his mistress for five years. He liked her because she was gentle, retiring, unsure of herself. But then, he said, it became oppressive. He felt as though he were too much of a father figure, always having to encourage her: to take courses, to apply for better jobs. "But you set that up," Alix had said. "Of course you were a father figure! You were almost twenty years older than her." "I don't think that's what I was looking for," he said. "At some level you were—or you liked part of it, but not all," she insisted. "With you it's different," he said. "We're equals. I can discuss anything with you." "But I'm still younger, not threatening. You haven't really broken the mold." "Well, looks are still important to me. Is that so terrible?" He would smile wryly.

Why was it she could remember that conversation almost verbatim, though it had taken place at least four years ago, and not remember the conversation with Giselle except to have the feeling that it had been unpleasant? *She said some pretty terrible things; I guess I blocked it out.* Suddenly the plane gave a dip. Alix sucked in her breath and inadvertently clutched the arm of the man sitting next to her, a heavyset businessman who said quietly, "Don't worry. It's nothing."

She drew back. "I'm so sorry. I just—"

"It's a little turbulence," he said. "I fly this route several times a month. It's not uncommon."

"I'm flying out for my brother-in-law's wedding," Alix said. "My sister died five years ago . . . Do you think he's waited long enough?"

The man looked taken aback. "Five years is a long time."

"For what? What do you mean?"

"Well, just . . . Men usually like living with women unless . . ." He seemed flustered.

"Are you married?" Alix demanded. He was wearing a paisley tie; his skin was rough and reddened.

"Yes, I am, for twenty-seven years." He seemed proud of the statistic.

"And you would marry—remarry—within five years if your wife died?"

He hesitated. "I think I might, yes." He laughed. "All these questions! You'd make a good lawyer."

"I *am* a lawyer."

"Are you? You don't look like one." He smiled, as though he were complimenting her.

"What do I look like?" Alix asked. For some reason his answer seemed important. "I mean, what profession did you think I belonged to?"

"An actress perhaps, or a dancer."

A dancer! *I don't belong to the ballet lineup.* What a strange comment. Alix fell silent, ignoring him.

When she arrived at the hotel, she had only an hour until it would be time to set out for the wedding. She rented a car; it was only a half hour's drive. But already she was feeling it had been a mistake. *I don't want to see him get married.* She thought of just spending the night and then flying home. Impulsively she tried Luke at his office again. "I'm in Denver," she said gaily. "Did you get my message?"

"Yes. I don't understand. Why go to the wedding? A day ago you were saying—"

"Yes, I probably shouldn't have," Alix said. She sighed. "I just . . . well, here I am. I'll go, then I'll come home."

"I would have liked to go with you."

"Would you? I never thought you liked Michael especially."

"I don't. That is, I never knew him very well, but I would have liked to be there, for your sake. It's going to be difficult for you, seeing him with another woman, don't you think?"

Alix looked around the room. "Well, it's been five years . . ." In her mind she saw Pam galloping on her horse. She remembered the dream about Michael getting married and in the background the sound of galloping.

"When do you intend to fly back?" Luke asked.

"Tomorrow, I guess."

"Look, why don't I fly out tonight? I can't make it for the wedding, but I'll stay over with you and maybe tomorrow we can drive around, spend the weekend. Give me the phone number of the hotel."

Alix did that. Then she hung up and began dressing for the wedding. It was a nice idea, thoughtful. Tonight he would be here. They could make love. Maybe they could conceive a child. Many children are conceived when people make love under unusual circumstances, in hurricanes or snowstorms or in exotic places. Because they're more relaxed. She hadn't brought her diaphragm.

When she was finished dressing, she looked at herself in the full-length bathroom mirror. A dancer, an actress. The skirt of the dress was very full, she was wearing low heels, her dark hair was pulled back in a chignon. She did look pale, a bit too thin, but otherwise all right, elegant. Would she look much older to the children, whom she hadn't seen since Pam's death?

When Alix arrived at the house, there were already at least one hundred people outside, having drinks, talking. It was a bright clear day, the sky almost too blue. *I don't know anyone.* She felt panicked. *You know Michael. Find him.* She got a drink, some champagne and then looked through the crowd until she saw Michael. He had grown a beard and was still heavy. He was wearing a suit with a gaudy vest, leather with silver doodads on it. Next to him was a plump, rosy young woman with shoulder-length reddish brown hair. She was wearing a white dress, almost to the ground. Wasn't that odd? For a second wedding? And to have all these people! Alix had expected it to be small, intimate, a few close friends and family.

"Hi, Michael," she said softly, tugging at his sleeve.

"Alix! How great! I didn't think you could make it. Where's Luke?"

"He'll be flying out tonight."

"Terrific." His voice was so loud, booming. "This is my fiancée, Stacey King. Stacey, this is Pam's sister, Alix Zimmer."

Alix had expected Stacey would look embarrassed, but she just smiled broadly. "Nice to meet you, Alix. It's such a beautiful day, isn't it?"

She seemed like a total dimwit, a fool. "Is this your first marriage?" Alix asked. Michael had turned away and was talking to someone else.

"Yes," Stacey said, beaming. Her nose was shiny where the sun had melted her makeup.

"I didn't expect such a large ceremony for a second marriage," Alix said. "So many people!"

"Yes, all our friends."

Our? How could they have acquired this many friends so quickly, before they were married even? Were most of these people friends Michael and Pam had had? Was that what she meant? That she was just stepping into an already existing niche? "Are you going to be living here?" Alix asked.

"Yes. We may add on a few new rooms, just in case."

Alix squinted. She fumbled in her bag for her sunglasses. "In case of what?"

"In case we . . . add on to the family, have children." At that moment, someone came up and grabbed Stacey by the elbow.

Alix stood there feeling stunned, almost sick. They were already planning a family? It was as though Pam hadn't existed. *I shouldn't have come. I betrayed her by coming. Forgive me, Pam. Please.*

The ceremony was held in back of the house. The ranch was far enough from the city to be so quiet that when the minister spoke the words, each word rang out almost theatrically in the stillness. Then Alix began hearing the pounding. It was Pam, galloping. *No, that was a dream. This is real. This is you, it's your heart pounding, probably.* Alix looked up. It seemed to her that in the distance she could actually see someone on a horse, galloping, too far away to see if it was a man or a woman. *Maybe I can save her. If I can get there before she reaches that tree.* Turning, Alix began to run. It was hard running on the earth. The grass was tall, and her heels sank into the ground. The bright blinding sun made it hard to see, even with her sunglasses. "Pam?" she cried. "Pam?"

Finally, just as she thought she was going to collapse, someone caught up with her. It was a man in jeans and a cowboy shirt, a cowboy hat. "Miss? Where are you going?"

The strange thing was that, although she'd been running so fast and hard that her dress was plastered to her body, the figure on the horse was exactly as far away as it had been when she started to run. "I want to stop her!" she cried, panting, leaning on him for support. "I'm afraid she'll be killed."

"Who?"

"That person on the horse." She gestured toward the open field which seemed endless.

"Where?" He squinted toward the horizon with her.

By now the figure was almost invisible. Maybe it was just a tree. "It's too far away," Alix said, a feeling of desolation creeping over her. "And it's too late. She died anyway."

"Miss?" He was deferential, kindly, an older man, his hair was white. "Why don't you come back and sit in the shade and have something cool to drink? It's real hot out here."

"Yes," Alix said gratefully. "I'd love that. Thank you so much. I'm Alix Zimmer. My sister used to live here."

"I know," the man said.

When she said she didn't see why a hospital would be necessary, Luke explained. "A lot of people think these things are chemical, mood swings, depression. And this hospital, Nash, has an excellent drug program. I've spoken to several people about it. One man said his wife came home a new person. They found the right drug and it changed her life."

They were sitting in their living room. "I don't want to be a new person," Alix said. "I don't want to change my life."

"Yes, but darling, you aren't. Something's happened. You've been having these . . . well, like at the wedding."

Alix frowned. "I can't remember. What happened at the wedding?"

"Don't you remember? You thought you saw Pam, you went running off, trying to stop her from being killed."

Dimly Alix saw the wide field, the peculiarly blue sky, the hazy tiny figure on the horizon. "I think that was heat stroke," she said. "It was incredibly hot. I should have worn a hat."

He was silent a long time. "I think it was more than that."

Alix felt a milder version of the desolation she had experienced in Colorado. "I suppose I resented Michael's marrying again. I was trying to pretend Pam was still alive. Maybe I willed her back into existence, however briefly."

Luke was silent. He seemed embarrassed and sad, unusually inarticulate.

"Is it that you think I'm crazy?" Alix asked. For some reason the conversation didn't bother her. She understood his concern. It was as though they were talking about someone else.

"No, crazy is such a perjorative word. I think you're upset. A lot of things have been crowding in on you. You've been working so hard. And maybe that invitation to the wedding set something off."

"Yes, perhaps," Alix said vaguely. She wasn't sure. It was true lately that things had seemed heightened, sometimes in a way that was exciting or at least unusual, at other times in a way that seemed scary and incomprehensible. "If I were mystical, I would probably feel I was reaching some other plane of reality." She smiled.

"But you're not. Normally you're a very rational person."

"Yes." That was true. Everyone had always said it of her, admired her for her coolness, for her organization. "I certainly haven't been an underachiever," she said wryly.

"Of course not," Luke said, surprised. "Quite the opposite."

They sat in silence. Alix looked around the large, beautiful living room, at the prints they had carefully collected over the years. Luke liked old photographs and they had several, framed, over the desk. "I suppose being in a place like that, the hospital you describe, could be restful."

"Exactly!" He looked relieved, pleased. "That's the whole point of it. You go somewhere where all your needs are cared for, where you have an excellent professional staff who have helped other people with these same kinds of problems, and where they have access to all the most recent drugs."

"And I could get out whenever I wanted?" Alix asked. "I mean, I'd be entering voluntarily, so . . ."

"Of course."

She thought of her mother and her breakdowns. She had been too young to understand at the time what was happening, only that her mother would "go away" and then come back. But she remembered a terrible quarrel between her parents over the fact that her mother had had shock treatment and had found it frightening. Her mother had begged her father not to let that happen again. It was strange, how this scene, which must have happened when Alix was young, seemed to appear out of nowhere. "They won't give me shock treatment?" she asked anxiously.

"Darling, this is a modern place. It isn't like those horrible movies one sees, *One Flew Over the Cuckoo's Nest*. Everything is done with the patient's consent."

It was tempting, appealing, the idea of sorting everything out, of coming to terms with what seemed at times too horrible to even contemplate: that Gerald was actually gone forever, that Pam was gone. When she would come out, in a few weeks, she would be able to think of them and not writhe inside. "Well, I'll start packing," Alix said calmly, getting up. "It won't take long."

LEO
THE LION

That morning, before Noah set out for school, his wife, Selma, shoved the announcement at him. "This came yesterday," she said. "I forgot to show you. Should we go?"

His brother, Leo, was going to be feted, to be honored at the public library in New York, he was going to be a literary lion. "I suppose we should," Noah said. "Would you like to?"

"I'd love to." Selma's eyes shone as they always did when Leo was mentioned. She had been Leo's girlfriend; that was how Noah had met her. Of course it had been years ago when he was a senior at City College and Leo a freshman on scholarship at Harvard. He could still remember his mother's ecstasy when that letter had arrived. "A scholarship at Harvard!" Leo had always had dozens of girlfriends, enough to spare, too many. Even in junior high, when Noah had only been gazing thoughtfully and timorously at the few possible girls in his high school classes, Leo was getting phone calls from girls almost every night. Their father was furious. "What is this? Boys should call girls, not the other way around. You're only eleven!" To which Leo would smile sheepishly and say, "Times have changed, Dad." Nathan, their father, would point at Noah. "No one's calling *him.* Why not? Haven't times changed for him? He's *supposed* to be going out. You're still a baby."

Leo had never lorded it over Noah about his girls. He seemed to find it slightly incomprehensible himself. He wasn't a sports star; he wasn't really good looking. He was skinny with red hair and freckles and a devilish grin, and had a way of clowning around that seemed to put girls at their ease. But it must have been more than that. He had some knack, he always had. A knack for living. Had there been justice in the world, it would have been divided up. Leo would have gotten the girls; Noah would have been the scholar. But Noah's grades were erratic, he daydreamed in class, blanked out at exams. Whereas Leo, with that same devil-may-care ease, got A's in everything, top scores on his SATs. Trying to explain math problems to Noah, he would say, "I don't know. I just look at the problem and the answer appears. I can't tell you how I get it. The numbers just interact in a certain way." Now that Noah was forty and Leo thirty-six, it was the same. Noah was teaching biology at a high school in Brooklyn which was constantly on the verge of extinction. Leo was a psychologist and the author of three books, one of which had recently become a best-seller.

"Well, call him," Noah said, finishing his coffee. "Tell him we can come."

Selma looked surprised. "Why should I call him? Why not you?"

"He likes to hear your voice."

She smiled, touched her lips. "No, you always say that. Look at his wife. I'm surprised he invites us to these affairs, even. We must seem so schlumpy compared to his friends, to the circles they move in . . ."

"We're family." Noah found Leo's wife, Eloise, nerve-wracking. She was director of marketing at a large import-export business. Tall, with high cheekbones and prematurely white hair, she always wore brilliantly colored clothes and bright red lipstick. Leo was unfaithful to her; Noah had never known if she knew or cared. There was something icy and imperious about her. But Selma was right. Suddenly he saw the two of them entering this posh party with famous people. Selma in whatever dress she wore, even if she bought a new dress especially for the occasion, would look frumpy, self-conscious, shy, would shred her napkin in her lap as she always did. Years ago when Selma had fallen for Leo "like a ton of bricks," as she admitted, he had known that she would never fit into the world into which he was going. He had been like an arrow, already released from the bow, racing toward the bull's-eye in the center of the target. Selma fit perfectly into Noah's world. He had gotten her on the rebound, but it had been a perfectly choreographed rebound, Selma accepting, understanding, he, Noah, relieved, overwhelmed with gratitude at his luck. *Leo the Matchmaker.* "Look, I know your taste. And she's a sweet girl. There's nothing wrong with her. It's just . . ." He didn't have to finish the sentence. Noah, Selma herself, could have finished it for him.

"I hate it when I get Eloise on the phone," Selma said. She was fussing with her greyish brown, curly hair. In five minutes she, too, would leave for her job at Sports World where she was an administrative assistant to the president. "Sometimes, I know this is petty, but I get the feeling she hates me, just because Leo and I once . . . Some women are like that. They can never forgive, never forget."

Noah was sure Eloise, if she had the time or inclination to be jealous or enraged, had many more relevant, closer at hand targets than a woman in her late thirties who, even seen with the eyes of love, was plump—sweetly maternal, at best. Not like Leo's last girlfriend, a twenty-eight-year-old brunette with blue eyes and a flawless figure who had been the copy editor on his last book. Noah always felt mixed about meeting Leo's girlfriends, but Leo always wanted him to meet them. Why? To flaunt? To brag? To mock, somehow, Noah's twenty-year fidelity to his wife? "I just like getting your reaction," Leo would say. "You know me. You know the real me."

Did he? Noah wasn't sure. But did he know the real Selma either, after all these years together? Did he know anyone, or even want to? On mornings like this everything seemed grey and shaky. "I don't think she bears you any ill will," Noah said gently.

"Oh, you don't understand!" Selma said. *"You* never bear anyone ill will, so you don't understand what people are like. People are sharks, sweetie."

"I know." That was exactly the way he felt going to work sometimes, as though he were lowering himself, naked, into a pool of sharks: the principal, Hal Garofolo, who was trying to get the school in shape, trying to weed out what he called "dead wood," and

Loretta Rauch, the guidance counselor who had been at the school as long as Noah had, who had been there when he had had his breakdown ten years ago. He tried not to look any of these people in the eyes because he saw there such a ghastly mixture of pity, cruelty, and contempt that, on some days, it could render him almost mute.

That was how his last breakdown had started. He had come into class one day and was unable to speak. It had been an ordinary class, on photosynthesis; he had his lecture notes, his diagrams, but when he opened his mouth the words came out wrong. The sentences were scrambled; they didn't fit together. When he saw this was happening, he stopped and tried giving an impromptu quiz, but the students were already looking at him curiously. Most of them were not good students, but they had a kind of streetwise quickness. Clearly they were delighted to see an authority figure—which to them he was even if he didn't see himself that way—falter, crumble. The therapist he had gone to for years afterwards had said it was connected to the beginning of Leo's success. Leo's first book had just come out; he was appearing on talk shows. At night Noah and Selma would watch, Selma entranced, Noah uneasy as Leo babbled on. No topic threw him. He fielded the most devious questions deftly, casually, seemed almost to enjoy the talk show hosts who were the most openly hostile and baiting. "Yeah, I love it," he admitted to them privately. "It's just a game. I'm better at it than they are. It's a lot of fun." Leo who could talk about anything and Noah who could talk about nothing even in the little area that he had chosen as his own.

Selma, nervous before she had any idea how far Noah's breakdown was going, would question him, uncomprehending. "But they're facts," she would say. "Can't you just get up and repeat them, just by rote, till it comes back to you?" When he would say that looking into the eyes of his students made him nervous, she would say, "Don't look at them! They don't care. Look at the wall!" She was so practical, so calm. She even offered to go in and teach for him; she had a teaching certificate and had been a biology major in college. Noah wouldn't have cared if she had; he was beyond shame, humiliation at that point, but the principal wouldn't allow it. "It's against the rules. Where will it end? If one wife comes in, everyone's wife . . ." Erasmus Drum. A tiny wizened man who had been principal for thousands of years, before the neighborhood had become predominantly black and Puerto Rican, who remembered the school's days of glory. One year, when the reading achievement tests were the lowest in Brooklyn, he came to school with a black armband on and insisted all the other teachers wear them too. Noah had thought anyone would be an improvement on Drum. He hadn't anticipated Garofolo with his beady glistening eyes, his moist hands, his booming voice. Looking back, the days of Erasmus Drum seemed almost nirvana.

Entering the school building, Noah went first into his office to deposit his coat. Loretta Rauch's office was next to his. He knew her office hours well and tried to time his appearances and exits not to coincide with hers. But this morning he was a little late because of the discussion about Leo. She was already seated at her desk, looking at some papers. Maybe she'd be too absorbed to see him, to hear him. But she looked up.

"Noah! How's it going?"

From anyone else that innocuous "How's it going?" would have meant nothing, but Loretta always said it meaningfully and he, no matter how "it" was going, whether he felt sick unto death of all mortal things or right as a trivet, just mumbled, "Great!"

But she was emerging inexorably from behind her desk. "There's something I've been saving to show you. I was going to leave it on your desk, but now that I've caught you . . . do you have a minute?"

"Just a minute." His class began in ten minutes.

"Well, remember how you were saying once that maybe those troubles you had might have been due to some connection between your blood pressure pill and that antidepressant your doctor gave you?"

God, what a memory she had. It was over a decade ago. "I'm on a different pill now," he said. "I'm no longer seeing that doctor."

She had bright greenish eyes, her lids tinted a variant of the same green. Sometimes she reminded him of a parrot with her dyed orange-red hair and tweezed eyebrows, high voice. "No, what I mean is, there's this writeup in *Newsweek* where they talk about a man who had that very problem—two drugs, one for blood pressure control, one for depression, and they collided. He was in terrible shape. But then they figured out that's what it was, they gave him new medication and now he's fine."

Noah pretended to glance at the article. "That's wonderful," he said. "I'll look at it later."

"It's called 'New Hope for the Hopeless'!" she cried gaily, as though he were hard of hearing, as though the small office were an auditorium.

Noah tried to smile. "I'm not hopeless," he said.

What a horrible phrase, what a horrible woman. New hope. I hate articles like that. Why does she do this? Is she a sadist? Can't she imagine I want to forget all that? She's like a vulture. No, she's just kind. She knows you went through a bad patch. She wants to be consoling. Everyone seemed to him Janus-faced. He saw both sides flashing back and forth: the kindly, the menacing. Maybe both were there and, depending on your mood, you picked up on one or the other.

He walked into class. They were doing Sex Education. Last week Garofolo had taken him aside. "Look, we don't want any trouble with the parents," he said. "I know it's not written anywhere that you have to, but don't just give them the facts. Give them morality. Tell them about responsibility, the guys too. Scare the shit out of them. It won't work, but at least they won't be able to say we didn't try."

Noah would have guessed ninety percent of the class were sexually active, maybe more. They were sixteen, seventeen, but most of the boys were easily half a foot taller than he, hulking black kids who looked as if they could have lifted a piano with one hand and hurled it across the room. Two of the girls were visibly pregnant. They sat knitting, not even pretending to take notes. Teaching them about birth control, warning them about AIDS, seemed a practice in irony. Looking around the room, he saw their alert, contemptuous eyes fixed on him with humor. *Scare the shit out of them.* The truth was, they scared the shit out of *him.* They knew more about life already than he ever would.

"Last week we were talking about methods of birth control," Noah said. "I think you all have a pretty good notion what they are, but just in case you've forgotten, I'll write them on the blackboard." He saw his veiny white hand writing: "1) condoms, 2) the pill, 3) diaphragm, 4) IUD, 5) sponge." When he was finished, he turned to them again. Ronnie, a stout black girl with straightened black hair, was waving her hand wildly. "Yes, Miss Gooder?"

"Mr. Epstein, how come you don't list the rhythm method? That's how my mother had me, by rhythm."

The class laughed.

Noah cleared his throat. "Well, as I discussed last time, the rhythm method is not really scientific. In this class we're discussing scientific methods to prevent conception."

"So are you, like, saying, even if we're Catholics and don't believe in birth control, we can't even *try* to not get pregnant?" She rolled her eyes.

"That's a good point," Noah said. He liked to use that phrase, even when almost none of the points raised were "good" or had much to do with whatever he'd been talking about. On the blackboard he wrote: "6) chastity." "Anyone like to define that?"

Crosby Barnes, one of the kids who looked like he could hurl a piano across the room, said, "Not doing it."

"Could whoever wants to make a contribution to class raise their hands?" Noah looked at Crosby. He was sitting with his arms akimbo. "Mr. Barnes?"

"Like I said, just not doing it. That's one way not to get pregnant." He laughed. "Not that I have to worry 'cause I ain't gettin' pregnant *any* way I do it."

The class laughed again.

"Is that true, though?" Noah said. "Is that the way all the men in the class feel?" He was aware of being ingratiating by calling them "men." "Do you feel if your girlfriend, say, gets pregnant, it's, as Mr. Barnes said, nothing to worry about?"

Todd O'Malley, one of the few white kids, a policeman's son, raised his hand. "You'd have to worry about paying for the abortion."

"Who says?" another boy called out. "Why can't *she* pay? *She's* the one pregnant."

"Well, why don't we vote on that?" Noah said. "How many of you feel it's the responsibility of the man who got his girlfriend pregnant to pay or help pay for her abortion?"

A few hands straggled up. For some reason votes made them nervous. They had the feeling there was a "right" and a "wrong" answer. "None of you girls who aren't raising your hands would want your boyfriends to help pay if you got pregnant?" He looked searchingly around the room.

"We might *want,*" Coralie DiMarco said, "but that won't make them *do* it. What if they don't have the money?"

Ronnie was waving her hand again. "What if we don't *believe* in abortion? Then what?"

"Then you have the child," Noah said. "I was talking about a hypothetical example." Blank faces. *Never use words with that many syllables.* "What I was really trying to talk about was the issue of responsibility, of taking responsibility before you have sex by using one of the forms I've listed, and taking it afterward, should something go wrong."

"Chastity's for girls," Crosby said. "That won't help *us* none."

"It's for nuns," Todd said. "They're not allowed."

Noah looked at the boys in the class. "None of you—the possibility of practicing other forms of sexuality other than intercourse, but waiting for that until you are sure you're in love or want to get married—that doesn't seem a feasible alternative?" Blank faces again. God, what was wrong with him this morning? *Feasible alternatives!*

Crosby was looking at him with his mocking expression. "What kind of activity do you mean, Mr. Epstein?"

Noah knew he was asking in hopes of embarrassing him. "Kissing? Oral sex?" he said.

"What's that?" Crosby's eyes glittered with malice.

"What's kissing?" Noah said, trying to smile. "Would anyone like to try and explain to Mr. Barnes what kissing is?"

"I meant the other."

"Oral sex? Would anyone like to define that?"

Silence.

Then one of the pregnant girls, a shy Puerto Rican named Angie Cortez, said, "It's with your mouth. Oral is with your mouth. But, Mr. Epstein, guys don't want to do just that. They want to do everything! And they don't want to use *any* of the methods you've put up there. They say condoms aren't comfortable and, well, they just don't want to cooperate. *That's* the problem."

Noah sighed. As usual, the discussion was wandering all over the lot. Sometimes Garofolo actually sat in a class, to see how it was going. "How about it, guys?" He hated himself for resorting to trying to act or talk like one of the students to ingratiate himself with them. "What Ms. Cortez is saying, in effect, is that you just don't care if your girlfriends get pregnant or not? Is that true?"

Sherman Skinner, a bright, chubby boy from Jamaica who still had a slight accent, said, "If you love her, it's different."

"If you love her," Noah repeated, "you're willing to take precautions, to use condoms or, perhaps, to even abstain? Otherwise, who cares?" He raised his eyebrows.

"It's their problem," Crosby said, unwrapping a slice of raspberry Bubblicious gum. "If they don't wanna do it, who says they have to?"

"Yeah, but guys pressure you," Ronnie said. turning to look at him. *"You* know that. They make promises—this, that. Then once they got you—vamoose."

Crosby laughed. "Who, me?" He was chewing lustily.

Noah glanced down at his notes. *Why am I here? Why do I have this fucking job?* "What about AIDS?" he said. "Are any of you aware of the nature of it as a disease?"

"That's for fags, man," Todd said with a slight swagger. He was the football hero of the school and had probably lost his virginity at twelve.

"Is it? According to *The New York Times,* one out of about every *twenty* human beings in this city has AIDS. That includes men *and* women. Heterosexual men and women can get it without knowing it, if their partners are intravenous drug users or have gone to prostitutes."

The silence that fell over the room this time had a more anxious quality to it. "Intravenous how?" Crosby asked, munching.

"AIDS can be spread by the virus going into the bloodstream," Noah went on. "People who use drugs that require the use of needles are particularly at risk." *How many of them did that apply to? Already! In their teens!*

Ronnie raised her hand. "Mr. Epstein, it seems sometimes like you're trying to just scare us. Is that right? Scare us to not have sex?"

"Not scare," Noah said carefully. "I don't want to scare anyone. Sex is an important part of everyone's life, an exciting, wonderful part. But, as I've tried to indicate, there are dangers involved for everyone. If you don't think about those dangers at the time, you may be in big trouble later."

"Man, I'm gonna be a nun," Crosby said. He grinned.

"You're not even Catholic," someone yelled from the back of the room.

"You can be chaste, even if you're not Catholic," Angie said. Her hands were crossed primly in front of her on her desk.

"Girls been chasin' me since I was nine years old," Crosby said. "But then, I learned how to run."

It was nearly time for the bell to ring. "I've Xeroxed an article about AIDS that appeared in the *Times,*" Noah said. "Would you all look at it and see if you have any questions?" He handed the stack of sheets to the class.

Gradually, after picking up the sheets, they all filed out. He had a period break before his next class. *My life is a farce, this class is a farce.*

No, life is what you make it. If I can reach one of them, two . . . He had considered at times trying to get a job in a private school, but the salaries were disastrously low. They were barely scraping by already. If they'd had children, they would have been at the poverty level.

"Mr. Epstein?" It was Angie. She was tiny, four feet nine, maybe, and slender with olive skin and soft black eyes. Her pregnancy seemed grotesque, unfair. *Who had it been? Someone in this class?*

"Yes?"

"You know how you were talking about nuns in class?"

He hadn't been, but he just nodded.

"I've been thinking maybe, after this"—she gestured toward her stomach—"maybe I'd like to become a nun. But do they take girls who've had babies?"

Noah smiled. "I don't know, Angie. I'm not a Catholic. I'm Jewish."

"Don't they have Jewish nuns?"

"No, they don't."

Her eyes grew round. "So, what do Jewish girls do if, you know, they don't want to have anything to do with men that way?"

"I suppose they just . . . lead chaste lives."

"But then men keep pestering them. They don't pester nuns."

"I don't know, Angie. But you *are* Catholic, so that won't be a problem for you. It must be hard, though."

She was silent. He found it difficult to read the expression in her sorrowful, beautiful eyes. "Sometimes I pretend you're the father," she said very softly, so softly he wasn't sure he had heard her right.

Jesus. "I don't think that's such a good idea," Noah said, panicked.

"You don't have children . . . and I pretend that maybe you wanted them, but maybe your wife couldn't. I pretend you'd be happy . . ." She trailed off, looking wistful.

"Angie, look, pretending isn't good. It gets people into trouble. You could get *me* into trouble. Try to connect to reality."

The look of despair that came over her face was so unvarnished that he was pierced with recognition. "I do, I do try."

Noah felt he might collapse. "Reality is all we have," he said shakily. "I'm . . . not the way I appear to you. In a sense I'm a fantasy figure. If you knew me in real life, you'd recoil in horror."

Angie just stood there, clutching her books, fragile, yet tenacious, unable to recoil. "You get nervous in class. They tease you. I feel sorry for you."

"I'm fine," Noah said. "Really. And you'll be fine too, Angie. I think the idea of becoming a nun is a fine one. Speak to the guidance counselor about it. She'll give you the proper information." Gathering up his papers, he rushed from the room.

Oh God, no. Why this? Why now? A pregnant student in love with him? Garofolo was waiting like a hawk for a chance to pitch him or transfer him. *You get nervous . . . I feel so sorry for you . . . Was it that apparent, then?* He'd thought he was doing well. Today had been a little unruly, but how else could you run the class? He knew he had always evoked pity in women. The maternal instinct. They wanted to baby him, nurture him. What a trap, for everyone. If he and Selma had only had children. But after two miscarriages, she'd said she couldn't take it—the disappointments, the waiting. And then there'd been that horrible time they had decided to adopt, had actually gotten a baby, had it for one day when the "real" mother had changed her mind. How he had avoided breaking down then was a miracle. Maybe because Selma, who was usually the practical, calm one was a wreck herself, weeping all day. He remembered that one day as though it were branded into his memory, the way the baby had looked lying in the crib. They had even picked a name: Simone Rachel.

Why is life like that? To change her mind after one day! Evidently seeing the baby had produced some change of heart. Or maybe her boyfriend had decided to marry her after all. That had been five years ago. By now they were probably divorced. At parties when people showed photos of their children or the topic came up, Noah saw the wounded look in Selma's eyes. Another way in which he had disappointed her, not been the husband she had expected. Leo had three kids, two at Hunter, for which you had to pass some incredibly complex entrance exam, another at Dalton. Full-time help. Eloise boasted that she had only gained ten pounds with each birth and had returned to her size six figure in one week after each child.

He returned to his office to glance over the notes for his next class. Loretta Rauch was gone. Her article "New Hope for the Hopeless" was still on his desk. He shoved it to one side. There was a rap on the glass door. It was Garofolo.

"So, how's it going?" God, how he hated that genial affability, that phony heartiness. The man would fling a five year old from a ten story window and not even look back.

"Fine, fine," Noah said.

"How'd it work, with the morality bit? Did they get the point?" He was half sitting on Noah's desk, his fat ass cutting into the wood.

"I think so," Noah said cautiously. "We'll discuss AIDS tomorrow."

"AIDS?" Garofolo frowned. "Isn't that going a little too far?"

"Well, don't you think they should know? It's a growing problem . . ."

Garofolo shook his head. "No, that's the gay community. These are kids, these are teenagers."

"It isn't just the gay community," Noah said. "There was an article in the *Times*—"

"The *Times!* Look, Epstein, remember where you are, okay? Give these kids what they need, a few facts, a little morality. They can't understand *The New York Times*. These aren't college bound kids."

"I know, I just thought—"

Garofolo lowered his voice. "Let me give you a piece of advice. You're a nervous man. I'm not saying there's anything wrong with that. I understand you once had a few problems there, coping, what have you. Just try to take it easy. That's all. It's simple, really. Set realistic goals."

Noah shuddered inwardly. This man was after him somehow. Why? "I do try," he said, attempting to keep his voice at a monotone, not to seem emotional.

Suddenly Garofolo's eyes lit on the "New Hope for the Hopeless" article. "Hey, what do you know? I was just reading this the other day. I was going to save it. My brother—he's had a few mental problems." He tapped his head, in case Noah didn't know what that meant. "Not that he's hopeless, mind you, no one's hopeless. That's my motto. You call someone hopeless, that's giving up on them. Right?"

"I agree," Noah said. He felt hot, sweat was collecting at his back. "Was your brother ever hospitalized?"

"Yeah, poor sucker. You name it, he's had it. Shock treatment. Listen, there's stuff he *still* can't remember, to this very day! But it made him calmer, a lot calmer. He's functional. What more can you ask?"

"Nothing," Noah said dryly. "You can't ask more than that."

Garofolo glanced at the article again. "And look at me. We had the same parents, same mother, same father. And I have the constitution of an ox, I sleep like a baby at night. Where's the justice in life, huh?"

Noah shrugged.

"So, like I say, take it easy," Garofolo said, getting off the desk and heading out the door. "Take care."

Ten more minutes to class. Noah looked down at his notes. Was the man a sadist, or was he simply abnormally hypersensitive? He thought back on their conversation. Maybe it had all been inadvertent, his catching sight of the article. *Why didn't I throw it out? Did he know I had shock treatment? Does he know I have a famous brother? He must know. He was taunting me, like the kids in class, but on a more sophisticated level. What if he finds out Angie Cortez is in love with me? "Hopeless. No one's hopeless." But I didn't even give Selma a kid. And Leo has three . . . Probably Garofolo was just a needler, not a sadist. We all enjoy watching other people crumble. I enjoyed visiting Leo in intensive care after his heart attack, seeing that expression of terror in his eyes. Seeing him helpless, when he seemed in perfect health, jogged, worked out on an electric bike during the winter.*

But then he'd recovered and was fine. *And so are you! You once were sick and now you're fine.* He had once seen the notes on himself in the hospital. Paranoid schizophrenic, they had read. Incurable. None of the antidepressants had really worked. He still took Elavil, but more because it made Selma happy to feel he was on something. Probably she was still afraid it would happen again. It was one of the many taboos in their marriage, one of the many topics never mentioned: children, breakdowns. He wondered if all happy marriages like theirs were actually minefields scattered with unmentionable topics. What did Eloise and Leo talk about? About his mistresses, Leo said, "She doesn't want to know, so she doesn't know." He was so practical about everything! He picked beautiful, racy women. He didn't have tiny, fragile Puerto Rican teenagers fantasizing that he was the father of their child. If women were attracted to Leo, it was for the opposite reason they were attracted to Noah. They saw him as competent, resourceful, energetic. No one wanted to baby him.

Take care. An innocuous remark. But it was also valid. He had to take care. Two people, no, three had already made mention of his nervousness: Loretta Rauch, out of what she interpreted as concern, Angie Cortez out of love and a desire to nurture, Garofolo

out of a vulturelike desire to strike. Three totally different people
had seen it, seen through his careful disguise of quiet competence,
his talking slowly, his holding himself in check. What did they see?
What was there so palpable that even a teenage girl could see it?

He got through the rest of the day. It was easier. The other
classes were straight biology, overseeing a lab, the science club that
met as an extracurricular event once a week. But those three remarks stayed with him all day, like seeing himself in a three-way
mirror and being horrified at how he looked from the back, from the
side. What a wonderful world it would be if people never told you
what they "really" felt, never felt they had to confide, to "show
concern," if privacy were respected.

Are there Jewish nuns? He could not, for the life of him, imagine
Angie Cortez engaged in the sex act. How could anyone have done
that? Her body was like a child's, her voice like a ten year old's. And
at night, lying in bed, his face loomed up before her as the fantasy
father, he who probably would have fucked up as a father as he had
in all other areas. But he was gentle, kindly. Yes, she saw true facts
about him, just didn't connect them to their real sources, his inability to connect or understand the male world in which it was assumed
he would function, fit in—the back slapping, boasting, hearty world
in which men sparred verbally or socked each other. That world was
as alien to him as it was to most women. Sometimes Selma would
ask him, "What do men talk about when they're alone?" He couldn't
tell her. When he was alone with most men, he scarcely listened to
their conversation. It was like being with animals in the zoo. In his
head he turned off the sounds. They were noises, that was all.

He wondered sometimes how many men like himself there
were—not gay, not effeminate, not especially at ease with women,
but representative of some hideous middle ground where both
sexes seemed to him mysterious and alien. He read of people who
changed their sex and that always amazed him, that people had the
illusion that being another sex would make any difference. Who
were they fooling?

Leo said it was a game—relations between the sexes, work,
marriage, and once you looked at it that way it was no problem. It
wasn't a matter of trying to understand; it was just a matter of
figuring out the rules, even if you knew they were corrupt or crazy,
and then just playing by them, the way Leo outwitted talk show
hosts, the way he outfoxed women, the way he seemed to make his
wife happy while cheating on her constantly. But all that took, not

only a kind of cast-iron cynicism, but energy and a feeling it was worth it. The fact was, Leo got a kick out of all that, he enjoyed it.

I wouldn't know how to enjoy it, even if I could somehow learn to do it.

At dinner that night Selma said, "I just realized, the night we have to go to the library for Leo's party, it's your birthday. What should we do?"

Noah shrugged. "How old will I be?"

Selma looked at him with a smile, frowning.

"Seriously. I know I'm in my forties. I just can't remember."

She was silent for just one second. "Forty-one," she said quickly. "Did you really not remember? Or were you just joking?"

"Birthdays aren't a big deal to me. You never feel the age you are anyway. I've never gotten the point." He understood her concern, and wanted to deflect it.

But Selma was still gazing at him with her softly perplexed expression. "It seems a pity, though. It's your birthday, but we'll be celebrating Leo's book."

"I didn't write a book."

She stood up to clear the table. "We should read it before we go. Everyone there will have read it."

"I don't know," Noah said. "You can't tell. The party isn't just for him, is it? I thought they were honoring twenty people, something like that." He followed her into the kitchen with the margarine container, which he replaced in the refrigerator.

"But I feel we should read it," Selma said. She was unpeeling Saran wrap from two containers of butterscotch pudding. "I feel ashamed not to have read it, but it was so . . . I wasn't sure I understood what he was saying. That's why I wish you'd read it. You could explain it to me."

Noah laughed. "You're as smart as I am. I probably couldn't make head or tail of it. It's all idiocy anyway."

Selma brought the pot of decaffeinated coffee into the dining room and poured a cup for each of them. "Idiocy? What do you mean? It got such good reviews, Leo's so brilliant—"

"It's words," Noah said. "A lot of words spinning around." He loved the way she made butterscotch pudding—with chopped almonds and bits of apple scattered in it. He poured some heavy cream over the top.

"All books are words," Selma said. "And important people

think it's a good book. And he's your brother. If my brother had written a book, I'd read it."

Selma's brother was a tax accountant who did their taxes free every year. "Really? Even if it was on tax returns?" Noah tried to joke.

"But Leo's book is about sex," Selma protested. "Anyone ought to be able to understand that. That's different."

"Sexuality," Noah corrected her. "Sex everyone knows about. Sexuality is the big deal. The 'philosophy' of sex. Otherwise it's in, out, on top, on bottom, once a week, once a month . . ."

There was a pause. Selma was toying with her butterscotch pudding. "My boss was making those remarks again today," she said. "Suggestive remarks." She widened her eyes. "What should I do? I don't want to lose my job. I'm married! He *knows* I'm married. I talk about you every day."

Selma's boss, Mr. Manucci, was in his sixties, overweight, bald. If Selma had been unmarried, or married and of a different temperament, he would have had the perfect setup. But she always froze in terror when her boss came on to her. Maybe it was some kind of turn on, observing her fear. "Just ignore it," Noah said, as he always did.

"He looks at me in this creepy way . . . Why? He has a wife, he has grandchildren even. I feel so ashamed when he looks at me." Selma had lovely clear skin and in that way looked younger than her late thirties, but because her hair was greying and she wore little makeup she looked her age, thirty-six. What was Mr. Manucci's fantasy about her? That she would lie there terrified, throughout? "And he's Catholic. Isn't it a sin for them?"

"They go and confess," Noah said. "Then they can do it again. It's a great system, actually. Jews just stew in their own juice." He thought fleetingly of Angie Cortez. "Students fall in love with me from time to time. I just ignore it."

Selma put down her spoon. "You never mentioned that. Do they really?"

"Not very often." Already he regretted bringing it up.

"Anyone special? Right now, I mean."

It seemed so innocent he decided to mention it. "Her name is Angie Cortez. This sweet little pregnant Puerto Rican girl, weighs about ninety pounds. She said she imagines I'm the father of her child." He smiled.

But Selma was looking at him, horrified. "But you didn't—"

Noah just stared at her.

"Noah, you can't have. You didn't—with a student?"

"Are you kidding? I told you because it's so pathetic, just to make you understand about Mr. Manucci, that people get these yens, these incomprehensible yearnings. It's all in their head. It has nothing to do with the real me. If she knew the real me, she'd run screaming for the hills."

Selma's face relaxed. "No," she said. Her voice became soft, dreamy. "You seem gentle, sweet. Probably she doesn't know men like that in real life."

"The tip of the iceberg."

"What is?"

"My being 'gentle and sweet.' "

"You *are.*"

He was always so torn about this, about the way in which Selma, with such care and artfulness and naïveté created a personality for him, woven of bits and pieces of reality. The parts that didn't fit, she discarded, like swatches of cloth the wrong size. It touched him and at the same time infuriated him. Was the person he really was so terrible that she had to avert her eyes, had to look frightened if he ever brought up anything concerning his real feelings? *Yes, you were mad, you were locked up. To live with that, she has to evade, deny, forget.*

In bed later, he slid his hand under her nightgown, caressing her breasts, her large, round, burnished nipples. They rarely made love during the week. They were both too exhausted, distracted. He wasn't even sure that was what he wanted now. Perhaps he would just hold her, caress her. *Sweet, gentle.* God, how he loathed those words. Selma's arms were around him, but in a way that gave no hint of which way she wanted to go. "What would you like?" he whispered. "Are you tired?"

In reply she unbuttoned his pajama top and rubbed her hand over the hair on his chest. "I'm so glad I have you," she murmured.

Meaning what? As opposed to Mr. Manucci? Never think in bed. Noah knew that was a mistake. He forced the image of lecherous Manucci from his consciousness as Selma reached down tentatively to stroke his balls, circling the tip of his penis. She was always so tentative that at times it was like some version of torture. They had gone through difficult times in their sex life, times when his penis seemed to have decided to become a vestigial organ. It lost its sense of identity, why it was there, what it was for. Now, feeling himself grow hard, he had a sense of almost hysterical relief. Angie

Cortez's dark limpid eyes drifted in front of him. *Whatever works, it doesn't matter.* As he made love to her, her body became a slender, child's body, terrified by Mr. Manucci, or simultaneously, Angie, terrified by whoever had done it to her, and he was both of those men and also himself, the fantasy lover who would dissolve their fears and make them happy.

Selma didn't come. Caught up in his own fantasies, he didn't try as hard as usual to hold back.

"Let me caress you," he said, afterwards.

"I don't know, I guess I wasn't in the mood." She sounded so sad, so far away.

"Tell me if that's the case. I didn't need to. I just—"

She was pressed against his chest, her voice muffled. "But I wanted to make you happy. You seem so strange sometimes when you come home."

Noah was silent in the darkness, which could shift so quickly from protective to terrifying. "Yes." He meant that he knew he seemed strange. But Selma interpreted it as meaning that he appreciated her desire to make him happy, that she had succeeded.

The party of the literary lions was on a Saturday. Noah's mother, Roz, was going. She was seventy-eight and had had two heart attacks, but, as she put it, still got around. Lately she'd been "keeping company," again her own words, with a widower her own age, maybe two years older. His eyesight was bad, so she drove the two of them to plays, to movies. They had agreed to pick her up and take her to the Forty-second Street Library with them. Her friend, Horace Carnow, was also attending the party.

"Sit in the front, next to Noah," Selma said, getting out of the car.

Noah's mother was in her ancient seal coat, a thin scarf over her precisely set, teased hair. Her hair was white, but she went to the beauty shop once a week to have it curled. Noah wondered, as he had often, if she and Horace were lovers. He was a courtly old man, stout, whereas his mother was very slender. He had brownish teeth—he still smoked a pack of Camels a day. Selma thought it was wonderful that his mother had found a male companion, at her age; imagine, it was a miracle! It was true. Glancing at his mother, she looked radiant. "I'll sit in the back with Horace," she said, beaming at her companion. He beamed back. Selma glanced at Noah as if to say: "It's okay, then?"

In the car, Horace, in his loud booming voice, said, "Hey, this is quite something, huh? That's some brother you've got. Six books! I haven't even *read* six books."

"We've been reading it aloud at night," his mother said. "What a style. What erudition! I couldn't even understand some of it. We had to look up words. It was like playing Scrabble."

Selma turned around to face them. "How did you like it? I haven't . . . finished it yet." She was evidently too ashamed to admit she hadn't even started it.

"Well, it's philosophy," his mother said. "What gets me so mad is Helen Gertler—you remember her, Noah?—I met her at the supermarket and she said, 'I hear Leo has this best-seller on sex.' Sex! I told her it's *not* about sex. It's about sexuality. That's a totally different thing."

"He's got a philosophy of life," Horace agreed. The smoke from his cigarette was fumigating the car. "That's the main thing. Not many young people have these days. He's thought about things, about life."

"He's like my father," Roz said. "A scholar. He loves ideas. That runs on one side of the family."

What ran on the other side? Madness? Idiocy? Incompetence?

"I have great respect for anyone who can write a book," Horace said solemnly. *Why was he yelling?* "It's a miracle."

"Any book?" Noah couldn't resist saying. *"Thinner Thighs in Thirty Days? Color Me Beautiful?"*

He was disgusted to hear these petty, envious words issuing from his mouth, but his mother blithely ignored them. "Leo is not concerned with the body," she said, "but with the soul. He's not conventionally religious. He doesn't go to shul as often as I might like, but that's because he has it all inside."

This was a mistake. It was such a set piece. Bringing his mother, it being his birthday, Selma in her new bright blue shiny dress that clung too tightly to her hips. "God, I hate driving at night," he said suddenly, almost to himself.

There was a pause.

"Do you want me to drive?" Selma asked nervously. "Are you okay?"

Streetlights were flashing in front of him with dizzying brightness. "Would you? Thanks." Noah pulled over and changed seats with his wife.

"What's the problem?" Horace asked loudly. "I don't get it."

"He has trouble driving at night." His mother was also talking at twice her usual decibel level. "He has problems with his nerves."

"I hate driving at night," Horace continued. "I hate driving, period. Six months ago I almost killed six people. Suddenly I was driving and the car went up on the sidewalk. There was a young mother, children. I could have been a mass murderer."

"That's different," his mother said. "You're eighty-one. Your eyesight is bad. Plus, you didn't kill anyone."

Now that he wasn't driving, Noah turned to look in the back of the car. Horace and his mother were holding hands. Do I care if they're lovers? His father had been dead for over a decade. He had always assumed his mother would want to avoid sex because of her bad heart. Once she had told him that she and his father had had a "sensational" sex life. He always remembered that word: sensational. "Every chance we got," she said. Had she meant that literally? They would have had dozens of chances a day after his father retired from work.

"Noah, you look funny," his mother said. She said it not critically, but calmly, as was her wont.

"Funny how?"

"You're not in a tuxedo, you're just in a suit. This is a big occasion. There'll be toasts . . ."

"It didn't say black tie."

"I want Leo to be proud of us. We should be proud that he invited us. Many famous men, once they've made it, they forget their families, they're ashamed. Not Leo. He sends me copies of all his books, he calls, he comes to visit. He doesn't have a swelled head. Does he?" For some reason she turned to Horace for corroboration.

"He's a great guy," Horace boomed. "But he ought to write simpler, so I could understand."

Noah admired men like Horace Carnow. They seemed so at ease with themselves, admitting to possible crimes (*almost a mass murderer*) to ignorance (*I haven't even* read *six books*), and seeming not to relinquish thereby any sense of self-esteem. *It comes from within,* as his mother had said in relation to Leo. But that wasn't true. Leo was all effort, you could almost see the sweat break out on his brow in his desire to impress, to please. It worked, that was all. But the effort was there. It seemed to Noah that if he had had the choice, he would have chosen being like Horace Carnow. His wife of fifty years had died so he'd found another "wife," or mistress or woman friend, not a cutie pie twenty years younger who would give him a coronary, just a warm, friendly woman his own age with whom he could share some laughs, affection, good times. He accepts life as it is and he'll never write a book about how he does that. Yet that was the book Noah wanted to read, not Leo's high-flown philosophic idiocy about narcissism and modern society.

After searching, they found a parking space within walking distance of the library. By the time they arrived, the room was filled with a babble of noise and laughter. His mother was wrong. Most of the men were in suits, not tuxedos. Even Leo, glimpsed from afar, was in a dark pinstripe; Eloise, oddly, was in a tuxedo. Her hair had been cut boyishly short, a look that might have been attractive on a woman half her age. But Noah always sensed she wanted simply to be eye-catching, not to look merely pretty or appealing, Selma's simple aim. For some reason Selma had no idea of how to dress to advantage on occasions that were anything but everyday. For work she looked feminine and attractive in wool dresses or tweed suits, but now, in the garish blue satiny dress she looked hopeless, dumpy. Leo, at twenty, had known that was how she would look twenty years later, had known that he would want, at such a party, which he had known would take place, a chic, almost frighteningly chic wife who could flash smiles on and off like a traffic sign.

"Mom! Noah! Great you could come." Leo looked both elated and totally at ease, as though being honored, being a "literary lion" was an everyday event for him. "This is Diana Trilling and—what did you say your name was?" he asked a charming young woman at his side.

"Eve Chasin."

Leo put his arm on Eve Chasin's white braceleted arm. "Eve reviews for the *Voice*," he explained.

"What voice?" asked Horace, lighting up a Camel.

Everyone smiled, not sure if he was making a joke.

"And Diana," Leo went on smoothly, "you've read her book on Mrs. Harris . . . Jean Harris."

Selma looked petrified, as though this were an oral exam and if she failed she would be sent home on the spot. "The one who killed the diet doctor?"

Mrs. Trilling smiled graciously.

"I felt so sorry for her," Selma said, licking her lips. "He treated her so badly!"

"But she picked him," Leo said, having no doubt treated just as many women just as badly in his time. "Does that justify murder?"

"Yeah," Noah found himself saying. "*I* think so. Guys like that should be shot."

Again there was nervous laughter, slightly different from that which had greeted Horace's remark.

Eloise tapped Leo on the shoulder. "There's Norman," she said. "We should go over and say hi . . . Norman Mailer," she explained to the four of them, as though they were Vietnamese boat people who had just come ashore.

With a swift motion she and Leo turned and plunged into the crowd. Simultaneously Mrs. Trilling and the young woman, Eve Chasin, also turned, as though in a choreographed dance. Selma clutched Noah's arm. "These are such famous people," she whispered. "I don't know, I feel so nervous. What if I have to sit next to one of them?"

"I'll take care of you," Horace said cheerfully, patting her. "I'm famous. I was once mayor of Dartington, New York. Mailer ran and lost."

"For mayor of Dartington?" Selma said, bewildered. "I didn't know that."

Finally a bell rang and everyone trooped into another large room where there were many round tables. To discover which table you were assigned to, you had to find your name. Noah had assumed the four of them would be seated with Leo, but as it turned out they were all separated. Even Leo and Eloise were at separate tables. He glanced over at Selma, but a friendly looking middle-aged woman, hopefully someone's wife, was chatting with her. Whew. He didn't have to worry about his mother or Horace, who could each take on Norman Mailer, Diana Trilling, or anyone present without even trying.

There was paté, then roast chicken, white wine, salad. He wasn't especially hungry, but ate just to have something to do. The room was warm, but he realized taking off his jacket would be indecorous. Then he became aware that the woman next to him was also not eating, just sipping her wine thoughtfully and gazing off into space. Their eyes met. She smiled. "I'm Ava Bernier," she said.

"Noah Epstein." She had a face that couldn't be easily categorized, large near-Eastern black eyes, an aquiline nose, thin lips, and closely cropped curly black hair flecked with grey.

"Who are you connected to?" she asked. Her voice was so soft that, though they were sitting very close, he had to strain to hear her.

"My brother, Leo Epstein. He wrote *Sexuality Today: The Clash of Instinct and Culture.*"

Ava Bernier gave a half smile. "I've heard of it. I haven't read it, I'm afraid. I don't read a lot of nonfiction. I'm a poet."

"Why are *you* here?" Noah asked.

She laughed nervously. "I'm . . . well, I'm one of the people this is for."

"One of the literary lions?"

"Lionesses, I guess." She lifted her wine glass again, and sipped.

"That's quite an honor for someone so young." It sounded trite, but he didn't know what else to say.

"I'm forty-one," she said. "I'm not *that* young, really . . . and you know, it's funny. Today's my birthday and I keep feeling I ought to feel so up, so excited or happy, and instead I've had such a terrible feeling of gloom and apprehension all day and even more now. Everyone I talked to before seemed so false and strange. Probably I'm projecting. Probably *I'm* false and strange." Now that she was talking, she spoke very rapidly and intensely, keeping her eyes fixed directly on him.

"It's *my* birthday too," Noah found himself saying. "I'm forty-one."

Ava Bernier smiled, her eyes widening. "That's so strange, isn't it, our being placed next to each other. I suppose if one believed in fate, one could say it was fated. But I'm just not sure I do. Do you?"

"Pardon me?" His wine glass was being refilled, yet he hadn't been aware that he'd been drinking.

"Do you believe in that kind of thing," Ava Bernier said in her rapid, soft voice, "things being predestined, meeting the right person at the right time, or the wrong person? I know I'm not putting this right, but do you believe things happen for a cause, or do you think they just happen?"

Noah shrugged. "I'm not religious," he said, feeling that was inadequate. Should he have said something else? Something more eloquent, expressive? If she hadn't seemed so nervous herself, he would have felt more anxious about being placed next to one of the guests of honor. "I don't read poetry," he said, "or I'd probably know who you are."

She smiled sadly. "Well, no one does, really. Or hardly anyone. I don't even read it much myself. Because if it's good, I feel so disheartened at how far I fall short, and if it's bad I think, why did this idiocy get published?"

"Yes," Noah said. "I know what you mean." He felt he did know what she meant, though of course nothing of what she was saying applied to him or his life.

"I hate to be rude and this isn't a come on," Ava said, "but are you married?"

Noah pointed to his ring. "My wife's over there, in the blue dress."

"I can't really see without my glasses. I asked because, well, you look almost uncannily like a man I recently, or fairly recently stopped seeing. When I first saw you, my heart almost stopped. Talk about strange coincidences!"

"Perhaps my face is so much like many people's that—" Noah began, but Ava interrupted him.

"No! The opposite. You have a unique face. You're the only two men I've ever met in my life with that expression. It's hard to describe. Dreamy, but also acute in some funny combination. I thought you were some hideously famous writer and I was terrified."

Noah laughed. "Hardly. I teach biology in a lousy public high school in Brooklyn."

"But you have contact with real life," she said continuing to gaze at him as though mesmerized. "I admire that so much. I started publishing when I was in my teens and that's all I've ever done— write and teach. I know *nothing* of the real world! Nothing!"

He drank some more wine, conscious at the periphery of his mind that his wine glass still seemed to be at the same level, even though he'd been drinking steadily since he sat down. Perhaps, while they'd been talking, the waiter had been stealthily refilling the glass. "You're lucky," he said. "The real world isn't all it's cracked up to be."

"That's what Ferris said, my lover or former lover or what have you. He was a lawyer."

Noah tried to imagine the kind of man she might have been involved with who, at the same time, would look or be like himself. He could not imagine such a man. "Why are you no longer seeing each other?" he asked gently.

"He was married," she said. "Didn't I say that? I thought I did

. . . That was why I asked you if *you* were married because it seems, for some sickeningly obvious reason, that every man I've ever been even *mildly* attracted to, starting with my father, of course, was married. I was hoping you might be an exception."

He just smiled and shrugged.

Her face was so close to his he could see the faint gleam of perspiration on her pale skin and a thin blue vein that throbbed on her temple. "Are you *happily* married?"

"Yes."

Ava laughed. "Goodness! Without a pause, even, without a qualifier. That's incredible! Don't tell me you're faithful too?"

He nodded, slightly sheepishly.

"How long have you been married?"

"Fifteen years."

She was staring at him in amazement. Suddenly he felt she was beautiful, or maybe he was just getting drunk or was drunk. "Really, that's so . . . twenty years! The same person for fifteen years! And it doesn't get boring, stylized, claustrophobic? You don't feel you're going mad with the sameness of it all, the same body, the same movements?"

It seemed to him he had never had a conversation exactly like this before. On the one hand, their being in a public place with all these people; on the other hand, her battery of intense questions, as though she were disrobing in public. He didn't know if he felt more anxious for himself or for her. "I have other problems," he said. "Perhaps that's why I don't even think along those lines. I had a breakdown once, I was hospitalized, and I'm terrified of it happening again. So it takes all my energy to stay on an even keel." He knew he must be drunk to be saying these things to anyone, but especially to a total stranger.

"Yes, I had a breakdown too," Ava said, as though his confession had been mundane, as though he had merely confessed to preferring Paris to London. "Of course, poets do. It's pretty common. And yes, I know what you mean, about the even keel. I'm sitting here and I *should* be happy. I'm reasonably young, reasonably attractive, Ferris claimed—if he can be believed about anything— that the sex he'd had with me was the best he'd ever had, I'm published, I've won prizes . . . and yet here I am. I feel almost too queasy to eat, I'm drinking too much, I'm babbling away to you—"

"They keep refilling the glasses," Noah said. "I've had too much too."

After a moment, Ava said, "Listen, I don't think . . . I'm afraid I can't stay here any longer. I'm really afraid I may faint."

Alarmed, he said, "Shall I go down with you and get you a cab?"

She was getting out of her seat. "No, I'll be okay. But if you ever want to see me again, tonight even or at any time, just . . . This is my address and phone." She stuffed a slip of paper in his hand and vanished.

Noah sat there, stunned. If it hadn't been for the slip of paper in his hand, and the empty chair beside him, he might have guessed that she had been an apparition: her white face, black dress, red lips. *Why would she give me her address? I said I was married, I said I was faithful.* He glanced guiltily across the room at Selma, who was still talking to the middle-aged woman. *Was I flirting with her?* He realized that he was not only drunk, but very dizzy. *Steady. Take care.* He drank some cold water. When he looked up again a moment later, he saw a man two tables down vomit quietly into his plate. No one noticed. The man sat there, dabbed at his drooling mouth and a waiter came over and removed the plate. Noah looked at the rest of the guests. There was something demonic and frightening about the scene, everyone overeating, overdrinking, laughing raucously. It was as though they were in ancient Rome, waiting for some Christians to be brought in and torn apart by lions. Literary lions.

Suddenly he leapt to his feet. With difficulty he crossed the room to where Selma was sitting. "What's wrong?" she said, alarmed.

"Nothing, I'm just a little . . . dizzy. I drank too much. Look, I'm going home. I'll see you later."

"I'll come with you." She started getting out of her chair.

"Don't. The ceremony hasn't even begun yet. Leo would be hurt. Just drive Mom and Horace home. Do you have the keys? I'll take a cab."

Clearly she wanted to stay. "Take it easy, sweetie."

Take it easy, sweetie. Sweetie . . . darling. The words circled in his head as he went down the long flight of stairs. He thought of the man vomiting. Was *he* that sick? No, it was the heat, the noise. Once outside he took a deep breath of fresh air and felt better. And then for some reason he removed from his pocket the slip of paper on which Ava Bernier had written her address. It was in Greenwich Village. What had she said? *"If you ever want to see me again, tonight, or . . ."* Had she actually said tonight? Why tonight? She had been feeling sick. Or maybe that was an excuse. She just couldn't live up to the occasion. He thought of Leo, of the hundreds of times women must have slipped such pieces of paper into his hands, the hundreds of secret assignations he must have had, the whispered excuses to his wife. *"You have a very unique face . . . dreamy, but acute."* Fatal. What was fatal was a woman seeing him as he wanted to be seen, hearing his worst secret and not recoiling, sharing his worst secret, she having had a breakdown herself.

He was just drunk enough so that the back and forth, should I, shouldn't I that he normally would have gone through, the sane, rational part of himself finally struggling to the helm, seemed blurry. *". . . boring, stylized, claustrophobic . . . the same body, the same movements . . ."* He had evidently decided because he found himself in a cab, speeding down to the Village, not even aware of having hailed it or having given the driver the address. *She may be asleep. Then I'll just go away.*

It was a walk-up, on the second floor of an attractive brownstone on a small old-fashioned street paved with cobblestones. He knocked. Ringing seemed too harsh somehow. It was silent inside the building. If she was asleep . . . He would just knock once more, then go away.

When she opened the door, she was in a black robe, loosely tied, barefoot. She didn't seem surprised to see him. "I've thrown open *all* the windows," she said, leading him in, as though he had been there dozens of times. "Wasn't it stifling in there? Maybe it's the medication I'm on, but I really thought I might just pass out."

Noah, having been divested of his coat, sat down awkwardly in an arm chair. "What medication are you on?"

"Tofranil. Oh, I've tried everything and frankly I think if one swallowed different colored M&M's every day, it would have the same effect or lack of effect. Do you take anything?"

"Elavil."

She swept back her hair. "Oh yes, I tried that once too. I forget all the names. But then suddenly one will meet someone who claims this pill or that one saved their lives."

"People claim that about a lot of things," Noah said. "Religion—" He was going to say "sex," but stopped. What was odd was that sitting in that crowded room with her talking in her hushed voice, the connection between them had seemed so intimate. Now that they were actually alone in her apartment, it was the opposite—a sense of strain, discomfort, of being watched. He had thought she would be sexually aggressive. Hadn't she said or implied that she had done this many times, that all the men she'd been involved with were married? Didn't "all" have to mean "many"? He had been assuming, somehow, that she would know he was a novice, that she would do something bold such as cross the room and kiss him directly on the lips, letting her bathrobe slide open. Instead she just sat on the couch, halfway across the room, watching him with an expression as wary as the one he was sure was on his face.

"I don't do this kind of thing normally," he finally blurted out, because the silence was so agonizing.

"Yes," she said vaguely. She looked around the room, then sighed. "My headache's gone, I feel so much better. I should never have gone, probably."

"But it was in your honor," Noah said.

She shrugged. "I asked my sister if she wanted to go and she said she didn't think she could get a baby-sitter. She's never read one of my books," she laughed bitterly.

"I never read my brother's books either," he confessed. "Sibling rivalry, I guess."

She sat forward, her face resting in her hands. "Are you horribly envious of him, of the life you assume he leads?"

"Yes, I guess I am. He's my younger brother so it's worse, somehow. And it's everything, not just that he writes books, but he has a glamorous wife—perhaps you saw her, she was in a tuxedo—he has three kids and we have none, he has mistresses . . ." He ran out of steam, hearing his tinny, pathetic voice running on in the quiet room.

But Ava said softly. "There are so many men like that. I don't think they're worth the paper they're printed on. You're real."

Noah sighed. "I'm not sure." Suddenly he felt exhausted, not only not aroused, but almost dizzy, not in the way he had been at the party, just emotionally wiped out. "Is there any chance I could lie down?" he said. "I feel terribly zonked suddenly."

"Of course." She led him toward her bedroom, a smaller room in back with a large bed in the center of it. "Just rest," she said. "I'll be inside."

Noah lay down. The bed seemed wonderfully comfortable. Ava drew a comforter over him. "Rest well," she whispered.

He was too exhausted to figure out what was happening. Possibly he had misinterpreted her slipping the paper into his hand.

Perhaps all she had meant was that he seemed a nice person to talk to, not predatory like the other men she knew. Instead of being chagrined, he felt an enormous relief; he fell asleep.

When he woke up, however much later it was, he was naked and Ava Bernier was naked, sitting on top of him, moaning softly. They were making love, he was inside her, yet he had no memory at all of any events leading up to it, of her getting into bed with him, of either of them taking their clothes off. She seemed to be coming, the sound she made was like pigeons cooing. He was terrified that he would come too, that if he did he would be akin to a murderer. He felt like an innocent man who wakes up to find a dead body next to him, his own hands covered in blood. "Please stop," he begged, pushing her away. "Please."

She reared back, then disengaged herself and, in the semidarkness looked at him in concern. "Is something wrong?"

"I'm married," he gasped. "I've never been unfaithful to my wife." His heart was racing so fast he thought he would explode. "Jesus, I think I may be having a heart attack."

"Really? What's happening? What should I do? Should I call an ambulance?" She was still naked, crouched next to him in bed.

Noah grabbed her arm. "Look, could you promise me one thing. If I—if anything happens, please have the hospital call my wife."

"What's the number?"

Horribly his own phone number eluded him. He saw the numbers in his mind, but they whirled back and forth. Finally with great effort he forced them back into their proper order. She wrote them down on a pad.

Almost about to pass out, Noah said, "Could you not tell anyone you were with me, even if I die on the way to the hospital? Just bring me there, dead or alive, and then . . . go away."

"Of course." He lost consciousness before he could see her dial the phone, just glimpsed her bare buttocks and legs, white, gleaming in the half light.

When he regained consciousness, Noah looked around the room. He couldn't believe it. He was at home, in his own bed. He was wearing pajamas, sun was streaming in the window. Selma was just peering into the room. "How about some muffins?" she said cheerfully. "I just made some from that new mix. There's coffee too."

"What time is it?"

"Eleven. You must have been exhausted. I should be—I didn't get home until two. We went to Sardi's afterward." She smiled, as though at a happy recollection.

He felt he had to be careful, not to give anything away. "Where was I when you returned?"

"Right here . . . in bed. You didn't have time to take your clothes off, I guess. Poor thing. Did you drink too much?"

His mind raced through various possibilities. Ava Bernier had brought him to the hospital and he was fine so they had dismissed him, sent him home? Or perhaps she had brought him home? Was it possible the whole thing hadn't happened, that he had never gone to her apartment after all, he had just left the library, hailed a cab and gone home by himself? But certain details were etched sharply in his mind: her black robe, the street lamps near her apartment, her mentioning that she took Tofranil, the comforter, her sexual cooing, his trying to remember his own phone number . . . *I've been saved. Somehow I've been saved.* He felt peaceful, purged.

Selma came in with a tray of warm muffins, buttered, with honey, mugs of hot coffee. *If she knew . . . What does it matter, she doesn't. And you never really—It's over.* "I can remember so little about the party," he said cautiously. "Did you happen to see who I was sitting next to? I can't remember even talking to anyone."

"I think it was a dark-haired woman," Selma said. "Yes, Leo was saying something about her. I think she writes poetry. He said something—what was it—that she was a Sylvia Plath clone, always dressed in black . . . that she'd had some emotional problems." She looked away as she always did at the mention of the topic.

"Yes, now I remember," Noah said. "We talked about her poetry."

Selma reached over. "She must have given you a copy. I found it on the night table. Here it is."

Noah took the slender volume entitled, *Night Terrors.* He opened it. Inside was written in a fine delicate script, "To someone special whose life is valuable. Take care, A." Guiltily he closed it. Had Selma seen the inscription? Evidently not or she would, surely, have mentioned it. "I never read poetry," he said, putting it aside.

"Still, it was a nice thought," Selma said. She was eating a muffin, her lips buttery and smooth. "Wasn't it odd, Eloise wearing a tuxedo? Do you think she's gay?"

"No, of course not," Noah said. "Why would you think that?"

Selma looked embarrassed. "It's just sometimes, don't take this

the wrong way, but I get the feeling Leo may not be sexually satis-
fied, that that part of his life may be . . . incomplete."

"Did he make a pass at you?" The bastard.

"Oh no, nothing like that! Just sometimes he looks so wistful
and he makes these remarks about how much he envies us, our
relationship."

"Leo said that?" Noah half smiled. What bullshit.

"Money isn't everything, fame isn't everything," Selma said.
She leaned over and hugged him. "We're very lucky."

On the way to school the next day Noah could not stop thinking
about Ava Bernier. He could call her and ask what had happened,
but he didn't want to. That might just start something up. Leave it
be. God or someone had decided to protect him from himself. He
thought of what she had said: "You're real." But she had said that
because he had been different with her. Whether it had been the
wine or the way she had acted, he had allowed himself to be open,
unguarded, not the stiff, petrified person he usually was. Perhaps
that was the secret, that when you tried to be "normal," to fit in, you
didn't, but if you were open, if you threw caution to the winds,
people would love you.

At school, instead of slinking quickly past Loretta Rauch's office, he called out loudly, "Hi! Have a good weekend?"

"So-so." She looked surprised. "You?"

"Fantastic. A big party for my brother. Leo Epstein. He's the
author of *Sexuality Today.* There was a celebration honoring him and
some others at the Forty-second Street Library. I sat next to a
woman poet, Ava Bernier. She gave me an inscribed copy of one of
her books."

"Lucky you," Loretta Rauch said. "We rented *The Big Sleep* to
play on our VCR and Hal fell asleep in the middle."

The real challenge was his Sex Ed class. Up until now he had
been so nervous about getting it right, giving them the facts, not
being either too extreme, or too vague. But that was all absurd.
They knew it all anyway or would just ignore it. Today he would
treat them as equals, talk to them man-to-man (or person-to-per-
son), with a kind of winning directness, not losing sight of the fact
that he was the teacher and they were the students. He would
somehow break through their boredom and sense of hopelessness
about their lives.

He spent the first half of the class going over the AIDS article he had handed out which, predictably, almost no one had read. Then, smiling, he set the article face down on the desk. "Enough facts!" he said expansively. "What have we really been talking about in this class?"

Dead silence.

"Sex?" someone offered.

"Meaning what?" Noah said. He felt elated, excited.

Clearly they thought he was making a joke. "You know," Ronnie said. She was wearing a bright yellow sweatshirt with a black tic tac toe board on it. "Doing it . . . men and women."

"Yes," Noah said, "but we're really talking about love, aren't we? That's the taboo word, the word we never mention. We talk about doing it, fucking, making it, what have you—but we never talk about the spiritual side, sharing ourselves with another human being, letting our essences merge, letting our souls conmingle."

The faces that were watching him, the eyes that would normally have made him nervous, now made him feel buoyed up. "Take me," he said. "I was twenty-four before I lost my virginity. Pretty old, huh? And yet do I regret it? Do I regret having waited that long, having waited until I met the woman of my dreams, the woman with whom I've shared my life?"

At that moment the back door of the classroom opened. It was Garofolo. He sat down heavily in a vacant seat, barely fitting his bulk into it. Usually his appearance would have petrified Noah, but this morning he just waved and said, "Hi, Mr. Garofolo. You're just in time. We're talking about love, love and sex, and how they are one, how they come together."

Garofolo's face was impassive. He locked his fingers together on the desk in front of him. It struck Noah that he looked like Lionel Barrymore.

"I was just saying how I was a virgin until I got married," Noah went on. "I know that's unusual today. Most young men can't wait to score, to prove their manhood. It never occurs to them that you can prove it by waiting, by regarding the sex act as a sacred act, as something very akin to a religious act . . . Now I want to share with you something that happened to me last night. It was an unusual experience, a spiritual one. I was at a party, a party to honor my brother, Leo Epstein, the author. It was a big room and I was placed at a round table next to a lovely young woman who happened to have the same birthday I did. Isn't that unusual? In fact, we were both forty-one, that very day. We talked, she was a poet—did I mention that?—and we both felt this mysterious kinship that one does feel, that we all feel occasionally in rare, special moments. Perhaps we fell in love. That can happen sometimes when you least expect it. A sudden awakening of buried feelings, finding a kindred spirit. I drank some wine, perhaps too much, who can say, and then she left. This woman, despite the fact that this party was partly in her honor—she was a poet, is a poet—had to leave out of anxiety, out of what one might call emotional problems."

Suddenly Garofolo yelled out. "What the hell is this? What are you talking about?"

Noah tried not to let this rattle him. "Love, love and sex is my theme, Mr. Garofolo. And you'll see. Please listen. Please be patient. As I say, she left, slipping a piece of paper in my hand with my address on it. I mean with her address on it. 'You're real,' she said. 'Most men are not worth the paper they're printed on.' I thought that was an interesting metaphor. Men, paper . . ." He was drifting. Garofolo's interruption had drawn him off course. "She saw my inner spirit, is what I'm trying to say. But can you say this was merely sex? Can you say if, by chance—I'm not saying this happened, I don't think it did, but can you say if the two of us had ended up in bed, our bodies joined, was that the merely physical act it appears?" He paused. No one had an answer.

Suddenly some of the confusion he had felt waking up in his own bed Sunday morning came over him, the same confusion he had felt standing on the library steps with the slip of paper in his hand. "To tell the truth, I'm not sure what happened. But I am sure of one thing. It was love. The sacred union of two bodies, two souls. Do you know what I mean, Mr. Garofolo? Has that ever happened to you?"

Garafolo leapt out of his chair. "This is crazy," he said. He turned to the students. "Don't pay any attention to this. It's—" Inexorably he made his way to the front of the room. "Class dismissed," he yelled. "Go to your home rooms! Get going! Out!"

The students remained motionless, as though wondering if the whole episode was some kind of test. Noah was terrified. He knew only that he had made a miscalculation. To be that open with just anyone, with someone like Garofolo who had the sensitivity of a wart hog, how could he have done that? Gradually the room cleared. Garofolo grabbed Noah by the arm. "What's wrong with you?" he said. "Have you gone around the bend?"

"I was just—You said to bring in morality," Noah stammered. "How it's connected, love and sex. You said not to just emphasize facts. You said *The New York Times* was too complicated."

Garafolo stared at him. "Listen, Epstein, come back to the office with me. You know your wife's number? Her office number?"

"Sure," Noah said. "She works at Sports World."

"Okay, well, listen, she'll have to come and get you. Are you okay now? Are you still— Do you want some tranquilizers?"

"I'm fine, Mr. Garofolo," Noah said. "I take a pill, Elavil, which is supposed to—"

They were at Garofolo's office. He led Noah in, still clutching his arm as though if he didn't, Noah would run away. "Look, I've got a meeting to go to. Will you promise me you'll stay here till your wife comes? Not move an inch? Promise?"

Noah tried to laugh. "Where would I go?"

He sat down in the chair near Mr. Garofolo's desk. Outside the door he heard Garofolo say to his secretary, "Don't let him leave, do you hear me? If you have trouble, call the security guards. Tackle him, anything. He's out of control. He could be dangerous."

"Yes, Mr. Garofolo," the secretary squeaked. "I'll do as you say."

Dangerous? Sitting in the office, Noah thought back on the class. He had been misguided, certainly, overly optimistic, perhaps he had shown a lack of judgment, but in what way dangerous? He hadn't attacked anyone, hadn't even shouted. Right now Selma was on her way over here, and then what? He would go home, Garofolo would, no doubt, transfer him to another school, maybe suggest a "rest cure." Maybe that was the answer, a real rest, if only they could afford it, going to the Caribbean for a week or two, lying on the beach. Money. He hated thinking it was the key to everything, but the fact was they couldn't afford the Caribbean.

Hadn't it been Garofolo who was dangerous, the way he had charged up the aisle, his face red, his voice thunderous? Enjoying his own sense of power, his ability to intimidate. The students must have thought he was crazy. And poor little Angie Cortez. He hated the idea that she had witnessed what had happened. She was so delicate, so gentle. What did she know of that kind of brutality?

Suddenly it seemed claustrophobic to Noah sitting motionless in Garofolo's office. He stood up and tried to open the door. It was locked. He knocked on the door.

"Yes?" came the secretary's timorous voice.

"This door appears to be locked," Noah said, trying to smile, even though she couldn't see him.

"Those were Mr. Garofolo's orders, Mr. Epstein," the secretary said. "I'll open it when your wife comes. She should be here any minute."

"I don't get it," Noah said. "What do you think I'm going to do? Break furniture?"

There was a pause. "I have to do what Mr. Garofolo said," his secretary murmured.

Noah was standing close to the door. "Look, Miss . . . what's your name?"

"Miss Neilson."

"Miss Neilson, could you do me a favor? Could you go to my office and see if Loretta Rauch is there? She's the guidance counselor. Her office is right next to mine. I'd like to speak to her."

Hesitantly, Miss Neilson said, "I'm not allowed to leave my desk, Mr. Epstein."

"Well, get one of the students then, will you? Or some assistant?"

"I . . . I don't know."

Noah rattled the door handle. "Miss Neilson, do you want to get Ms. Rauch, or should I break this door down?"

"Oh . . . well, I'll ask someone. I'll—" She scurried off.

Shit. These women were like mice, fearful, empty-headed. God knows where she'd gone. But about five minutes later he heard Loretta Rauch's voice on the other side of the door. "Noah?" she called cheerfully. "It's me."

"Loretta? Thank God. Listen, can you open this door? It seems to be locked. I don't know what's going on."

"Evidently Mr. Garofolo wanted it locked," Loretta said in a strained voice.

"Okay, but you know me. We've shared an office for fifteen years. Am I violent? What the hell does he think I'm going to do?"

There was a long silence. "Why do you want to get out?" Loretta asked coyly.

"Would you like being locked up?" Noah asked. "It's humiliating, it's insane."

"I gather there was some incident—" Loretta began.

"Just open the door! I swear on all that's holy, I just want to *talk* to someone."

He heard murmured whispers, then the door opened. Loretta Rauch in a bright orange suit and big, frightened eyes, stared at him. "Are you all right?"

"I'm fine." He sighed, frowning.

She came close to him. "Do you mind if I just close the door, just so—" she indicated Miss Neilson, "we can talk privately?"

"Sure, whatever. I felt like a caged beast in here."

Loretta sat down in the chair he'd been sitting in while Noah paced the room. "What exactly happened?" she asked, crossing her legs. "I don't understand."

Outside it was sunny, a lovely April day. "Some kind of . . . It was a Sex Ed class. I was trying to explain what love was, what sex was, how they differ . . ." He trailed off.

"So, why was that so—"

Noah shrugged. A terrible, overwhelming sense of desolation settled over him. "I fucked up somehow. I don't know how, I really don't. Suddenly he was charging at me like a mad beast, in front of all the kids. It was so humiliating, so—" His voice cracked. He bent over, covering his face with his hands, weeping. "What did I do?" he murmured, almost to himself. "What have I done?"

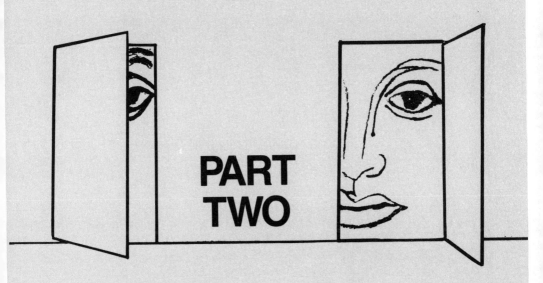

PART TWO

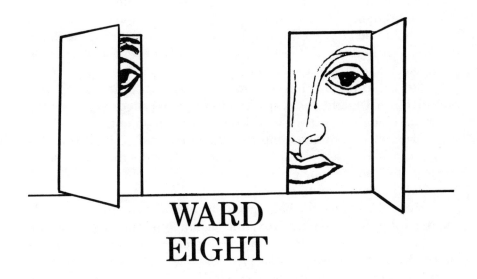

WARD
EIGHT

No one saw Stern as he crossed the hospital grounds on his way to Ward Eight where Roxanne was staying. Grieff had gone home. Stern passed the tennis courts where some patients were playing. Like a country club. That was what everyone said about Nash, at least it was the image they tried to put forward in their brochure. Even the grass was rolled up, carted away, and laid down again, like carpet, so it would never dry up or be any less than that bright iridescent green.

Why am I going to see her? I want to reassure her, she's upset, tell her that the wedding announcement was—what? A mistake? No, no need to go that far. Just reassure her that she's still a part of my life, that I'll always love her, no matter what.

He was still wearing his white coat. He wanted to appear as a doctor, checking up on a patient, not as a visitor. The nurse at the main desk looked up at him. His name was on his coat. "Can I help you?"

"I'm Dr. Stern. I know it's a little past visiting hours, but I was wondering how Ms. Arlen was doing. I believe she was admitted three days ago."

The nurse glanced down at her notes. "She seems to be doing nicely, a little distant, doesn't talk much. I believe it was reported that she made a phone call today."

Stern hesitated. "I'm an old friend of Ms. Arlen and I just wondered if I might speak to her briefly. She called me, I was the one she made the call to. It will only take a moment."

"Dinner is in fifteen minutes," the nurse said, "but, if you like, her room is 103. Keep it short, Dr. Stern. Her doctors don't seem to feel she's up to much contact yet."

"Of course, I understand."

He walked down the hall, feeling a kind of excitement, not only at the thought of seeing Roxanne again, but out of disobeying Grieff. *My life is my own. He's not my fucking father, not my surrogate father either. The hell with him! Has his life with women been such a paradigm?*

Roxanne was sitting by the window. All the windows were barred, something he had never noticed, but because she was here, he did notice and found it strange. Her hair was loose, concealing her face, which was turned away. She was looking out the window. As he stood in the doorway of the room, she turned.

Stern tried to interpret her expression. She didn't look surprised or fearful, just stared and the two of them were caught, their eyes locked, like two wrestlers unable to disengage. "Is it all right—" he said very softly. "I wasn't sure if you wanted to see me."

She shrugged.

Taking that as assent, Stern entered the room. Usually, for work, she fastened her hair up on the sides with two large tortoise-shell barrettes. Now it was totally loose, like the Lady of Chaillot. The only times he saw her hair that way was in bed. He sat down in a chair, facing her. "I wanted to see you," he said. He kept his voice very low. He felt afraid that what he was doing was wrong in every way, for her, for Sydney, against hospital rules. "Do you want to see me? I don't want to upset you."

She said nothing.

He looked down, began again. "I know I should have told you about the wedding announcement. I suppose I was hoping you wouldn't see it, which was absurd really, because it's a reality. It's a choice I felt I had to make. I just need some kind of stability in my life. I wasn't sure we were really good for each other. That goes both ways. I hoped I would be freeing you, somehow, to find another man. You always said as long as I was unmarried, you would feel tied to me."

Again she just shrugged.

"The kind of closeness we had was so explosive," Stern said. "Look, look where it's landed you! And I'm in trouble too. One of my patients died. An overdose. It was a mistake, it could happen to anyone, but it's also been the strain, thinking about you, trying to put you out of my mind. I haven't been concentrating well."

With one hand in a slow, languorous gesture Roxanne drew her hair back and swept it behind one ear. She kept her eyes fixed on him, but still didn't speak.

"Maybe you're thinking this is egocentric, assuming that everything you do is connected to me. I know it isn't. Maybe you have some new man in your life. I want you to. I feel jealous, even though I know I'm not entitled to, but you deserve someone, someone so much better than me."

Roxanne was in a hospital gown. He hated seeing her in the rough cloth, in this room with the barred windows. Her nightgowns were beautiful imported silk, lace. And something else was different. He was used to seeing her with eye makeup. He liked watching her put it on, the black line above her lids, the sweeping gesture with which she lengthened her eyelashes so that they looked so long they almost looked false. This way she looked younger, more innocent.

"I kept wondering why you called yesterday," he said. "I felt it must be because of the wedding announcement, but you said that wasn't it. I guess I want to think you really meant it when you said you wanted me to be happy, that you really are that generous, that you want my happiness as much as your own. I believe that about you."

Her expression changed just slightly. Was it cynical, bitter? "I thought once the wedding announcement was out, once it was public knowledge, that I could let go of you, at least in my mind. Maybe it's too soon. When I make love to Sydney, you're there, you're always there. Sydney doesn't know. She'll never know. But I feel I should let go of you. I feel as long as I think of you, you'll know somehow, and it will keep you from being free."

Roxanne spread her hands.

Stern leaned forward. "No one will ever know me the way you

do. But I can't live with that day after day. You can understand that, can't you? Remember how you once said you had a fight with your best friend in high school and you didn't want to make up with her because she knew you inside-out?"

Staring across at her, Stern had the sudden feeling she wasn't hearing anything he said or that, possibly, he wasn't speaking, just thinking things he thought were being transmitted. "Remember when we first met, when we were about to go to bed together that first time and you said, 'Can you handle this?' I didn't know what you meant. But I sensed it would be extreme, something that would draw me out of myself. I'm afraid I still want that. Maybe I'll always want it."

At that she looked down. Stern was afraid she was going to cry. Her hands were locked together; her hair almost concealed her face. He saw tears falling on her hands, but she didn't seem to notice, didn't seem to know she was crying, made no sound. "Don't cry, Roxy, please," he begged. More than anything he wanted to go over and fling his arms around her, run his hands through her hair, hold her, carry her out of here, carry her to safety. But if he touched her, he was lost.

"Darling," he said. He had to let his words touch her. "Please don't . . . It tears me apart. I can't bear it. I love you too much. It's terrible to watch you suffering this way."

Still the tears were falling, falling, her hands wet.

"I know I shouldn't be here," he said. "I'm not your doctor. Do you have a good doctor? You need to get well, to heal yourself, to rest. I'll check into the medication they're giving you. I want you to rest, to become your old self again. Don't do it for me. Do it for yourself. Will you? Will you, Roxy?" He was leaning forward, on the edge of his seat.

When she raised her head, her face still wet with tears, her voice was barely above a whisper. "You bastard," she said.

Stunned, Stern left the room.

He had been looking forward to this weekend, to just this moment, driving to Philadelphia. It was a short enough drive, yet long enough so that by the time he arrived all his concerns about Nash, his patients, whatever was happening in his life seemed far away, on another planet. Although there had been times when he resented Sydney's unwillingness to transfer to Manhattan, to look for a job there, in another way he liked it. In Philadelphia with Sydney and her parents, he could play a part and play it well.

As he drove, he imagined Sydney and her parents sitting watching a video of the scene that had just taken place between himself and Roxanne, his meandering, babbling digressions, trying to explain, justify, and her unbridgeable silence. She must have been listening to him the way he often listened to his patients: what bullshit, what rationalizations, what phony promises, heard and reheard so many times. Then he imagined Sydney and her parents, their faces. But this isn't the Stuart we know, the good old Stu who plays squash with Sydney's bisexual brother, Darryl, and gives him wise advice on life and women, the Stu who always pays Sydney's mother a gallant compliment on her latest silk dress, who embraces Sydney with the proper mixture of affectionate warmth and decorous restraint, the Stu who manages to exchange gruff pleasantries with Sydney's father about politics. Twice Mr. Sutton had voted for Reagan and was finally getting disillusioned. Bush was his man now because, in so many ways, Bush was a carbon copy of Tilden Sutton himself, encased in forms and rituals, henpecked in that particular WASP way which one escaped by going to "the club"—the Yale Club, the Princeton Club. No one ranted in this family. Stern could imagine them in an Agatha Christie novel: Someone had been poisoned and every member of the family had deep-seated reasons to poison everyone else and the detective would have to pick and pry through all those layers of gentility to discover the true culprit.

Sydney had made a mistake. She was marrying outside her caste. Not so much that Stern was not wealthy enough or didn't have a good enough job, but that he was dissembling. She knew nothing of his family—fortunately both his parents had died long before he met her. He had swept aside his crazed father and obsequious mother and created fantasy substitutes; warm, down to earth "simple people" who had cared for each other and for him. If she only knew! If she knew how uneasy he felt at the hospital, how dangerously close he had come to doing something lethally foolish, enough not only to get fired, but permanently destroy his professional reputation. Even with his patients there was the constant fear that they could see through him, saw him as a poseur, a phony, saw his attempts at Freudian detachment as patently false. No one was sitting in on the sessions, of course. The patients were powerless, but he found it hard not to see them, even more than his colleagues, as antagonists who could, in some palace revolution, overturn all he had painstakingly built up over the years.

From the beginning, his euphoria with Sydney was due to the relief he got out of seeming to fool all of them into feeling he belonged. He liked the person he became in Philadelphia, he liked "good old Stu." Was it an illusion that he could spend a lifetime playing that role until he got so good at it he could do it in his sleep? He saw himself interviewing prospective suitors for his and Sydney's daughter's hand. Would they find him as icy, as impenetrable and as admirable as he found Tilden Sutton? Would they let him win at tennis, but just barely, so as not to offend his pride? Would he console Sydney when she found the box of birth control pills in their daughter's bureau drawer—or by then perhaps something more efficient would have been discovered.

He realized that all his thoughts were of the future. Roxanne was the past. Going to see her had been one final pull of his old self; he was almost glad of her parting shot delivered with such cool aplomb: *You bastard.* It was self-protective perhaps, but accurate. He talked of breaking from her, but in the talking itself he was doing the opposite—clinging, hanging on, nurturing the baby part of himself who couldn't face losing her. Now it was done—she was lost to him, and if he really meant what he said, he would leave both of them free to pursue their separate destinies. Roxanne would find her Sydney, someone who would make her feel the sense of peace he had never been able to give her.

Friday evening the tradition was that he let himself into Sydney's apartment, left his briefcase and clothes there—he already had duplicates of most essentials like his shaver—rested, if there was time, and met Sydney at her parents' home just outside the city at eight. Sydney came straight from work—she always worked long hours. She didn't even bother to call him, nor he her, unless there was a change of plan.

The Suttons had a dining room, a room reserved exclusively for dining which struck Stern as strange, having grown up in a tiny railroad apartment where meals were usually gobbled in the kitchen. It was a large room, with dark blue wallpaper, several tastefully selected prints of the kind that you noticed and then forgot. A few were extremely valuable—signed editions or originals—he forgot which. The table was dark polished wood. Always, there were candles: off white—tapers really, they were so tall—burning in their pewter candlesticks. Along one wall was a buffet. There was a family servant, Lear, who had been with them since the Suttons were married.

This particular evening Sydney's younger brother, Darryl, and his fiancée, Winifred, were joining them. Sydney had been after Stern to "have a talk" with Darryl who had been gay, "on and off" for the five years since he graduated college, but who was now, in the family's opinion, reformed. The question was whether to inform Winifred, just so she would know "what she was getting into." Winifred was thin, almost anorectic, Stern thought, with beautiful hands and long polished nails. She had been a student at the Belzone School—Sydney had introduced them—and now gave recitals of Schubert lieder in her fragile but lovely voice. In Stern's opinion they would make love once a year and Darryl would discreetly return to having a monogamous gay lover, probably a married man like himself, with whom AIDS would not be a danger.

Darryl worked at the *Philadelphia Inquirer.* Over the appetizer, a cucumber tarragon soup, he looked over at Stern. "You're having problems over at Nash, I hear," he said.

Stern thought the remark was good natured. Everything everyone said always sounded that way and also sounded the opposite—it was hard to tell as an outsider. "It's all under control now," he said tersely.

"What problem?" Sydney asked. She was in a pink dress, a little too young for her, with a string of pearls. At the end of her work week she always seemed a bit tense, on edge.

"A patient overreacted to a particular drug," Stern said, glancing at her reassuringly. "It's not that uncommon. There are so many possible side effects."

"Yeah, but didn't he die?" Darryl said. He laughed. "That's quite a side effect."

"He was alcoholic," Stern said. "There were a lot of complicating factors. Sometimes our nursing staff isn't as scrupulous as they might be in the exact dosage. And of course the smallest error can, in very very rare cases, be fatal."

Sydney looked horrified. "I hope they're firing that nurse!"

"Yes, it's being looked into," Stern said. Lear was removing his soup bowl.

"You mean she's still on duty?" asked Mrs. Sutton, startled. "The nurse who gave the fatal overdose? How can that be?"

Shit. Had he gotten into this feet first? "She's a very competent nurse, normally. It's hard for an outsider to understand, but there are extraordinary pressures working at a place like Nash. Occasionally, at a weak moment, people make mistakes."

Winifred laughed hysterically. "I'd go crazy working in a place like that. Doesn't it get to you sometimes?"

"I try not to let it," Stern said. "You learn a certain detachment. It takes time."

"It seems to me that what those people need," Mr. Sutton said, "is to learn a sense of structure. That's the thing. Not drugs, not therapy which, pardon me, Stuart, is just whining on about things we all have to deal with every day. They need to learn control."

Sydney was helping herself to green beans and roast pork. "Yes, but Daddy, if they knew that, they wouldn't *be* there. These are crazy people, not just neurotics."

"Crazy people, neurotics, schizophrenics," Mr. Sutton said. "It's a lot of jargon. I read an article the other day which said a group of perfectly sane people were placed in one of those places and not one doctor could tell the difference between them and the crazy people. Not one!"

Off and on Stern had the feeling that Mr. Sutton loathed him. Sometimes he felt it was because he was a Jew, sometimes because he was a psychiatrist, sometimes because he was taking away his beloved daughter, and sometimes simply out of sheer malice. "Not every mental hospital is the same," Stern said, trying to act calm. "It's a matter of training."

"Life is training," Mr. Sutton said.

Sydney adored her father. She admitted he was rigid, had a bad temper, was "prejudiced," though she never spelled out the particular ethnic groups toward whom those prejudices were directed, but she also was of the opinion that deep down he was "an old sweetie," whose heart, which she assumed existed, was in the right place. She adored her mother, too, in fact actually used that word about both of them: "adore." About her mother, she admitted that she was old-fashioned, and perhaps hadn't done all with her life that she might have, that she had hidden talents (Sydney was convinced her musical ability came from her mother), that she could get needlessly hysterical (for instance, at the slightest mention that Darryl's sexual development was even slightly off course), but that she, too, was a "total darling." And Darryl—well, Darryl did have problems and maybe, yes, they were due to Daddy's being a bit too stern and strict, not being quite such an "old sweetie" with him as he was with

Sydney, but all that would be straightened out once he was married. Sydney was tickled to death (again her words), that she was the one who had been able to find someone to suit Darryl, who had seemed so hard to please. Stern was sure Darryl had reached a point where he was ready to succumb to the relentless family pressures: Winifred could have been Jane or Susan or Lulu, or anyone.

They got through the meal, chatted briefly over brandy in the living room. Stern arranged to play squash with Darryl the following afternoon and then he and Sydney set off for her apartment in a cab, called by Lear. He had recently seen *The Purple Rose of Cairo,* in which the characters get stuck in their own movie. One of them, out of sheer boredom and curiosity, did escape, briefly. That was how Stern felt. Each weekend was like the same set of vignettes. At times he felt he was as replaceable to Sydney as Winifred, he assumed, was to Darryl. It all depended on his mood. In certain moods it was a relief, feeling he could just play a part he knew by heart, and at other times he was pierced through with a sense of deadness, suffocation.

Friday night, for instance, they never made love. This had never been agreed on, but the few times in the beginning he had made anything that could be interpreted as a pass, Sydney had said she was just too exhausted after her work week, that if they waited until Saturday evening it would be more fun for both of them since they would both be "in the mood."

At the apartment, he got into pajamas and watched her sit, naked, with perfect posture, at her dressing table, removing her makeup. Like Roxanne, Sydney was petite, barely over five feet tall, but whereas Roxanne's body had a womanly fullness, Sydney's could have been that of a preadolescent girl, delicate, barely formed. She was like the nymph in the old White Rock commercials, unaware of her nudity, or unaware that nudity and sexuality were connected. Inadvertently he kept flicking back and forth from Sydney, naked at her dressing table and Roxanne, in her hospital gown, her dark hair screening her face, her tears falling. The irony was that watching Roxanne, fully clad, he had felt perversely aroused, willing, had it been possible, had she allowed it, to make love to her right there. And now, alone in his fiancée's apartment, seeing her round behind, her small breasts, the line of her back, he felt nothing.

She slipped a short cotton nightshirt over her head, flipped off the light and got into bed beside him. It was funny—the Suttons were so rich, they could easily have afforded the most extravagant nightgowns, but when he once bought Sydney something like that, something more akin to what Roxanne, on her meager salary, always wore (the store, appropriately enough, was called Wife Mistress), she had gently explained that it wasn't her taste. Maybe if you were rich, you didn't need silk. "And when you make love, you don't wear clothes, so I've just never seen the point," she explained. Grieff insisted Sydney wanted to be ravished, that all of it, the Friday night taboo, the sitting naked at her dressing table, the sexless cotton gown was a peculiar attempt at a come on. When Stern explained that he had been rebuffed the few times he had made a pass, Grieff insisted that was nothing. "Just keep going, she wants to be overwhelmed, they all do."

He's been divorced three times, what does he know? But he did feel aroused, whether from the violent scene with Roxanne (it struck him in retrospect as violent, though she had sat as motionless as a statue and said only two words), or just from some pent-up hysteria of the past week with its threats, deaths, panics. He stroked Sydney's breasts and let his hand slide down between her legs to test if she was moist. He wanted to bury his head there, lick her gently, feel her body writhe back and forth in pleasure, but she just sighed and said, "Oh Stu, I just can't . . . I'm so exhausted, it's been such a week."

She had a week! What did she know of weeks in her music school with its well-heeled parents and obedient students? "Please," he begged. "For me. I need to . . . I feel desperate."

"I'll just be lying here, I don't have the energy to respond."

"That's okay."

But it wasn't. She was dry. He had difficulty entering, even thought of abandoning the effort, but finally pushed through. And then she lay there with her legs straight out, her hands lightly touching his shoulders, and let him have his way with her. He came fitfully, it was barely one step above masturbation.

"Was that all right?" she asked, seemingly without irony.

"It was fine." He felt immobilized by despair. How could he endure this relentless passivity for a lifetime, this altruistic "giving in," where there should have been passion, joy? He thought of how he and Roxanne would wrestle sometimes; they both knew how to almost hurt the other. Being so close to that edge was exciting for both of them. Sometimes they veered too close to the limits. Once he pulled her hair so hard she screamed. Another time she bit him so hard that she drew blood. *You don't want that.* Sydney was like

Desdemona; you would smother her with a pillow. *Go to sleep, forget all this.*

Darryl was a better squash player than Stern; in fact, he had been on the squash team at Yale. He was tall and thin, in much better shape than Stern and yet he had the same ambivalence on the squash court that Sydney had in bed. Maybe it was some hidden defect in the genes of the Sutton family. Darryl wanted to win, but he didn't. He would play brilliantly, and then make a string of foolish errors, laugh at his own clumsiness. Stern wondered if this male ritual, the two of them in this enclosed space, the smell of sweat, half naked bodies, was any kind of turn-on for Darryl. Stern won three games out of five. He let himself pour out the tensions of the week and played better than usual.

Afterward, Darryl slapped him good-naturedly on the back. "Nice going . . . I wasn't concentrating too well out there."

They showered and then had a light lunch in the club. At times Darryl looked eerily like Sydney, the bright pale blue eyes and a kind of spacey intenseness, earnest but not quite there simultaneously. "Hey, I saw your wedding announcement," he said. "Nice. Nice going. I guess Win and I will have to do that soon. She wants a fall wedding. Her parents got married in the fall."

"Sounds like a great idea," Stern said. *What was? Weddings? Weddings in the fall?*

Darryl bit into his chicken salad sandwich. "You waited quite a while," he said. "I mean, Sydney said you were thirty-eight. I'm just twenty-eight."

"I know."

Darryl looked off at the players who were in a court right in front of them. "I don't know if I could wait that long," he said. "I think, like Dad said, I need the structure."

"But relationships outside marriage, long-term ones, can provide structure too." Stern felt more than ten years older, almost avuncular.

"I guess." A shade of melancholy crossed Darryl's face. "For me they were never . . . They were more passing things. Sex alone—"

"They don't have to be based primarily on sex," Stern said. "Relationships outside marriage, I mean."

Darryl frowned. "Then why not marry? If you're going to cheat? Not you, I just meant in general."

Stern looked off evasively. "Maybe not everyone is suitable . . ." he began again. "There are some people one shouldn't marry, one knows that, and yet one feels some kind of fascination. But as I say it's more than sexual, though it's that too." He felt protected, even in being this cautiously confiding, because he knew Darryl would never refer specifically to being gay, and thus there were definite fixed limits.

Darryl seemed intent on the conversation. "And then what?" he said. "I mean, after marriage? I know what you mean, but can one give that up, what you've been talking about, that kind of intense relationship where, as you say, it may be all wrong, too dangerous? Won't one always miss it?"

"Probably." *This is Sydney's brother. Don't go too far.* "I'm not the right person to ask," he added. "I'm not married yet. I've had ten more years of freedom than you. You get tired of being jerked around by your emotions—at least I have—scenes, screaming. Maybe when you're young that kind of intensity is a turn-on, but at my age, you want peace, security."

Darryl was silent. "Sydney's great," he said. And then after just a moment, "Winifred too . . . I'm lucky."

"We both are."

Their eyes locked and suddenly both of them smiled. "Listen, forgive me if this sounds, I don't know what," Darryl said, "but don't you, at some level, feel trapped, feel like they're about to nail you in your coffin? I don't mean because it's Sydney you're marrying, but doesn't marriage in general, the idea of it, frighten you?"

"Sure," Stern said, laughing.

Darryl's blue eyes flickered. "And, well—this is all off the record—what do you think about afterwards? What do you think about monogamy?"

"If it can work—" Stern began.

"Can it? Do you think it can?"

Stern shrugged.

As though the shrug had been an answer, which in some ways it had, Darryl rushed on, "And you don't think that's unfair to the—the person you're marrying, starting off with those doubts?"

"Maybe they have doubts too."

Darryl raised his eyebrows. "I don't think women do, somehow. I think for them it's easier."

"I guess we have to live with our doubts. Maybe we *are* our doubts. I see marriage as a structure, but within it each person finds his own way of existing. Without that it's not a structure, but a cage."

Darryl looked pleased. "I like that. That's a good image. Not a structure, but a cage."

Just don't die of AIDS. But Darryl didn't strike him as self-destructive. He would be as ultra careful as, no doubt, Tilden Sutton might have been had he engaged in extramarital relationships.

Later Sydney asked him if he and Darryl had had the talk about the future that she had been urging on him. "Yes, we did," Stern said. "I think we did."

Sydney looked at him sharply. "What do you mean, you 'think' you did? Either you did or you didn't!"

"I mean he never refers directly to being gay so there's a certain amount of evasion—" *On both sides.*

"He *isn't* gay!" Sydney exclaimed. "He was bisexual, at the very worst. Don't say gay—that's a label. I know he's slept with Winifred, and she thinks he's a wonderful lover." Her lower lip trembled.

"Well, whatever he is, whatever one calls it, I tried to reassure him it would be fine"—Stern tried to seem imperturbable—"that we all have doubts, but one can live with that."

Her eyes widened. "What kind of doubts? What do you mean? Do *you* have doubts?"

Jesus. "Sweetheart, I don't mean . . . All I meant was everything is a tradeoff in life—love, work. Like you said when you decided against being a harpist, you were giving up one thing for another."

He felt he sounded reassuring, warm, kindly, but she went on in the same tense way. "But what are *you* giving up for marriage? *I'm* not giving up anything!"

"I meant it in the most abstract way . . . freedom." He saw himself in a maze of words, groping his way out. "It's an abstraction, but even as that it's meaningful, at least to some people. To Darryl, perhaps."

Sydney's eyes were still hurt. "You're being so vague! Do you mean freedom to have sex with other people? What are you talking about?"

"No, of course that's not what I mean." He watched her warily, afraid to entangle himself further.

She was silent for what seemed a long time. "I know you used to see someone, someone at the hospital, a nurse."

"That was years ago."

"I saw her photo once in your drawer. She was beautiful."

"Not really. Dramatic, intense, but screwed up, *hopelessly* screwed up. I just found out last week she'd made a suicide attempt."

Sydney whirled around. "How did you find out?"

"She's at Nash." What in God's name was wrong with him? How could he have said that?

"Did you go to see her?"

"No. Why should I? We haven't— Our relationship was over years ago."

"You don't think the attempt was connected to her seeing our wedding announcement in the paper?"

"How could it be? I tell you, we haven't . . . We're friends, at best. For all I know she's engaged herself."

"But when you speak of her, you sound so emotional, like there's still some tie." Deny, deny her eyes pleaded.

"There isn't!" Stern shouted, impatient. "Won't you believe me? She almost dragged me under, we almost dragged each other under. If I hadn't met you—"

The expression on Sydney's face was ironical. "So I saved you from a fate worse than death?"

"In effect."

"Well . . . I guess I never had any relationships like that. Men like that scare me—brutal, crazed men. I had one friend in college who always ended up with them and I never understood it."

He held her close, kissing her, relieved they had somehow navigated the shoals. "You're such a darling, such a sweet wonderful darling." *You crazy fool. Are you trying to dynamite your whole life to bits?*

Monday morning Dr. Szell informed him that a new patient had been admitted over the weekend. "Suicidal?" Stern asked.

"Not in any literal sense. She signed herself in. We'll have her appear at rounds later. But could you interview her? I thought since Luise Browner was dismissed, this might be a good candidate for you. She'll be tricky. Very intelligent, a lawyer in a big Manhattan firm."

"Married?"

"Yes, she came in with her husband. I've set it up for you at nine-forty."

"Terrific. I'll give you a report at lunch."

Another woman patient. Lately Stern had had more women

than men. He felt he was more at ease with women. With men he could get drawn into feeling competitive or, more often, if they were weak, being unable to repress a kind of contempt.

An intelligent woman lawyer sounded perfect, not psycho, not on drugs, not a basket case. What was she doing in a hospital, though, if all she was was neurotic? There must be more. He looked forward to finding out.

When she entered his office, she looked around intensely at everything, including the portrait of him over the fireplace. Was that just her lawyer's training, taking it all in? She was somewhere between attractive and not: a thin face, beaky nose, expressive eyes, dark hair tied back in a careless way. Her height and her dancerlike posture made her seem imperious.

He stood up. "Ms. Zimmer. I'm Dr. Stern."

She shook his hand. Her hand was icy cold. "I know."

"Please have a seat." After she was seated, he said, "This won't be a real session, though I will be your doctor. I just wanted to get a few facts straight about why you were admitted here."

"I admitted myself," she said. Her chin lifted. "I'm a voluntary admission." It was clearly important to her.

"I see. You felt a need for something more than therapy?"

"My husband . . . felt I was getting out of control." She hesitated. "There were some incidents over the weekend. I was afraid he was right."

"Could you give an example?"

Many patients refused to look at him. She stared right into his eyes. "My brother-in-law was getting remarried . . . in Colorado. My sister died five years ago and he sent me an invitation to the wedding. I didn't know whether to go. I thought I might be betraying my sister. Of course it's been five years, but . . . I shouldn't have gone. It was a mistake."

"Because it *was* a betrayal?"

"It was upsetting for me. I had the feeling my sister was there. Actually I saw her, or I may have seen her. It's not clear to me." She frowned.

"When did she . . . appear to you?"

She looked out the window, as though trying to conjure up the image. "During the ceremony. It was like a recurring dream I've been having. She died falling from a horse and in my dream she was on the horse, galloping, and during the ceremony I heard that sound, of horse's hooves galloping, and I thought I saw her, far off.

They live on a ranch. I thought if I could reach her in time, I could save her from dying. I wanted so much to save her!" Her voice broke.

"But you didn't?"

"No, I never . . . I never reached her. I ran and ran, but she was always just out of sight. Perhaps it was a hallucination." She changed from dreamy to almost crisp.

Stern took some notes. "You were very close to her?"

"Quite close but . . . it's not just her. Everyone has been dying, it seems. First my father—that was a more natural death, of emphysema, then my sister, then my mother which, again, was what you might call 'natural.' It was cancer, but she was seventy-eight. And then . . . well, that's all really." Her expression was alert, but wary. She touched her throat.

"When did your mother die?"

"Four years ago, a year after my sister. It was so terrible, that she had to live to see that." Her voice was shaky, her hands clenched into fists.

"So, you think it was your brother-in-law's remarriage that triggered your breakdown?"

There was a long silence. "In part," Alix Zimmer said finally. "And."

Again a long silence. This time she looked away. "Other people have died too, outside my family."

"Anyone in particular?"

"Someone at work . . . an older man who was like a mentor to me. So perhaps it was like my father's death all over again, though he was nothing like my father." She stared challengingly at Stern. "He was my lover, in fact."

"What did *he* die of?"

"A heart attack. Not while I was with him. He—he'd had a bad heart for a long time, but we still— His doctor had said sex was safe if—" Suddenly she covered her face with her hands and began to weep.

Stern let her. Then very quietly he said, "But despite that, you feel somehow responsible for his death?"

"No, no, not at all. It's not that."

"What is it then?"

She tried to stop weeping and then blurted out. "Where will it stop? Everyone is dying!"

"How is your husband's health?"

"Fine. But you're right. He, too, could . . ." She was breathing heavily, trying to get back in control.

"Did your husband know of this relationship?"

"No!" She cried this out so loudly he almost jumped.

"How long had the affair been going on?"

"Five years." Again that challenging look.

"So, it was a love affair, not just a—"

"Not just a what?" she said sharply.

"It was not primarily a sexual relationship?"

She gazed at him, into him. "It was everything."

Shit. Why this? Why now? Grieff said that was a common fantasy, that patients seemed to hook into your own life, their neuroses often seemed perfect mirror images of whatever was happening to you. "Perhaps you feel betrayed by your lover, by his dying?"

Almost inaudibly she said, "I feel . . . alone."

"Despite your husband?"

"Yes."

Stern felt he was handling the session well, winning her confidence, so that he was surprised when seemingly casually she said, "That's an interesting portrait of you on the wall."

Often patients, as you came close to dangerous material, started commenting on the furniture, the weather. "Interesting in what way?"

"Everyone's face has two sides, two aspects of their character." She held up her hand, covering one eye. "If you look at the left side, you see a calm, withdrawn person." She moved her hand. "If you look on the right side, you see something tormented, like a frightened horse about to rear up." She looked at him questioningly, seeming to want confirmation.

"How does that make you feel, your assumption that I have these two sides to my character?"

"Good in that you'll be able to understand both sides of *my* character." She hesitated. "Bad in that I'd like to imagine you as more in control. What if you have personal problems as complicated as mine?"

"How would that make you feel?" He tried for jocularity.

"Profoundly uneasy. But perhaps everyone has these double edges, sides to their character one doesn't anticipate."

"Like your brother-in-law? The fact that he remarried?"

"Oh, I know he was entitled to do that. It had been five years, after all. And certainly Luke, my husband, is reliable, not two-faced, but—" She broke off.

Stern watched her. "But you feel you are not? You feel you've betrayed his trust by this relationship you mentioned?"

"No, I don't think of it that way."

"How *do* you think of it?"

She was faltering, close to the verge of breaking down again. "There aren't that many people one can love in that way, that deeply." Once again she covered her face with her hands. "Why did he die?"

Stern waited a moment as she sat, her face covered, not weeping, but clearly unable to speak. "I'm afraid we'll have to stop here, Ms. Zimmer. But on Friday we can—"

Suddenly she sat up. "Friday is in three days! Don't I see you every day?"

"No, I have other obligations, other patients."

"Who do I see, then?"

"Well, there are interactions with the other patients, planned activities. Therapy, however, is twice a week."

She seemed agitated, trembling, her eyes bright. "But I don't see the point, then. I could get more therapy than that on the outside! Why am I here?"

Stern tried to smile. "We'll discuss all that. I have another patient now."

His next patient, Wolcott Fish, now back on lithium, was almost alarmingly calm, tedious, already thinking of his rope factory, plans for the future. As a "normal" man he was dull to the point of incomprehensibility. Stern was able to listen, nod, let his mind flash back to the preceding session with Alix Zimmer who had stirred up some intense, conflicting emotions which he tried to unravel.

There was a slight physical resemblance to Roxanne, more manner than looks, a combined sense of intelligence and controlled hysteria. He thought of the abrupt yet unerring way she had analyzed his portrait. No patient had ever remarked on it or seemed to notice it. He had talked to Grieff about this fear, of being "found out" by a patient, of the dread that one could turn the tables on him, unmask him. "But no one's in the session but the two of you," Grieff had argued. "Who'll believe a patient in a mental hospital under those circumstances?" He was right, it was a foolproof situation.

Perhaps it was that a woman with that kind of intuitive sharpness had the power to get through to him on some primitive sexual level. She had made him feel endangered, wary. Her personal life was clearly a tangle of confused relationships. Whom did he identify with, feel sorry for—the deceived husband or the lover whom she was unable to stop thinking of even after his death? What had she said? "What if you have personal problems as complicated as mine?" Or the same as mine? Two lovers, an inability to choose between them, caught, no solution.

In rounds Ms. Zimmer was more silent, withdrawn. Stern questioned her a little, and then met briefly with Szell. "What about the hallucinations?" Szell said. "She didn't mention those when she was admitted."

"I don't know if that's been a pattern," Stern said. "Let's put her on Thorazine. She seems borderline hysterical."

"Fine. I don't believe that's been tried on her. Check the charts."

Stern enjoyed interacting with Mortimer Szell. He was like a Jewish version of Sydney's father, so encased in rituals that there was never any danger that a real person might leap out at you. He seemed to have an absolute lack of curiosity about everyone on the staff, and not only didn't gossip but barely seemed to know who the staff were, what their names were, even though he had worked with many of them for decades.

Going downstairs for lunch, Stern felt a tap on his shoulder. It was Grieff. "Hiya. How'd you find your girlfriend?"

Stern froze. "Do you want to have lunch?" Having lunch with Grieff was the last thing he wanted, but he also was petrified someone might overhear their conversation.

"A quick bite maybe," Grieff said.

As they drove to the restaurant at the foot of the hill, Stern said, "How did you know?"

"Am I wrong?"

"Don't play games. Tell me how you knew."

"For starters, I know you. And I checked, just out of curiosity. I made a bet with myself—heads you did it, tails you wouldn't. It was pretty even-steven. I thought, can he be *that* dumb? And then I thought, sure, sure he can." He grinned.

"You're wrong," Stern said. "She didn't call in order to start something up again. When I went there, she didn't say a word. *I* did all the talking."

"Silence is a weapon."

"I know."

"No tears?"

Stern looked for a parking space. *Damn this man, was he psychic or what?* "Sure, tears."

Walking to the restaurant, Grieff asked in his seemingly detached, but also impish way, "Total silence, huh? No parting shot?"

Stern hesitated. *Why do I always tell him the truth?* "You bastard," he said.

Grieff laughed. "Is that what *she* said, or what you're saying to me?"

"Both."

"Look, kiddo, it's your life. You get some kind of kick out of it. You were involved with her for six years. She knows you—that's an attraction."

Stern just shrugged. "I felt aroused, sitting there, watching her weep. She sat with her hair loose, her cheeks wet. It was like a painting, like some incredibly beautiful painting that takes your breath away."

"Would you have fucked her if you could've?"

A long silence. "I hope not."

"In other words, yes?" Grieff shook his head. "Well, I don't know. Things must be slow in Philadelphia, huh? Or was it the wedding announcement? Did that make you feel trapped?"

"I wasn't aware that it did." Of course, as they both knew, it was the things you weren't aware of that counted.

They ordered. Grieff, who should have been on a diet, ordered a pastrami sandwich and dumped three containers of cream in his coffee. He smoked and ate alternately or even, it seemed, simultaneously. "How's the new patient?"

"Interesting, hysterical—"

"She seemed pretty withdrawn in rounds."

"Both. Somehow she reminded me of Roxanne." He described the incident with the painting.

"Not bad for a first session. She has you by the balls already, huh?"

"Just slightly."

"I thought women with X-ray vision scared you shitless."

"You used to say that was paranoid, that no one has X-ray vision."

"I'm talking about how she affected you. What has reality got to do with it?"

"Look, I can handle it, okay? Get off my case!"

Grieff looked amused. "*Your* case?"

"Her lover evidently had a bad heart. She wasn't with him when he died."

Grieff snorted. "I'll bet she wasn't. She probably ran for cover and let the ambulance pick him up, D.O.A."

"It isn't clear yet."

"Women, women. They're wonderful, really. I truly couldn't live without them, despite the fact that they've caused me more *tsuris* than a hurricane. They should be running the world, no question. What powers of manipulation! So subtle."

Stern was barely hungry. He sipped his Diet Coke. "Sydney's not like that. She's totally straightforward."

"She still sit around naked and claim she's too tired for sex?"

"I truthfully don't see that as manipulation," Stern said. "Repression, maybe."

Grieff laughed. "Stuart, my boy, you're wonderful. Four years of intensive analysis and in some ways you're like a five-year-old boy. No, make that a five *month* old."

"I don't want to go through life, my personal life, analyzing everything to death. It would destroy any pleasure I could get."

"Your choice. For me it's the *only* pleasure. Without it I'd shoot myself by late this afternoon."

"We're different, then."

"Maybe."

You will never win with this man. Stop trying. He will see through everything. He is inside you. Curtly Stern paid the check and didn't talk to Grieff all the way back to the hospital. Grieff sat back and whistled, "I'm Gonna Wash that Man Right Outa My Hair."

Alix Zimmer's husband, Luke James, came to see Stern while she was in occupational therapy. He was a tall, handsome man, with an ascetic, refined face, beautifully dressed in a grey suit, a thoughtful manner. Stern knew only that he was in the art history field and that he and Alix had met in college. Most of the sessions had been spent talking about Gerald Lehman, or avoiding talking about him.

"My wife seems upset about the small amount of therapy," James began. "She says it's only twice a week, less than she would get on the outside. Is that true?"

"Mental hospitals aren't just for therapy," Stern said. "We provide an atmosphere, an oasis, if you will, of rest and tranquillity where the patient can shut out the concerns of the everyday world that have been troubling him or her. Concentrating every day on problems might be highly counterproductive."

James nodded. "Yes, well I can see that . . . Alix has been working terribly hard, she's a very high-pressured person, so it stands to reason she wants to be cured just as rapidly."

What did he know of his wife? Anything? "Has she always been high-pressured or is that a recent development?"

"She was always that way to a certain extent. And I admire it, I admire her intensity and drive. She made partner in her firm, the first woman to ever do that, at thirty-four. But since then, perhaps to show she deserved it, she's been overworking, late hours. I feel she's been under too much strain."

And fucking her boss. "You've never thought of having children, I gather?"

James frowned. "Well, that was one recent thing that seemed to precipitate what happened. I came home one evening and found that Alix had left work early and completely rearranged the furniture in the living room, actually dragged the harpsichord into it, in order, she said, to see if we could set up a nursery in the music room. She wanted to get pregnant immediately! It was so sudden . . . Not that I'd mind, but I felt we should talk about it. I don't know, really, where the idea came from."

"Perhaps all the deaths in her life," Stern suggested. "She talks about that a lot."

"Birth eradicating death?" James looked off, bemused. "Yes, that's an interesting theory. It's possible . . . Another incident, as perhaps she's mentioned, was her brother-in-law's remarriage. I blame myself for that. We'd received the wedding invitation and Alix expressed not the slightest interest in going. In fact, said categorically she didn't want to go, couldn't bear to see another woman taking her sister's place. I felt that was a good decision. Then suddenly I came back to my office after a meeting and there was a message from my secretary that Alix was on a plane going to Colorado, for the wedding." He looked bewildered.

"You joined her there later?" Stern asked. She had been vague about this and it still wasn't clear to him if James had been there for the wedding itself.

"The second I heard from her, I flew out. But by then she was . . . well, highly excited, as I said, talking about having a child." He hesitated. "She even thought she had seen Pam, her dead sister, at the wedding. In her imagination, of course, but evidently to her it seemed real."

"Has she had other hallucinations?"

"Never."

"Well, we have her on a drug that ought to control that tendency, should it recur," Stern said. He looked at James who sat, legs crossed, gazing back at him with respectful attention. "Were there any other incidents that, as you see it, might have led up to this? She's mentioned the death of her sister, her parents . . ."

"No," James said. "I don't think so, really. But then having one's whole family wiped out that way would be a terrible trauma for anyone."

"No other deaths outside the family?"

James thought. "Well yes, actually, now that you mention it, someone at her firm, another partner, Gerald Lehman, who had been very helpful to her in her career. He had a heart attack a few months ago. Perhaps Alix had some reaction to that, though it was certainly not noticeable.

"What was their relationship?"

"I suppose mentor-protegée, really. I think he was about a decade older. A brilliant man who, I believe, had an unsettled private life, a mad wife, something of that sort. No, mad is too strong. A recluse, is what Alix once said."

Stern looked right at him. Men like this aroused some kind of rage in him, their impeccable manners, calmness, detachment. "Was there ever any sexual jealousy on your part?"

"None whatsoever. He was a short, physically unattractive man. I know men like that can be sexually dynamic, but he . . . he wasn't Alix's type."

"So you think her sense of loss in relation to his death is more what she might have felt for her father, had he been a stronger person?"

"Definitely."

Stern was silent. *God, talk about denial!* He decided to take another tack. "Are you faithful to your wife, Mr. James?"

"Is this confidential? You won't repeat anything to Alix?"

"It is."

"Yes, I am."

Stern smiled.

"Why are you smiling?"

"Well, I just wondered why confidentiality would be needed in that case."

"I want to know the context in which our conversation is taking place."

"I see. So, for you the marriage has been a happy one in every way, including sexually?"

"Yes."

"And for Alix? Would she say the same thing?"

James hesitated. "Well, now, of course she's not quite herself, but normally, yes, I think she would say she was happy. I think a lot of her energy goes into her work. Alix's passion, if you will, is for her work."

"Not for you?"

James smiled. "Of course, for me, too. But between the two I don't think there's a lot of excess space. Which is why I wondered about her desire to have a child. It seemed to me it would pull her in too many directions."

Stern glanced at his watch. "I think Alix will be coming back from O.T. now, if you'd care to see her."

"Of course. I miss her terribly. It's difficult for me, having her here."

"That's understandable." Stern walked with him to the door.

"Could you give me any rough estimate of how long you feel the treatment will last?"

Stern shrugged. "I really can't. This absorption with death could indicate she herself is deeply tempted with the idea, with joining these loved ones, as it were. But we have to understand that further."

James reached out and shook Stern's hand. "Thank you for this time. It's been helpful."

Stern watched him walk down the corridor. He felt the way Grieff probably felt on hearing that he had gone to see Roxanne. Are we all so blind if we love someone—such willful, crazy blindness?

At times he wished he knew someone in the city who was as good a squash player as Darryl. There were days when the outlet of tension would have been wonderful. Instead, today he jogged, though he found it tedious. When he came in, sweaty, light-headed, the phone was ringing. It was Sydney. "Stu?" She sounded excited.

"Yeah?" He was out of breath, cleared his throat.

"What's wrong?"

"I've been out jogging. Let me just sit down a sec." He sat in the chair in the kitchen, reaching for a glass to pour himself some orange juice.

"I have the most super news! Win and Darryl are announcing their engagement in two weeks!"

Stern swallowed the juice. "Great, that's wonderful."

"I think your talk with him really helped. He said something about how it gave him perspective. He looks up to you so much. I think you're like an older brother to him."

Stern thought back to the conversation over lunch. He couldn't remember having said anything especially profound, but maybe it was all in the timing. "I'm glad," he said lamely.

Sydney paused. "The thing is—we won't do this if you'd mind, but Mother and Daddy and I were talking and it suddenly occurred to us—it could be a joint wedding. What do you think of that? It's not to cut corners or save expenses, but they just feel it would be so nice, it's such a nice coincidence that both of us have found people. I think they were giving up on both of us." She laughed. "But if you'd rather—"

Stern had a quick image of the four of them, side by side. How did joint weddings work? Did the couples speak in unison? Was the whole ceremony repeated twice? "It's fine with me . . . Any way you want is fine."

"I know *you'd* rather just go off to City Hall and make no fuss at all, but it's for them. Mother is such a darling and Daddy too, underneath, and they'll be so happy. Win is a blonde like me so we can have all the bridesmaids in pale mint green, or maybe pale blue, we haven't decided."

"You look lovely in pale green," he said.

"*I* wouldn't be in green!" Sydney said sharply. "The brides-maids. I'll be in white, of course!"

"I'm sorry," Stern said. "I forgot. Of course."

Sydney sighed. "I guess the brutal fact is men don't care about all this. They think it's trivia. And it is, in one way. But in another it's not. It's like with dying. You don't just toss people in bags. You have a ceremony. Even more now that we're older than most people when they first marry. We've both waited so long to find the right person, I think it's even *more* important to mark it as a ceremony." She laughed again, or rather trilled. "And I don't know about you, but for me this is it. I'm never getting married again so it is a once in a lifetime thing."

"For me too," Stern said. What he liked with Sydney was that even after a hard day at work, he could talk to her almost as though he were on automatic pilot. He neither believed in most of the things she did, nor did he disbelieve. He thought they were all charming myths and, as such, were as valid as anything.

Suddenly Sydney's voice dropped. "There's just one thing," she said.

"Umm?"

"Well, Darryl felt, and we all agreed, that he had to be frank with Win about his past, you know, his . . . And she was great, she really was. She *couldn't* have been more understanding. She just wants him to take a test for AIDS, just to make absolutely sure. What do you think? Mother and Daddy think that shows a lack of trust."

"What does Darryl think?"

"He's willing to do it. I guess he feels pretty confident he's fine. And, well, if he wasn't, he'd want to know too."

Stern was beginning to feel clammy and sticky sitting around in his jogging clothes. "What's the problem, then?"

Sydney sighed. "It's not a *problem,* I guess. It's just it's like they're starting their marriage under a kind of cloud."

"Even if he gets a clean bill of health?"

"Just the idea . . . Just the thing of, her always wondering if maybe one day he might . . ." Her voice trailed off.

"One day any of us might do anything," Stern said, beginning to get irritated.

"What do you mean?" She sounded so startled, he immediately retreated.

"Nothing."

"You must have meant *something!*"

"Sweetie, I'm—I'm sitting here feeling all sweaty and uncomfortable. I wasn't thinking."

But Sydney, as always, was relentless. "Are you implying there's no difference between them and us? That one day you might suddenly decide to have a wild fling with someone like that psychotic nurse you used to see?"

"No," Stern said curtly. After a second he added, "She wasn't psychotic."

"Well, schizophrenic, unhinged, whatever."

"I said no!"

There was a silence. He realized he would have to work harder at winning her back. "Darling, we have a clean bill of health, both of us, physically as well as morally. Why not delight in that? It can't be as though we were two teenagers. Of course, we've had other involvements. But that—at least for me—is what makes me able to appreciate you, that it took so long to find you, that I was almost giving up hope . . ."

He could feel her melting over the phone. "Yes, that's how I feel too."

"I'm sorry if I was curt. Things at Nash have been rough lately. I've had a new patient and I had to meet with her husband. It all takes a toll."

"Of course," Sydney crooned, not really interested any more than he was interested in what went on behind the scenes at the Belzone School of Music.

He hung up, feeling relieved, both to get off the phone and at having redeemed himself for the momentary lapse. After a hot shower, he felt better. When the phone rang again, it was nine, Sydney's usual time for calling. "Hi, sweetie," he said. "I didn't think you'd call again.

After a pause Roxanne's voice said, "It's me."

Stern was silent. "Hi," he said warily.

She was speaking haltingly, in soft, broken sentences. "I'm sorry I was so upset when you came to see me the other day. I wanted you to know I appreciated your coming."

"Well, of course," Stern said. His hands were trembling. "It was upsetting for me too, to see you like that. You don't belong in a place like that, with bars on the windows."

" 'If you might endanger your own life or those of others,' " she quoted from the form patients had to sign before entering Nash.

Stern looked out the window. "You wouldn't really . . . endanger your own life, though, would you? Wasn't it just a—"

"A what?" she asked quickly.

He knew he had to be terribly careful, much more than he usually was. "You were in a certain mood," he said, as though to a patient, "a mood of despair. But now—"

"Yes?"

"Aren't you better now?" he asked anxiously, as though pleading.

"I think I'm better," Roxanne said in her slow, languorous voice. "But I feel safer here, for the moment."

Again he hesitated. "Would you—would you like me to visit you again sometime?"

"Should you? Aren't you about to get married? Aren't you trying to cut all ties to me?" She laughed bitterly. "Your unsavory past."

"It wasn't unsavory," Stern said.

"How *do* you think of it?" Her murmuring voice was a million times more intimate than Sydney's had been.

"As the great love affair of my life."

"And now?"

He saw himself darting back and forth between a kind of compulsive honesty and a desire to hide, not knowing which would be a better tactic, which would help him more. "Now I have to . . . Look, Rox, I *am* getting married. I can't . . . It's all settled. The announcement. But it's not just that. I need that other life. I need order, stability, things I know you have contempt for."

"Why should I have contempt for order and stability?"

"You think I'm settling for a rigid, empty, surfacy kind of life. Maybe I am. Maybe that's at bottom what I really need. And if you have contempt for that, for me, I'd understand. At times I have contempt for myself."

Roxanne laughed her throaty, quavering laugh. "I would *love* a rigid, empty, surfacy kind of life. It's been my lifelong ideal. It just hasn't come my way."

"You could've—" he began, but she interrupted him, knowing what he was going to say.

"Those men bore me!" she cried. "They *sicken* me! I don't want some stuffed trophy sitting in his pin-striped suit in my living room and pumping me once a week or every other day on vacations. *You* want that. Fine! *You* want your sickening little thin-skinned Philadelphia virgin who'll grind her teeth in bed and go shopping every Saturday with her mother and fiddle around at some innocuous job—"

"Stop!" Stern shouted. "You're getting upset, and it's not true. Sydney isn't like that."

"You yourself said she was!" Roxanne cried. "Do you deny it?"

He felt as though someone's hands were around his throat.

"Look, I said certain things. You're distorting them for your own purposes. I love Sydney—"

"As much as you loved me?"

"In a different way."

"Do you love making love to her as much?" Her voice was high pitched.

"Rox, please . . . don't. You're getting hysterical."

Suddenly there was silence. He wondered if she'd hung up. "Are you there?" he asked softly.

"Sort of."

Stern took a deep breath. "I will love you forever and I'm going to marry Sydney. I would like to see you again, but only if we can both accept that as a given, not something to argue about or defend or anything else. It's reality."

She sighed softly. "Reality," she repeated. And then, "Okay."

"Sleep well, darling." He hung up before realizing how wrong those final words had been. He was counseling her to accept what was and he was not accepting it. So what else is new, as Grieff would say?

The trouble was that at some not very deep level he was touched at Roxanne's reaction to his getting married, at the depth of her feeling for him. If he could control reality, which would he choose? Never seeing Roxanne again, making a clean break, or having it both ways? He had said what part of him wanted—order, stability—but another part of him feared and dreaded it. At times, picturing that life—dinners with Sydney's parents, squash games with Darryl—he felt the same kind of pleasure he might have watching a rerun of *The Philadelphia Story,* on late-night TV. At other times he saw it as a kind of death. He knew so many men who moved inexorably through a non-life, too frightened to change. But those were men who had married young. He'd had all these years to do the other, to "get it out of your system." He had always wondered if that expression made any kind of sense. What was "it" and where was that "system"?

If he were God, if he could be himself and God simultaneously, creating any kind of solution possible, he would have Roxanne marry a male Sydney. She said she despised men like that and he knew some of the doctors who pursued her at Nash and other men from other parts of her life: her Upper West Side nuclear freeze group, her photography classes. But if he could, he would have created someone boring, no threat to him, but not impossible, someone who would give Roxanne the kind of stability he was convinced she needed much more than he did. And then, maybe even children. And they could also have each other, in whatever way, if not as lovers, then as friends: perfect symmetry. They would each have their Sydneys, their structure, and within that structure their own intimacy would flourish, but not destroy the other.

But he was not God and perfect symmetry existed, if at all, probably only in mathematical equations.

When he told Alix Zimmer she was to go for a CAT scan, she looked terrified. It was toward the end of the session. "Why?" she cried. "I don't . . . I don't have any symptoms. What would make you think—"

"These hallucinations you describe," Stern said, "most likely are just mental aberrations, but we have to check. You could have had some kind of stroke. People do have them without realizing it. Your behavior seems to have been erratic in several areas. We need to rule out any possible physical symptoms."

Her eyes were wide with fear. "Do you really think that's a possibility?"

"Not likely, perhaps, but possible until we rule it out."

"No, I mean a likelihood? Do you think it's likely?"

"I can't commit myself on that. We'll get the results immediately and I'll let you know."

She seemed stunned, or maybe just frightened into silence. For the rest of the session she sat there, immobile, staring out the window.

MISSING
LINKS

Alix's fear about the CAT scan was so great that for the first time since entering Nash, she felt paralyzed. In the twenty-four hours from the time Dr. Stern informed her that the CAT scan would be necessary to the moment she got ready to leave to have it performed at a nearby hospital, her mind was like a blizzard with thoughts drifting and darting around and around, up and down, sideways. Could she really have had a stroke without realizing it? Had, in fact, her behavior been that bizarre? She remembered all the events up to entering the hospital both dimly and sharply, more like an especially vivid dream that you remember years later, than like a piece of reality. What was disturbing were the missing links.

The lunch with—what was her name?—Giselle. She saw Giselle's face, the necklace, but their conversation seemed to have been wiped out. She could recall being in the cab, going home, and not knowing how she had gotten there. *Dear God, please, don't make it a stroke or something with my brain.* It wasn't just the pain she feared, but the terror of losing her mental faculties. It was the one thing she prided herself on beyond anything else. Her emotions seemed to her unruly, often absurd. But even now, for instance, she could remember perfectly the conversation with Bernice Daley, the woman who wanted her sister to bear her child, could practically have recited that conversation by heart. Could a person who had had a stroke do that? Surely not.

Just to test herself, she began reviewing all the other events. The wedding, for instance. She could remember the man on the plane, their conversation. *Okay, now replay that conversation in your mind. What did he say and what did you say?* The plane had jolted. She had inadvertently clutched him and he had said turbulence was common on these flights. Then she had told him she was flying out for Michael's remarriage. She must have told him how long it had been since Pam had died because he had said: *Five years* is *a long time.* She remembered his paisley tie, his reddened, rough skin. They had discussed marriage and he had told her he had been married twenty-seven years. She had asked him if he would remarry within five years if his wife died and he had laughed and said he might. It was then he had said, "You'd make a good lawyer," and had told her she looked like an actress or a dancer. She remembered having the thought: I don't belong to the ballet lineup, because she used to tease Gerald about picking women with romantic names: Daphne, Giselle.

She felt a flicker of pleasure and pride. *Look how well you can remember that. How many people could with such an unerring eye for detail? Surely someone with a stroke couldn't. Or could they? Was it something that could come and go? Now think of the wedding. Think. Did you really see Pam? Did you really see her?* Alix sent herself back to the wedding. She remembered the heat. In her mind's eye she gazed at the horizon. There had seemed to be something moving. But that could have been the heat. She had read articles on how on very hot days objects seemed to shimmer and move—something to do with the quality of the air. Perhaps she had seen something, some person riding, or even just a tree, waving in the breeze, and her guilt at being there had made her assume it was Pam. *Perhaps I was pretending to be mad as an escape from feeling grief at Gerald's death. And you pretended well. Now you're here. But I can still leave. I'm a voluntary patient. I must remember that.*

She dressed in street clothes to go to the hospital and was accompanied downstairs by one of the nurses, named Kefaldis.

There was something peculiar about her. Alix wondered if she drank on the job. She wore a wig which was never on straight. Didn't other people notice? There was something flaky in her expression. If the nurse had been a witness in a trial, Alix would have assumed she was on drugs. But surely in a hospital they would test people for that.

A man was driving the van that was waiting downstairs, but Nurse Kefaldis opened up the back of it which contained a stretcher. "Hold out your hands," she said to Alix. She was holding a pair of handcuffs.

"Pardon me?"

"Hold out your hands. I've got to get you ready."

"For what?" Alix's heart was thudding. "Why do you need to handcuff me? I thought I was just going for a CAT scan."

"Regulations," the nurse said, snapping the handcuffs on Alix's wrists. "We have trouble with a lot of the cases around here. You'd be surprised. One of them bit me once. Straight through the skin, like a mad dog. I thought I'd have to have a rabies shot."

"But I'm not violent," Alix said, half laughing in bewilderment. "I—"

"Regulations," the nurse repeated. She pointed to the stretcher. "Lie down. I'll sit beside you."

Petrified, Alix lay down. "Do you really think I'm about to do something violent?"

The nurse just smiled her funny smile. "Never can tell. That's one thing I've learned in fifteen years on this job. You never can tell. Sometimes it's the quiet ones you have to watch out for." She pulled back the sleeve of her uniform. "See those marks? He bit me clear through the skin. And I've got tough skin, I can tell you."

Lying flat on her back, her hands together in handcuffs, Alix felt a calm terror. *I'm a prisoner. Only this is worse than prison.* The thought was too frightening for her to contemplate; it vanished into the air. But it was with her as she had her CAT scan done. The process itself was painless, the doctor who performed it largely silent. *If this proves I haven't had a stroke, I have to get out of here. Otherwise I'll be reduced to a terrified automaton through being treated this way.*

When the procedure was completed, they got back in the van and once again Alix lay down. She looked over at the nurse. *Jesus, straighten your wig, lady.* "Did you ever see *Hannah and Her Sisters?*" she asked conversationally.

"Who?" said the nurse.

"It's a Woody Allen movie, *Hannah and Her Sisters,* I just wondered if you had seen it."

"I might have. What of it? I see so many I forget, especially now that I have a VCR."

It was strange having a conversation with someone while lying flat on your back with your hands in handcuffs. Alix had interviewed prisoners hundreds of times. *If I get through this, I will know what it's like.* "Well, I was just thinking of the scene where Woody Allen goes, that is, the character he's playing goes for a CAT scan, to see if he has a brain tumor, the parallel with my own situation."

Nurse Kefaldis sniffed. "Yeah, well, you never know. My sister—she was never sick a day in her life and one day, whomp. My mother's over there visiting her, going to take her to the beauty shop like they do every week and she goes in and there's my sister, dead as a doornail. Heart attack. Here today, gone tomorrow. So you never know, do you?" Her conversation was laconic, as though she were talking about a complete stranger, not her sister.

"I guess you don't," Alix said. After a moment she asked, "Do you like your job?"

"What?" The nurse gave one of those odd glances which seemed to indicate her mind had been in orbit somewhere.

"I was wondering—you said you'd had this job fifteen years. Do you enjoy the work?"

Nurse Kefaldis shrugged. "Well, you've got to work, right? I mean, unless you're married, and then even then. You'd be surprised how many friends I have who, they have kids, they're married, *plus* they work. I'm lucky. I just have the work."

"I'm a lawyer," Alix said after a moment. She folded one hand over the other, touching the metal.

The nurse looked at her suspiciously, as though she had just announced she thought she was Catherine the Great. "Are you now? Fancy that."

Or was it that she thought Alix was boasting? "Do you not believe I'm a lawyer? I just ask because you sounded somewhat ironical."

"Sure, why shouldn't I believe you?" The nurse smiled. "I believe and I don't believe. That's what this job is all about. Otherwise you'd go crazy."

Alix looked at her. She felt a strong impulse to say, "You would look more attractive if you'd straighten your wig," but she decided not to mention it. Perhaps the nurse had cancer or had gone bald at an early age. It had to be a delicate subject.

In the group therapy session that afternoon, conducted by Dr. Wishnick, there was a new patient. Dr. Wishnick always seemed bubbly and eager to please, more like a nursery school teacher than a doctor. "Now, I thought Noah Epstein, our new patient, might introduce himself to us and tell us a little about what's brought him to Nash, and then we might all tell him about ourselves." She beamed at all of them.

Alix looked at the new patient. He was medium height with thinning dark hair and soft, anxious dark eyes, glasses. For some reason her heart went out to him, which it had not done to any of the other patients. He smiled nervously. "Well, I'm, uh, Noah Epstein. I teach—I used to teach—biology in a high school in Ocean Park, Brooklyn. My brother is Leo Epstein, the author of *Sexuality Today*. I don't know if any of you have read it. It's an excellent book. Actually, I haven't read it myself, but it's gotten excellent reviews. It was on the best-seller list."

Dr. Wishnick's eyes grew round. "Goodness, that's exciting. A best-seller! Has anyone here read Mr. Noah's brother's book?" She turned to Noah. "By the way, we tend to call each other by first names here, but it's up to you. Which would you prefer?"

"Either is fine," he said.

"But which would you *prefer?*"

"Noah's fine."

"Has anyone heard of Noah's brother's book? I haven't myself, but I get so terribly behind in my reading. It's awful. I always mean to catch up." She looked over at Elton Koriaff, a tall, hulking seventeen-year-old boy who was evidently "in" for a criminal charge which his parents had had changed to "temporary insanity."

"I don't read nothing," Elton said. He had a teasing, baiting smile which seemed simultaneously ingenuous and all knowing.

"I've read it," Alix said to the new patient. "I thought it was pretentious and absurd, really. I don't blame you for not reading it. Is it because you're jealous of him or because you're not interested?"

He looked over at her with just the barest trace of a smile. "Both, I suppose."

"Well, Noah," Dr. Wishnick said, "you say you teach biology.

Were you having some problems with that? Would you like to share with us exactly what happened to bring you here?"

It was like Show and Tell, Alix thought, only what you showed and told about were psychotic breaks, neurotic problems. Noah Epstein spoke slowly, haltingly. "Yes, I . . . I had trouble teaching. That is, I didn't see it that way. I was teaching Sex Education to a group of eleventh- and twelfth-graders and it's often hard to impart the complexity of that subject."

Elton Koriaff grinned. "That's my favorite subject, man. That ain't complex. That's easy."

There was an elderly woman in the group therapy session. Her name was Tamara Grace and she had been a grade school teacher. She was tiny and spunky; evidently her "episode" had come on a few months after her husband's death when she'd made a scene in the lobby of her apartment building. "I know just what Mr. Epstein, Noah—excuse me, I have trouble with first names, it's my generation—means because I felt the same way. I remember the day our principal came in and said, 'Tamara, you have to teach them Sex Ed. It's been voted in.' This was in Georgia, mind you, a very conservative district. So I sat there at home and I practiced and I practiced saying words like penis and vagina over and *over* just so when I had to say them in front of my class I wouldn't blush red as a beet. And you know what? Well, it *was* hard at first and then after a while I thought, those are just *words*—penis, vagina . . . and why should we be scared of words?" She looked around at all of them. "Or even of what they symbolize!"

"*I* ain't scared," Elton said. "Never saw one yet that scared me."

Dr. Wishnick blushed. "I know what Noah and Mrs. Grace mean. It *is* hard, calling a spade a spade or in this case a— Mr. Koriaff, why are you laughing? Have I said something funny?"

Elton was doubled over with laughter. When he caught his breath, he said, "I guess every time we start talking about sex, all I can think of is your nipples, Ms., I mean *Doctor* Wishnick. Because I can see them plain as day, and I always wonder, is every man in this room getting as turned on as I am or is it just that I'm a horny little bugger with a filthy mind?"

At that Dr. Wishnick froze. "I don't think that's relevant," she said.

"So, how come you dress like that?" Elton asked.

She ignored it. "We were discussing Noah's class, his problems teaching it and I feel we should give him the courtesy, the common courtesy, to let him continue." She looked over at Noah Epstein.

Alix thought how everyone in the room had had the same thought about Dr. Wishnick's see-through blouses and how only Elton Koriaff, perhaps out of youthful naïveté, was willing to mention it. In the time that she had been at Nash she had gotten a glimmering of the unspoken rules. If you talked about what you saw or observed, you were considered crazy or a troublemaker. She knew she could be confrontational and was trying to rein this in. At times it was extremely difficult.

Noah Epstein looked at Alix. "I wanted to be honest," he said. "That was probably foolish. Mr. Garofolo, our principal, said I should instill morality into these kids, but you should see them. Most of them are already sexually active, several girls—little girls— are pregnant. I thought somehow if I talked about myself, I could reach them. But maybe I went too far. I displayed lack of judgment."

"That's why you're here," Dr. Wishnick said gaily. "To be cured of that."

Alix cleared her throat. "Who said you displayed lack of judgment?"

"Mr. Garofolo."

"How did he know?"

"He was sitting in on the class," Noah said. "He does that sometimes."

"And do you respect and trust him to that extent," Alix said, "simply because he's an authority figure? Maybe he was acting unjustly. Maybe he had it in for you for some reason."

Before Noah Epstein had a chance to reply Dr. Wishnick said to the rest of the group, "What do we call that?"

Leroy Demos, another group therapy patient, was a drug addict with beautiful green eyes like cracked marbles and a tremendous reddish beard. He was amiable most of the time but occasionally hysterical. "Shit," he said. "That's what *I* call it. Pure unadulterated shit. Men who love coming down on people they can control."

Dr. Wishnick smiled patiently. "No, there's a technical term for what Alix has referred to. We all know it, we've used it often." She looked around at all of them. "What is the word?"

There was silence.

"Paranoia?" Tamara Grace suggested gently.

"Right!" Dr. Wishnick looked delighted. "That's what we call it when we have the feeling we're being unjustly persecuted."

Leroy Demos was glowering at Dr. Wishnick. "Yeah, but how about when we're really *being* unjustly persecuted? What then, lady doctor?" He only called her that when he wanted to get her goat.

"My name is Dr. Wishnick."

"Sharon?" he taunted.

"Dr. Wishnick," she replied firmly.

"Hey, but you said you wanted us to use first names," he went on. "So, how come—"

"Among the patients—" she began, and then stopped. Blood had suddenly begun flowing in a bright stream from Leroy Demos's nose. "Oh my God!" Dr. Wishnick jumped to her feet. "Oh no! What's wrong?"

Leroy Demos, unperturbed, brought forth a filthy handkerchief from his pocket. "Just a nose bleed," he said. "I get 'em all the time. Too much excitement, I guess."

Dr. Wishnick pressed her hands to her cheeks. "What should we do? You'd better come with me, Mr. Demos."

"I'm fine," he said, though, in fact, the handkerchief was already soaked with blood. "Chill out, Sharon."

She grabbed him by the shoulder. "Come!" she ordered. To the others she said, "You can return to your rooms. I'm terribly sorry."

After the two of them had left Elton Koriaff said, "Did you get a look at that guy's handkerchief? Man, he must have been carrying that around since the dawn of time! Since before."

"Poor Dr. Wishnick," Tamara Grace said. "She gets upset so easily."

"She gets a kick out of it," Elton said. "I bet it made her day. Anyone who wears see-throughs like that is asking for *some* kind of excitement."

"You shouldn't speak that way about the doctors," Tamara said. "It's disrespectful."

Elton rose lazily to his feet. "Lady, I may not know much about much. But I know when a lady is asking for it and when she's not. I may have flunked eleventh grade, but I could get a Ph.D. in *that.*" He sauntered out of the room.

"Young people," muttered Tamara Grace. She gathered herself together and left also.

Alix looked over at Noah Epstein. A smile of saddened complicity passed between them. "I'm sorry that you're here," she said.

"That is, for you. You probably don't know what it's like. This session was pretty typical of the kind of therapy you get here."

The expression that crossed his face was disturbing. "Yes, I know," he said. "I was in one of these places ten years ago."

Alix was shocked. "You were? And you came back?"

"I was signed in by my wife."

"Why?"

"She was scared—Garofolo convinced her I was out of control."

"But you weren't!" Alix cried. "Not from anything you've said . . ." When he didn't reply she said, "I'm going to get out of here. I had no idea what it was like. I'm a voluntary patient and I'm applying for leave this afternoon." She described the incident where she had been handcuffed, her feeling of uneasiness with Dr. Stern, who seemed so erratic—with his trembling hands and wild expressions, alternating with bitingly sardonic put-downs.

Noah Epstein listened to her with his look of gentle, resigned intelligence. "You can't get out," he said quietly.

"What do you mean? I'm a voluntary patient. It said, the form I signed when I entered, that I could leave at any time." She tried not to sound as alarmed as she felt.

"If they want you out. You didn't read it properly. No one does. The way it really works is, if two doctors here say you should stay, you stay."

There was something about his calm, uninflected voice that terrified her more than threats might have. "Why would they do that? she asked.

"Why does evil exist?" Noah Epstein asked with a wry smile.

Alix stared at him. "But—I can't believe what you're saying is true. There's no way out of here?" She remembered having had that thought while lying on the stretcher: *This is like being in prison, but it's worse than prison.* "I'm sorry, I can't accept that. It's too . . . And then how could you, knowing it, allow them to put you back in?"

"I felt I deserved to be punished." He also said this in that uninflected voice, as though he were repeating something by rote.

"Why?" Alix got up from her chair and went over to him. "What had you done?"

Suddenly he buried his face in his hands and wept, loud racking sobs. "I don't know," he sobbed. "I don't know."

Alix put her arms around him. "You didn't do anything," she

said softly. "Please. I can tell. You're a good man. You're a gentle, sensitive person. I'll get you out of here. I'll get us both out."

They were like that, she with her arms around him, holding him as one would a child, he sobbing, but more softly, when Dr. Stern opened the door. He looked startled. "What is going on here?"

"Mr. Epstein got very upset," Alix said, frightened in spite of herself.

"Isn't it for the staff to deal with this, Ms. Zimmer? Or do you now consider yourself capable of taking on staff functions?"

"Dr. Wishnick had to leave abruptly in the middle of a group therapy session," Alix said. She hated the way she had crossed over from being so courageous and bold with Noah Epstein to being a cringing coward with Dr. Stern.

"I believe you were told to return to your rooms," he said. "Perhaps it would be a good thing if you did that now." Moving closer to Alix he said, "And we can discuss this episode in our session later today."

Noah Epstein stood up and walked, like a wind-up toy, to his room. Alix's room was on another corridor. *What if he's right? What if there really is no way out of here? Can that be? Perhaps he was just upset . . . but he hadn't seemed, on any level, a cruel man. Please, God, let what he said not be true. I don't believe in you even now, but let it not be true.*

As she sat in her room, waiting for dinner, Alix kept seeing Noah Epstein's soft, imploring eyes—you couldn't call a man's eyes doelike, but they were, like a deer spotted by the hunter who knows it's a matter of seconds until the shot is fired. *Why does evil exist?* She thought of the line from *Hannah and Her Sisters.* "How should I know why there are Nazis? I don't even know how a can opener works." That was her world, a world of spacious Manhattan apartments, intelligent people, wry quips about life. This was a world no one had told her existed, which she would not have believed existed even had they told her.

She thought of her feeling when Dr. Stern had entered the room. How she despised herself for knuckling under that way! Dr. Wishnick seemed to her ludicrous, but Dr. Stern frightened her. *You have to knuckle under. That's the way you'll get out.* But whenever she was with him, his tendency to twist her words created in her a compensating desire to fight back. *Okay, but do it subtly. You were playing right into his hands then. How could I have known he would enter the room at that point? I was just trying to comfort Noah Epstein. Anyone can enter at any point. You aren't in your world anymore. Privacy no longer exists. Learn the rules, or you're doomed.*

No, I can't start using words like that. Doomed. Evil. Luke will come. I'll talk to him. He'll get me out. This is all silly. She remembered having seen *One Flew Over the Cuckoo's Nest* with a group of friends and how everyone had thought it was far-fetched, the characterization of Nurse Ratched something out of Brecht. She remembered saying, Kesey was clearly misogynistic, the whole thing was a male fantasy. Lobotomies? It was just a castration fantasy on the part of a man.

The other reaction she had had when Dr. Stern entered was of being interrupted in a moment of unallowed physical intimacy which had sexual overtones. She didn't find Noah Epstein sexually attractive. She had only two types, she felt, Luke and Gerald. Either a tall, slim, reserved preppy gentile or a jokey, fun-loving, intelligent Jew. Noah Epstein was crushed. Whether it had happened before he entered the hospital the first time, she didn't know, but the expression in his eyes was one of passive despair. To the extent she could stop thinking about her own dilemma, she feared for him.

"Well, we have good news," Dr. Stern said at the beginning of the session. "I have the reports from your CAT scan and everything seems to be in order. No physical problems."

"I knew that," Alix said calmly.

"Really? How did you?"

"Well, on the stretcher, as I lay there, it came to me that I had feigned madness to escape my grief over Gerald's death."

" 'Feigned'? You did a pretty good job. Managed to terrify quite a few people."

Alix recalled the man on the plane asking if she was an actress. "When I say feigned, I don't mean I was consciously deceiving anyone. I believed it myself."

"Believed you actually saw your dead sister?"

"I saw something . . . and I think now it's possible it was an actual person, maybe just a cowboy on a horse, but my guilt at being there took over, somehow."

Dr. Stern stared at her. "You say you 'knew' the CAT scan would be normal? How?"

"I just tested my own reasoning and found it to be sound."

"You seem to have a lot of faith in your own judgments."

"Yes, I do," Alix said. "That's my profession. I have to continually make judgments about people who sometimes aren't telling the truth.''

"And the judgments made by the staff here strike you as faulty, less accurate than your own?"

He's baiting you; don't trip. "Not necessarily."

Dr. Stern smiled at her. "When I entered the room in which your group therapy session was being held, you were embracing one of the new patients, Mr. Epstein. Were you aware of the sexual connotations of that action?"

Alix hesitated. "He was desperately upset, weeping. I wanted to comfort him."

"What got him so upset?"

"What we were talking about." *Be careful, be careful!*

"Namely?"

"He said he felt he needed to be punished, and I told him he didn't."

"Who gave you that authority, Ms. Zimmer? Do you know anything about Mr. Epstein's case?"

"Not in detail, no."

"Yet you felt you had the authority to intervene in his care?"

"I wasn't intervening!" she cried.

He was silent a moment, looking right at her. "I was outside the door and heard you say to him, 'I'll get you out of here. I'll get us both out.' Could you tell me what you meant by that?"

It was like playing chess. *But this isn't a game. You're in a mental hospital. Forget the truth. Try only not to let him trap you.* "Mr. Epstein said something that surprised me," Alix said. "He said patients, even those admitted voluntarily like myself, could not be released if two doctors felt they needed to stay here."

"That seemed to you unjust?"

"Of course! When I signed in, I was under the impression, as I think all voluntary patients are, that I could leave at any time."

"And you would like to leave now?"

"Yes."

"You feel cured, after just a few weeks?"

"Yes, I feel . . . I feel much better."

"And you don't feel the doctors here have the ability to make that judgment?"

Every question was double-edged. "I think it should be up to the patient."

"You think Leroy Demos and Noah Epstein should be allowed to walk out of here today, should they decide to do so?"

Alix's heart was thumping. She placed her palms down on her skirt. "I thought Mr. Epstein said he was placed here, that he *wasn't* voluntary."

"So, you feel voluntary patients should be allowed to leave at any time, but patients who are not voluntary should not?"

After several moments she replied, "Yes."

"Then why did you say to Mr. Epstein, 'I'll get you out of here?' This is assuming you have magical powers to perform that action. Did he strike you as a man ready to resume life in the outside world?"

"Perhaps that was a hasty remark," Alix said. "I was basically trying to comfort him."

"You don't feel the remark shows some delusions of grandeur? 'I'll get both of us out of here'?"

"If taken literally, perhaps."

"Do you often say things which come across to the listener in one way but which you interpret in another?"

"I don't know how Mr. Epstein interpreted my remark. I believe he took it as I meant it, as a desire to comfort him."

"I meant myself as the listener," Dr. Stern said.

"You were eavesdropping," Alix couldn't resist saying. "That's different."

"Why do you think patients are put in a hospital, Mrs. Zimmer?"

"Could you call me Ms. Zimmer, Dr. Stern? My husband's name is James. I use Zimmer professionally; it's not my married name."

"As you wish. Would you like to answer my question? Shall I repeat it?"

Alix wove her hands together. They were cold. She was afraid he might notice they were trembling. "I thought it was to be in a safe, quiet, comforting environment where they would receive the best professional care."

"And you don't feel that's been true so far?"

"I didn't say that."

"Do you feel it's been true?"

"I think I would be capable of functioning in the outside world."

"And if the doctors here do not believe that?"

"On what grounds?" Alix cried.

Dr. Stern looked at his notes. "I met with your husband, Ms. Zimmer. You're aware of that?"

"Yes."

"He seemed very concerned about the way you'd been acting prior to your admission. He said you'd been high strung, erratic. I question whether he would want you home right now."

"I'll have to discuss it with him," Alix said. "I'm sure he wants what he feels is best for me."

"Aren't you really saying you're confident about your ability to manipulate him? That you despise him at some level for allowing you to do this, but need it as a source of power?"

"No, I'm not saying that," Alix said. "Luke is strong in his own way. His methods may be different than mine, more passive, per- haps, but he can be extremely determined when he wants."

"Then perhaps you ought not consider leaving the hospital quite as much of a fait accompli as you appear to."

Alix tried to speak normally. "Can you give me any idea how long you feel I might be here if I don't apply to leave?"

"Several months at a minimum. I wouldn't even want to begin considering it until I had seen a major change in your behavior."

"Months?" This time she couldn't conceal her dismay, her voice rose.

"Many patients are here for several years," Dr. Stern went on smoothly. "Remember *you* have the key. We want to let you out."

"Could you just tell me in what way my behavior justifies a stay of that duration? Am I mad? Have I been acting crazy?"

He laughed quietly. "Oh, Ms. Zimmer, you know those terms are alien to us—crazy, mad. Those are jargony, useless terms, used to put people in mental straitjackets."

"And sessions like these are not?"

"Your seeing them that way may be a major part of the prob- lem."

By now she knew she could never win. Instead of answering, she said, "If I wanted to leave Nash, what would be the procedure?"

"Well, you can apply to leave, but, if two doctors feel you should stay, and I think I should advise you that in your case they will, you would have to take the case to court. Your husband would have to take care of the details, he would have to be willing to assume full responsibility for you if you were released."

"Thank you." Alix rose to leave.

Outside Dr. Stern's door, she realized her legs were so weak, she could scarcely move. Rather than trying to return to her room, she sat down on a sofa in the hall. *All right, look, on the one hand you're terrified. And that's a natural reaction to what's happening. He's trying to terrify you. And instead of really trying to outwit him, you're trying to convince him, to argue. You acted on the assumption that he was the judge and if you presented your evidence, he would listen and render a just decision. Now you know that's not so. But would it have mattered what I said? He wants to keep me here, wouldn't he have taken anything I said and twisted it somehow? I've got to speak to Luke, convince him. He loves me. He's a just, kind person. If he sees that I'm unhappy, if he sees what it's really like here, he'll help me get out.*

Alix knew defendants who had passed lie detector tests simply because, while totally guilty, they were convinced of their own innocence. But she knew the opposite was true too, that innocent people could with astonishing ease become convinced of their own guilt. She thought of Noah Epstein saying, "I deserve to be punished." The quality that helped her professionally, her frankness and desire to confront reality head on, were problems here. *You have to subdue your pride. Grovel, pretend, agree to anything. Don't be assertive or honest, or, above all, angry.*

But what if it were a fixed game? What if there truly were no way out? No, You know your mind is clear, you know your brain is fine, you didn't have a stroke, you don't have a brain tumor. Act. The man on the plane thought you were an actress. Be one.

When she woke up in the morning, before she opened her eyes and saw the window with bars on it, Alix thought she was at home, that in another minute she would get out of bed, saunter into the kitchen, make the coffee, warm the croissants. *I was having another one of those bad dreams. Should I try to remember?*

Then she opened her eyes. *No, I'm here. It's not a dream. Oh my God, it's real.* She closed her eyes again. This time she willed herself back, as into a fantasy, into the simple, often repeated reality of walking into the kitchen, making the coffee. Life in all its simple, prosaic reality. No one appreciated it until it was gone. *If I can get out of here, unharmed, I will appreciate it. Don't say if—say when.*

She knew that what she feared most was being kept here indefinitely, her will undermined by the insidious therapy sessions until she either ended up accepting Dr. Stern's view of her or came to feel, like Noah Epstein, that she deserved to be punished. She remembered her mother's fear of shock treatment. Alix had always assumed that was something that could only be done to severely depressed patients, could only be done with their consent. But she had also assumed as a voluntary patient that she had rights, which evidently she didn't. Did she have any legal rights here that couldn't be subverted by the medical establishment?

Stop. You're just frightening yourself. Act calm. Stay away from Noah Epstein. Let him solve his own problems. Or if you want someone to talk to, just talk to him casually, as though you'd met at a party. He's a sympathetic, nice person. Don't go beneath the surface.

In a break after the session in which they sat, trimming animals out of colored paper and pasting them on sheets, Alix called the Mental Health Service. The phone was in the hall. Doctors and nurses passed by all the time, but there seemed to be no alternative. "I wanted to know, if one applies to leave a mental hospital—I'm a voluntary patient at Nash—what would be the procedure?"

"You'd have to hire a lawyer," came the male voice at the other end, polite. "The hospital will have one also. And, if they feel you should stay, they'll have two doctors testify to that effect at the trial."

"And whom will I use as witnesses?"

"If you were in therapy before, you could use your outside doctor, if he's willing. That's the most effective, we've found."

"I wasn't in outside therapy."

There was a pause. "Then it's more difficult."

"Could you give me some rough idea, of patients applying to leave this way, how many succeed?"

"If two doctors feel the patient should stay, not very many, I'm afraid."

"What if one's spouse agrees to take full responsibility for one's condition?"

"That's a first step, certainly. Without that, it's not even worth trying."

"I see." Her mouth was dry. "Thank you."

Visiting hours were in the early evening. Waiting for Luke to arrive, Alix, sitting in the large waiting room, watched Noah Epstein with a woman she assumed was his wife, a round-faced, sweet-looking, dumpy woman. They seemed to be talking amiably. They seemed . . . Jesus, everything here was *seemed*. She sat watching them. She was tense about seeing Luke again, especially after Dr.

Stern's revelation, knowing that his help would be so crucial to her leaving. She glanced at her watch. Seven-fifteen. He was late; he was always late. She was always early. Opposites attract.

Then she saw Noah Epstein and his wife walking across the room toward her. "Alix, I wanted you to meet my wife, Selma," Noah said. "This is the woman who was so nice to me the other day."

Alix felt a kind of revulsion. Her pity for him had gotten her into trouble. She wanted to keep it at bay, although she felt it again. His wife knew nothing, never would—a simple sweet, uncomprehending woman who had married a complicated, tormented man. Why? Not knowing? Or wanting to cure him as he had, surely, wanted to be cured? "It's lovely to meet you," Alix said. "I was just waiting for my husband."

"Oh, you're married?" Selma said. She seemed relieved. Why? Surely, she didn't think Alix was going to seduce her husband in a mental hospital. *Stranger things have happened, kid.*

"I've been married twelve years."

"We've been married fifteen," Selma said. "That's so rare these days, isn't it? But we both come from families where our parents were married forever. I guess we're just old-fashioned."

Her babbling, bubbly style grated on Alix's nerves. Noah stood by his wife's side, silently. *He loves her, she loves him, none of that will matter here.* Out of the corner of her eye, she saw Luke and stood up. "Oh, there's my husband," she said. "I have to speak to him privately." She walked, her heart beating wildly, toward Luke, who looked, as always, handsome, restrained, not like a man visiting his mad wife in a mental hospital. *That's not what he's doing. You're not a mad wife!* "Hi," she said, feigning lightness.

He embraced her. "Darling, hi . . . how are things?"

Alix looked around. In the large room several couples were talking, but they were spaced fairly widely apart. If they went into her room, she knew it would be easier for doctors or nurses to "eavesdrop," as Dr. Stern had outside the group therapy room. "Let's talk here," she said. "I have something to ask you about."

They sat down in facing chairs near a window. Outside it was an exquisite spring evening, the sky a soft violet blue. *I will always hate spring from now on.* "Luke, I . . . I want very much to leave here. I've been here almost a month and I feel much better—"

"I'm so glad," he said, seeming genuinely pleased.

"I don't like the drugs they hand out, they only make my mouth dry, and the therapy seems useless. Perhaps I just needed a break, time to think things over."

"Wonderful," he said. "When can you leave? Shall I speak to Dr. Stern?"

She sucked in her breath. "That's the problem. Evidently you're not allowed to leave here unless the doctors feel you're ready to leave. Dr. Stern doesn't feel I'm ready."

Luke frowned. "Does he give any indication when you might be?"

"No. But I have the feeling I might be here a long, long time if it were left up to him."

"Well, doesn't it have to be left to him?" Luke asked. "Isn't that why you're here? These are the finest doctors of their kind in the world. Shouldn't we rely on their judgment?"

Alix looked into his serene blue eyes. "No, I don't think we should."

Luke was silent. "Well . . ."

Alix leaned forward. She kept her voice low, almost a whisper. "I called the mental health legal department and they said you can be kept here, against your will, if two doctors feel you need to be here, but if your spouse is willing to assume full responsibility for your actions, you have a chance of leaving . . . would you do that?"

There was a pause.

"I'd have to speak to Dr. Stern," Luke said.

"Why?" Alix cried. "I'm your wife, someone you've known and loved for fifteen years! He's just a doctor."

"But you're under his care. He has professional judgment." Luke reached for her hands. "Darling, of course I want you home. But not if you would be in the same state you were in before."

"I'm telling you I'm not . . . Do I seem strange to you?"

"But before you always seemed alternately normal and then, well, you know—you had those fantasies. You thought you saw Pam, remember?"

"I see now," Alix said very carefully, "that I was denying Pam's death. Michael's remarriage must have triggered some kind of guilt and grief. But now, well, I've come to terms with it."

He was still stroking her hands. "You've been through so much," he said gently. "It hardly seems fair."

Alix felt like leaping at his throat, like yanking her hands from his. "Luke, if you believe that, if you truly believe I've been through a lot, why put me through *this,* which is a thousand times more painful than anything I experienced in the outside world? They handcuffed me when I went for a routine medical procedure! They treat you like an animal, like someone who can't be trusted."

"That's terrible," Luke said. "Why would they handcuff you?"

"Because that's what it's like here! The patients are intimidated, terrified. The staff is unjust—" She stopped, hearing how extreme her words would sound to someone on the outside.

"And the drugs they give you?"

"All they do is make me feel dizzy and sleepy. Look, I've thought a lot about what happened, but if, as the price for getting out, you want me to see an outside therapist, fine. I'll see anyone. I'll see someone once a day. Just tell me what you want me to agree to." *Shit.* She was acting upset when she had wanted so much to appear calm.

"Why don't I ask Dr. Stern—" Luke began.

"Luke! Aren't you listening to me? As a lawyer, I meet hundreds of people and have to judge them. There's something profoundly wrong with Dr. Stern. At times his hands shake so much he has to conceal them under his desk. He's pursued by demons. I don't know what kind or why, but the so-called therapy sessions just allow him to try and get an upper hand with people who are vulnerable, in his power. He scares me."

"Poor darling."

"Do you trust my judgment?" she asked, recoiling from the endearment. "Just tell me that."

His blue eyes were evasive. "But you've been sick."

"I *was* sick"—she tried to keep her voice down—"now I'm fine."

"You seem so excited."

Oh Christ, what an endless vicious circle this is. If he went to Dr. Stern and repeated what she'd said, Stern would explain that she was paranoid and hysterical. *You're not acting. You're expressing what you really feel.* But she felt so desperate she could scarcely speak. "If you were here, instead of me, I'd get you out in one second," she said.

Luke thought a moment. "Yes," he said. "I know you would."

What did he know? Only that she was impulsive? That she trusted individuals over authorities? That that itself was part of her "madness"? "Just tell me one thing," she said. "Do you think I'm mad, right now? Do I strike you as mad?"

"No, but—"

"What?" She fixed her eyes on him avidly.

"Dr. Stern seems to feel—" Luke began.

"Luke, please. Let's not talk about Dr. Stern, okay? This is us. If you want a divorce when I get out, that's okay too. I can understand whatever you may be feeling."

"Of course I don't want a divorce," Luke said, taken aback. "I love you."

"Then get me out! Without your help, I'm trapped here. Don't you see that?" She felt bitter, totally shut off from him. He was worse than a stranger, someone who held her ticket to freedom and wouldn't, despite his avowals of love, do a damn thing to help her. Was this marriage for everyone? Did every man long, in his heart of hearts, to hold his wife prisoner? *Maybe he's enjoying this in some sick way? No, don't think like that.*

After that they just sat. Alix felt beyond conversation.

She felt as though the cords were being tightened around her, like some nightmare dream, where you keep trying different exits and all of them are blocked off. The sight of Luke, sitting there, so calm and impeccable and restrained, aroused in her such fury that she barely trusted herself to speak. Finally, when visiting hours were over, he stood up. "I'll do whatever I can," he said distantly.

"Thank you," she said, equally, if not more, coldly. They were a million miles apart, perhaps always had been. Was that why she had had the affair with Gerald? To be in contact with someone who, if he drove her crazy, did it by responding and reacting and caring, who let her know what he felt? *You weren't his wife. Love affairs are always different. Of course—they're more intense.* Could Luke be like that with another woman? Impassioned, carried out of himself? But he had always been drawn to women like her who did the "feeling" for him, warming himself around their flames. Now perhaps she was going mad for him. *You're not mad. Don't use their jargon.*

After Luke left, there was a half hour until dinner. Some of the patients went back to their rooms. The large central room became emptier. Noah Epstein came over and sat down beside her. "How did it go?" he asked.

She had promised herself to be detached and not get involved with him in any way, yet his warm dark eyes and kindly expression, after the session with Luke, melted through her. "It was terrible," she said. "I can't describe it."

"I know," he said.

When she spoke to him, she felt as though he understood, but also that he had that deadly passivity which frightened her. "I'm beginning to wonder if you're right," she said. "Perhaps there's no way out of here."

"Did you ask your husband to get you out?"

"Yes."

"And?"

Alix sighed. "He believes the doctors—it's so ironical, really, I married him for that, in part, that quiet obedience to authority. I'm so—confrontational, bristly. I grate on people's nerves—"

"Or the opposite," Noah said.

"Or the opposite," Alix agreed. "But here both get you into trouble." She hesitated. "When I tried to comfort you the other day, Dr. Stern, who was listening outside the door, assumed I was making a pass at you."

He smiled. "That's flattering."

Alix shrugged. "Your wife seemed . . . nice." She looked up at him. "Are you happy together?"

Noah glanced away with what seemed a guilty expression. "Yes," he said finally.

"Why did you take so long to answer?"

He looked away again. "I had a strange experience. It was one of the . . . strange things that happened before I came in here. I was at a party and a woman gave me her phone number and address. Ava Bernier. Have you heard of her? She's a poet."

"I don't read poetry," Alix apologized.

"I felt queasy and left the party early, went to her apartment. I don't know why. I don't do things like that normally. But when I got there, she didn't seem especially . . . Nothing happened, really. I felt dizzy and she let me lie down on her bed and put a quilt over me."

Alix smiled. "I don't think that counts as adultery."

Noah was visibly upset. "No, but . . . there was more. I . . . please don't think I'm this kind of person. I don't want you to hate me."

"I don't hate you," Alix said, trying not to smile. He seemed so naïve, pathetic almost. Yet there was no male boasting.

He was having trouble speaking. "I started . . . I came to and we were . . . it seemed we were making love, but I didn't remember taking my clothes off or . . . So I stopped, right in the middle. Does that still not count?"

"I don't think it counts," Alix said. She would have said anything to calm him. She also felt it to be true.

"But I was—we were—"

"It doesn't count!" Alix repeated. "It happens to everyone. Really."

"No!" Noah cried. "My wife would never—if she knew, she would hate me. She'd never trust me again. My brother does things like that, fucking other women, exploiting them. I hate that! I've never wanted to be that kind of man." His face contorted with disgust.

"You're not," Alix said firmly. "You're not that kind of man. You weren't 'fucking' anyone. You were just . . . you felt attracted. She indicated she was available. You'd had a little too much to drink. It's so minor. Truly."

"If you were my wife, and you knew, would you forgive me?" Again he acted as though her word was law. It was both flattering and amusing, given that she had never felt more powerless in her life.

"Does your wife know what happened?"

"No, but—"

"I would forgive you," Alix said. "Of course she would forgive you. She loves you. To love is to forgive." It sounded banal, but she half believed it and also wanted to comfort him.

He fell silent.

"Look," Alix said impulsively. "I had a love affair for five years. If anything 'counts,' that should. But I don't think I'm a monster."

"Did your husband know?"

"No." She smiled bitterly. "But I feel being here is unraveling our marriage. I see it happening already."

Noah frowned. "The only thing I really fear is their giving me shock treatment."

"Can they without your consent?"

"If Selma feels it will help . . ."

"Talk to her!"

"She's like your husband. She feels they know best."

"But if you knew all this, how could you return?"

He shrugged. "It was a terrible mistake."

"Are you saying anyone here can be given shock treatment if their spouse signs a form?"

"If two doctors agree . . ."

"That's their trump card, isn't it? But you had it once. What was it like?"

"It was horrible. There are things I still can't remember." He seemed frozen into a kind of otherworldly place.

Alix stared at him, wanting to call him back, but felt herself sinking into the same mood of uncommunicative despair.

A moment later, one of the nurses came in and announced dinner was ready. During dinner many of the patients were silent. Some talked in a sporadic way. Alix found herself at a table with Tamara Grace and Leroy Demos. She didn't especially feel like talking, just silently ate the fish, mashed potatoes, and peas that were placed in front of her. Dormitory food, tasteless.

"I saw your husband at visiting hours," Tamara said. She always applied her makeup with an unsteady hand—smeared eyeliner, globs of pink blusher. "He's so handsome!"

"How do you know it was her husband?" Leroy said. "Maybe she's got a boyfriend."

"It *was* my husband," Alix said. For some reason Leroy Demos didn't revolt her, though if she had met him anywhere else, she would have backed off.

"I love tall blond men," Tamara said dreamily. "My husband was a tall man. He was so handsome. Women used to come up to him. One woman came up to me once and said, 'I'm going to try and steal your husband away.' I said, 'Good luck!'" She beamed.

Leroy was stuffing large chunks of meatloaf into his mouth. Some pieces stuck to his beard. "So what happened? Did she get him?"

"Oh no," Tamara said. "He would never have done a thing like that."

Leroy shrugged. "How come?"

Tamara seemed flustered. "He wasn't that kind of man."

"We all are," he said. He winked at Alix. "Right?"

Although she half agreed, Alix disliked the way he was baiting the elderly woman. "No, I don't think all men are the same . . . *or* all women."

He seemed indifferent. "Hey, I hear you got Stern," he said suddenly. "The Mad Dog Killer."

Alix started. "What?"

"That's my nickname for him. I call Wishnick 'See-Through.' I call Stern 'Mad Dog.'" He grinned.

"Why do you call him that? Is he your doctor?"

"Naw. But he bumped off a patient a couple weeks ago. Almost bumped two, but one got lucky. They let her out pronto."

There was a gleam in his green eyes that made it hard to tell if he were telling the truth. "What exactly do you mean?" Alix asked.

"How can you call Dr. Stern a mad dog?" Tamara said. "You're a very rude young man." She stood up. "I want to move to another table."

"So move," Leroy said, waving her off.

The elderly woman took her plate and moved to another table.

Alix said, "Could you explain? Or were you just joking?"

"You haven't heard? It was in the papers. An accidental overdose, they called it. It made the *Times*. Stern gave two patients an overdose of Thorazine. Ever hear of it?"

"Yes, but—"

"One of them, Blades, a big Jamaican guy, tossed off. Tough cookies." Leroy stood up to get dessert, which was a slice of pound cake and an orange.

Alix followed him. "How can that be? I mean, how could that have gone unnoticed?"

"Oh, it was noticed all right. It got in *The New York Times,* I told you."

"And he's still giving drugs to people?" Alix's heart started thudding again.

Leroy grinned. "Oh sure, it happens to the best of us, right? No time to read all the fine print. Stern's in thick here. Friends in the right places. He's a doctor, baby. They're big men. They wear uniforms."

They sat down again. Leroy bit into the thick skin of his orange. Then, spitting out a chunk, he patted Alix's arm. "Don't worry. You're not on anything vicious, are you?"

"Thorazine."

"Just a little garden variety murder, but it's not like that happens every day around here."

"Isn't there malpractice?" Alix asked. "It would sound—"

"He lucked out. Blades had no relatives in the U.S. and Quinones didn't know up from down." He began munching on his orange, crunching on the pits. "Don't you like oranges? They're good for your skin. You're too pale."

"Do you want mine?" Alix asked. She didn't feel hungry. She

sat and watched him devour the oranges. *Look, he could be just inventing this. Remember this is a mental hospital. Some of the people . . . Or maybe drugs have affected his ability to think.* "Do you . . . have the clippings about the murder?" she said.

"Sure, want to see them?" His eyes sparkled. "Come to my room and I'll show you." He was pretending to be lascivious.

"Why don't you bring them to the main room and show them to me there?"

"Scared?"

"No, I'd just—"

"Honey, I'm horny as sixteen buffalos, but you're married and I never go near married ladies. That's a sacred rule for me. Never. One, once, pulled off every stitch of her clothes and went on and on—how her husband didn't understand her. She had a nice body on her too. But I said, 'No sir. Put your duds back on.'"

"Okay, just for a minute," Alix said. She knew they were being watched and, though she trusted Leroy, she didn't trust what the nurses would make of it.

Later in the evening she followed him into his room. He pulled the clippings out of the drawer. April 18th. The day of Michael's wedding. There were just two short articles.

DRUGS AND HEAT PROBED IN HOSPITAL DEATH

The chief medical examiner's office is probing the death of one patient and the near death of another who may have succumbed to a combination of heat stroke and the effects of powerful tranquilizers administered during last week's heat wave.

The patient who died reportedly had a temperature as high as 108 degrees Fahrenheit—the highest measure on a body thermometer. Normal body temperature is 98.6 degrees.

The investigation was ordered because death from hyperpyrexia, or heat stroke, is rare. The drugs allegedly involved included Thorazine and other potentially dangerous antipsychotic drugs usually prescribed to calm patients. The drugs also reduce the body's ability to perspire and rid itself of accumulated heat. This side effect was aggravated by room temperatures in many of the medical facilities, which averaged 90 degrees or more during the heat wave, sources said.

Dr. Stuart Stern, of the Nash Institute for Mental Health, defended the use of powerful tranquilizers, but would not discuss the specific cases.

In the interview in the second article, Stern was exactly as Alix would have expected: eerily detached, as though the death of the patient had been a minor "unfortunate incident." Leroy was watching her. "Cute, huh? He's a real mad dog all right. Ever seen him foam at the mouth?"

"No."

"Watch him in your next session. It's just at the corners, a little foamy stuff. It could be the drugs he takes."

Alix tried to laugh. "What?"

"He's an off and onner. Just a little grass. Nothing like Kefaldis. She takes liquid coke right on the job. Boy, if I could get her to share some, I'd sell my fucking soul."

Alix was staring vacantly at the articles. "How can you possibly tell something like that?"

Leroy smiled his wicked, knowing smile. "Baby, you're a lawyer, right?"

"Yes?"

"So, you know what a courtroom is? You know a judge when you see one?"

She nodded.

"Okay, so drugs are *my* specialty. I gave them the best years of my life. I can look into anyone's pupils and tell you in five seconds what they're on, how much, when they took it. It's like anything else. You get a sixth sense."

Alix was trying not to believe him. "But wouldn't the authorities, wouldn't someone higher up here notice?"

"Baby, baby, these *are* the higher-ups. They close ranks. Or maybe some of them don't notice, sure— You know how people close ranks, don't you?"

Of course she did. It happened all the time at her firm. Nothing overtly corrupt, but if someone was a partner and some hanky panky occurred that could be concealed, they did it without thinking, "for the firm's sake," but also because, after all, he, or she, was human. "Somehow, Dr. Stern doesn't seem the drug-taking type," she said.

"How would *you* know? What's the type? We all have our addictions. Some to the weed, to alcohol, to saintliness. I had a wife once, and *her* addiction was being a saint. I'll take a druggie any day over that." He laughed his hoarse, barking laugh.

Despite herself, Alix laughed too. Luke was a would-be saint; she knew what he meant. "Well, thank you," she said. "What you've said is disturbing, but I think I'd rather know."

Leroy grinned. His teeth were crooked, badly in need of cleaning. *"Your* addiction is the truth, right? That's a dangerous one. Watch it. Especially here."

Alix went back to her room, thinking about all he had said. Mad Dog. Killer. Closing ranks. Drugs. But especially she thought of what he had said about her, which seemed the one incisive thing anyone had said since she had arrived here. *"Your addiction is the truth."* It *was* dangerous. She used it out of pride, because she prided herself on it and also because she always had used it and it was a natural reaction for her. Every time she tried to "act," her pride got the better of her.

A nurse peeked into the room. "Honey, bingo's about to start."

"I'd rather just sit here," Alix said, trying to smile.

"No, that's how you got here."

"Pardon me?"

"You got here out of brooding. That's no good. Bingo'll get your mind off your troubles."

"I'm not brooding. I'm just thinking."

The nurse marched into the room and grabbed her by the arm. "Same thing. Going round and round in circles. That's no good. *I* know. Not that I've ever had mental problems, but even if I'm down, I just go out and roller skate and it takes my mind off. That's what you need." She was dragging Alix, as though she were a young, stubborn child.

"I can walk myself, thanks," Alix said stiffly, pulling away.

Bingo. Good God.

She hadn't worn makeup since she arrived at the hospital, but decided that, to appear "better," she would. She had washed her hair, fastened it with barettes, and put on some eye makeup and lipstick. She sat down in her usual chair, about six feet from Dr. Stern.

"Your husband says you're quite concerned about leaving," he began. "He said that was all you could talk about."

"I was," Alix said, "but I've thought it over. Perhaps it's best to stay until I'm really ready, until *you* feel I'm ready." *Pretend you're twenty years old. He's one of your professors. You admire him, but are a little frightened of him.*

"I didn't have the feeling you had that much faith in my judgment."

"I tend to be headstrong," Alix said. "It's hard for me to put my faith in other people unquestioningly. But I see that's a problem."

"Was your husband upset at your wanting to leave the hospital?"

"A little, perhaps."

"Do you think that may have been part of your motive in raising the topic?"

"To upset him?"

"To get a rise out of him, one way or the other. After all, he has a certain power over you now, and that must be galling."

"I don't think of relations between the sexes as power plays."

"How about a desire on your part to inflict pain on him?"

"Pardon me?"

"Is it conceivable that your madness itself—or shall we say your erratic behavior—was partially designed to punish him?"

"For what?"

"For being weak, for tolerating your infidelity."

"He doesn't know about that."

"Perhaps. Or perhaps he does know and is keeping you in the hospital as punishment."

"Luke isn't a punitive person. He feels I'm better off here—for the moment."

"And your lover with the weak heart. Weren't you also, unconsciously, inflicting pain on him by the affair itself, knowing it would have to lead to his death?"

It was hard for Alix to speak. "Yes, perhaps I was." *Lie, lie.*

He was leaning forward eagerly. "You enjoy inflicting pain on men? Acting seductive and then going in for the kill, as it were?"

"Perhaps unconsciously." She felt dizzy. *Shit. Don't keel over. Just keep your cool. Lies are necessary.*

Dr. Stern leaned back. He looked at her appraisingly, as though they were on a date. "Are you aware of acting seductively with me?"

Alix looked surprised. "No, I wasn't."

"You've put on makeup, fixed your hair in an appealing manner. You're talking more softly, acting more feminine—if I can use that word without offending your feminist sensibilities. May I?"

Alix just nodded.

"Is your acting seductive with me conscious?"

She shook her head no.

"Perhaps your hope is that if you win me over, as you won over your husband and lover, I will release you. Your hope is to manipulate me as you manipulated them."

"No," Alix said. "I simply wanted to try to look attractive, as I would if I were not here."

"Pretending you're not here?"

"Not pretending. It's for myself." She looked away, then back. "In fact, I was wondering . . . I see that some patients are allowed to do some office work and I would like that, if you felt I was ready."

His half smile was sardonic. "It wouldn't be demeaning for a woman like yourself, a lawyer who made partner at thirty-four, quite an achievement, to do mere filing?"

Rage was blurring her vision, but she said steadily, "No, I think I'd enjoy having something to focus on, some structure to my day."

He didn't respond to that. "And how do you feel the Thorazine is working?"

She hesitated. "I think perhaps it is. I feel calmer."

"Is the dosage affecting you in any way?"

"Not so far."

"Perhaps you could tolerate a higher dosage then?"

"I don't think that's necessary," Alix said. Just then she noticed that there was a slight white foam at the very corners of his mouth. She thought of Leroy's nickname: Mad Dog.

"Why are you smiling?"

"I just thought of . . . something, a happy memory, something with Luke."

"It looked like a vindictive smile, as though you had a secret."

Alix shook her head. Was he stoned today? Unlike Leroy, she had no way of perceiving that. "I have no secrets."

"Really? I would have thought quite the contrary." As he showed her to the door, he said softly, "I like your perfume."

Immediately after the session they were taken as a group to another hall where they were allowed to sit and draw or paste colored paper onto other pieces of paper. Alix was hardly aware of her surroundings. She trimmed a giraffe out of green paper. In nursery school the only animal she had liked drawing was a giraffe. As she trimmed one after the other, she replayed the session. It seemed to her she had done what she had told herself to do: She hadn't been confrontational, she had acted calm. Was it just a double whammy? If you were excited at how you were being treated, you were "agitated" or "paranoid." If you were calm, you were "out of touch with reality."

She thought of Stern's murmuring, "I like your perfume." Who was being seductive? Another trap. If the price of getting out was having sex with Dr. Stern, she would have done it in a minute. But she knew that if she did, he would either never tell, or use it as a way of keeping her here longer. She wondered if he was married, not that it mattered. God save his wife, or his girlfriend, or both.

The aide came over and looked at her string of giraffes. "Why, that's charming! Look at that! Why don't you try and paste them onto this sheet of paper?"

Afterward they trooped back across the bright green lawn. It was a perfect spring day, the air warm, but with a cool breeze. Back at their respective offices, Silas Foss was at his desk, Giselle was typing, Luke was looking over prints. There was a world of people who simply functioned, were happy, unhappy, mad, sane, and no one knew of this world. She hadn't known about it. And if I ever return to the world, will I just forget because the memory is too painful? *Don't say "if." Believe you will get out. You must believe that.*

When Luke next came to see her, they were allowed to stroll on the grounds. She was continuing to dress as she would have on the outside. He looked at her appreciatively. "I've always liked that dress."

Was he truly unaware of what a charade this was? But she would enter the charade. "Yes, I have too."

"I'm glad you're looking so much better. You must feel better."

"Yes."

He smiled. "Soon you'll be home again."

"I don't know. Dr. Stern hasn't said anything about that. He indicated it would be months before he would even consider it."

"That's absurd! Why would you need to be here for months?"

"I don't know."

"Perhaps you misunderstood him."

The sky was so blue, so blankly, uncaringly blue. "I don't think so. But I did ask if I could do office work on the grounds. There's very little therapy. Otherwise it's just trimming paper animals out of construction paper. Having any kind of work, no matter how menial, might be good for me."

"Of course," he said. "But not menial. You have a fine mind. Don't they realize that?"

"Why would they be insisting I stay here if I have a fine mind?"

"That's just temporary. I'm sure in a week or two—"

"Luke, he said it would be months. I didn't misunderstand him. He said for some it was years."

"That's preposterous. I won't stand for that."

"What will you do?"

"I'll insist they let you out."

"I thought you believed in their judgment."

He was silent. "It's so quiet at home," he said. "I miss you. Every night I sleep with one of your nightgowns."

Don't react. Don't grovel. "I miss you too."

"When this is over, it will just seem a bad memory."

She couldn't reply.

"Are any of the patients nice?" he asked. "Any potential friends?"

In its own way this conversation was worse than the sessions with Dr. Stern. Luke was talking, acting, as though everything she had said had never been said, as though she were here on a pleasant trip, to meet new and interesting people. But she would not be confrontational, not here. When she was out, she could scream her head off or just leave him, whichever felt most needed. "There's a nice man named Noah Epstein," Alix said. "He's a biology professor."

"Oh? Where?"

"At a high school . . . his brother is an author. I read one of his books."

Luke smiled at her. "All the men must think how beautiful you are."

She didn't reply.

Then, from a distance, she saw Noah and his wife strolling toward them. "That's him over there," she said. "Would you like to meet him?"

"Sure."

Noah was clutching his wife's arm as though he were an elderly man. He looked bent and strange. Selma had that same smile plastered on her face. Did she ever not smile? It made her look like a Halloween pumpkin. "Noah, Selma, this is my husband, Luke," Alix said.

Noah straightened up slightly. "He's feeling a little down," Selma said cheerfully.

Always Noah evoked the same feeling in Alix: an instant sense of connection and compassion and a drawing back at his seeming to give in to both his depression and his surroundings. *He's two people, and you react to both. Everyone is at least two people.*

"What I told Noah is things always feel worst just before you get better," Selma said. "It's a sign good things are about to happen."

"Yes, I've always found that," Luke said.

Why hadn't he married a woman like that? A smiling woman who made banal, cheerful remarks and had a smile that never vanished. But he loathed such women, always had. "Perky," was the most damning remark Luke could make of a woman. He disliked slim, sleek, well-mannered blondes. When they had seen *The Turning Point* years ago Alix had asked him who he would pick if he had to choose between Shirley MacLaine and Anne Bancroft. He had looked at her in amazement, as though it weren't even a choice. "Shirley MacLaine would drive me crazy." "But Anne Bancroft looked so brooding, so tormented," Alix had replied. "At least you'd always know what she was feeling," had been his response. Was that his illusion about her, that he always knew what she was feeling? Had he ever known?

It was like a stylized scene from a tea party: the bright sun, two smiling couples, exchanging attempts at small talk. "Aren't the grounds lovely here?" Selma said, indicating the tennis courts, the rows of flowers.

"Yes, it really *is* like a country club," said Luke.

"That makes such a difference," Selma went on. "I feel very calm when I come here. And the doctors are so understanding."

"It's the finest hospital for mental problems in the world," Luke said.

Alix felt almost crippled at the irony of it. Had he met her elsewhere, Luke would loathe this woman because he was aware that nothing she said was real or true. Yet he stood there exchanging inane remarks, the same untruths and absurdities, the same denials. Her eyes caught Noah's and, even though he was clearly not there in some sense, a glint of understanding flew out at her. "It's a prison," she heard herself say, "only there's no parole."

It was as though she hadn't spoken. Selma just glanced nervously over at the tennis courts. "I've always wanted to learn how to play tennis," she said, "but I'm such a klutz at sports. In high school I was terrible. I have a balance problem."

"*I* play," Luke said. "It's one of my favorite sports. Alix is very good too." He beamed at her.

"They say exercise is so good for getting your mind off things," Selma babbled. "I always tell that to Noah . . . my job isn't demanding like his, but I think we both should exercise. His brother, Leo Epstein, the author, works out in a gym every day! Even when he's away on tour for a book!"

"Admirable discipline," Luke said.

"That's how Noah and I met," she continued. "I used to date Leo. But he's so, well, he's an intellectual. He always made me feel so . . . like I didn't know what to say."

Jesus, and he felt guilty for half fucking that woman poet? Oh, Noah, you deserve a thousand women poets, blonde, brunette, red-haired! You deserve . . . Again Alix looked at him, but now he was staring into space as though he weren't there, as though they weren't there.

"I feel a little weak," he said suddenly. "Maybe we should go back."

To Luke and Alix, as though Noah weren't there, Selma said, "They have him on Haldol. I think the dosage is too strong. It makes him dizzy."

Alix laughed mirthlessly. Again no one noticed or at least seemed to notice. They let Selma and Noah walk ahead. Seen from behind, they looked like a couple where the man was thirty years older. He was clinging to her as though he would literally fall to the ground if she let go. "He seems—" Luke began.

"Yes," Alix said. Suddenly she turned to him. "He was in a hospital ten years ago and they gave him shock treatment. It's obviously destroyed part of his mind."

"He doesn't seem all there," Luke concurred. It was as though they were strolling through Central Park, discussing some stranger they had observed.

"He's partly there," Alix said. "At times he can be sensitive and wonderful. Perhaps it would be easier for him if he didn't have that side as well."

They were near the building again, in a grove of flowering trees. Suddenly Luke grabbed her and pressed her close to him. She could hear his heart thumping wildly. "Alix," he whispered.

Alix let herself be held. "What?" she said coldly.

"I want you back so badly."

"Then get me back."

At that he recoiled and let go of her. They didn't speak for the rest of his visit.

She looked out the window and watched him leave. *He's hand-*

some. Tamara Grace was right. Courteous, handsome, loving. *He wants you back.* And all she could feel was a wish that his car would go up in flames, that he would somehow understand what pain was, even if just for one second. She hated, more than anything, the person she had become here. Outside she had felt occasionally sad, tormented, but she had been connected to people. Now all of that seemed to have faded away. The knowledge that Stern was a "mad dog," the accidental overdose (who knew if it was even accidental), didn't surprise her or shock her. *This is the world as it is. Before you were protected from knowledge. Nothing has changed except your perceptions.*

Noah had come over to sit beside her. He moved so quietly, sometimes she didn't hear him. He looked better, pale, but otherwise okay. Perhaps his wife made him sick, perhaps his clinging was just what he did with her, playing out their mutual roles. "Your husband is handsome," he said.

"Yes," Alix said.

"I felt ashamed I was so . . . weak seeming. He must have thought I was grotesque, pathetic."

"Why do you care what he thought?" she said bitterly.

He was speaking in that intent, passionate way he had, though his voice was soft. "I *do* care," he said. "I hate being perceived as a weakling, by Selma, by men like that, men like my brother who function so effortlessly in the world. I want to be one of them."

"Why?" Alix cried. "Your brother's a phony, and he writes phony books and my husband is dead inside and he'll never know it or come to terms with it. *Why* do you want to be like that? I don't want to be like your wife. God, she's a robot!"

He was offended. "No," he said stiffly, drawing back. "She's not. I'm lucky she married me. She's put up with so much. Any other woman would have left me years ago."

Alix touched his shoulder. She felt she loved him as she might have loved a brother, had she had one. "Oh Noah," she said, hopelessly.

He let her touch him, accepted the caress as it was meant. "We're lucky," he insisted. "Not everyone is married to such good people."

"Lucky," Alix repeated.

They sat together until the nurse came by and announced that it was time for dinner.

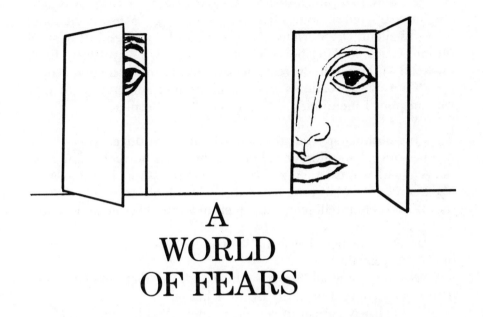

A
WORLD
OF FEARS

Sometimes Dr. Stern reminded Noah of Leo. It was nothing specific—Leo was taller, clean-shaven, his eyes were brown, but there
was a sense with both men that they were in control of their lives,
personal as well as professional. Though Dr. Stern didn't wear a
wedding ring, Noah assumed he was married. He imagined his
petite, delicate, glamorous wife, their elegant suburban home, even
their children, who he decided were two teenage sons, proud of
their father for his accomplishments, maybe a bit awed by him, a bit
competitive.

He felt unable to evaluate whether Dr. Stern was likely to be
monogamous or not. Nonetheless, he had told him about the incident with Ava Bernier. As with Leo, Noah had the feeling that Dr.
Stern regarded him as a fool, an incompetent both in career terms
and with women. Had he brought Ava Bernier up in order to show
that, at least occasionally, women were attracted to him?

Dr. Stern, also, seemed not to have heard of her as a poet. Why did that matter? After all, she'd given him her book. She *was* a poet. But he wanted Dr. Stern to say, "Oh, Ava Bernier? Goodness, and she was attracted to you? That's very flattering." Most of the time, if he was silent, Dr. Stern was also. At times he seemed just to stare off into space, looking bored or vacant. Today his eyes were fixed on Noah as though he were a speck of matter under a microscope.

"One of the patients here reminds me, sometimes, of that woman poet I mentioned," Noah said. "Ava Bernier?"

"Yes?"

"It's nothing specific, they don't really look alike. Ava—I only met her once, I shouldn't call her Ava, but Miss Bernier sounds too . . . Ava—what was I saying?—oh yes, Ava had short hair and Alix, Ms. Zimmer, Alix has long hair. No, it's not looks so much, though they both seem intelligent, but I feel they both like me and understand me."

Dr. Stern leaned forward. "Do you feel Ms. Zimmer is coming on to you sexually?"

"No, no, not at all. She has a husband. I've met him. He's very handsome. There'd be no reason for her—"

"You clearly appeal to certain women. And her husband isn't available to her sexually. I found her with her arms around you. Wasn't that a sexual gesture?"

"I don't think so," Noah said. "I thought, well, that she was trying to comfort me."

"The staff has noticed that you talk to her fairly often. What do you talk about?"

Noah hesitated. "Things."

"Things?" Dr. Stern echoed.

"Our marriages, our spouses, life—"

"Sounds like you cover quite a lot of ground. And how does it feel when she touches you? Are you aroused?"

"No!" Noah felt annoyed at the conversation. "She doesn't touch me in that way. I can tell the difference."

"Can you?"

Suddenly he wondered. Could he, really? Had he been able to tell with Ava Bernier? "She—she's an attractive woman," he stammered.

"Have any fantasies about her? Any dreams?"

In fact, he had a dream in which he was with Alix, but once he was awake, the memory had vanished. "I did dream of her once, but I can't remember the dream."

Dr. Stern leaned forward, as though this were significant. "How did you feel when you woke up?"

"No special way. I tried to remember it, but I couldn't."

"Ever imagine her undressed? What she'd look like? Her body?"

"No . . . at least not that I'm aware."

The expression on Dr. Stern's face was a slightly contemptuous one. Or was that Noah's imagination? "I miss my wife," Noah blurted out suddenly.

"Do you?"

"Yes, very much. I . . . want to just hold her. I think of that a lot." A shot of pain flew through him.

"Not fuck her?"

Noah was startled at his using the word "fuck." "If it could be the way it was . . ."

"Meaning?"

"Just that sometimes I haven't, it's been—"

"Impotent?"

"I wouldn't use that word," Noah said.

"What word would you use?"

He shrugged.

"Maybe your fantasy with Ms. Zimmer is that with her it would be terrific, that you'd really be a hot shot with her, like your brother is with his girlfriends."

"No," Noah said. "She would frighten me . . . in real life."

"How so?"

"She's so . . . sharp, quick. I can't describe it exactly . . . She wouldn't be soothing."

"That might be fun," Stern smiled.

"For some men, possibly."

Stern cleared his throat. "The staff have noticed Ms. Zimmer seeking you out, coming on to you. She's begun wearing makeup, dressing nicely since you arrived. But you haven't noticed?"

"I perceive she's an attractive woman, but I don't feel that's for me."

"Despite the fact that it coincided with your arrival?"

"Despite that. And she has a husband, she has a lover—" He broke off, sorry he had mentioned that since he had felt it was a confidence.

"Is her lover still alive?"

"I don't know."

"Maybe he's dead. Maybe she's looking for a new lover."

"I don't get that feeling."

Stern sighed. "You seem to have trouble accepting yourself as a sexually attractive male, Mr. Epstein. Yet women clearly *do* find you attractive. You said there was a student at school—"

Angie Cortez. God, how long ago that seemed! "Are there Jewish nuns?"
"My problems aren't with women," Noah said.

"With who, then?"

An image of Mr. Garofolo charging through the classroom came back to him. "With men, powerful, functioning men—Mr. Garofolo, my brother, you . . ."

"Men you also hate?"

"No, I don't hate them, I envy them."

"Isn't that the same thing?"

"I don't think so."

Dr. Stern got up. "Your wife said you've been complaining of dizziness."

"Yes, the Haldol seems—"

"Maybe we'll have to think of something else, then," Dr. Stern said.

The therapy session was just before dinner. After dinner, though Noah would have liked to sit and read, they were taken to a recreation hall where there was bowling. Some of the patients were playing cards. He noticed Alix Zimmer sitting to one side, with her habitual detached, watchful expression. Yes, she was attractive. No, he didn't think of her that way. Perhaps for men like Stern or his brother that was impossible, the idea that you could find a woman attractive, but not want to "fuck" her, as he put it, not even in fantasy. He tried, deliberately, imagining himself in bed with Alix Zimmer. She was angular, she would have a lovely body. But she wouldn't have that maternal sweetness Selma had, that warmth, cradling him, nurturing him.

He couldn't tell if Dr. Stern had been warning him not to interact so much with Alix. His remarks were usually indirect. He had made it seem as though she were being the aggressor. Yet she sat there now, staring into space, seeming unaware he was there. Of all the patients, she was the only one he felt was a kindred spirit, although outside the hospital they would have nothing in common. *You're not here for that. You're here to get well.*

Alix eventually came over and sat at his table. "You don't bowl?"

He shrugged.

"I'm not great at sports," she said. "My husband is. Skiing, squash. He was a sports hero when we met at college."

"I can imagine."

"I loved his looks. My father was this little harrassed man, obsessed with 'doing the right thing,' stoop-shouldered, practically blind without his glasses. He wasn't literally an immigrant, he was born here, but he could have been. He felt a stranger here and so, despite trying to fit in, he never did. And when I first saw Luke—it's such a cliché, but he really looked like a god to me. He had such seeming ease in his body, just in the way he walked—" She broke off.

Noah couldn't tell if her mood was wistful or bitter. He didn't say anything. She seemed in a semi-reverie. Around them the bowling balls knocked against each other, there was clatter and noise like static on a radio.

"What it was," Alix said, as though he had responded, "was that I felt so amazed. There I was—skinny, with a big nose, awkward with men, brainy—and this tall, handsome man 'deigned' to love me. Deigned! That was how I saw it. When he could, technically, have had thousands of blonde cheerleaders or what have you."

"Yes," Noah said. "I felt the same with Selma. She's a little plumper now, but I always liked that in women, a certain soft roundness. So many women nowadays are so bony—" He stopped, afraid she might take this as a reaction to her own body which was certainly, in his opinion, overly thin. She didn't react, though, so he went on. "When I saw her naked the first time, it was like seeing a Renoir come to life. Her skin was so rosy, it glowed." He never spoke like this to anyone, but here it seemed natural.

"Why did she get fat?" Alix asked abruptly.

Noah started. "She's *not* fat. All women put on some weight as they get older. Most men too. I still find her beautiful."

He expected a sarcastic rejoinder, but Alix just said, "Good."

"I suppose I caught her on the rebound," Noah said wistfully. "She was dating Leo and he, well, dumped her. I was there. That's how it happened."

Alix's face wrinkled with disgust. "Thank God for her!"

"Why?"

"Your brother's a monstrous person. She would have been disastrously unhappy with him."

Despite himself, he loved hearing her attack Leo. "How do you know? You've never met him."

"I've seen him on talk shows. He's an ass. Worse—corrupt, cruel. He probably fucks every woman he can lay his hands on." Her mouth was curled in a contemptuous line.

How did she know? "It's true, Selma wouldn't have been happy with Leo. He would have left her behind. She wouldn't have fit into that sophisticated world he moves in."

Alix was staring at the patients who were bowling as though they were alien beings who had descended from another planet. "I never understand games," she said. "Games or sports. Do you?"

"Not especially."

Then, without a break, she said fiercely, "Why do you always defend everyone? You defend your brother, your wife, why don't you allow yourself to have critical thoughts about them?"

When she became angry, her eyes flashed at him and he noticed the quirky tilt of her black eyebrows, which gave her a devilish look. "What good would that do?" he said wryly.

"It would do *you* good," Alix said, seeming determined to convince him.

"How? They're all I have—my family, my brother, my wife. I can't just trade them in like an old car."

"Sure you can. Lots of men do. Your wife, anyway. You could walk around the block blindfolded and come back with a dozen wives—ten, twenty years younger."

Something about her cynicism appalled him. "I don't *want* that, I told you," he said, his voice rising. "I just want Selma. I want our old life back, I want what we had. Maybe to you it's nothing, just a useless, stupid, humdrum life. But it was my life!" He was shaking, his blood pressure soaring, he could tell.

"But you're throwing it away," Alix insisted. "Why are you here where all they'll do is try to destroy what crumbs of self-confidence you have? Why don't you make her get you out?"

Noah's heart was racing. "I— She wouldn't. I acted . . . I acted strangely, inappropriately. I did things." It started coming back to him, and that feeling of horrible dizziness began to make the bowling alley tilt precariously, as though the bowling balls were rolling from the ceiling, about to knock people on the head.

"Tell me what happened." Alix was so close to him he could see each hair of her straight black eyelashes, her thin lips which were chapped slightly, the lipstick wearing off.

He described the incident in class, Garofolo charging down the aisle at him, locking him in the office. "I was out of control," he said, "saying those things to a class of semiliterate black teenagers. What was wrong with me? I was crazy."

Alix grabbed his hands. "You *weren't* crazy. You wanted to make contact. Okay, maybe your judgment was off, but did you harm anyone? At most, they didn't get what you said. That principal just had it in for you. He was waiting like a vulture for something to nail you on. Don't you see? Men like that live to trample. That's how they get their kicks. You *didn't* do anything wrong."

Noah was exhausted. At times he felt she was like a ventriloquist saying everything he felt or had thought, but at other times he wanted to run when she opened her mouth and such ugly, uncompromising words poured out. Her vehemence terrified him. Suddenly a nurse appeared. "Now, how about you two?" she said jocularly.

"How *about* us?" Alix said.

"You two is just sitting there! I don't see you bowling. I don't see you playing cards, even. You're not socializing. You're not doing nothing."

"We're socializing with each other," Alix said sarcastically.

"That's no good," the nurse said. She was plump, with curly hair and round glasses. "You need physical exercise, the both of you. Look how pale you both are!" She took Noah by the arm. "I'll show you," she said. "It's not hard."

"I feel quite dizzy," he said truthfully. "I'd really rather not."

Alix leapt to her feet. "I'd like to learn," she said. "Would you show me?" She followed the nurse to the bowling alley.

Noah watched them go with relief. Alix excited and frightened him. Without her, this place would have been hell. He would have felt totally isolated. But at times her insistence was like a dentist's drill. She darted back and forth so strangely, at times having that cynical, harsh bluntness: Why is your wife fat? Your brother is a monster. And then suddenly becoming dreamy, kind. Like right now—she had perceived he was dizzy, though he hadn't said he was, and had rescued him from having to bowl, though he knew she loathed bowling. But no, he didn't want to be in bed with her. Ava Bernier had been softer somehow, at least to the fuzzy extent he could remember her. But the moment he thought of her, his mind leapt ahead to that moment when he had become aware they were making love and he had felt like a murderer with blood on his hands.

That image was all that stayed with him: blood, murder, a feeling of panic.

To calm himself, to draw his mind from these thoughts, he watched the bowlers. He watched the pattern of lines and shapes, the alley, the dark balls, the moving figures. He had tried bio-feedback once to control his blood pressure and he tried in a vague way to do that now. Lines, shapes, figures, dark and light. He tried to disconnect the word "blood" from "blood pressure" because blood brought back that image, that moment in bed, her cooing . . .

That night, in bed, he pretended Selma was with him, not that they were making love, or were about to, or that they had done it, just that he was there with her arms around him, holding him, the smell of her hair, her skin. *Please let me return. That's all I ask.*

A week later Dr. Stern evidently decided Noah was well enough to see his entire family. During the session he didn't mention it, but at the very end he said, "Tomorrow your brother and mother are coming to see you. Can you handle that?"

"Yes, I think I can," Noah said.

He tried to remember what had happened the last time he was hospitalized. He couldn't remember either his mother or brother visiting him. Why? Leo had been in Italy with his family, on some island. And his mother? Oh yes, it was that his father had just had his first heart attack and she was afraid the stress would be bad for him. Why she hadn't come alone he couldn't remember, maybe she was afraid to leave his father by himself. Or maybe she had never told his father he was there, even.

When he saw the whole group of them approaching, he felt apprehensive. Selma was in front, an anxious, trembling smile on her face, wearing a bright pink dress. His mother and Horace Carnow were arm in arm, both looking well fed and solid, pleased with themselves and the world, undauntable. Leo, strangely, had an uneasy expression, as though he wasn't sure what he was getting into. Next to him was Eloise—why her, also?—with a bright, generalized smile, looking all around as though it were a big party and at any moment some celebrities might appear and rescue her. Norman? Diana? Where are you?

"So, how's it going?" Horace boomed. Of all of them, he was the one with whom Noah felt best. His reactions seemed so simple, almost primitive. Mental illness must seem as alien to him as the behavior of sea slugs.

"It's going well," Noah said. He was feeling better today. They had switched his medication; his blood pressure, which had zoomed disastrously high the night of the bowling, was down again.

Horace looked all around the room. "Where are the crazy people?" he asked.

His mother was in a navy suit with a thick gold bracelet around her wrist. "They aren't crazy," she chided. "These are just people with mental problems, that's all."

"So, why're they here?" Horace asked. "Why're they locked up?"

"They're not locked up," Selma said. Clearly his loud, booming voice bothered her. "They're here because they want to be. They need help. And they get it here. That's what places like this are for."

Horace sat down. He was smoking one of his cigars. "So, are you getting help? Is it working?"

"Well—" Noah began.

But before he could finish, Horace said, "What I don't get is no one here looks crazy. I thought they'd all be, you know, doing funny things. Or be thinking they were Teddy Roosevelt."

"That's a cliché," Leo said smoothly. "Things are much more complicated."

"Huh? What do you know?" Horace looked around. "Not much to look at." He winked at Noah. "Where are the pretty girls? Got any of them?"

"Horace, stop!" commanded Noah's mother.

"He's supposed to get well, right?" Horace said. "To get well you need beautiful scenery, and pretty girls come first." He started singing, "A Pretty Girl is Like a Melody."

"You're eighty-two years old," Noah's mother said. "Much too old for talk like that."

"Am I blind? Am I dead?" Horace rejoined cheerfully. The fumes of his cigar wafted toward Noah. "This bother you?"

"No, I'm fine," Noah said.

Leo leaned over. "I'd like to talk to Noah a minute alone," he said. "Could I?"

Noah stood up. For some reason he remembered when he had been eleven and Leo eight, and their father had spanked Leo, one of the few times he had ever laid a hand on either of them. Noah couldn't remember the occasion, just Leo's lusty howls and his own furtive pleasure which he disguised by running off and hiding in the closet. "Are you—how *are* things?" Leo asked.

"They're fine," Noah said, recoiling.

"Noah, come *on.* You had a breakdown. You're in a hospital. What happened? Was it something about the party at the library? Did something happen there?"

"No, nothing happened." Could Ava Bernier possibly have gotten in touch with Leo, told him everything?

"Tell me," Leo said soothingly. "There's no need to hide anything."

"I can't," Noah stammered.

"Why not?"

Noah gestured toward Selma and the others.

"Let's go to your room, then." He strode back and said to the others, "Noah and I need to talk a minute. We'll be right back." Pointing to a deck of cards on the table, he said to Horace, "Play a little poker."

Horace grinned. "Is it allowed?" He started shuffling the cards.

Noah hated his room. It was like a box, dark, with one narrow window. He hated the feelings he got in that room, of such terrible loneliness and fear. He sat on the bed. "What do you want to know?" he asked guardedly.

"What happened," Leo said. "You said something happened at the party. What was it?"

"Did I say something happened?"

"Noah, come on! You said you couldn't speak in front of them. Now we're alone. Tell me!"

"Why?"

"Because I want to know. I'm your brother, for Christ's sake. I care. I care about you." He looked away. "Was it . . . Selma told me later it was your birthday. Were you hurt we all forgot? I'm sorry. That was inexcusable."

Noah shrugged.

"What, then? Selma said you left early. Did you feel dizzy?"

"A little."

"Did you go straight home?"

Suddenly Noah felt enraged. "Why does it matter? *You* fuck women right and left every day of the week! What the hell difference does it make if once, once in my life I—" He stopped, horrified.

"Once in your life, what?" Leo looked bewildered. "You made it with some woman at the party? Oh right, Ava. You were sitting next to her. So what? She said, 'Come back to my place,' you went, you—"

"Stop!" Noah yelled. "Shut up!"

Leo grabbed his hands. "What's wrong with you? I don't care, nobody cares. What's the big deal? Does Selma know?"

Noah's heart began racing again. "Leo, please." He could hardly speak. "Don't tell her. Do you promise? She would hate me. I didn't even *do* anything. I just lay down on the bed. I never even took my clothes off. I swear to you. Do you believe me?"

"Sure, I believe you."

"I came to and we were . . . I was inside her, she was making these sounds, but I never . . . I love Selma. Do you believe me?"

Leo sighed. "Christ, of course I believe you." He looked impatient.

"Then how did it happen?" Noah begged. "What happened? I was lying there, asleep, and suddenly—or do you think it didn't happen? Do you think I imagined the whole thing?"

Leo gazed out the window. "It probably happened," he said in a bored, irritated voice. "But out of guilt you repressed it, and then you had some after-reaction, some guilt attack. You went bonkers." He smiled. "What's Ava like? A friend of mine, Ferris McCauley, had a long thing with her. He said she was pretty—"

Noah felt wiped out, as though he'd been running and running. "She writes poetry," he said flatly.

"Yeah," Leo said. "I've read some. A touch gloomy, a touch Plathish, but not bad. Sometimes women like that . . ."

Noah said nothing. He almost forgot Leo was there. There had been a pleasure in his seizure of rage, though he knew he would pay for it later. "I don't understand how you do it," he said.

"Do what?" Leo said impatiently, drumming his fingers on the bureau top.

"With women," Noah said. "I don't . . . How do you do it?" He was really curious, sincerely so.

Leo frowned, then laughed. "How? You mean the mechanics, how often, you mean why—I don't get your question."

"How do you live with yourself?" Noah asked.

Leo grinned. "Do I have a choice? Someone else I can live with? Okay, you want to know? It's simple, really. Terribly simple. Other things in my life aren't. But this is. I married El. For five, six years, I can't even remember anymore, we were monogamous, which meant I did it to her, she lay there like a beached whale and faked orgasms, or maybe really had them sometimes, who knows, she did have Actor's Studio training. I used to think maybe she was pretending to be a boiled onion. It was hard to tell. But I thought, or tried to think: this is marriage, or maybe it'll get better, or nothing's perfect. The usual clichés. And then one day a little light bulb went off in my head which said, 'This is shit! You're a jerk. Give the lady a break. There are dozens, *hundreds* of women out there who would love to go to bed with you, married women, single women.' And so there were, and, believe me, El has never been happier. Maybe once, twice a year we do it for old times' sake and she does her boiled onion thing, and we cuddle and I say, 'I love you,' because it's true. I love her, she loves me. Only now she doesn't have to lie there in fear and trembling, wondering, 'Is this horny jackass going to pounce on me again?' She can use all her energy for shopping, for her life, her *real* life."

Noah was watching him. When he was ten, or maybe nine, he taught Leo to play checkers. He remembered Leo sitting forward, his round freckled face, his ginger hair which had darkened over the years and gotten thinner. He saw Leo's eager face, his bright eyes, and recalled how he would say, "Can I jump you now? Can I jump you?" And he, still clinging to the vestiges of his superiority as older brother, would say, "No, Leo, not now." But probably someone, seeing them even back then, would have seen who was ultimately going to make it, or who wasn't, who would get ahead, and who wouldn't. Leo had learned when to jump, all right. It was he who hadn't.

"Is yours what you'd call an open marriage?" Noah asked.

Leo shrugged. "Open? Closed? Who knows? I mean, we don't sit around talking about it. I don't come home and say, 'I just had a great fuck with a beautiful redhead in Chicago.' I'm not a sadist. And she's not interested, like I said. She doesn't care. So she knows, but no details. Just like I don't question her about how many pairs of shoes she has, or whether she bought two or six suits at a fashion show, because *I* don't care."

Noah wove his fingers together. Sadness was coming at him from somewhere like a cloud. "Selma and I could never have that kind of marriage. Selma trusts me absolutely, totally. If she knew about Ava Bernier . . . She didn't call you, did she?"

"Who, Selma?"

"No, Ava."

"Why should she call me?"

Noah shrugged. "Just because . . . I don't know."

"Noah, look, your marriage is something else. It's touching, it's sweet, maybe it's also a little sick, who's to say. But for a woman like Ava to get a yen for a guy at a party and act on it, what's to call about? This isn't front page news. Do I call you when I have a cold? When I have an ingrown toenail?" He shook his head. He was pacing up and down the room. "I don't *get* you. Why are you here? Why again? What's it for? Life is what you make it. If you want to make yours into a fucked up melodrama, do it. But I just don't get *why.* Can you explain it to me?"

"No," Noah said. "I can't . . . I don't understand it myself. Certain things frighten me, I guess, more than they should. I try to overcome those fears and I seem to end up doing things other people feel are inappropriate."

"So, stop!" Leo yelled. "Use your head. Everyone has fears. Big deal. Figure out what people want out of you, and do it. Christ, is that so hard? So you fucked, or almost fucked some woman you're not married to? Jesus, if every man who did that ended up in a nuthouse, they'd have to tear down the whole state of Nebraska and use it just for mental hospitals."

As always, Leo was oversimplifying and, in doing so, making Noah's breakdown seem even more shameful. Not only was the event, minor, insignificant to Leo, but Noah, at forty-one, had no idea of how to handle himself in the real world, never had, never would. He stared hopelessly at the floor.

"So, is being here doing you any good?" Leo said. "Is it helping?"

Noah shook his head. "It's terrible."

"Then get out!"

"I can't. The doctors have to feel you're normal."

"Then act normal!" Leo was out of breath, he was so exasperated. "Act however they want you to. Lie. Do whatever . . ." Clearly to him it was as simple as his relationships with women outside marriage. A game. *Can I jump you.*

As Noah rose and they returned to the central room, Leo said more softly, "Hey, sorry if I was a little rough. I just want you to shape up, you know? You're so—you're smarter than me, there's so much you could've done with your life, there still is. You just give up."

Noah nodded. Leo was like a bird swooping down from the sky and saying, "Flying is easy. Just spread your wings and fly." *But I don't have wings.* "Spread your arms and fly." *But I'll fall.*

As they approached the family group, Noah saw that Eloise was talking animatedly with Alix. For some reason the sight of this made him anxious. He didn't want Alix to meet his family. She was wearing a black dress and looked paler than usual except for the fact that her lipstick was bright red. Her dark hair was loose down her back. Eloise charged over to them. "Leo! This is the most amazing coincidence! Alix—Alix, this is my husband, Leo Epstein, Alix Zimmer—Alix works at the same firm Sid went to for his divorce."

"What do you know?" Leo said, eyeing Alix in the way he eyed all women under the age of sixty who weren't grossly overweight.

Eloise turned to Alix. "The reason Sid went to your firm was that his niece, Giselle, works in the same building and had a—well, she had a man friend, a . . . someone she was involved with who worked at your firm, Gerald Lehman. Did you know him?"

"Yes," Alix said, almost in a whisper.

"Did he do a great job for Sid! He *worships* him. Said he was the most brilliant man he ever met. Give him our best when you see him."

"He died," Alix said. She stood there very stiffly, her arms at her sides. Noah wondered why her husband wasn't visiting today.

"Oh." Eloise was momentarily at a loss. "I guess we haven't been in touch with Sid for quite a while. Still, small world."

Alix nodded.

Horace was playing solitaire as Noah's mother watched. He began singing softly, " 'It's a Small World,' " and she found herself unexpectedly touched.

"Hush," Noah's mother said affectionately, with a mild rebuke. Noah thought of how, when his father used to horse around in public, she wore the same expression, a mixture of impatience and affection. Horace looked up at Alix. "So, who're you visiting? Your husband?"

"I'm a patient here," Alix said.

"No!" He looked bewildered. "A young, pretty girl and they have you locked up?"

Noah's mother sat forward. "Horace, this is not a place where they lock people up! Why can't you understand that? It's a *hospital.*"

"You mean you can just leave at any time?" Horace asked.

Alix had moved so that she was standing right beside the table. "No, you can't leave. You *are* locked up. They can do anything they want to you."

There was a silence. Everyone looked uncomfortable.

Horace looked over at Noah. "Is that true?"

Noah half shrugged, half nodded.

"I don't like that," Horace said. "Locking people up. I'm going to speak to someone. Where's the nurse? Where's the doctor?" He leapt up to find one.

Noah's mother went after him. "Horace, stop! You don't know anything about it. There are rules and regulations. You can't just go barging into things like that."

"It's your son," Horace shouted, angrily. Suddenly he reached out as a nurse rushed by. "Nurse!"

"Yes?" said Nurse Kefaldis.

"Listen, I'm a visitor here. I just want to get something straight. My girl friend's son is a patient here and he says he can't get out, that the doctors can do anything they want to him. Is that true?"

She smiled brightly. "Whatever works," she said, and began walking away.

Horace went after her. "What? You didn't answer my question. Can they leave or not?"

"When they're well, they leave," the nurse said impatiently. "We give them drugs, we take care of them. They don't leave till they've learned to behave in the outside world. Otherwise the world would be a mess with people doing crazy things all the time."

"The world *is* a mess," Horace said.

The nurse walked off. Horace stood there, looking bewildered. Noah's mother took him firmly by the shoulder. "Horace, you can't change the world. Now sit down and play cards again."

Horace walked slowly across the room and sat down, but heavily, without his usual bounce. He looked up at Alix. "Want to play some poker?"

Alix smiled. Her face lost its rigid expression, became soft. "I'd love to."

"Anyone else?" Horace asked.

"Sure, I'll play," Leo said. "How about you, Noah?"

"Okay." Noah wasn't good at card games, but he enjoyed poker.

Although the four of them were seated, Eloise said, "How about bridge instead?"

Horace reached for his cigar, which had been burning in an ashtray. "Nope, poker or nothing." He began shuffling the deck.

A moment later the same nurse approached. "Gambling is not allowed," she said, and snatched the cards out of Horace's hands.

"Gambling?" Horace stared at her. "Who's gambling? We're not playing for money. We're playing for fun."

Without a word she walked off with the cards.

Leo laughed. "Boy, I hope I never meet *her* on a dark night."

Alix smiled at him. "She's one of the better ones."

Noah, watching, hated seeing Alix flirt with his brother. Or was it flirting? If she hadn't been wearing red lipstick, perhaps it would have seemed just friendly. Selma had been sitting across the room, talking to someone, another wife. She walked over and sat down beside them. "Where's your husband," she asked Alix, "that nice man we met the other day?"

"I guess he had better things to do today," Alix said with a defiant look.

Selma was nonplussed.

"What profession is your husband in?" Leo asked in the caressing voice he used with women.

"He's an art curator," Alix said. She seemed poised, but a little tense. She touched her wedding ring self-consciously.

"And you're a legal secretary, like Giselle?"

"No, I'm a lawyer," Alix said. "I'm one of the partners."

Leo whistled. "Wow. Impressive. You look so young."

"I'm thirty-six," Alix said.

Leo looked up at Eloise. "Hey, El, did you hear that? Ms. Zimmer, Alix, is a partner. Not bad."

"Thank you," Alix said.

Noah, watching them, wondered if Leo, had the circumstances been otherwise, would have slipped her his card and arranged an assignation. Or maybe he would, in any case. And Alix? She said she'd had a lover. Would Leo be her type? Noah hoped not, but it was impossible for him, with his fiercely ambivalent feelings about his brother, to tell. He felt Selma reach out and take his hand. That small secret gesture was so like her, so endearing. Neither of them spoke, but she held his hand, and for that brief time the fears moved back, and he could have been at home, free, well.

When it came time for them to leave, she took him aside and said softly, "I'm sorry we didn't have time to talk. There were so many people . . . Was it all right they all came?"

"Sure," Noah said. He felt he would have sold his soul for an hour alone with her, holding her.

"Are you getting better?" Selma asked. She asked that every

day when they spoke on the phone. And every day Noah said, "I think so," as he did now.

They embraced and then she moved off with the others. There were generalized good-byes. Horace was smoking another cigar. His mother said, "Get better. It's Leo's birthday next month. We'll have a nice party."

"Great seeing you," Eloise said, hugging him perfunctorily. She waved at Alix, who was still sitting at the table. "Nice to have met you. Give us a ring when you get out."

"Right," Leo said. "Come to my birthday party. Tell your husband. You're both invited."

When they were all out of sight, Noah felt a simultaneous sense of relief and desolation. Alix sat quietly, like a mannequin. Her aquiline nose was like the profile of a statue, her mouth severe, despite the shiny red of the lipstick. The black dress made it seem as though she were in mourning. "Families," he said, wryly.

"Mine are all dead," she said. "My father, my mother, my sister . . . but yes, I know what you mean." She looked down at her hands. "I liked your father."

"That wasn't my father," Noah said. "He's my mother's—well, they go around together, they're a couple. He's eighty-two and she's seventy-eight."

"Do they sleep together?"

"I don't know."

"He seemed so energetic, so caring. Even your brother wasn't as repellent as I expected."

"I never said he was repellent."

"He cares about you, I think, in his way. Odd marriage. Does his wife know, or doesn't she care?"

"Know what?" Noah asked, not sure why he was pretending he didn't know what she meant.

"The way he comes on to women." She shook her head. "I kept feeling his legs trying to clasp mine under the table. God! Trying to make a pass at a patient in a mental hospital! That's either desperation or chutzpah, or a little of each."

"More the latter," Noah said. After a second he added, "Did you find him attractive?"

Alix frowned. "Sexually, you mean?"

"If you met him on the outside and he acted that way, would you?"

He was afraid she would consider the question rude, but she said pensively. "I don't . . . do that kind of thing."

"I thought you had a—there was someone other than your husband." He hoped he had not misunderstood her.

She gazed at him. "I was in love with someone for five years."

"But you never actually—"

"No, we did. But your brother does it as an indoor sport. In a funny way I admire that. I'm such an uncasual person. A friend of mine once said of a man she slept with, 'It was about as intimate as a handshake.' And I thought, how amazing, to be able to do something that intimate and regard it that way. I always feel I'm taking my life in my hands. But then I haven't had much experience. Luke was my first."

"Selma was for me, too," Noah said.

"She loves you," Alix said, as though he had asked, "she just doesn't understand you."

In bed that night Noah pondered Alix's remark. Did anyone understand anyone? Did he understand Selma? He knew what Alix meant. Selma was simple, direct, sweet. Perhaps she didn't understand with an intellectual's knowledge, she hadn't read Freud, she hadn't ever been in therapy herself. But she understood that he was suffering. Wasn't that enough?

Selma. The thoughts of her turned from contemplations to a dark, painful yearning, as though his heart were being squeezed by an inexorable hand. He had failed her. All she wanted was an ordinary husband like anyone else's. She didn't mind that they lived the way they did, that his salary was low, that they couldn't afford the kinds of vacations and extras she would have had if she had married Leo, or someone like Leo. Alix was right. Selma would have been unhappy with Leo, but she might, had she not married Noah, have married a Leo who was kind to her, who loved her, someone who wasn't a fool, an incompetent jerk. It was as though self-loathing were a medication, a time-controlled capsule whose effects he could feel seeping into his system.

I love you, Selma. At least know that.

He was lying on his side, still dazed by longing thoughts, when one of the night nurses peered into the room. Noah feigned sleep as she approached the bed. She leaned over and touched his forehead. "Feeling all right?" she whispered.

"Yes, I'm fine," Noah said. He had taken off his pajama top

because the room had started to seem warm. He was sweating, but his skin was cool.

"You'll get cold," she said. "You better put your top back on."

Noah struggled to sit up, groping for the pajama top which he had tossed on the floor, but the nurse, a young blonde, picked it up for him. She had a coarse face with heavy brows and a flattened small nose, full lips. "Here, I'll help you," she said. She started putting the pajama top back on him, buttoning it gently, her hands seeming to caress his neck and chest as she did. He felt himself getting an erection, and recoiled, ashamed.

To his horror the nurse reached down and touched him where he was stiff, almost as though she were feeling his forehead to see if he had a fever. "Don't be ashamed," she said. "It's natural. You miss your girlfriend."

"My wife," he whispered, wanting her to leave, but transfixed by her.

Without changing her tone, the nurse stroked him gently. "You just feel lonely," she said. "This'll make you feel better."

Torn between excitement and dread, he let her caress him. Afterward, he turned on his side, coiled in a ball, appalled, wanting to vanish into the darkness. "Now, you sleep well now, you hear?" she called out as she left the room.

Alone, he felt the darkness was both a kind of protection, and a cave in which he lay, helpless. Why had he let her? Using Selma, using his desire for her. Why did women sense these feelings in him so easily? He hated the nurse, but hated himself still more. *Please let me get well. If I get out of here, I'll make it up to Selma. I'll be a better husband. I'll make our lives the way she wants, I'll do anything.* But sleep, when it finally came, was simply escaping from one darkness into another.

He had made up his mind. When he next saw Dr. Stern, he said, "I want to go back to teach."

"When? This afternoon?"

"As soon as I can." Noah leaned forward earnestly. "I think I can do it. I think that will prove to me that I'm well." He was trying to take Leo's advice: act well, seem strong, play the game.

"And if it fails?" Dr. Stern said. "Won't that make things even worse? Won't you be humiliated?"

Noah tried not to be daunted, though he was sure Dr. Stern was right. "I won't fail. Selma can bring me my notes. You see, I just—I made certain mistakes. That was what went wrong. My judgment was off. They're underprivileged kids, and most of the staff regards them with such contempt. Perhaps I share that, but I also wanted, somehow, to try and reach them, to—"

"—be their savior?" Dr. Stern interjected.

"No, I didn't think of it in those terms," Noah said. "I just wanted to communicate."

Dr. Stern looked at him curiously. "Mr. Epstein, has anything happened since you arrived here, which you feel has clarified your judgment sufficiently that you feel able to undertake such a project? You still seem quite nervous and agitated, not only to me, but to the rest of the staff."

"Yes, I know," Noah said, his heart starting to race, "I know I do seem that way, but, despite that, I—my thoughts are clearer. I know what went wrong. I talked about it with my brother."

Dr. Stern cocked his head to one side. "Oh, your brother. Is he such an expert in psychology on the basis of a few pop books?"

"He *is* an expert, yes," Noah said, feeling the usual mixed feeling at having Leo's accomplishments so lightly dismissed. "Not only because of his books, but because of his life. He knows how to live."

"And what were his words of advice to you?"

Noah felt a need to protect both himself and Leo. "Nothing specific, really. But he gave me a sense that it was possible. He said he thought I was wrecking my life and that I should just stop." He tried to smile.

"As simple as that?"

Noah tried to meet his gaze. "Yes, he feels it can be simple. It's simple for him."

"What's simple? Life?"

"Yes, and . . . well, I talked about what happened, or might have happened with that woman poet I mentioned to you, and Leo said it happened all the time, that it was nothing to worry about."

Dr. Stern frowned. "What, exactly, was nothing to worry about? Losing consciousness? Making love to a woman and not being able to remember how it happened? Waking up in bed the next morning and not knowing how you got there? Your brother must know unusual people."

Noah felt the session was going all wrong. "He meant guilt," he stammered. "That guilt was normal. He said I forgot out of guilt."

"Well, it's nice to have a simple explanation, isn't it?" Dr. Stern said. "Just wave a magic wand and no more guilt. And then one can go out and do it with countless women? Betray one's wife? Betray her trust?"

At that, Noah remembered the night before, the nurse caressing him. He felt felled, as though Dr. Stern had seized him from behind and started choking him. He sat motionless, numb. "You're right," he said. "I have. How could I?"

Dr. Stern just watched him. "How could you?" he repeated.

"She saw I was excited," Noah said, as though in a trance. "I had taken my pajama top off and she offered to put it back on. Then she reached down, and—"

"What are you talking about?" Dr. Stern said sharply. "How did you get in pajamas when you were at her house? This doesn't make sense."

"Last night," Noah said, looking away. "I meant last night."

"What happened last night?"

Noah told him. Dr. Stern's face wrinkled with distaste. "Are you saying one of the nurses . . . ?"

"I don't want to get her into trouble," Noah said. "She was only trying to be kind. She saw I was lonely. I should have stopped her."

"Why didn't you?"

"I—it happened so quickly." He bent over, weeping. "I love my wife so much, I had been thinking of her, pretending . . ."

"And this is how you show your love? By letting another woman bring you to orgasm, a nurse, a member of the staff?"

"It was wrong," Noah said. "I know that. I knew it then."

"But you were unable to help yourself?"

"Yes."

"Yet you expect to go out into the world and teach your class, a situation infinitely more difficult, requiring much greater powers of judgment and control? What about that student you mentioned? The one who's in love with you. What if she were to approach you alone as you've indicated she has? Could you trust yourself?"

"Of course," Noah said, horrified. "She's a student. She's—"

"But was allowing a nurse to do what you allowed her to do any more appropriate?"

"Angie is a teenager," Noah said, amazed Dr. Stern didn't seem to understand the difference. "I'm not real to her. Nothing like that would happen, I can swear to you. But if you're afraid, I would just go, teach the class, and return here. I wouldn't be alone with anyone, even for a minute."

"I'll have to think about it," Dr. Stern said. "Perhaps, as a trial measure, you should go on an outside trip with another patient—just to test your powers of control and judgment."

"That would be fine," Noah said eagerly, relieved.

"Perhaps a trip with—who would you like to go with?"

Noah hesitated. "With Alix Zimmer," he said.

"Fine," Dr. Stern said, unexpectedly. "That should be a good test. If she comes on to you, you'll know how to handle it?"

"She won't," Noah protested. "We're just friends."

Dr. Stern smiled with what seemed to Noah barely veiled contempt. "Good," he said, getting up. "That's settled then."

Noah emerged from the session confused as always at how the conversation had drifted so far from where he had intended it to go. Of course, that was what therapy was, supposedly—letting one's thoughts wander—but he always felt as though he were an animal treading lightly on what looked like piles of leaves. Somewhere a pit lay craftily concealed by the hunters. If he wasn't careful, he would fall and a steel trap would encircle his leg. He had flash images of animals caught in traps, dying in agony as the steel bit into their flesh, even trying to yank off their leg in order to escape.

No! Why was he thinking that way? *These thoughts are paranoid. He's a doctor, not a hunter. He wants to help you. Stop thinking of yourself as a victim. If you do, you'll become one. He's willing to let you out. He must trust you to some extent. Or was it another trap? What if Alix did make a pass?* He should have suggested someone else, someone neutral who knew nothing about him, to whom he had confided nothing. Alix was the wrong choice.

Alix is your friend, no more, no less. And he's right. It's a test. Don't act confiding with her, just act neutral, discuss neutral things. It's a matter of steps. One step at a time . . .

Nurse Yvonne Chen took Noah and Alix into Rigsville, the town adjoining the hospital. They were allowed to remain off the grounds for an hour. It was a brilliant spring day with a fresh breeze. "What would you like to do?" she asked them when they had gotten off the bus.

He was afraid Alix would say something strange, but she just said, "Why don't we have an ice cream soda in that place over there? It looks nice. Is that all right with you, Noah?"

"It's fine," Noah said.

The ice cream shop was odd in that the decorations, as well as the prices, seemed left over from the 1940s. There were advertisements for root beer floats, egg creams. They looked dusty, as though they might have been there all along, rather than having been put up recently as a bit of nostalgia. Noah slid into a booth and Alix slid in on the other side, next to the nurse. The waitress came and they ordered. Alix asked for a chocolate ice cream soda. Noah ordered just a glass of seltzer.

"Oh, come on," Alix said, smiling mischeviously. "Live dangerously. Have a hot fudge sundae."

"I couldn't," he said. "My digestion."

The waitress looked at the nurse, who smiled and said, "Just water for me." Then she stood up. "I have an errand to do. Can you both stay here while I'm gone?"

"Of course," they said in unison.

She checked her watch. "I'll be back in twenty minutes."

"That'll give me time to really savor my soda," Alix said. The minute the nurse had disappeared, she grinned at Noah. "Here's our chance. Let's run off together!"

Noah's heart sank. "Don't," he whispered.

"Don't what?"

"Don't talk like that. This is a test. They may have someone listening. We have to act normal."

"Noah." Alix sighed. "I didn't mean it literally. Relax. Let's enjoy our bit of freedom. Why not?"

Although he had sworn not to mention anything that was important to him, he told her about Dr. Stern's promise to let him teach if this outing was a successful one.

"I don't trust him," Alix said.

"Why not?" Noah said. "He's a doctor. He's here because he wants to help us."

"The way he helped the two patients he killed?" Her eyes glittered with rage.

"What?"

"He killed one patient, sorry," Alix said. "The other one managed to live. He's a mad dog. That's what Leroy Demos calls him—Mad Dog. Have you noticed how he foams at the mouth?"

Noah felt afraid that she was crazy. "How could he kill two patients, or almost? That would be illegal."

She laughed. "Depends on how you define it. We're chattel, property, specimens." Seeing his terrified expression, she reached out and touched his trembling hands. "Look, forget I said that. I think it's a great plan. You can do it. I know. You'll teach the class and then you'll go home and you'll be fine."

At her touch, Noah drew back. He looked over his shoulder to see if, possibly, the nurse was watching outside.

"What's wrong?" Alix said, puzzled.

He put his hands in his lap. "They don't want you to touch me," he said, hating himself. "They feel it's wrong."

"In what way?"

"That it's sexual," he said, not looking at her, "that you might be making a pass at me."

He had thought she would get angry, but she just looked at him sadly. "Noah, you're so—you let people manipulate you. It's strange. Your brother is the opposite. He manipulates others all the time. He can't stop. But you—you're too ingenuous. You put yourself in danger, don't you see? You're playing into their hands."

That was, in effect, what Leo had said. "I don't mean to," Noah said. "I just—I have poor judgment at times."

"You don't!" Alix cried. "Listen to me. Your judgment is fine. Don't let them rip you to shreds. Look, I'm not going to talk to you as much once we get back. Don't think I'm turning against you, or acting cold. It's part of a plan I have . . . So this is the last thing I'll say to you. Please fight what's happening. I've been so afraid for myself, but when I see you, I feel more afraid. They can destroy you. Don't let them."

Noah had forgotten his fears that the nurse might be outside. He was transfixed by her words, by her intense stare, feeling almost as though she were trying to hypnotize him. "What is your plan?"

"I can't tell you, and you must swear to me you won't mention this conversation to anyone, especially not to Dr. Stern, ever. Do you swear that?"

"Yes."

As they sat there, both charged up by the conversation, the waitress brought their orders. In silence Alix removed the maraschino cherry and ate it. "I love these," she said dreamily, as though the circumstances of their being there were totally different, as though they were two singles having a blind date on a beautiful spring day. For a second Noah allowed himself to toy with that notion, the two of them unattached, free, never married. Would he, under those circumstances, find Alix attractive? He recalled saying to Dr. Stern that she was too sharp and his response, "Some men like that." As she was right at this moment, dreamy, distant, her hair softly shining, her eyes downcast, he felt she was lovely. But when he thought of her as she had been a few moments earlier, giving him advice, however well intentioned, he knew it would never work. She would loathe him for being weak, he would recoil from her vehemence.

Catching his eye, Alix half smiled. "What were you thinking?"

"That we were on a date, that neither of us was married . . ."

She sighed. "A pleasant thought."

Suddenly he turned serious. "But could you live without your husband? Isn't he crucial to you, to your very existence?"

Alix was slowly spooning up the whipped cream which was on top of her soda. "Crucial to my very existence? I hope not. I would hate to be that dependent. I'm too dependent already."

"I like that," he said. "I like the sense that someone . . . that I matter to someone."

She stared at him thoughtfully. "You don't have to be married for that."

Was she thinking of her lover, whoever he was, whoever he had been? "I do," Noah said.

He was afraid she would shoot back a contemptuous reply, as Dr. Stern would have, but she just said. "That's sweet." Then she looked around. "You know it's funny, at first I really did think that she was leaving us alone as some kind of test, to see if we'd try to escape, but I think she literally had errands to do."

The thought horrified him. "If you escape, they can catch you."

"How? With bloodhounds?"

"They can—they can punish you. They can give you shock treatment. You aren't thinking of escaping, are you? Don't! It's terribly dangerous."

Alix didn't reply. "I haven't had an ice cream soda in so long. It tastes wonderful. This is like a date, you're right. Only I hardly dated, ever. I met Luke when I was so young. I would hate that part, starting over, having to be charming to new people, pretending, being sexy—"

"But you—" he began, and then stopped, feeling to say anything about her lover would be an intrusion.

"That wasn't pretending," she said.

At that moment Nurse Chen returned and slid in next to Alix. She was holding a paper bag, so evidently she really had been doing an errand. "Everything good?" she said in her softly inflected voice. "Having a good time?"

"It's delicious," Alix said.

"I have to watch my weight," said the nurse. "Otherwise I'd join you."

"You're so slim!" Alix exclaimed.

Noah looked at the two of them, two lovely women side by side. The Oriental nurse had smooth, almost poreless skin and delicately curved brows, too doll-like for his taste. But Leo, no doubt, would find something in both of them to be attracted to. It's a matter of attitude. He assumes all women are available and so, to him, they are. He never bothers checking for wedding rings; it's irrelevant.

On the way back to the hospital, Alix was silent. Noah found himself wondering what she had meant earlier when she'd spoken of having a plan, of the fact that from now on she wouldn't speak to him as often or as openly. It was curious. She was afraid for him because of what she thought of as his passivity, and he was afraid for her because of her rebelliousness, her desire to flout authority. He remembered a patient who had escaped and been brought back the last time he had been hospitalized. It had been a man, but all Noah could remember was his ashen face and staring eyes. He prayed that would not happen to Alix, not only for her sake, but because seeing it would horrify him.

For days before he was to be allowed out to teach, Noah went over the notes Selma had brought him. Sometimes, when she came on visits, she would test him, he would give her pretend lectures on various topics, like methods of birth control, or AIDS. They had agreed it was less important what he lectured about, than that he prove he could do it, take the right tone. "I think I was too personal before," he told her. "I have to stick to just the facts."

"I've outlined it for you," Selma said. She had circled the key points in red: Chastity. Celibacy. The importance of restraint. "I think it's that they want you to be like a parent, but talking to them about things their own parents might not want to talk about. Just be yourself."

Of all advice, that was the most incomprehensible to him. Hadn't it been by being himself that he'd gotten into trouble? "I'll try," he said.

Selma looked at him with her shining eyes. "Your only problem is that you worry too much," she said. "You always do things fine, but you *think* you're doing something wrong."

"No," Noah insisted, touched by her belief in him. "I actually do sometimes do something wrong."

She squeezed his hands. "Everyone does, all the time. I do, every day. But the difference is, I just figure I've done my best, and the next time maybe I'll do better. Promise me not to let yourself think thoughts like that, okay? Promise?"

"I promise."

The one most terrible thought Noah had was that Mr. Garofolo would sit in on the class. He was sure that, if nothing else, might upset him. But on the morning he was to set out, Selma said, "I'll be in back of the class, sweetie. Just look at me if you feel nervous."

"Will anyone else be there?" he asked anxiously.

"Just Loretta Rauch. And she likes you, Noah. Really. She told me how awful she thought it was that Mr. Garofolo had you locked up that day."

Noah shrugged. "I guess he thought I was dangerous."

Selma's mouth was severe. "That's absurd."

The other patients knew why he was leaving for the day. They watched him curiously. Alix, who had been staying away from him, touched his shoulder lightly. "Good luck," she said.

Selma was driving him to the school. She had brought a fresh set of clothes, a tie, a jacket. It was hot, but the air conditioner had broken down long ago and had never been fixed. Noah rolled down the window.

"Pretend this is an ordinary day," Selma said.

"Yes," Noah said.

He tried remembering what an ordinary day was like. There must have been hundreds, thousands, of days when he had come to class half consciously, read from his notes, gone through the motions, not even thought about doing well, or doing badly, having no concept of what that meant. His previous breakdown had taken place over the summer when school was not in session, and by the time he recovered, another session was beginning. *Pretend that's what's happening now. You've had a bad experience, but it's just like an illness. You're a little weak, convalescing, but fine. Selma is right; Leo is right. Everyone does wrong things, but they don't let it bother them; they just go on, they don't brood, analyze, chew it over.*

At the sight of the school building, he cringed. It looked so formidable, like a prison, the heavy ugly brick building, the streams of noisy, yelling kids. If only he'd chosen a different profession, one where he didn't need to deal with people. His father had owned a small jewelry store and, as a child, he occasionally sat in the back, drawing, while his father dealt with customers. But they came in so infrequently that he thought his father must hate his job. He always had classical music on the radio, which he turned down when a customer came in. Now, Noah realized that it was when there were no customers that his father was happiest, when he could sit quietly, polishing or fixing some intricate piece of jewelry, immersed in his work and the music, almost oblivious to Noah's presence. When Noah's mother badgered his father about opening a larger store in a better neighborhood, he would always say, "I'm content with things as they are." She always snorted at that, taking it as an excuse, but perhaps he had genuinely, as Noah felt he himself never had, come to terms with his own deficiencies and had no need to put himself in a situation where the pressure might bother him.

Too late for that. He *was* in such a situation. *But you like kids. That's why you chose teaching.* He would look at the kids he liked, or at Selma. He was sorry Loretta Rauch was going to take part, but perhaps that was inevitable, and, according to Selma, she was on his side. It was she, in fact, who was waiting at the doorway as they came in. Selma was holding his arm. "This is wonderful," Loretta said. "We're so glad to have you back!"

"Thanks," Noah replied weakly. He had forgotten how noisy it was, like a zoo. Probably when you came in every day you got used to it.

He and Selma followed her back to her office. His office was changed. Clearly someone else was using it. That fact, perfectly natural, disquieted him. Was there any point in today, really? Garofolo would never let him back as a teacher. *Yes, the point is to show you can do it, to return to the scene of the crime. No, not crime. Just to return, to start over—you can get other jobs.*

Loretta was patting her face with a handkerchief. "Isn't this weather ghastly? Usually it isn't until June that it gets this way." She looked down at her handkerchief. "Whoops, my face is coming off." To Selma she said, "You're lucky, you just need powder."

Selma smiled. She was nervous, Noah could tell. Like him, she was dressed too neatly. New shoes, a new handbag, as though they were auditioning for some kind of play. He glanced at his watch. Ten minutes until the class started.

"Now, Noah," Loretta said. "The main thing is, don't worry

about a thing. I'm not sitting in to spy on you, or check up on you, or anything! It's only to make you feel at ease. Just ignore us."

"Then why are you coming to class?" he asked, knowing his voice sounded belligerent.

She flushed. "Oh, well, I thought . . . we thought it might make you feel better."

"No," Noah said. "I think I'd rather not have you sit in, if that's possible."

She looked at Selma. "It isn't possible. I have to, but I won't say a word. I promise. I don't even know that much about the subject you're talking about. It's not like I'm an expert. I'm not there to judge."

"Not even my behavior?" he said. "Isn't that why you're there?"

Selma took his arm. "Don't, Noah. . . . We're glad you could come, Miss Rauch."

"Thank you." She looked relieved at this intervention.

Walking to class flanked by the two women, he felt annoyed with himself at his outburst, yet also angered by arriving that way. How could he pretend it was a regular class with the two of them sitting there? *Don't look at them. They'll be in the back. Pretend they're not there.*

Selma and Loretta parted from him and moved to the back of the classroom. He went to the front and sat down, pretending to consult his notes. Selma's red circles and numbers flew up at him. Then he became aware that Angie Cortez was standing in front of his desk. He looked up. "Hello, Angie," he said.

She smiled with her radiant, otherworldly smile. "I had my baby," she said.

"I'm glad. Was it a boy or a girl?"

"A boy. I named him after you. Is that all right?"

"I'm very honored." He wished she would move away.

"It's good that you're back, Mr. Epstein," Angie said. "I heard you were sick. Are you better now?"

"Yes, Angie," Noah said. "I'm better now."

Who had been teaching the class in his absence? What had the other teacher been lecturing on? He should have checked, or had Selma check into that. *It doesn't matter. Lecture on anything you feel comfortable with.* Turning to the blackboard he wrote down the five main methods of contraception. The classroom was, as Loretta had predicted, swelteringly hot, though it wasn't yet nine in the morning. "Hi class!" Noah said when the bell rang, and they quieted down. "It's good to see you again."

Ronnie, the stout black girl who always sat up front, said, "Are you going to be our teacher again, Mr. Epstein?"

"I hope so, Ronnie."

She stood up. "Here's something we did for you while you were gone." She placed a stack of handmade cards on his desk. Some had flowers, others just writing. He flipped one open. "Get well soon. We miss you." For a moment, his heart fluttered. He tried to speak. "This is very . . . Thank you," he murmured, trying not to lose control. Then he pointed to the board. "I thought today we'd go over the various methods of contraception," he said.

"We did that already," Crosby Barnes said. "We know that stuff."

"Do you?" Noah said. "Well, why don't you explain to us what the different methods are, Mr. Barnes."

"Who me?"

"Yes, you."

"I'm not a girl, though."

Noah turned to the blackboard. "Are all these methods for girls?"

Crosby looked uncomfortable. "Not the first one."

"Tell us about that one, then, how it's used, what it's for." Noah liked his own commanding, take-charge tone.

Crosby wrinkled his nose. "Well, it's this rubber thing. You put it on—"

"When?" Noah interjected.

"When, you know, you're about to do it, and then, when it's over, you take it off. Only I personally don't like them. I wish the girl would do her part."

"What do you consider the girl's part to be?"

"One of those other ways. She ought to go to some clinic or whatever. Rubbers are nasty things."

"But they're useful for more than just birth control," Noah said. He looked out at the sea of teenage faces. "Does anyone know what other purpose they serve?"

Todd O'Malley raised his hand. "AIDS," he said.

"Right," Noah said. "Good for you, Todd. But what is the best method of all?"

They stared at him. Angie shyly raised her hand. "Being a virgin," she said.

The class laughed.

Undaunted, she went on in her quiet voice. "Even if you've done it, you can still go back to being a virgin, being *like* a virgin."

Afraid she would be ridiculed, Noah said, "You mean the best method is either abstaining, or making love with only one partner, someone whom you love and trust." Inadvertently he glanced back at Selma. Her face was intent.

"Yes," Angie said. "Like your wife, or your husband."

Like a winged creature flying in the window, a flash memory of Ava Bernier appeared, not her so much as the feeling he had had in bed with her, that his hands were covered with blood. Noah looked down at his hands. In fact, some of the ink from Selma's notes had come off on the palms of his hands, which were streaky and red. He forced himself to look up. "If you betray someone, you will die," he said.

The class fell silent, ominously so.

"You will be punished, I mean," Noah said. Again he looked down at his hands.

Angie asked, "Will God punish you?" She looked frightened.

"Yes," Noah said angrily. "God, or whoever you believe in, or don't believe in. You, Angie, were punished. You had a child out of wedlock, and that will follow you all your life wherever you go, just as my sins will follow me."

"Oh," she whimpered. Her small white face crumpled. She began to cry.

Suddenly Noah felt he had done a cruel, an unjust thing. Why single her out in front of everyone? Moving from behind his desk, he went over to her desk and knelt at her feet. "Forgive me," he said. "That was wrong."

Angie was still crying quietly. Noah put his hands out and took hers. "Please forgive me," he said. Then he noticed with horror that the red ink on his hands had come off on hers. Her skin was so fair that the red stains looked worse, like ugly sores. "Oh my God," Noah said. He buried his face in his hands.

The next thing he knew, Selma had come forward and was pulling him to his feet. Loretta Rauch moved to the front of the room. "Students," she said. "Mr. Epstein is very tired. He's been ill . . . Will you all wait here while he goes to rest?"

"No, I'll be fine," Noah said. "I was just—it was the red ink. It looked like blood. Please, let me continue."

Loretta's face was blotchy with agitation. "No, do stop, Noah, you can't go on."

"I can," he said. "Leave me alone. Let me teach. That's all I ask. I'm not trying to take your job away from you. Why are you trying to take mine away from me?"

Selma tugged at him. "Noah," she whispered.

The class was beginning to murmur among themselves.

Noah turned to the class. "Do you want me to teach?" he yelled. "Tell me. We'll have a vote, a show of hands. All in favor of my continuing to teach, raise their hands."

Most of the hands went up. He turned triumphantly to Loretta Rauch, who was still standing at his side, clenching her fingers. "See!" He pointed to the get-well cards piled on his desk. "*They* want me to continue. Just because you, or Mr. Garofolo, have different ideas about teaching, why does that allow you to disrupt my class? *You're* not a teacher, *he's* not a teacher."

"This is my duty," Loretta Rauch said, obviously trying to keep up her own courage. "I'm here to—"

"To what?" Noah bellowed. "To make a mockery of this class! That's all! To humiliate me in front of my students. Well, it didn't work, so why don't you leave?"

She stood there uncertainly. "I—"

Again Noah turned to the class. "Does anyone here want Ms. Rauch to stay and supervise this class? If so, please raise your hands."

The class, uneasy, just sat there.

Noah pointed to the door. "Leave!" he ordered.

Looking over her shoulder, she scurried out. Only then did Noah notice Selma, who was standing to one side, pale, her eyes large. "Darling, sit down," he said. To the class he said, "Class, this is my wife, Selma. Whenever I talk to you about love, about what it means, I'm talking about her."

The class applauded. Selma, red-faced, looked at the ground. The sight of her so flustered and anxious made Noah's heart turn over. Suddenly he did, in fact, feel physically exhausted. He sat down. "I have been ill," he said in a much softer voice. "That's true. I'm on certain drugs that weaken my system."

Ronnie raised her hand. "I thought you told us not to take drugs, Mr. Epstein, that they aren't good for you."

"You're right, Ronnie, they're not. But doctors believe in them, and so—but let me just say, because I fear Ms. Rauch is going to reappear any moment, let me just tell you how happy I am to see all of you again, what a pleasure it is to teach you. Teaching is my life. It's all I have." His voice started trembling. "That's why I hate it that they're trying to take it away from me, that they—"

The next moment the door to the classroom burst open. It was not Miss Rauch, but two huge, burly security guards who came in and hoisted Noah up by the arms and started carrying him out the door as though he were a piece of furniture. "Stop!" he yelled, humiliated. "I'll go. I was finishing up anyway. Selma! Help me!"

Selma ran beside the burly men, trying vainly to get their attention. "Please let him down," she begged. "He's not dangerous. He's a peaceful man. He's weak. He's been ill."

But she might have been a moth fluttering in the air; they totally ignored her, just carried him out the front door of the building where they deposited him on the steps. It was only then that they turned to Selma. "You got a car, lady?"

She nodded, petrified.

"You get this guy out of here, and back to the nuthouse, understand?"

Selma nodded. Both she and Noah stood there, stunned.

"Get going," one of the men said again, "or we'll call the police."

Silently, they both scurried down the steps and toward the car. Selma unlocked it and got in behind the driver's seat. Noah got in next to her. She turned to him, on her face an expression so sorrowful that it was more painful than anything that had happened thus far. "Oh, Noah," she whispered. "How could you?"

At that she burst into tears and flung herself into his arms. In one way there was a delicious, immense comfort in holding her, in comforting her, as though the security guards had been muggers from whom he had rescued her. But the thought that he was the cause of her distress, that he had made her suffer, destroyed the pleasure. "Oh, Sel, I love you so much. I just—having them spy on me, treat me like a criminal—"

She was quieting down slightly. "But why did you say those things? About death and punishment, making that little girl cry?"

"I shouldn't have. It's just—how will she learn, otherwise? She's so fragile. She lets people take advantage of her. Her child is a boy, and she's named him after me. She loves me, Selma, but it's a pure love. Do you believe me? I've never laid a hand on her. I never would, not in a million years."

"Of course I believe you," she said.

They sat in despairing silence in the car. "It was the ink," Noah said, half to himself.

"What ink?"

"You used red ink. It came off on my hands. It looked like blood, somehow. That was what upset me."

Frowning, Selma started up the car.

"Where are we going?" Noah asked, startled.

"Back to the hospital."

He grabbed her hand. "No, please, I don't want to go back. I can't. Please don't make me."

Selma looked frightened. "But I have to, Noah. It's against the law not to. I promised. They said, 'Bring him right back after class.' They could put me in jail!"

He took her hands. "No, no, they couldn't, they wouldn't. Don't you see? They're trying to frighten you, the way they tried to frighten me. I see it all now. I've talked to Leo, I've talked to Alix—that patient you met. They both say my judgment is fine. They say my problem is I'm too self-critical, too honest. Play the game, they say."

"Yes, that's true," Selma said. "But—"

He knew he was squeezing her hands too hard, but he couldn't let them go. "Let me go home with you," he begged. "We can start over. I'll get a new job. Maybe one where I don't have to deal with people so much. I could enter the jewelry business like my father. My cousin still owns the store. Maybe he'd let me help out and then gradually, if it goes well, we could become partners."

Selma's face was still worried. "But that's in Cleveland," she said.

"So? We'll move. We'll sell our house, and buy another. We can make it. Maybe Leo will lend us a little." He felt excited, wanting to win her over.

"It might be a good idea," Selma said, "but not now, Noah. We have to check into it. We don't know if your cousin wants another worker. And you've never had any experience in that line of work."

"I can learn," he said. "I'm not a fool. I used to watch my father. I know more than you think. I might have to start at the bottom, but so what? We have each other. Isn't that all that counts? All I need to make me happy is you. That's all."

Selma hugged him. "Oh, me too," she said. "I love you, Noah. I just want you to get well. But I have to take you back to the hospital. After that we can talk to the doctors. When they think it's time for you to leave, you can leave."

"What if they never think it's time?"

"They will, of course they will. We have to trust them."

It occurred to him that he could make a break for it right then, run away, hide somewhere, start a new life somewhere on his own, but that would mean leaving Selma behind, and she was his lifeline. Leo would say it was naïve, foolish, but without her, he felt he would cease to exist. "All right," he said. "Let's go back, then."

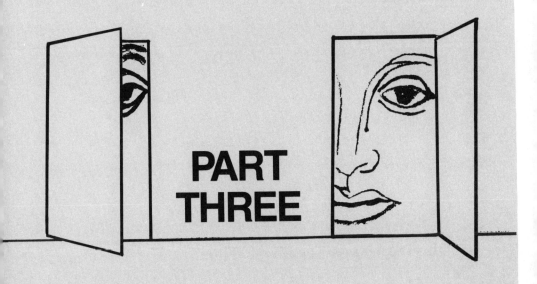

PART
THREE

SEVENTH
HEAVEN

Grieff had had a stroke. Stern learned about it early Monday morning when Szell stood up and in his flat, unemphatic voice said, "I'm afraid I have to announce a sad event which took place over the weekend. Dr. Grieff has suffered a stroke." He paused for emphasis.

"How serious is it?" Sharon Wishnick asked.

"It appears to be fairly serious, but of course it will be weeks before the doctors are sure how permanent the damage has been. At the moment he is able to communicate mainly in writing. His verbal or vocal capacities are evidently severely impaired."

"Would it be all right if we visit him?" Sharon went on.

Szell stretched his neck, a gesture Grieff used to say reminded him of a giraffe. "I think visits, one or two each day, might be a good idea. But it's important that he not be tired. His capacities to interact are, of course, limited. I've been to see him myself and I had the feeling he was pleased to see me."

Chaskes stood up. "What about his case load? Will that be divided up?"

"Yes, we'll work on that . . . For the meantime, let's try our best to carry on as usual. Dr. Grieff has been with us for many years. He knows that the institution is more important than any mere individual. That is what he would want."

Stern thought how in some ways Grieff would have been content to see Nash burn to the ground and watch most of them go up in flames inside it. No, too strong, but there was little love lost between Grieff and most of the other staff. He lacked Szell's graciousness in getting them to accept difficult decisions. He could be cantankerous, brusque, baiting. He regarded most of them as fools.

When the talk reverted to their patients, Stern took the floor. "I'd like to suggest a series of ECT treatments for Mr. Epstein. Ever since he returned from his attempt at teaching, he seems almost catatonic. He hardly speaks in the therapy sessions. We've tried various other drugs on him. Nothing seems to make a dent."

"Didn't he have a series like that the last time he was hospitalized?" Bernard Menschel asked. "They don't seem to have helped."

"On the contrary," Stern said. "Before he had them he was agitated, nervous. After them he was much calmer, able to engage again in teaching. It gave him ten years of life."

"Has his wife agreed?"

"She will. She sees he's in bad shape. She wants him to get better. We won't have any problems with her."

"An equitable decision," Szell said. "Well, I see our time is running out." He glanced at Stern. "Could you stay on, Dr. Stern? There's something I want to talk to you about."

"Certainly." Stern had half an hour until his first patient. He waited impatiently as the rest of the staff filed out. Through Sharon Wishnick's blouse, from the back, he could see the fine line of her bra strap. It was the kind that slid into a hook. He thought briefly of Roxanne's breasts, of her slipping out of her bra, smiling at him . . .

Szell closed the door so that they were alone. "Well," he said, "I was sorry to have to break the news of Dr. Grieff's illness to you. I know how close you were, that he was both a mentor and a friend."

"Yes," Stern said. "I'm terribly sorry to hear about it. I'll try and see him tonight."

"He'd like that." Szell cleared his throat. "This is a difficult matter for me and, of course, nothing is decided yet, and I hope you'll regard anything I say as being in the strictest confidence."

"Of course," Stern said.

"The fact is," Szell went on, "we don't really know to what extent Dr. Grieff will recover or, if he does, whether that recovery will permit him to continue his duties here as associate director. Or, I should add, whether he would wish to continue. He has a private practice, as you know."

"Yes," Stern said. Though he also knew Grieff's practice had fallen off in the past ten years.

Szell's grey eyes were like stones, unreadable. He had a small wart on his left eyelid. "I appreciate your devotion and fondness for Dr. Grieff, and of course I've enjoyed having him as a colleague, but the fact is that in the past, oh, shall we say, half decade, he has angered and upset many of the staff here by his perfunctory, often irritable or jocular manner. I realize that he's simply trying to be direct, to, as he might put it, 'cut the crap,' but not everyone appreciates that style in a director. Someone more guarded, discreet, is often preferable."

He paused, as though wanting a response.

"He tends to pride himself on the very qualities you were referring to," Stern said. "Perhaps that's part of the problem."

"Yes . . ." Szell looked temporarily distracted again. "Here's what I want to suggest, Stuart. And naturally, any reaction you have, any decision need not be made right now. You can think it over. There's no need for a rush decision. What I wondered was would you consider taking over Dr. Grieff's position as associate director?"

Stern's heart began thumping. He had had fantasies along these lines for years, but knew Grieff would never step down. "Wouldn't that depend on Dr. Grieff's recovery?"

Szell looked away. "Well, it's hard to know how to put this. It *is* such a delicate matter. But I have to say that, recovered or not, I'm not positive we are serving the institute's best interests in having Dr. Grieff in this position. Nor his, ultimately. Partly I think all institutions need new blood, as it were, new ways of looking at things. What I thought was that in the interim period, while Dr. Grieff is recovering, you might temporarily take over his position. Then, as things progress, if you feel happy with the job and we feel happy with you, we might indicate to Dr. Grieff that he could return, as many psychiatrists do at his age, to private practice exclusively. It may well be that he would want to step down, in any case, not only as a result of this illness, but just wanting to ease off a bit. And needless to say, I can't imagine anyone he would be happier to see take over his job than you."

How little he knew Grieff, how this conversation would horrify and appall him. "I'm going to see him later in the day," Stern said. "Should I mention anything about this?"

Szell shook his head emphatically. "Absolutely not. He's still very ill. Any excitement, news of any kind must be totally kept from him. I would go to see him just as a friend of whom you're fond. No talk of Nash at all."

"That was what I intended, actually," Stern said.

"He asked after you," Szell said. "Clearly you're like a son to him. He's made that remark to me many times."

"Yes," Stern said, "I know." He wished that the conversation with Szell had taken place after he had been to see Grieff, or that he had simply taken on the job of acting associate director without knowing the plan to ax Grieff. He could pretend, he would certainly try to, but Grieff had that uncanny way of being able to see through him. Getting the job would be a major promotion. Sydney would be ecstatic. And he had to admit that the thought of not having to see Grieff at work, of only seeing him once every few months for dinner was a wonderful one. No fear that he would peer into the office with his mischievous smile, his probing remarks. If he was truly Grieff's son or his symbolic son, anyway, wasn't cutting the umbilical cord long overdue for both of them?

Thoughts of Grieff led without a pause into thoughts of Roxanne. She had called him three weeks earlier. Every day he had wondered how she was doing, if she had been released yet. Every day he moved to the phone, sat there, receiver in hand, and then set it down. Now, impulsively, he darted into his office and called her ward. "This is Dr. Stuart Stern. I was wondering if you could tell me whether Roxanne Arlen is still a patient in your unit?"

"No, she was released a week ago, Dr. Stern."

"I see . . . Thank you."

So, she was at home, presumably. Or, who knows, maybe she'd gone somewhere on a trip, to rest, to rethink various plans. It disquieted him to think of her at home, even though he had wanted her out of the hospital. He had thought that having her sick and in such close proximity was worse. *But you only went to see her that once. You used some sense. You held back. Even when she called, you restrained*

*yourself, didn't suggest seeing her, said only that you wanted to remain friends
. . .* Then he remembered calling her "darling" at the very end of
the phone conversation. *But that was a natural reflex. You'd used that
term of endearment with her so many times.*

She was at home now, or could be. Therefore, technically, he
could call her or go to see her. *But you won't. You know better. She had
a crisis, it passed, she's come to terms with her life, with losing you, to the extent
that was the cause of her breakdown. Leave it as it is.* What if her doctor
had fallen in love with her? Who had her doctor been? Should he
try to find out? *No, it's over, what does it matter? The last thing she'd do
would be to get involved with another doctor at Nash. She'd have more sense
than that.*

His first session of the day was with Alix Zimmer. Stern recalled
Grieff's comment right after his first session with her. "She has you
by the balls already, huh?" The battle of wills she had set up between them made him wary. All his life he had been drawn to strong,
insightful, iconoclastic women, but if they became sexually involved, he felt a certain pride in subduing that. Roxanne understood him, but she loved him, so it was a winnable battle, with
pleasure in its tensions. What galled him about Alix Zimmer was the
contempt she could not keep out of her glances and expressions, no
matter how hard she tried. It was like a chess competition stalled in
the end game, both players canny, careful, locked in combat. If he
allowed her to be released, she would have won. So he hesitated,
and the game continued.

"So, are you enjoying your work at the counseling center?" he
asked. He had allowed her to go there three times a week to do filing
and minor clerical jobs.

"Yes, I am," she said. "It's been good for me."

"Doesn't it make you feel depressed? Those women are hardly
your intellectual equals."

"They're competent. I don't think they need to be brighter than
they are."

"But to take orders from women who are half as bright as you
are must be, on some level, humiliating."

"I'm not that arrogant." With a slight smile.

"No?" He smiled back.

"I know my talents, but I don't want to take over the world."

Stern crossed his legs. "Ms. Zimmer, for some reason, though you've never discussed it in these sessions, after initially befriending, more than befriending, Noah Epstein, you seem to have totally dropped him. Is there some reason for that?"

She hesitated. "I wasn't sure I was good for him."

"In what way?"

"He appears to have a lot of women in his life giving him advice—his mother, his wife. I don't think he needs another."

"How about the pleasure you derived from the relationship?"

"What pleasure?"

"Why don't you tell me?" He paused, pencil in hand.

"He's a thoughtful, intelligent man, weak, but—"

"Like your husband?"

"Not really, no."

"Like your former lover?"

She flushed. "No, Gerald was much more sure of himself, iconoclastic. If I had any feeling about Noah, it was that he was like a brother I might have had. I supposed he aroused a maternal instinct."

"You're speaking in the past tense. He's still a patient here."

"I decided my behavior was inappropriate. He seemed to have the feeling I was coming on to him."

"Were you?"

"No. But if he felt that, it seemed wise to desist with even friendly overtures."

"Why do you think he felt that?"

"He seems naïve about women. I don't think he knows how to interact with them casually, as I do with men all the time at work."

"But it was an interaction at work that led to your five-year love affair, wasn't it?"

"No, that was completely different."

"In what way?"

"Gerald was someone who—I think one knows at once what one is feeling, if the person is a member of the opposite sex, whether one acts on that or not. I've never felt sexually attracted to Noah."

"Nor to anyone else since you've come here?"

"No."

"You don't miss being sexually active?"

"I think that part of me is still dormant."

"Does that frighten you? The thought that it might never return?"

"I think it will return."

"With your husband? Or with another lover?"

"With my husband, I hope."

He cleared his throat. "You seemed very eager to leave when you first arrived here, Ms. Zimmer. You haven't discussed that in some time."

"No, I—I realized I had to get myself in shape first, that when I did I would be released."

"Do you feel you're in shape now?"

"Yes."

"So, you expect to be released shortly?"

"I hope I will be."

"The staff doesn't seem as confident about your progress as you appear to be. They find you're still unwilling to share your thoughts, even with the other patients."

Her eyes flashed angrily. "Yet when I did, with Noah, it was interpreted as a sexual come on. Heads you win, tails I lose."

"Is that how you see it?"

She hesitated. "Only sometimes."

"Isn't there a cost to being the way you are now?"

"Not for me."

"You don't feel isolated, alone, estranged from your husband, fearful he may have found someone else?"

"No."

"Perhaps that's part of the problem," Stern said. "Most other women in your position would have those fears."

"I'm not most women."

He had stopped thinking that she was like Roxanne. Only occasionally something in their proud, bristly clashes reminded him of some of the denouements of their worst quarrels when, after violence and screaming, Roxanne would look at him exactly as Alix Zimmer did now, with black, scornful eyes. "You don't think that's an arrogant remark?"

"No, I don't."

"Your husband is handsome, he interacts with women all day, some of them surely attractive, appealing, perhaps younger than yourself. None of that worries you?"

"No."

"Because you wouldn't care if it did happen? You'd feel it would even the score, as it were?"

"I don't think of it in terms of keeping scores."

"And the possibility of other women?"

"That's always been there, it always will be, for anyone."

"But now that you aren't sexually accessible to your husband, wouldn't he be at greater risk, more vulnerable?"

She was obviously trying to hold herself in. "I don't think so. I hope not."

"You feel that his love for you is so strong that nothing can shake it?"

"I can only hope it is."

"It wasn't strong enough for him to get you released, though, was it?"

"I don't believe that was out of lack of love."

"What, then?"

"He believes the doctors here know what's best to get me well."

"And you believe that too?"

She hesitated. "Yes."

Stern was shocked when he saw Grieff lying in the hospital bed. He was leaning back, the bed propped up just slightly, but he looked half his normal size, tiny, shrunken; his round face like a child's, white; his hair disheveled. Only his eyes retained his alertness. Or did they? Perhaps that had gone also. If so, it would be easier.

Stern sat down next to his bed. "Hi," he said. "This is an awful mess you've gotten yourself into."

Grieff pointed to the bedside table. On it were a small pad and pencil. Stern handed it to him. Grieff wrote slowly and then showed the note to Stern. It said, "Talking difficult. Mind if I write?"

Stern said, "Not at all. How are you feeling?"

"Rotten," Grieff wrote back. "Scared."

"The doctors seem to feel you'll recover," Stern said. "It just may take time."

"Doctors!" Grieff wrote.

"How've they been treating you?" Stern asked.

"Like a patient," Grieff wrote. "Like shit."

Stern hesitated. "We miss you."

Grieff wrote, "We?"

"Everyone at Nash. Me especially."

Grieff just smiled ironically. Then he wrote, "Did Mort announce my illness at the staff meeting?"

Stern nodded.

"What did he say?" Grieff wrote.

"That he hoped your recovery would be rapid, that we should all try to carry on normally."

Grieff wrote, "Who's going to be acting director?"

Stern hesitated. His inclination would have been to lie and say, "No one," but the truth could get back to Grieff and, in any case, having an acting director was a normal procedure. He pointed to himself.

A slow grin spread over Grieff's face. "Excited? Happy?" he wrote.

Stern shook his head.

"Your nose is longer," Grieff wrote.

Stern just shrugged.

When Grieff took the pad again, he wrote for a long time, slowly. Stern finally took the sheet; it read "Szell will try to offer you my job. Refuse it, okay? He's looking for an excuse to ax me. This is perfect."

Stern raised his eyes. "Of course," he said.

He was not aware of having paused, even momentarily, before his reply. But there passed across Grieff's face an expression so knowing, so sad, so cynical, that it was clear he perceived everything that had happened. He lay there, just staring at Stern and finally a slow, weakened version of his old grin flickered at the corners of his mouth as though to say, if nothing else, he could still take pleasure in his ability to take the world's measure. Then he leaned forward and replaced the pad and pencil on the bedside table.

"Tired?" Stern managed to ask.

Grieff nodded and then closed his eyes. Watching him it was clear to Stern that he was not asleep, but also that he would not open his eyes again while Stern was present. Slowly Stern got up and left the room.

Because daylight savings time had started, it was just light enough to jog, although the shadows were deepening by the time Stern reached the park. But after leaving the hospital, he had felt a sick, hollow feeling, self-disgust annihilating his hoped for feeling of freedom. *You had to take the job; you couldn't afford to turn it down. You didn't cause his stroke. His erratic behavior brought on what happened . . . But what about my own erratic behavior? Who will shield me now?*

He ran doggedly, wanted to exhaust himself, going beyond his usual limit. The result was that when he staggered back to his apartment, he felt almost dizzy with fatigue. He took a long, hot shower, letting the water beat down on his body until the heat got to him and he had to emerge. After dinner, a heated-up casserole and a glass of wine, he felt restored. Not ebullient, but infinitely better. It wasn't nine, but he called Sydney.

It took a long time until she answered. When she finally did, her voice was muffled, hoarse and groggy. "Oh, hi, sweetie."

"How are you? You sound terrible."

"I am, I'm a mess. I thought I might be coming down with something, but then I felt better. This morning I had a hundred and one, and I've literally just slept the day away . . . But, 'twill pass."

"Poor darling."

"I know. I get sick so seldom, I forget what it's like. How are you? I hope you didn't pick it up from me over the weekend."

"I'm terrific," Stern said. Then he told her about his promotion, first mentioning Grieff's illness.

Sydney had met Grieff a few times. "What a tragedy!" she said. "How terrible for him."

It disturbed Stern that her first reaction was to Grieff's illness rather than to his promotion. "I went to see him tonight. He seems fine mentally. He just has trouble speaking. He had to write everything down."

"But what if he recovers? Daddy's best friend had a stroke and was just like that, and now he's right as a trivet. Wouldn't he want to go back as associate director, then?"

"Well, it's partly that his manner evidently irritates a good many of the staff. And, as Dr. Szell said, they feel a need for new blood, new ideas."

"I suppose," Sydney said languidly. "I can't help but feel it will be a terrible blow to him, the fact that it was done behind his back that way."

"Are you saying I shouldn't have accepted?" Stern said. "I thought you'd be delighted. It's such an important step for me."

"No, of course you should have accepted," Sydney said. "I'm just sorry for him because I think as men age they're aware enough of losing their powers, and to be let go so brutally . . . Well, maybe I'm being sentimental. This is the way the world works. 'Brutal' is too strong . . . I'm just so zonked. Once you come next weekend, we'll have a proper celebration."

"I hope I can do a decent job," Stern blurted out. "I could be getting in disastrously over my head."

"Oh, of course you'll do a wonderful job," Sydney said. "Did you tell Dr. Grieff that you would be taking over?"

"No, Szell seemed to feel it would be better to wait until he recovered."

"Still," Sydney said, "I can't imagine there's anyone he'd rather see in the job than you. He's helped you so much all along the way."

"Yes," Stern said.

She sighed. "Sweetie, I think I really better sign off. I can hardly speak I'm so tired. But congratulations. It really is wonderful news. I'll tell Mommy and Daddy. They'll be in seventh heaven."

"Take care of yourself," he said.

Of course, Sydney's being ill had affected her reaction to the news. But it still disturbed him. He had wanted her, with her usual sunny, ebullient manner, to make it seem unequivocally splendid. It was her almost resolute perkiness he depended on, as though it would shield him as well as her. He had never let her see through to the fears of failure that had dogged his life with such hideous persistence from adolescence on. He loved her for her not probing into what his family life had been, for seeming to accept him as he hoped to appear. But his colleagues? Was he safe now? The investigation into Blades's death had quieted down. Perhaps the appointment would silence it finally.

When the announcement was made at the staff meeting the following day, that Stern would become acting director, Dr. Menschel asked, "Is there any indication of when Dr. Grieff will be able to return full time?"

"Not yet," Szell said. "But I'll be seeing him and will keep you informed."

Stern had the feeling some of them suspected what was going to happen. Jonah Welch came over after the meeting and clapped him on the shoulder. "Hey, nice going."

"It's a temporary thing," Stern said quickly.

Welch winked. "You never can tell . . . play your cards right and you'll be running the place before too long."

Stern smiled nervously. He knew that the hardest part would be the first year or two since at that point the staff would still consist mainly of doctors who had started when Grieff was associate director. But in five years time he would be totally accepted, assuming he did a reasonable job. Meanwhile he would try at all costs to act low key, unobtrusive. No drugs ever, especially not at work.

He had a meeting with Noah Epstein's wife toward the end of the day. It was to get her permission for the ECT schedule which was to begin in two weeks time. She sat nervously at the edge of her seat, wide-eyed, twisting her wedding ring around and around. "It's just . . . I don't think Noah wants the treatments," she said. "He's afraid they hindered his ability to remember things, that they might have caused some of his problems."

"But, Mrs. Epstein, don't you feel that having ten years of recovery, as your husband did, is a pretty stunning refutation of that?"

"It wasn't permanent though," she pointed out.

"Perhaps it can't be." He paused. "I think we may have to face the fact that your husband will always have a difficult time functioning in the world as it is. That, as you know, is the case with many gifted, sensitive human beings."

Her face lit up. "Yes," she breathed, "you're right. Noah is— he's almost too sensitive to things in some ways. It's such a pity that something so good, being sensitive, can cause someone problems."

"Well, clearly he's been fortunate in many ways, having such an understanding and sympathetic wife. We find that, in the end, that does more good than anything modern medicine can devise."

She looked troubled again. "I want to think that. It's not that I don't think I'm understanding or sympathetic, but I really *don't* understand Noah. We've been married all this time and I still don't. The way he thinks, why he gets so agitated, his mood swings . . . And that makes me feel I'm a failure as a wife, that perhaps he would have been better off with someone more intellectual, more—"

"On the contrary," Stern intervened, "acceptance and love far outweigh intellectual understanding. The fact that you will stand by him, no matter what—that's all any man wants or needs."

"Is it?" She smiled tearfully. Then she looked around the room. "But now that it's over I wonder—do you think it was a good idea to have Noah go back and try teaching again? It seems to have made him so much worse. If I'd known that—"

"How *could* you know? *We* didn't. Here at Nash we always try to balance what we feel is good for the patient and what the patient wants. Your husband seemed caught in a kind of bind, a crisis of self-identity, if you will, and he was insistent that going back to the scene of the crime—I believe he actually used that phrase several times—would be the cure. Alas, that was not the way it turned out."

Again she began twisting her wedding ring. "I think maybe I shouldn't have been in the room. Or Miss Rauch, the school counselor. You see, Noah does have rapport with his students. They love him. They really do. You should have seen the lovely notes they wrote to him when he was ill. But having us there, judging him, I think that made it harder."

"But wasn't that one of the conditions of the school," Stern asked, "that a school official be present? And we felt your presence might have the opposite effect, might be a stabilizing influence."

Mrs. Epstein sighed. "Yes, I'd hoped so . . . but I still wonder, wouldn't it be better for Noah just to go home? I could look after him."

"But you have a job, don't you? And if he's unemployed you'll certainly have to continue working."

"Yes, but I could call him during the day," she went on. "He seems so terribly unhappy here. He was crying the other day as though he couldn't stop."

"Mrs. Epstein," Stern said, "let's face it. Your husband *is* terribly unhappy. That has nothing to do with his environment. It has everything to do with his state of mind. Here he is being cared for by professionals. He is being watched so that, should any desperate thought occur to him, he would be protected. At home—"

She gasped. "You really think he might—"

"Yes, I'm afraid I do. And the effect shock treatment often has, which is so miraculous, is to smooth out all these despairing, troubled thoughts. They simply are erased from the brain, as it were, and the patient, without knowing why, has a wonderful sense of calm and quiet."

She stared out the window. "Well . . . I guess it has to be done then. Should I tell him?"

"No, I think we'd better handle that . . . but if you could sign these release forms for us, that's all that will be necessary." He slid the forms toward her and she obediently signed.

Then she stood up. "Thank you," she said. "You've been very understanding."

"Thank *you.*"

Women like her reminded him of little mice, scurrying hither and thither, easily moved in any direction. Those like Roxanne, with her bursts of temper and arrogance, were more appealing to him, but there was the whiplash of dealing with that day by day. Hopefully in Sydney he had a liveable combination—liveliness without excess intensity; a mind of her own, but no wayward impetuosity.

What happened that evening seemed to happen by chance. He reached for his address book to look up the name of a tailor someone had once recommended who made custom-designed suits. The tailor's name was directly above Roxanne's. Next to her name he had scribbled various different numbers: work, home, her mother, vacation numbers. His intention when he became engaged was to buy a new address book and throw this one away. He had had it for ten years. In some ways, though it contained nothing but names and addresses, it was like a diary of his past, women he had seen briefly. Now he was transfixed by the list of phone numbers near Roxanne's name, the several addresses. He found himself remembering the apartment she had lived in when they first started seeing each other. The bedroom had been so small that her bed took up almost the entire room. He remembered his first glimpse of the bed—it was an extra long king size, and the boldness of that gesture seemed, even then, both an invitation and a promise. Now she had a much larger bedroom, which doubled as a study, so that the same bed seemed much smaller. Sydney still had a single bed and he often, after they made love, slept on the pull-out bed in her study. *Tomorrow I'll buy a new address book.* He closed this one.

The trouble was, her phone number was as engraved on his memory as his name. For several moments he sat there. It reminded him of the time he had gone on a diet to lose fifteen excess pounds he had gained during medical school. He would sit trying not to think of food, and all he would be able to think of were things to eat. Even reading, visions of apple pies, sundaes, glasses of milk would float in front of him, making him unable to concentrate. And now all he could see in his mind's eye was Roxanne, naked, clothed, washing her hair, lying in the sun on her terrace, slicing melon, lighting candles, reaching out to him . . .

Without allowing himself to censor the motion, he reached for the phone and dialed her number. *Let her not be there. Let someone be with her.* "Hello?" came her soft voice.

"Roxanne? It's me, it's Stuart . . . I, I heard you had been released from the hospital. I'm so glad."

"Thank you," she said. She laughed lightly. "It was a relief to get out."

"How are you doing? Are you—"

"I'm well," she said. "Just resting, really. I quit my job, but I won't start looking for another one right away. I may go away for a while. I feel I need a change."

"Yes," he said, "that sounds like an excellent idea."

There was a moment of silence.

"And you?" she said.

"As well as can be expected," he said.

"What does *that* mean?"

"I'm fine." He looked down at the address book. "I wasn't sure I should call you. I don't want to do anything that might cause you any pain . . . but I think about you a lot. I guess what I was wondering was—would you like to see me?"

"Yes, I would," Roxanne said in a voice he couldn't interpret. "That would be lovely."

His heart started racing. "As I said, I—"

"Stuart, I know!" Roxanne said. "Please don't make me listen to that speech again. I *know* you're getting married. I know the whole thing. Can you promise me that if you come, you won't refer to it?"

"Of course," he said. "As long as you understand that—"

"I understand everything," she said.

What did that mean? "Well—" he began.

"Look, I have priorities too," she went on. "This isn't going to be come over for a farewell fuck, okay? You get that?"

"Of course, I didn't—"

"It's over. We both know that. I don't want any anguished crap about your being torn, or deep down, feeling undecided. I don't want one *word* about that! Do you understand?"

"Yes!" *Why could they, even now, not have a civilized, calm conversation?*

They arranged that he would come over Thursday evening. He didn't say he couldn't come on the weekend because he would be visiting Sydney. On the one hand, he wondered what this meeting was for, if they would not make love and not refer to his future with Sydney. But basically he felt she was right. They had had a thousand variants on the scene in which they broke up, resolved never to see each other again, scenes which had ended tearfully, erotically, with slammed doors and screams. It would be perfect if somehow this could be something different, quiet, calm, the emotion that flowed between them recognized, but not acted on. *Just be adults, civilized adults!*

He had once read that for most men there were two kinds of women—those who appeared beautiful or desirable the first time you saw them, and those who became more beautiful and desirable every time you looked at them. Roxanne, more than any woman he had ever known, was in the latter category. At this point he hardly knew if she was attractive or not. He had seen her looking ugly, her eyes puffed from crying, her hair wet and flattened to her head, her face distorted with anger, but there was always that other quality which made these seem like minor details, like a fleck of dust on an extraordinary painting. He was glad in many ways that Sydney's looks, lovely as they were, didn't affect and disturb him that deeply. When he saw Sydney's mother, he could imagine, with variations, how Sydney might look in several decades—the same delicate skin, fine bones, alert eyes, a certain feminine grace and dignity. But nothing that ever made his insides contract with longing or dread.

Roxanne was in slacks and a white shirt when he came over. He felt, uncontrollably, a feeling of disappointment. Somehow he had thought she might be in the silk bathrobe he had given her many years ago. It was black with shocking pink and purple dragons embroidered in heavy thread on the back. Both the dark color, the shimmer of the material, and the vivid design suited her. *Be glad. Don't be a fool. You don't want to see her in a bathrobe.* She wasn't wearing makeup and looked, he thought, paler than usual, but she had pale skin in any case. Her long, thick hair was brushed to one side, fastened with a barrette. "Hi, Stuart," she said.

It was warm in her apartment. She hated air conditioning, but the windows were thrown open and, because her apartment had a terrace overlooking the East River, there were cool breezes. "I hate this weather," she said.

"Yes, the heat is debilitating," he said. He moved awkwardly into the living room. It looked the same. For some reason she had always preferred that they come here rather than go to his apartment, although both apartments were the same size and both in good neighborhoods. At night she said it was because she didn't like having to go home when it was dark. But even when it was a clear pattern that they would spend the night together, or even the entire weekend, she still usually insisted they come here. In one way, he preferred it too. It meant that his phone would never ring with its intrusions of his other life. He wondered sometimes if she did it for the opposite reason, that she wanted him to know other men pursued her. Sometimes she would answer the phone, even when they were in bed together, and murmur something about being busy. Other times, she would let her answering service pick it up. If he would ask jealously who could be calling at that hour, she would reply sleepily, "Oh, Harry . . . or maybe Will."

Some of her boyfriends were ex-boyfriends whom she had known before she met him. Others she would meet during times when they broke up, and they would continue calling. One weekend she had gone on a retreat and started two new affairs: one with a priest from Montana who had been celibate for twenty years; another with a married English businessman. The priest wrote her long, pathetic, touching letters every day, and even threatened to leave the priesthood and come to New York to live with her. He did come on visits and once Stern had met him, a gentle man with pale blue eyes, who watched her with adoration. "He's such a darling," she would say, "but I couldn't bear the responsibility." The businessman sent her tickets to London, put her up at expensive hotels, took her to the opera. "Doesn't that make you feel like a kept woman?" he once asked, to which she replied, "You feel like what you are." Since neither of them, even when their relationship was most intense, had ever promised fidelity, he knew he had no formal right to complain, especially since he saw other women also, from time to time.

"Would you like a drink?" she asked.

"Just tonic is fine." He didn't want a trace of alcohol in his system, nothing that would prevent him from feeling and acting in a level-headed, unemotional way. As she poured it, he asked, "Have you started looking for another job or are you going to take a break?"

"Oh, I think I'll take a break," she said. She handed him the glass. Their hands touched briefly. "I'm seriously thinking of leaving the field, actually. Or at least trying something different."

"Like what?"

"Well, I have a master's in biology. I've thought maybe working in a lab could be interesting. Nothing with people any more. It's too frustrating. People get better, they get worse. I've seen half the nursing staff at Nash break down in one way or another, and I don't think that's exceptional. It seems like such a sham to me, somehow." She sat down, her legs crossed to one side.

Stern sat down in the chair, facing her. "A sham in that the cures aren't permanent?" he said.

"In that the whole system is a farce," she said. "No one knows what they're doing, and the higher up you get, the more confusion and deceit. Probably it's the world, but—"

"I'm not that cynical about it," Stern said.

She raised her eyebrows. "No?"

Carefully he said, "I mean I think anyone can be cynical, but still, as you say, it's the world. One does one's best and—"

"Yes, I know," she interrupted. "If you buy into the system, you have to believe in it, or pretend to. I just got sick of pretending, and of knowing everyone else was. It got to me, the daily deceit . . . but you're better at that."

He let the remark pass. "I've been promoted," he said. "Grieff is too ill to return to his job, he had a serious stroke, so I'll take over from him."

Roxanne ran her hand through her hair. She had evidently just washed it. It stood out in silky, electric strands. "Congratulations," she said dryly, in a tone that implied she knew all he had not said.

"Of course, it will make my leaving New York just about impossible," he went on.

"Why should you want to leave?"

"My marriage," he stammered. "Sydney being in Philadelphia."

"I thought that was one of the attractions," Roxanne said. "The double life. I thought you said living there all the time would drive you crazy."

He hesitated. It was impossible to have a conversation about anything which stayed on a casual level because she knew too much about him and because that was not how she ever conversed. "Perhaps it would," he said, thinking that to concede would be easier than to deny. "I'll have to see . . . I've never been married before."

"No?" Roxanne smiled. "I thought you might have been, somewhere in your dark, mysterious past."

"You know my past. I have no secrets from you."

"Don't you?"

"Not really. That was part of . . . well, should we even discuss this?"

"What are we discussing?"

"Our past."

"Why not? Since it's past, since we agree it's past."

Stern looked at her. He was wrong about her looking like Alix Zimmer. Her eyes were larger and had a golden light, even though they were brown. *No one will ever seem this beautiful to me.* "It's a fault of my character, perhaps," he said. "I didn't think I could live, day in, day out, with the kind of intensity we had. It was too explosive. But other men—"

"Yes," Roxanne said, "other men will love it. It will be just what they've always searched for." Her voice sounded bitter.

"How about Lionel?" He was the English businessman whose wife, since Roxanne had started the affair with him, had died.

"What about him?"

"You said he was single now. I thought—"

"Oh no, he's engaged. And he's like you. He wants stability and calm, quote unquote, and all the rest, meaning me, on the side. You and he have a lot in common, actually."

Stern set down the glass. "Anyway," he said, sidestepping, "you wouldn't have liked living in London, would you?"

"Probably not. And he traveled a lot so I either would have had to travel with him, become an appendage, or let him travel and fuck around the way he did in his first marriage. So it's all for the best, as you say." Her voice took on that acid edge again. "Not that he ever asked me, you understand."

"Men are fools," Stern said, unexpectedly.

Roxanne laughed. "Aren't they?"

"I just meant—"

"I know what you meant."

"We don't seem able to integrate emotion the way women do," he went on. "It's a pity."

"Yes, it *is* a fucking pity," Roxanne said furiously. "For us . . . but for you it's just a minor inconvenience, or not even that really, an advantage, because you can just have the double thing, as you say—one woman for this, one woman for that, however you choose to set it up."

"That doesn't solve everything,"

"Who said it did?"

The air was vibrating with the feelings he had hoped would not exist or, if they did, would be repressed. *Get a grip on yourself. Stop this. Start again.* He took a breath. "Some man will want what you have to offer," he said passionately. "Your beauty, your honesty—"

Instead of firing back a retort, she said almost in a whisper, "Will they?"

"Yes, I promise you. It has to be. What kind of world would it be, otherwise?"

Roxanne looked away. The dimming evening light cast soft

shadows on her face. "I don't understand the world anyway," she said. "I never have. I don't think I ever will. I see people making decisions that are sensible and right, and yet they don't make sense to me. I don't understand the way people live." She looked at him, as though appealing to him to explain it to her.

His heart flipped over. "We choose what we can handle," he said. "Most of us are cowards, we take the easy way out."

Roxanne leaned forward, her hair falling over her shoulders. "But I want that!" she cried. "I want the easy way out. I just don't seem to know what it is."

Leave. If you stay, you'll be caught. Leave now. But he sat there, transfixed by her voice, her pleading, anguished tone. "I'll never love anyone the way I loved you," he said.

"Loved?"

"Love."

She stared at him. "Yes," she said sadly, "I know."

Stern felt as though part of him had left the room, had gone home, and the part that remained was someone he wasn't responsible for, who would cease to exist once he left this apartment. "If you want me to break my engagement, I will," he said. "I'll do whatever you want. I'll never see Sydney again."

"All right," Roxanne said. "Do that. Call her now. Call her from here." Her eyes were aglow with excitement.

"Now?"

"Yes, right now! Or leave . . . and never come back." She walked into the kitchen and brought him the phone. "Here."

Without allowing himself time to think, Stern dialed Sydney's number. He prayed she would be out. "Oh, hi, Stu," came her voice, still a little hoarse from her cold. "I'm feeling *so* much better . . . How come you called now? It's only eight. Aren't you usually jogging?"

"I—" He looked up. Roxanne was standing, her arms crossed, her eyes enigmatic, watching him. "No, I will call later. I have to go now. Good-bye." He put down the receiver and then closed his eyes. "I'm sorry," he said to Roxanne. "I'm so sorry. I just couldn't."

He was shaking uncontrollably all over. He had thought she would rip the cord from the wall and hurl it at him, but instead she came over, knelt at his feet and laid her head in his lap. "That's okay," she said softly.

He stroked her silky hair over and over. "How despicable," he said, as though to himself. "It's just—"

"I understand," Roxanne said. "Don't explain."

"It doesn't change anything I said," Stern said, "or anything I feel . . . Do you believe me?" He lifted her face to look into her eyes.

"Yes, I believe you," Roxanne said.

They kissed, she kneeling in front of him, he leaning forward with her face in his arms. "Darling," he murmured. "My beautiful darling."

She stood up and began unbuttoning her blouse and unhooking her bra, still looking at him with that calm, transfixed expression.

"Should we?" he asked.

"Yes."

This is crazy. You know it's wrong. Why are you doing it? When she was naked except for her underpants, she came over and started unbuttoning his shirt. "You're cold," she said. "Your skin is so cold."

"Is this what you want?" Stern asked urgently. "Is it really what you want?"

"Yes," Roxanne said, touching his skin. "It *is* what I want. It's all I want."

They moved into the bedroom. The bed was made neatly and his mind leapt ahead and backwards, to other afternoons, clothes thrown on the floor, times when it had been so cold they had burrowed under the covers, times when their bodies had been moist from the heat even before they began. She had given him permission, and he tried to fight the feeling that he was doing something inexcusable and stupid. He forced that part of his consciousness to one side. How long had it been since they had made love? Months, weeks? What season had it been?

She touched and caressed him slowly, carefully, memorizing his body. Her movements seemed to him dreamy, as though they were both underwater. He let the feelings he had tried half successfully to repress well out of him, let the scent of her skin overwhelm him. He felt as though he were being sliced open; there was something violent and painful about it, along with the pleasure. *The last time, never again.*

When he came, he gripped her shoulders and let his mind dissolve. There was no room, he was no longer there, no one was there. He stayed inside her, wanting not to leave her body, wanting never to leave it.

Stern wasn't sure how much later it was when he awoke. The room was dark except for the streetlights he saw glimmering outside the windowed doors leading to her terrace. When the weather was lovely, they had often eaten out there or had an after-dinner drink by candlelight. "Where are you?" he called anxiously, disturbed at the quiet.

"I'm here," Roxanne said. She was half in the closet, slipping into the black bathrobe.

"Come back," he said. "I miss you."

What happened next took place so quickly and yet in an eerie kind of slow motion. He saw her move to the terrace doors and fling them open. "Good-bye," she called, lifting one hand, and then she was gone. She vanished. He never saw her disappear. She just wasn't there anymore.

For one second he thought she was outside, lighting the candle on the small wicker table, and even as he had that thought, he realized what had happened. "Please," he begged someone, getting out of bed, "anything else."

But there was no one on the terrace.

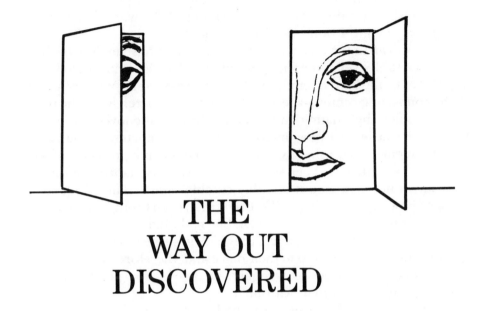

THE
WAY OUT
DISCOVERED

In one way Dr. Stern was right. It was demeaning and infuriating for Alix to go three times a week to the counseling center where she sat at a desk, organizing patient records according to a sloppily set-up filing system. In a week, in a day, had she been left alone, she would have reorganized the office. Instead she sat meekly and did as she was told.

The two women who "ran" the office were Mina Schulder and Wendy Nazon. Mina was a woman in her fifties, heavyset, with hair that looked like an inanimate object, dyed and set and sprayed into place. Her eyesight was bad, but she was terrified of contact lenses and spent most of the day taking her glasses on and off. If a man of any age entered the office she took them off, then put them back on. Usually she forgot them several times a day and then Alix would join in the playful search, locating them on a bookshelf or under a stack of papers. She was a widow whose husband had died five years earlier. When Wendy, a gawky blonde with an endless supply of

polyester pantsuits and ruffled blouses, complained of loneliness—
she had never been married—Mina would say, clasping her hand to
her chest, "You don't know the meaning of the word. There isn't
a day of my life I don't think of Gerald."

It was an unfortunate irony that her former husband's name had
been Gerald. Every time she spoke of him, Alix felt irritated, but also
a flicker of the kind of emotion she was trying to suppress. While at
the counseling center—she went for three-hour stretches—she tried
to be quiet, ingratiating, and friendly. In fact, she loved these moments because the two women, dense and incompetent though they
were, seemed astonishingly uninterested in mental problems of any
kind. Alix might have been someone who was hospitalized for cancer
or any other serious but possibly curable illness. They frequently
asked how she was doing or if she felt tired, even brought her cups of
water from time to time. Unlike Dr. Stern, though they knew she had
been a lawyer "on the outside," they had no suspicion that she didn't
enjoy the "work" she did in their office and, therefore, didn't regard
her as condescending or arrogant. Or maybe she just pretended
better with women than with men.

One spring day, when Alix had been in the hospital almost
seven weeks, Wendy put down the papers she had been sorting
through and looked out the window. "You know, we should feel *so*
lucky," she sighed.

"About what?" asked Mina.

"I mean, here we are," Wendy said. "We're in good health, you
had a happy marriage, you have two kids who are doing all right,
I may marry any day now—"

Mina looked up. "Any day? To who?" she asked eagerly.

"Oh, I didn't mean literally any *day.* I didn't mean any special
person. I just meant here I am, thirty-four, in my prime, and who
knows what could happen?" She laughed girlishly. "I guess it's just
spring. Spring fever or who knows what." She looked over at Alix
who was going over the stack of unpaid bills they had presented her
with. "Are you married?"

"Yes, I am," Alix said in her neutral voice. "I've been married
twelve years."

"Kids?"

"No . . . not yet." To imply that she had been trying to get
pregnant would make her sound more normal to them.

"You better not put it off," Mina said severely. "You're both in
your thirties. My cousin, Tilly, was like you two. Career, career.

Dating, whatnot. And now she's thirty-nine, she finally met Mr. Right, and she can't get pregnant! She's *desperate.*"

Wendy looked wistful. "I'm not even married, though."

"*Get* married!" Mina said. "You wait and you wait. It's the same with marriage. The longer you wait, the fussier you are, the less men. Then you'll be up a tree. I did it the right way. Marriage, kids, *then* career."

"Well . . ." Wendy looked uncertain. "You can't just marry someone in cold blood. You have to be in love . . . don't you?" She appealed to Alix.

"I think it helps," Alix said.

Mina shook her head in exasperation. "You tell yourself you're in love and you're in love! People make it into this big mystery. It's not! It's as simple as pie. You meet a nice man, he has faults—okay, so do you. You marry him, you deal with it, you get on with your life." She turned to Wendy. "You're waiting for Prince Charming. That's *your* problem."

"I'm *not,*" Wendy wailed. "I just want a decent, kind, honest, intelligent man. Is that too much to ask?"

"Yes!" Mina said.

Alix and Wendy looked at her in surprise.

"Wasn't Gerald like that?" Wendy asked. "Wasn't he decent, kind, honest, and intelligent?"

Mina raised her eyebrows. "Decent? Okay, sure he paid his taxes, he was as faithful as most men—"

"What do you mean?" Wendy asked nervously. "Wasn't he faithful?"

"He was faithful most of the time. I didn't follow him around like a bird dog. He was human. He did what men do. He was discreet. I had my life, he had his. We both loved the kids."

Wendy looked dismayed. "That's not romantic," she protested. She looked at Alix. "Is it?"

"Maybe it's realistic," Alix said.

"Is that how it is with your husband?" Wendy said.

"My husband is faithful," Alix said, "but I think that's largely a choice people make according to their inner needs."

Wendy looked from one of them to the other. "Gosh, this is so depressing. Probably you're right, but I don't *want* that. *I* want—"

"Something perfect," Mina finished for her. "And with that attitude, you'll be here in this office till doomsday."

This pronouncement left Wendy so depressed that she sat at

her desk for the next hour staring out the window. At four-thirty, Mina got up. "I have to leave early. Can you two handle everything?"

They nodded.

Alix had to leave at five. She had finished her work, but pretended she still had something to do. Wendy, who was trying to give up smoking, but allowed herself five a day, lit up a cigarette. "Can I ask you something personal?" she asked. "I mean don't answer if you don't want to."

"Sure," Alix said. "Ask away."

Wendy squinted at her. "How come you're here? I mean, did you have, like, a nervous breakdown?"

"Yes," Alix said, choosing what she thought was the simplest answer.

"What's it like? Sometimes I wonder if *I'm* having one."

Alix smiled. "I don't think you are. I'm not really positive what it was with me. I was very upset about various things, my sister had died and my mother died . . . I felt terribly alone somehow."

"Even though you were married?"

"Yes."

Wendy inhaled deeply. "So, it was like one day it all kind of came together? You just couldn't handle things anymore?"

"Basically."

"And has being here helped? I sometimes think it might be nice to go to a quiet, friendly place where they took good care of you and you didn't have to worry about anything, the way it is here."

"That's not the way it is here," Alix said. She stood up. "I guess I have to go back." After a moment she said, "Wendy, a friend of mine is visiting here and she wondered how she could get from here to the subway. Is it far? She doesn't have a car."

Wendy stood up and stretched. "I guess the easiest way is calling a cab . . . Here, I have the number of one that comes here." She looked it up in her phone book and handed Alix the slip of paper. "They come pretty fast, in about fifteen minutes. And then the subway's right down the hill."

"Where should she tell the cab to come?"

"Right in front of the main building. They pull up there all the time."

"Thanks so much," Alix said.

It was Monday. On Wednesday she would do it. She had had other conversations with Luke about getting her out and they had reached the same dead end. He felt the doctors knew what they were doing, it was only a matter of time. Finally Alix had stopped bringing it up because it upset her too much. *How did I live with him for twelve years? How did I handle this? He never controlled your life. You had a separate life, work, Gerald.* She didn't allow herself to think beyond getting out of the hospital. She had no idea what would happen to her marriage. Going through the absurd rituals of the hospital day, trimming things out of paper, playing bingo, she felt as a criminal must who is planning a bank break-in. She went over the details in her mind again and again. There would be no second chance. She had to get it right the first time. On the way to the counseling center there was a private phone. It was not in the same building as the ward, and none of the doctors or nurses she saw during the day were ever near it. It seemed to be used mainly by people from the outside, visitors.

One problem was money. She was only allowed to carry twenty dollars, which was to be used on snacks or magazines. It was enough for a cab and enough to get her somewhere else. The question was where. In the form she had signed, it stated that the hospital had rights over you for seventy-two hours after you left. How that number had been arrived at, whether it, in fact, meant anything, she wasn't sure. Noah had implied that some patients were "captured" and brought back. Since she had worked with the law all of her adult life, she decided to abide by this, whether it proved necessary or not. For seventy-two hours she had to stay somewhere safe. She had no credit cards or checks, so a hotel was out. The only person she could think of was Pam's daughter, Laurel, who was a senior at Wesleyan. Somehow Alix doubted Luke had been in touch with Michael. They had no relationship, had never written or called each other. And Michael himself wasn't close to Laurel, something Pam had often complained about, feeling he favored their son. *Anyway, I'll be able to tell by the way she responds when I call how much she knows. If she sounds funny in any way, I'll think of something else.*

The one thing Alix regretted deeply was being unable to say good-bye properly to Noah. Since he had returned from his failed attempt at teaching, he seemed in a daze, just sat hunched over, eyes blank with pain, staring out the window. Alix knew it was too dangerous to tell him anything directly, or even to talk with him in the intimate way she had at the beginning.

At what she hoped would be her last group therapy session, Dr. Wishnick went around the circle, asking each of them how they felt.

Alix had learned how to do this, how to sound perky but humble, mildly confessional but totally dishonest. "I've been feeling really well," she said. "Doing this office work is helping me. I like having that interaction with the outside world, even if it's not really outside yet."

Noah was sitting next to her. He hardly seemed to have heard.

"How about you, Noah? How have *you* been feeling?" Dr. Wishnick said.

He didn't reply.

"You and Alix came in at about the same time. Doesn't seeing her improve give you hope?"

At that he looked up at Alix. "In some ways," he said very slowly.

"In what way doesn't it?" Dr. Wishnick asked.

"Before I felt like Alix was my special friend. I loved talking to her. Now she's like a stranger."

God, why was he doing this? Why was he throwing his life away? Dr. Wishnick looked at Alix. "How do you feel about that, Alix? Do *you* feel Noah is a stranger to you?"

"No, not at all," Alix said. "I feel he's a very special, wonderful person. I want him to get better. I believe he can . . . but I suppose I've been selfish, just thinking of my own life and how to get it in order."

Dr. Wishnick beamed. "You see, Noah? Alix thinks you're a very special, wonderful person. Doesn't that make you feel good?"

He shrugged.

"How do the rest of you feel about Noah?" Dr. Wishnick asked. She looked at Elton Koriaff, who was sitting on Noah's other side.

"Well, no offense, but I think he's kind of an asshole," Elton said. "I mean he's just sitting there, not even talking, not even trying. He's like some dog lying in the middle of the road waiting to get run over."

"Squish!" crowed Leroy Demos. "Wow, I love that sound."

Dr. Wishnick frowned. "What sound do you love, Mr. Demos?"

"Hitting a dog or a squirrel when you're driving along at night. Whammo. All over." He grinned.

"Why is that a pleasurable feeling?" Dr. Wishnick said. "Could you explain it to us?"

"Life and death. Man, you take someone's life and what greater power can you have? So, like I see it, Noah here, he's getting some kind of kick out of flushing his life down the toilet. It's the same as me with squirrels, but *he's* doing it to himself." He made a sound like a toilet flushing.

"That's *not* what I'm doing!" Noah cried in despair.

Leroy made the sound again.

"Stop that, please!" Alix said.

Leroy's eyes were glittering; probably he had gotten drugs from someone. *"Pardonnez-moi,"* he said, bowing courteously. "Just my opinion, right? That's all I've got. That's all we all got." He started singing "Mad Dogs and Englishmen get stoned in the midday sun."

"Mr. Demos, this is *not* appropriate behavior," Dr. Wishnick said. "Why are you singing?"

"I feel good." He grinned. "I feel superdooperalaPeter T.Hooper."

"Why do you feel good? Could you share that with us?"

He leaned over and said in a whisper, "It's a secret."

"Yes, but here we have no secrets. We're among friends. We have nothing to be ashamed of. We would all like to know. All of us want to feel better."

"He's nuts," Elton Koriaff said dismissively. "He's stoned. Leave him alone."

"That's not possible," Dr. Wishnick said stiffly, recrossing her legs. "Where would he get drugs?"

"They fall out of the sky," Leroy said. "I tell you, man, this place is hopping." And he sang again, "Mad dogs . . ."

"Mr. Demos, I'm afraid I don't understand what your song means," Dr. Wishnick said. "Could you explain it to us?"

Alix glanced at Noah. He was somewhere else, his face blank.

Leroy had the expansive glee of someone who has left reality on a plane far away. "Lemme see. Mad dog . . . well, that's my name for Stuart, Stuart Stern, because he foams at the mouth and because he bumped off that patient, Blades. And you, Dr. Wishnick pardon me, Doctor—oh, the hell with it. You, I call See-Through because of those beautiful blouses you wear and on account of which I can sit here and listen to all this shit and just gaze on your beautiful breasts which, believe me, *are* beautiful. I can tell you that because I've looked. I can see through clothes, that's a fact. Now, Ms. Zimmer here, hers are nice, but small. Some men like them small— quality, not quantity—but I like them both ways, I like quantity *and* quality, and, Dr. Wish, you got both. And I want to say I think your husband is a lucky man. If I was him, I wouldn't go to work in the morning, I'd just lie there all day, just—"

"Stop!" Dr. Wishnick said. "Mr. Demos, either attend to this session or leave immediately."

He looked contrite. "I *am* attending. I'm free associating like the doctor said to do. Now your topic was Mr. Noah Epstein and the fact that he's lying there like a dead dog, like I said."

"*I* said that," Elton interrupted.

Tamara Grace had been silent. "I think this is cruel," she said. "I'm sixty-six years old and yet I have to sit here listening to crazy licentious men ranting on." She turned to Dr. Wishnick. "Make them stop!"

"Mr. Demos, please leave," Dr. Wishnick said. "You're upsetting Mrs. Grace."

Leroy Demos got unsteadily to his feet. "I'm sorry," he said to Mrs. Grace. "I didn't mean to offend nobody. I think yours are nice too." He stumbled out of the room.

There was a dead silence.

"I miss my wife," Noah said suddenly.

"Yeah," Elton said in a soft, dreamy voice. "I miss my girlfriend . . . Not just sex. I miss her holding me."

Suddenly Tamara Grace began to cry. "I miss my husband," she said. "He died five years ago and I still miss him so much."

For one moment, looking at each of them, having a flash memory of Gerald smiling at her, Alix felt her chest constrict. *God, don't let me break down. Please.* Looking at the floor, she tried to breathe evenly in and out, as a doctor who knew she had low blood pressure had once advised her to do if she felt faint.

As always, Dr. Wishnick seemed disconcerted by this display of emotion. "Well," she finally said brightly, "I think this is wonderful. All of you are feeling something, you're missing someone you love. The trouble with Mr. Demos, the sad thing is, he *doesn't* have anyone he loves or ever did love. That's why I think we should all be tolerant of him, of his behavior. If he had someone to love, if he was capable of love, he wouldn't act the way he does."

Why isn't she writing Hallmark greeting cards? As Alix caught the therapist's eye, Dr. Wishnick said, "You have your husband." It was in between a question and a statement.

"Yes, I do," Alix said.

"Married love," Dr. Wishnick went on, "is what we're all aiming for. When you're older, you'll appreciate that, Elton. It gives us stability, warmth, a sense that, no matter what, someone will always be there for us, someone on whom we can depend, someone who loves us more than we love ourselves."

There was silence. "Well!" she said, smiling. "I think perhaps we'd better stop now, but I feel today has been a very important session for all of us." She stood up, gathered her papers together, and left the room.

After she left, Elton whistled. "Man, I wouldn't marry my girl-friend if they put a gun to my head. All *I* want is—"

"We know," Alix said quickly.

He sauntered out.

She was left alone with Noah. *I can't say anything, I can't do anything.* Had he heard what Dr. Wishnick had said or what she had said earlier? She remembered her fateful words to him weeks earlier. "I'll get us both out." Now she knew it would be hard enough pulling it off for herself. Still, she sat there, unable to leave him in his despair, unable to speak.

Finally he looked up at her. "Thank you for what you said," he said in his slow, quiet voice.

Alix stood up. Without touching him, she tried to convey what she felt through her eyes. "Take care, Noah," she said softly and left the room.

Wednesday morning Alix ate breakfast feeling a bright, sharp-edged clarity, as though every motion she made, every word she heard was being engraved on her skin. Her fear was counteracted by a kind of wild excitement. She ate very little, moving the food around on her plate. The tips of her fingers were icy cold. Then she stood on line to get her medication. When she reached out to take the small paper cup and the pills, the nurse said, "Goodness, your hands are freezing!"

"I've had that all my life," Alix said. "The doctor said it was nothing to worry about."

"You have low blood pressure, don't you?"

"Borderline."

"Well, better take it to be on the safe side."

Shit, Alix thought. This was how crimes didn't work in movies—some unexpected snarl-up. But she had no choice but to wait patiently as the nurse took her blood pressure. "Sixty over eighty," the nurse said. "Well, it's pretty low. How do you feel? Any dizziness?"

"No, I feel fine," Alix said.

The nurse frowned. "Maybe you better stay here until the doctor comes on. You may need a change in your medication."

Heart thumping, Alix said, "I've discussed this with Dr. Stern, and he said he felt I was well enough to continue with the activities I've been taking part in. This morning I work in the counseling office. In fact, I'm due there now."

For a moment the nurse seemed indecisive. Then she said, "All right . . . but when you come back for lunch, let's discuss it with him."

"Gladly," Alix said. She took one quick look at the nurse whose wig was on, as always, at a slightly acute angle. 'Bye, she thought flippantly. But, in fact, she was tense with dread. She had gone over this plan a hundred times, had timed it, had calculated every possible mischance and how she would handle it. Now she walked out the door, down the steps, and crossed to the main building. The phone was right near the exit. It was five past nine, but she often didn't arrive precisely on time. Sitting in the phone booth, she dialed the number of the cab company that Wendy had given her. It was busy. Alix lowered her head, breathless. *Please.* She dialed again. "City Cab," came a brusque female voice at the other end.

"I wondered if I could have a cab pick me up at the main building of the Nash Institute," she said.

"What time?"

"As soon as possible."

"Let's see, it's nine ten. It'll be ten, fifteen minutes."

"Thank you," Alix said.

"Name?"

She hesitated. "James."

She decided to sit in the phone booth, holding the phone for ten minutes, then to stand just inside the front door. Probably it was absurd to have said "James," but she had a sudden fear that possibly the hospital gave out lists of the patients just for this reason. In the ten minutes she was there, no one passed by whom she knew. No one even tried to use the phone booth. A woman stopped and, seeing the phone was in use, walked on. Alix kept her eyes on her watch, looking at the second hand as it jerked around. It was a battery driven Timex, which she preferred to the elegant watch

Luke had once given her for her birthday. It was reliable, it always worked.

At nine-fifteen she stood up, replaced the receiver and moved to the front entrance. People were coming and going, doctors in their white coats, patients being led like people in a chain gang to their various activities, visitors. Then, as she stood there, she saw Dr. Stern. He was talking to another doctor. Alix moved back from the entrance. She darted into the phone booth. *No, it's not fair. Let him not see me.* Then she realized it would be more incriminating if he saw her in the phone booth. She got up and started walking very slowly in the direction of the counseling center. A moment later he passed her. "Ms. Zimmer?"

"Yes?"

"You're a little late for your work session, aren't you?"

"Slightly."

He gave her a long, hard glance and then said, "See you at your therapy session later."

She nodded. He walked briskly ahead of her, turned a corner, and was out of sight. In a panic, Alix rushed back to the front of the main building. There was a cab waiting. Putting on her sunglasses, she walked briskly over to it. "My name is James," she said. "I was expecting a cab."

The driver nodded. "Where to, lady?"

"Could you take me to the subway stop at the bottom of the hill?"

"Sure thing."

Alix slouched down slightly, her head bent. But as the cab moved down the hill, she turned and took a final look at the hospital. Everything was bright and beautiful, the flowers, the grounds. *Free, I'm free.* But she held her excitement in. This was just the beginning.

When she got to the subway, she paid the driver and took the train that went to Grand Central. Everything on the train looked strange to her. The people looked odd. She wondered what it was. She had been in the hospital so long that it was hard to remember there was a real world out there which, all that time, continued to function. A man was asleep on one of the seats, a homeless person. No one looked either more or less normal than the patients, but they looked alive. There was a kind of cheerful, blithe intensity to their casual bits of conversation. She felt as though she were watching a fascinating play.

When she got off at Grand Central, she looked for another

phone booth. All of them were busy, so she waited, still looking around her in a kind of daze. It was ten. Perhaps by now the counseling office had called to find out what had happened to her. Or perhaps not. They were so scatterbrained they might not think to call at all, and her disappearance might not be noticed for another two hours. But it no longer mattered to her. All she needed now was a place to stay for three days.

She called Wesleyan and got Laurel's number. She was living in a place called Womanist House. As chance would have it, she was in. "Laurel? Hi, it's Aunt Alix."

"Oh hi!" Laurel said. "How are you?" She sounded delighted to hear from her.

"I'm fine . . . I just wondered—I'm going to be up in your area for a few days at a convention and I thought I might stop by and see you if you aren't too pressed with work?"

"No, gosh, that would be super. I'd love you to meet all my friends . . . but I do have some work. How long can you stay?"

"Well," Alix pretended to think. "The conference is three days. If you have an extra bed, I might stay over with you and we could just meet for dinner. That way both of us could go our own way during the day."

"I have an extra bed in my room," Laurel said. "My roommate dropped out this semester. It's pretty messy, though."

"No problem," Alix said. "How's your father and his new marriage?"

Laurel snorted. "I should know? He doesn't know I'm alive."

Perfect. "I'm at Grand Central. Could you give me instructions on how to get there?"

She had enough money for the train ticket, but would have to take a bus after that. Possibly Laurel could lend her a little; she could invent something. On the train she took out a piece of paper she had brought with her. She wrote the date on the top. Then she wrote:

Dear Luke,

I've left the hospital. As I tried to tell you, I felt it was not only not helping me, but was making me feel worse. Actually, I've felt fine for a long time now, and am eager to resume normal life. I realize we may have to rethink our marriage, as well as everything else. Let's do that when we see each other. This is just to let you know that I'm safe. Presumably the hospital has no hold over me after 72 hours so for that time I'll be staying somewhere. I'll call you when the time is up.

She hesitated over writing "love" at the end of the letter, and ended up just putting her initial, "A." She put the letter in a stamped envelope and mailed it.

The three days with Laurel at Wesleyan were difficult. It was clear after their first lunch that Laurel had no suspicions and was, in any case, immersed in her work and her part-time job at the co-op. Evidently she was gay. Alix hadn't known that, but then she realized she had never talked a great deal with Pam about her children and hadn't even seen Laurel, except for the brief glimpse at the wedding, in a long time. Laurel seemed nervous about Alix's response to her being gay, which was a perfect balance to Alix's own nervousness. Even though she was out of the hospital, she realized she was still incredibly on edge. At night she slept badly, had nightmares that she was caught, woke up drenched in sweat. One night she cried out in her sleep and Laurel woke up. "Are you okay?"

"I'm fine," Alix said. "I just had a . . . bad dream."

"Want some hot milk and honey? That's what I always have."

"I can get it. Why don't you go back to sleep?"

"No, that's okay." Laurel got out of bed in her wrinkled T-shirt. She was tall, like Michael, and resembled him more than she did Pam. She had a strongly chiseled nose and mouth and bright blue eyes, brown hair in a pony tail. Only her speech, its rhythms and intonations, reminded Alix of Pam, a certain halting quality, as though it was hard for her to express exactly what she felt.

Alix sat in the kitchen while Laurel heated the milk. "I get bad dreams too," Laurel said. "Since Mom died. It's not so bad anymore. But I dream about her sometimes, still."

"Yes," Alix said, "I do too."

"Were you close?" Laurel asked. "You lived so far away."

"In some ways," Alix said. "Now I wish we had been closer. Pam hated writing letters."

"I know!" Laurel laughed. "Do you have any from her? Or any photos or stuff? I'd love to have them or see them, if you do. Dad didn't save anything."

"Yes, I have lots," Alix said. "I'll send them to you as soon as I get home." In the warm, quiet, intimate atmosphere of the kitchen, sipping the hot milk, she felt she could have told Laurel everything, and felt a strong desire to, but knew it wasn't worth the risk. Sipping the milk, she said, "This has been so good, being here with you.

There's no one left in the family, and not having kids is like a cavity scooped out of my life."

"Me too," Laurel said. "I get so angry when I think of it. Why wasn't it Dad?" She smiled. "I shouldn't say that, I guess."

"Why shouldn't you?" Alix said. "The only bad thing is denying what you really feel or who you really are."

"Do you think so?" Laurel said. "That's what Julie says. But I'm not that kind of person. I mean, I'm not that open or that confrontational. I guess I'm like Mom in that way. She always let Dad run roughshod over her. She said you were the spunky one. She really admired you."

Alix sighed. "I don't know . . . I was once."

"What do you mean?"

"I feel . . . flattened out somehow, as though all the spunk had been beaten out of me."

"By what?" Laurel seemed so genuinely curious that it was hard not to tell.

"Sweetie," Alix said, "there's a lot about my life you don't know, just like I didn't know about yours. And I'm glad we've had this chance to catch up. Right now there's a reason I can't tell you more, but some day I will."

"When?"

"Very soon. And when I do, you'll understand."

Laurel was looking at her curiously. "I had the feeling you were upset at Dad's wedding. I was too. I wished then I'd had a chance to talk to you. I saw you, but then it was such a crowd, I lost sight of you."

So she hadn't even known about what happened? Was that possible? *Even one's disgraces are less significant than one thinks.*

During the day she slept in fitful bursts or walked around the campus. The feeling of freedom she had felt leaving the hospital had vanished. Partly it was her anxiety about the possibility of being caught and forced to return. But it was also that she had forgotten, in her single-minded determination to get out, that what lay outside was real life, with all its confusions and ambiguities and terrors. No one had done a magic trick and made it all fall into place. What was gone was the feeling of anxiety. In fact, if anything, the world seemed flat and unexciting. Perhaps, having kept her real emotions in check so long in the hospital, they had forgotten how to function. *Do I love Luke? Do I want to preserve our marriage, assuming he does?* She would examine these questions and then let them slide away, as though they were minor decisions like whether she should let her hair grow long or have it trimmed.

On the third day she called him at work. His secretary, whom she hadn't spoken to since the day she had flown to Colorado for Michael's remarriage, answered. "Could I speak to Mr. James?"

"Who shall I say is calling?"

"This is his wife."

Probably Luke had told no one at work about what had happened to her. The secretary said, "I'll try and get him."

A few moments later, Luke said, "Alix! My God! Where are you? I've been frantic!"

Fuck you. Frantic for a few days of wondering where she was! "Didn't you get my letter?" she asked coolly.

"Yes, but I had no idea . . . The hospital has been terribly worried. They were afraid you might have done something desperate." His voice broke.

"I did do something desperate," Alix said. "I escaped."

"But you're all right? Where are you?"

"I'll tell you tonight. I'm coming home by train this afternoon . . . but Luke?"

"Yes?"

"Will you swear to me you won't inform the hospital that you've heard from me?"

"I have to," he stammered. "They made me promise. They have to know."

Alix paused. "Then perhaps you should decide, right now, on the phone, which means more to you, the doctors or our marriage. Because if you tell them, you'll never see me again. I'm not talking about suicide, just divorce."

There was a long pause.

"Well, if those are the terms," Luke said.

"They are."

"Then of course I choose you," he said. "What time will you be home?"

"Late afternoon."

"I can't wait to see you," he said in a soft voice. "God, I've wanted this for so long."

"See you tonight, then," Alix said.

Replacing the receiver, she felt a cool flash of rage like a white heat that melts and destroys without flames. *Our marriage is over. It was over before I entered the hospital. Now it's just that I see what I didn't allow myself to see before. Nothing has changed except my perceptions.* She felt neither despair nor grief—perhaps that would come later—but a kind of nostalgia for the way she had been before. Even her anxiety attacks, her hallucinations, her grief at Gerald's death, all seemed to her now a smokescreen she had created to shield herself from this moment of clarity: that she didn't love her husband, that their marriage was a dead, inert thing. Some people drank, others had affairs, some had breakdowns just because this flat cold perception was so hideous, as though all the color had been removed from the world and it was now black and white with certain shadings of grey.

Laurel lent her thirty dollars. "Are you sure that's enough?" she said.

"Positive." Laurel knew something was wrong and her sympathy, her kindness, her ability to give without probing was a balm to Alix. "This has meant a lot to me," she said, "being here with you." She hugged her tightly.

"For me too," Laurel said. "I never could be close to Mom the way I wanted. But now it's like I have a second chance." Then she frowned. "But, listen, gain some weight, will you? You're so skinny!"

"I will," Alix said. "I'll have doubled in bulk next time you see me."

"And maybe I'll have lost some," Laurel laughed with a laugh that was so much like Pam's it caught at Alix's heart. It was funny how small things like that brought a person back—bits of Pam scattered in her children.

The doorman greeted her just as though she was returning from work as always. Did anyone know, did anyone notice? Probably Luke, if he had said anything to anyone, had just said she was ill, or maybe not even that much. He would not leave work early. He hadn't the day his father died or the day she had been made partner. Knowing that, she had timed her arrival so that she would have an hour to be alone in the apartment. What struck her as she walked from room to room was how absurdly large and almost eerily neat everything was: the kitchen, the dining room, Luke's music room. Had he sat there in her absence mournfully playing Scarlatti on his harpsichord? She remembered that manic afternoon, dragging the harpsichord into the living room. There were still scratches on the polished wooden floor. *We could have it repolished. It needs it.* And then she remembered that she wasn't sure about the future.

Probably she would have to get a new job. She doubted, if Silas Foss knew that she had had a breakdown, that he would let her back. He had always been uncertain about allowing a woman to be a partner. Probably this had proved to him what he already felt: that women, in whatever way, were unreliable, couldn't be counted on, broke down or got pregnant or moved with their husbands to other states. Another job, another husband, another apartment. *Do I want another husband? Even assuming I could find one. What do I want?* Before, these questions would have thrown her into a panic. Now it was: *I don't really know and I won't for a long time.*

It didn't seem to her that the hospital experience had embittered her toward men. Dr. Stern was a disturbed and occasionally sadistic man, but so were many people in power whom she had seen in the outside world. She had just never been so completely in someone's power before. She felt prouder of her escape than she had of being made partner. It seemed the one brave thing she'd ever done in a not very adventurous life. Laurel had said, "You were the spunky one." Oh, but her spunkiness had been so mild, so within feminine boundaries! Even when she thought of her relationship with Gerald, she realized how much game playing there had been, how much he had enjoyed her youth, her subservience in the firm, his role as mentor. Nothing horrible in that, but certainly not the free, breaking-all-traditions love affair she had liked to think of it as. Just another man whom she had loved, fucked, catered to, admired, fantasized about. *That's all there is, kiddo. Luke and Gerald probably represented the best that was out there, for all their individual faults. And you are far from perfect, as you know. Yes, I know.*

Before Luke came home, Alix took a long hot bath and then changed into a fresh dress, put on clean makeup, shadow on her eyes, lipstick, blusher, washed her hair. She enjoyed the ritual for its own sake, but was disturbed at it familiarity. *This is exactly what you would have done a year ago, five years ago.* Had she just shed one skin in order to grow another identical one? When he walked in the door, she was sitting in the living room, leafing through a copy of *Architectural Digest,* sipping a glass of white wine.

He rushed over and clasped her tightly in his arms. "Darling."

She allowed herself to be held. He was handsome, of course, how could that have changed, his blue shirt matched his eyes, his

faintly greying temples. His heart was careening wildly. "Oh Alix
. . . I've missed you so terribly."

When they pulled apart, Alix said, "Shall we eat in? I haven't
prepared anything."

"I picked some things up on the way home." He smiled boyishly. "I want to cook you a real celebration dinner. I've learned a
few new recipes while you were away. I got shad and asparagus and
fresh strawberries."

While you were away. That was how it would be if she stayed.
She had been "away," now she was back. *Every marriage is like this.
Every person uses words and concepts differently. Why should yours be an
exception?*

She sat in the kitchen while he cooked. It was like the first
rehearsal of a play in which everyone had learned their lines, but not
exactly how to say them. Alix knew she was more silent than usual,
but she knew Luke would attribute that, in part correctly, to her
exhaustion.

"You've gotten so thin," he said as he whipped the hollandaise
sauce.

"Yes." Even the half glass of wine had made her feel almost
drunk. *I'm here. I'm not there. I did it. I made it.* A flash memory of Noah
went through her mind as he had looked when they sat alone in the
group therapy room, his head bowed, his eyes vacant. Would she
always remember or would she try to forget?

They ate by candlelight as they always had. Alix ate very slowly.
*I used to do this every night. Or no, not every night. Sometimes I worked late,
or pretended to.* All that flurry of activity. She thought of rushing from
Gerald's apartment, feeling as though everyone on the subway or
bus could tell from her flushed face where she had been, what she'd
been doing, that manic excitement.

"Are you glad to be back?" Luke asked. "You've been so
quiet."

"I feel very tired."

"Where did you go for those three days?"

"To Wesleyan. I stayed with Laurel. I wasn't sure really how
seriously to take the threat that they could hunt you down and bring
you back within seventy-two hours, but it didn't seem totally at odds
with their methods, so I decided to be on the safe side."

"You were a voluntary patient," he said.

"Meaning what?"

"Meaning—" He stopped. "Well, that's all behind us now."

Alix ate her fish. "I love Laurel," she said suddenly. "I never really knew her before. I'd never talked to her. She's been gay since she was in high school and I had no idea. I guess Pam felt ashamed, or maybe I just never bothered asking."

"She's so young," Luke said.

"Yes?"

He paused. "I meant it could be a phase."

"She just hasn't met Mr. Right?"

"Not everyone is as lucky as we were." He looked at her. "I've had a chance to realize in these months how lucky I am."

"In what way?" Alix asked.

"How special you are, what a special person. I didn't properly . . . appreciate you, how much you meant to me. I know I'm not good at expressing emotion. I never was, never will be. But I love you very much."

She wanted to be touched by this confession and felt instead just bitterness. "But not enough to help me when I was desperate, when I begged you to get me out?"

"Alix." He reached for her hand. "We'll never agree about that. I felt, I still feel that it was the best hospital that exists, that the doctors were only interested in getting you well, in doing whatever they thought would make you better."

"And is the fact that I was there, that I experienced it of no account?"

"Of course it is, but you were sick. That was why you were there."

"And am I sick now?"

"No, of course not."

"And why am I here?"

"Because you . . . They were going to let you out. You might have been out today anyway. Dr. Stern promised he—"

Alix looked down at her plate, not trusting herself to speak.

After dinner he took her in his arms again and began kissing her tenderly, her face, her eyelids, her hair. "You're so beautiful," he said. "I dreamt of you every night. I wanted you so much." They moved into the bedroom, took off their clothes, and made love. *This is stupid, insane.* But her body was needy. It swept aside all doubts and took what it wanted greedily. Only afterward, when consciousness returned, was there that cold, still feeling.

"I've thought a lot," Luke said, "of what you spoke of before you— About our having a child."

"Yes?" Alix asked.

"I think it's a good idea, I think we should. Not immediately perhaps, but once you feel totally well again, your old self. You're right. We need that bond, and—well, how do you feel?"

"I'd like a child, eventually," Alix said, though in fact she hadn't been thinking of it recently.

"A boy or a girl?"

"A girl."

"Yes," Luke said. "I'd prefer a girl too. But either would be fine."

She had thought she would get up after they made love, it was only a little past nine, but she found she was too exhausted to move. "I think I'll sleep now," she said.

"I'll stay up a bit." He dressed while she slipped into one of her nightgowns. Before he had left the room, she was asleep, falling into a black dreamlessness that was like an anesthetic. She woke suddenly in the middle of the night. It was as though she went from being asleep to being fully awake in one second, and in that second she thought she was in the hospital again. Then her eyes caught sight of the familiar objects in the room; she saw Luke sleeping beside her. *It's all right, you're safe.* She fell asleep again.

The next morning while they were at breakfast the phone rang. Luke answered it. "Yes . . . Oh hello, Dr. Stern, could you hold on one moment?" Covering the phone he asked Alix, "What shall I say?"

"You can say I'm home and that I'm fine."

"Yes, she's here," Luke said into the phone. "And she's feeling very well . . . Ummhmm. Certainly. That sounds . . . I'll ask her." He covered the receiver again. "Dr. Stern wondered if you might want to come up and see him for one final session. He's delighted about your recovery. He just thought—"

Alix stared at him in disbelief. "Tell him that if he dares to call here again, we'll have him subpoenaed."

"Dr. Stern?" Luke said. "Alix and I are about to leave on a month-long vacation . . . Yes, certainly, when we return, we'll be in touch if Alix feels she'd like to continue therapy on the outside. Not at all." He hung up and returned to the table. Looking pleased, he said, "Well, he said he knew all along you had it in you."

"Had what in me?"

"That you could recover and—"

"Then why did he want me to return to the hospital?"

"Oh just, you know, as a form thing, to see how you were feeling and so on. He really is very concerned about you."

"Do you really not understand what that was all about?"

"What?"

"The second I put one foot on the hospital grounds, he could have me recommitted. All it takes is the opinion of two doctors that you need to be there."

"But you don't," Luke said, puzzled. "You're fine."

"I was fine a month ago." She was shaking with rage.

Luke was silent. "Well," he said finally, "I have to go to work. And perhaps I was right, perhaps we would consider a trip somewhere. Why don't you think about it during the day?"

"Fine," Alix said.

When he had left, she read the *Times* slowly and carefully—the weather reports, the obituaries, the sports section. Everything seemed interesting, yet slightly remote. Then she went outside. It was hot, nearly eighty, but not yet oppressively humid. Alix walked slowly toward the park. Elderly people were sunning themselves on benches, lovers embracing under trees, mothers and tiny children romping in the playground. Wanting to be alone, she found a large flat rock which was partly in the shade. The fury that had enveloped her when Luke had been on the phone with Dr. Stern had melted away. She saw her anger as a hard rock which time would melt, the way a hard candy did until it was a sliver. But it would always be there, like a bullet lodged in her groin that couldn't be removed.

"Beautiful day, isn't it?"

She looked up and saw a tall, ginger-haired man in his thirties who had *The New York Times* under one arm. "Yes, it's lovely."

"Do you mind if I share your rock?"

She gestured to indicate it would be fine.

He sat reading the paper. Alix closed her eyes and let herself enjoy the warmth of the sun. "I don't think you know me," he said finally.

"No," she said. A pickup on her first day back? Curious, when men so seldom tried to pick her up, especially in the city.

"I work at Merrill Lynch," he said. "We used to go up in the elevator together every morning."

"Oh," Alix said. The elevator was always packed with people.

"I changed jobs about two months ago. That's why you haven't seen me lately."

"Where are you now?"

He mentioned another firm. "You still where you were?"

"I've been ill . . . I had a leave of absence." She smiled at him. "I think I may have to change jobs too."

He had a frank, snub-nosed face, freckles, wiry hair, the broad accent of a Midwesterner. Probably he'd played basketball in high school or college. "Pardon me if this is an intrusive question," he said, "but . . . have you gotten divorced? You aren't wearing your wedding ring." He reddened slightly. "I mean you always used to."

She had taken it off in the hospital and Luke had not appeared to notice. Now, looking down, she saw that there was still a faint whitish mark where it had been. "No," she said, "but I think my husband and I may be about to separate."

"Join the crowd," he said. "I'm one step further down the line. My wife and I had a separation, now it's final. We're just hacking over the custody arrangements. We have two kids."

"Do you want joint custody?"

"If I can get it . . ." He shook his head. "It can get pretty ugly. Do *you* have kids?"

"No."

"Well, maybe it'll be easier then. How long were you married?"

"Twelve years."

He whistled. "You must have done it young."

"Right after college."

"Yeah, I guess we all did it too young. Or maybe that doesn't matter much. I don't know anymore. I always wanted what my parents had—just a decent workable thing. I'm not a raving romantic. I didn't think I wanted what wasn't possible. But it all blew up in my face."

"Yes," Alix said softly.

"It's so damn ironical," he said. "All my friends, my married friends, say, 'Wow, you're so lucky, all those single women out there.' Maybe I was like that when I was married. And now I think— it's like something I've forgotten how to do. Date, make moves, all that shit. Do you do that yet?"

"I'm still living with my husband," Alix said. "I haven't even discussed it with him yet."

He looked startled. "You mean he doesn't know?"

She shook her head. "He thinks we're very happy together."

The man was silent. "That's what I thought. I mean, sure, I knew we had troubles, but one day whammo, my wife just said, this is it, out. It turned out she'd been miserable for years, so she said. I don't know, I must have been living in a dream world."

"Everyone does," Alix said.

Suddenly he seemed angry. "So, why're you leaving him, then? Have you found someone else?"

"No."

"So? What is it—you want space, freedom, all that?"

His bitterness was like shell shots flickering around her. "I'm not really sure what I want."

"So why break it up? I don't get it."

"There's no reason you should," Alix said softly. "It's complicated. We don't know each other. Every marriage is different." She turned away from him.

He was silent for several moments. "Sorry . . . I just—"

"You'll find someone," Alix said, "if that's what you want. Everyone who wants to does, especially men."

He laughed bitterly. "That easy, huh?"

"Sure." She stood up.

As she did, he also sprang to his feet. He had rolled the *Times* into an elongated cone. "Hey, listen, I know this is—this is my address and phone number. If you ever, well, feel like—"

Alix took the slip of paper: Nicholas Drakes. "My name is Alix Zimmer."

He grinned. "Yeah, I know."

Really, she wanted to find another rock where she could sit peacefully, but since he seemed to be remaining in the park, she walked out toward Central Park West and headed uptown. This was what lay ahead; confused, embittered men with vendettas against ex-wives, nice guys who felt they'd gotten a raw deal. She thought of him watching her in the elevator for months, noticing her wedding ring, how she had evidently been some kind of symbol to him. He had constructed a fantasy around her because she seemed unattainable. Or maybe it was because during the time she had been with Gerald she had thrown off, unconsciously, some aura of desirability which had vanished now. She looked down at her ringless hand.

She made an appointment to see Silas Foss at the end of the week. She decided, partly to let him off the hook, partly because it was what she wanted, to resign, sparing him the awkwardness of hemming and hawing and inventing some excuse to fire her. And it was strategy. If she bowed out gracefully, he was more likely to give her a good recommendation for another job.

He looked wary as she entered the office, but managed a cautious smile. "I'm glad to see you looking so well."

"Thanks," she said. "I'm feeling well."

"And what are your plans for the immediate future?"

"Well, I think perhaps I may take a few months off, to think. I'll stay in law. I'm quite sure of that, but I've felt for a long time that a fresh start in a new organization might be good for me."

The relief that crossed his face was so extreme it was almost ludicrous. "We'll be devastated, naturally, at losing you, but I agree we all reach certain crossroads from time to time. I felt that at fifty, but other friends I've had have made much more dramatic changes. Otherwise one gets into a kind of rut."

He didn't mention the obvious, that it would mean starting from the beginning again, an arduous struggle which might not necessarily result in her being offered a partnership. "How did the surrogate mother case turn out?" she asked.

"Oh, excellently, much better than we thought, in fact. The sister had some kind of change of heart. We were able to settle out of court."

"I'm glad."

He looked away, then back at her again. "I'm sorry you were working so hard at the end of—just before you— What I mean is, I was dimly aware that was the case, but there are so many things to attend to here. I kept meaning to have a talk with you, but I never had the chance."

Sure you did. But she only said, "I'm not sure it would have helped. I think one has to put the brakes on oneself. Probably I was overeager to prove myself, being the first woman partner and so on."

He smiled his urbane half smile. "It's always hard being the first, being in the spotlight."

"I'm glad I had the chance."

"I had some of your books and papers moved . . . if you want to go over them at your leisure." He stood up.

"Thanks, I'll do that. Maybe not today, but soon." She smiled, shook his hand.

"It's been a pleasure having you with us, Alix. And if you need my recommendation for a future job, please feel free to call on me."

"I will."

How quickly the world opened and closed. Gerald's death, her breakdown, were tiny events causing a few minor ripples. No one had thought to call or write her, even though, had she returned, everyone would have been warm and courteous. It was a male world into which she had managed to fit and now it would go on as before. For whatever reason she didn't feel bitter. Her life had not been destroyed. Only she had the power to do that, finally, and she had managed to resist.

But as she left the building she wondered how many people in the forty-story structure were feeling as she had that day, were clinging desperately to shreds of work, spouses, children, anything to keep from floating or swirling into the abyss. Not only in this building. In every building, not only in New York, everywhere. Some return and some are swallowed up forever. *Noah, return. Try and make it.* It was only when she thought of him that the feeling of blind rage returned and she wanted to go crashing into Silas Foss's office and say: *"Pay attention, notice!"*

But she only went off to find a coffee shop, where she could have lunch.

DO SHARKS
EVER
SLEEP?

At lunch Leroy Demos came over and sat at Noah's table. Noah recoiled slightly, he found the man repugnant with his blathering talk and disheveled appearance. "Hey man," Leroy said, winking at him, "I hear your girlfriend's flown the coop."

"What?" Noah just stared at him.

"Little Miss Lawyer. They're all in a state. She went off to do her work at the counseling office and never came back."

"Are you sure?" He was torn between elation and fear.

"Sure I'm sure. Go ask one of them. Or don't bother. They'll ask *you*. They probably think you're in on it. Were you?"

"Of course not." But he remembered Alix's saying when they had gone out for a soda, "I'm not going to be talking to you as much. I can't tell you the reason." And her sudden mischievous smile: "Let's run off together." That little moment in the group therapy room when they had sat together in silence, how she had touched him and said, "Take care, Noah." No, she hadn't touched him. *Don't add that. Oh God, they'll catch her, they'll bring her back. Alix, why did you do it?* He had warned her; he had begged her. Noah found he couldn't eat. He stood up.

One of the nurses came over to him. "What's the matter, Mr. Epstein? You haven't touched your food."

"I don't have any appetite," he said. "I'm sorry."

"You'll get weak, it's not good for you."

He brushed past her and went to his room. He felt angry at Alix. She would be caught, she would be punished, it was stupid. And they would believe he had been in on it, no matter what he said. Sure enough, when he had been in his room five minutes, Dr. Stern looked in. "Mr. Epstein?"

"Yes?"

"Have you heard that Ms. Zimmer has left Nash, against medical advice?"

"One of the patients just told me, at lunch."

Dr. Stern entered the room and stood over him. "The staff would like to interview you about this in ten minutes. We've called an emergency meeting."

"I don't know anything about it."

"We'll meet in the general meeting room," Dr. Stern went on, as though Noah hadn't spoken. "One of the nurses will escort you there."

An inquisition. The whole staff. The last thing on God's earth he wanted to do was to face all of them and try to parry their intrusive questions. But he was caught, no way out.

Nurse Kefaldis appeared shortly afterwards. She was carrying handcuffs, which she attempted to put on him. "What's this all about?" Noah said backing away. "I'm perfectly willing to go. Please put those away."

"Doctor's orders," she said briskly.

"I said put them away!"

The nurse grabbed him and put on the handcuffs. "None of that, understand? You don't stand a chance."

"At what?"

"Just follow me."

Humiliated, he followed her down the hall as the other patients watched. They turned a corner, went down some steps and entered a large room in which about six doctors were assembled. Noah turned to Dr. Stern, who was standing at the front of the room. "Could you have these removed?" Noah asked, indicating the handcuffs. "I have no intention of escaping. I've put up no protest."

"Nurse, you can remove these now," Dr. Stern said. "Please lock the door. You may sit down, Mr. Epstein, if you like."

"Thank you," Noah said sardonically.

"Well, without further ado, I'd like to proceed to the matter at hand. Ms. Zimmer was a patient here and she has escaped. Her husband has no idea where she is. Her life may be in danger. Can you tell us where she went?"

"No, I can't," Noah said.

"Why is that?"

"I have no idea where she went. I had no idea she was planning on leaving."

"Mr. Epstein, Ms. Zimmer was a special friend of yours. Dr. Wishnick has stated that in the last therapy session Ms. Zimmer had here, she said of you that you were special to her. You were seen together, alone, in the group therapy room after the session broke up. Do you expect us to believe that she would not have mentioned her plans to you at that time?"

"She just said one thing," Noah said.

"What was that?" Dr. Stern leaned forward eagerly.

"She said, 'Take care.' "

Dr. Stern paused. "Just those two words?"

"Yes, and those were the only two words she had addressed to me in over two weeks. She appeared to be avoiding me."

"Why do you think that was?"

"Perhaps she had contempt for me," Noah said shakily, "after I . . . Perhaps she had given up on me."

"Did she ever express contempt?"

"No, but—"

"But what?"

"I think she felt I was too passive, that I was somehow playing into your hands."

"Were those her actual words, 'playing into our hands'?"

"I can't remember." It was a though he were facing a group of Ku Klux Klanners, their white intent faces and beady eyes, the fervent gleam in their eyes.

"Mr. Epstein, remember, we are concerned about Ms. Zimmer's safety. We are afraid that she may have escaped here in order to take her own life. If you have any information that will help us to track her down, you will be doing her a favor."

"I don't."

"Did she ever, during the time she was confiding in you, express any feelings about her family or friends, anyone she felt she could trust or might turn to?"

"She never talked about that."

"What *did* she talk about?"

"Her marriage, her husband . . ." But he felt even saying this much was a betrayal.

"What did she say about that?"

"I think she loved her husband . . . perhaps she felt they were becoming estranged since she had come here. But she wasn't suicidal, I'm sure of that."

"How can you be sure?"

"She never mentioned suicide or even having thoughts like that. She thought I was—"

"You were what?" Perched like a hawk ready to pounce.

"Nothing."

"Mr. Epstein, I'm afraid we must insist you tell us everything you know."

"I have, damn it! She felt trapped here, she'd thought she was a voluntary patient and would be able to leave at any time. She was bitter when she realized she couldn't. As everyone is."

"Everyone?"

"Yes." It was as though Alix's spirit had possession of him and for one moment instead of fear he felt rage.

"You feel every patient here feels trapped, unjustly treated?"

"Most do."

"And why do they feel that?"

"Because we're forced to take medication that may not be good for us, because we're handcuffed when we're not violent, because we're treated like chattel, like dirt, because we know you murdered one patient, Dr. Stern, and almost murdered another. That's why." His eyes blazed.

"You're out of control, Mr. Epstein," Dr. Stern said.

Noah was silent.

In a gentler voice, Dr. Wishnick said, "I think Mr. Epstein has told us all he knows, Dr. Stern. I don't think we're getting anywhere."

"All right," Dr. Stern said. "But, Mr. Epstein, if any further thoughts occur to you that might help us protect Ms. Zimmer, you will let us know, I trust?"

Silently, Noah just stared at him, then turned and left. The nurse accompanied him back to his room. It was too late for recreational therapy. "Could I lie down a minute?" he asked. "I feel very tired."

She looked at him suspiciously. "No monkey business?"

"What do you mean?"

"I got enough to tend to, with one runaway. You stay right here, hear me?"

"I said I was going to rest."

He lay down on the bed and closed his eyes. He knew the nurse was remaining in the doorway of his room, watching him, for several moments. Then he heard her walk away.

Should he worry that Alix might do harm to herself? He knew she hadn't ever spoken of suicide, but not everyone did who had thoughts like that. Perhaps that was what she meant when she told him she had a plan. He had assumed she just wanted to escape, to resume her normal life, but what if her intention had been more ominous? She wouldn't have told him because he would have tried to dissuade her. Unwanted, horrible images of Alix, dead, implanted themselves on his mind. He saw her lying in an alleyway, unconscious in the back of a car from gas fumes, or methodically taking an overdose of pills. There was that eerily calm side to her nature. He could imagine her planning her own death as someone else might plan a vacation: taking all the steps, nothing violent or bloody, just a calm, dignified exit . . . But no, she was alive! He had to believe that. Until now he had worried most that she would be found and brought back to the hospital. Now, he prayed only that she would be alive.

During his session with Dr. Stern the next day, Noah felt almost unconscious with fatigue. When he had tried to close his eyes, images of Alix, dead, superimposed themselves on his consciousness. He had been up all night, fighting these demons.

"Have you had a chance to think about what we discussed in staff meeting any further?" Dr. Stern asked.

Noah felt as though he'd been running and running and the hounds had finally tracked him down. "Maybe you're right," he said. "Maybe she is dead. I knew she felt desperate."

"Why do you say that?" Dr. Stern said.

"I had the feeling she was thinking of escaping, though she never put it in so many words. But I never thought—"

"Say she *is* dead . . . How would that make you feel?"

"Terrible."

"But you didn't kill her, even if she did decide to take her own life."

"No, but I—I allowed it to happen. I could have prevented it."

"How?"

"I could have talked to her about it. We did have a rapport."

"Do you think you know her better than we, the doctors, did?"

"Perhaps I did," Noah said. "Perhaps with me she let down her guard, talked more freely."

"But perhaps she was using you, making you feel special, desirable, just to have an ally."

Noah turned from him. "Put me in jail then. If you think I killed her, arrest me. Take me away. I can't bear this thing of everyone watching me, thinking I'm a murderer."

"What makes you say, 'I killed her'? I never suggested that."

"It's the same, the same . . . If she's dead—"

"We don't know that she's dead," Dr. Stern said, "but I want to know why you jump so easily to a perception of yourself as her murderer. Did you ever have thoughts like those toward her?"

"No!"

"Toward other women—wanting to kill them, destroy them?"

"No!"

"How about that bout of unconsciousness you had in bed with that woman poet? Maybe that was connected. Maybe you had a flash desire to kill her because she, like Ms. Zimmer, had led you on and in order to escape that thought you blanked out?"

Noah leapt to his feet. "None of these things are true! Why are you tormenting me?

"Mr. Epstein, you seem extremely agitated. Can you manage to sit down and continue this session?"

Reluctantly Noah sat down. "She's alive," he murmured. "I know she's alive."

"Fine," Dr. Stern said. "Let's assume she is alive. Then what?"

"I'm not sure what you mean."

"How would you feel if you heard she was alive?"

"Terribly relieved, very happy for her."

"So you would assume that she took the correct action in escaping against medical advice, that now she is happily ensconced with her husband?"

"Yes, I hope . . . I hope she's fine," Noah said.

"And that it's fine that she escaped? Pretty clever, right? Outwitting all the doctors? Something you've thought of yourself, no doubt?''

"I told her not to escape."

Dr. Stern raised his eyebrows. "I thought you told us yesterday she had never said anything to you on the subject, only 'Take care.' ''

The hounds were circling, circling. *Tell everything.* "Once, when we went out together for a soda, when the nurse left us alone, she said, 'Let's run off together.' But she said it as a kind of joke."

"I see. Were you amused?"

"No. I told her it would be dangerous. I told her not to do it, that she could be caught, brought back—"

"But you didn't think to inform any of the staff here of that remark, though it clearly implies that even as far back as that Ms. Zimmer was planning to escape?"

"I thought it was a joke," Noah repeated.

"Mr. Epstein, if it was a joke or if you thought it was a joke, why did you bother to warn her not to do it?"

"I couldn't tell with Alix. It could have been either. All she really said after that was, 'Let's enjoy our little bit of freedom.' ''

"And you felt no significance in her wording, 'Let's run off together,' implying she wanted you to join her, that perhaps she had fantasies of a new life together with you?"

"That wasn't what she meant."

"Ms. Zimmer seemed pretty articulate to me. Why wouldn't she say what she meant?"

"She was joking around. I think what she meant was, as long as the staff has this illusion we're flirting, let's really give them something to worry about. Something like that. But we both knew it wasn't true. She knew I loved my wife, I knew she loved her husband."

Dr. Stern licked his lips quickly. "Did she mention any other men?"

"She said she'd had a lover. I think she said he was no longer living."

"And it never occurred to you that she might want to join him in death? That's a fairly common fantasy, you know, joining a loved one, being reunited in death."

"She never spoke of that." Suddenly Noah felt he was going to keel over with fatigue. He gripped the edge of his chair.

"Is anything wrong?"

"I'm exhausted. I can't stop thinking of her. I just can't talk about this anymore. I believe she's alive. I want her to be alive. Don't drive me to . . ."

"To?"

"I don't know."

After a moment, Dr. Stern said, "All right. Why don't you go to your room and rest? But I have to ask you one thing. Your wife suggested that you might be up to going home for a birthday celebration for your brother this weekend. Do you feel up to that, in your present condition?"

"Yes."

"I'm asking not only for your sake, but for your family. Your wife is anxious about your condition. If you were to act inappropriately, it would be difficult for her."

"I'll be fine. I can handle it."

The thought that had implanted itself in Noah's mind was that, after the celebration, he could stay at home, not return to the hospital. Alix had shown it was possible. By the weekend she would have been caught or some word would exist about whether she was all right. If she was all right, he was exonerated and he would escape himself. If she was dead, he would stay and accept his punishment.

Friday morning, just before the group therapy session, the only session they had had since Alix had left, Dr. Wishnick looked around the room and smiled. "Well, I have some wonderful news for everyone. Alix Zimmer has been found and she's fine. We were all very worried that she might have made a suicide attempt, but she's at home with her husband and doing splendidly."

Noah felt as though the room were flooded with light. He couldn't speak.

Elton Koriaff said, "Is she coming back?"

Dr. Wishnick shook her head. "No, she's going to remain at home."

"So, why can't we all go home?" he said. "What's so special about her?"

Dr. Wishnick fiddled with the bow on her salmon pink blouse. "It isn't so much that she's special as that, well, she evidently feels capable of functioning on the outside. We all have to hope that's true, that she can."

"Yeah, but the thing is, she has a chance. *We* don't."

"If the doctors feel a patient can function on the outside,

they're delighted to sign his or her release papers," Dr. Wishnick said.

"I think *I'm* ready to go back," Tamara Grace said timorously. "I feel fine."

"Me too," Leroy Demos said. "Never felt better in fact."

"How about you, Noah?" Dr. Wishnick asked. "Do you feel fine too?"

"Yes," he said, his voice trembling. "I want to leave also."

Dr. Wishnick beamed. "Well, this is marvelous, I'm so glad. You all feel ready to leave. That's wonderful news."

"Yeah, but when *can* we?" Elton said. "My doctor just keeps saying he has to see. It's been four months now."

Leroy Demos snorted. "Man, I've been here a year and a half. Four months is nothing."

"The point is," Tamara Grace said in her gentle, ladylike voice, "we feel ready, but it doesn't seem to affect what our doctors will let us do. Why *is* that?"

Dr. Wishnick's eyes widened. "Well, of course you all have different doctors, but in each case it's that we want to be absolutely certain that you *are* ready. Sometimes patients leave too soon and then there can be terrible reactions. People can have relapses, breakdowns—"

"But we're in here because we *had* breakdowns," Tamara said. "What Elton means is we want a chance to see if we can make it, now that we have stabilized and are on the proper medication."

Leroy Demos looked contemptuously around the room at all of them. "Boy, what dummies! You think you're getting out of this place? No way. Zimmer had the smarts. She left. She didn't wait for no doctor's permission. She walked off the fucking premises. I saw her."

Noah stared at him. "When?"

"When we were going to R.T. I saw her get into a cab in front of the main building. I knew she was flying. Don't think she saw me, though."

Dr. Wishnick flicked at one of her eyebrows. "Are you saying, Mr. Demos—Leroy—that you saw Alix Zimmer leave Nash and yet told no one?"

"You got it," he said.

"But we were all terribly concerned. We were afraid she was dead. Noah was questioned—"

Leroy rolled his eyes. "She wasn't dead. Come on, she wasn't the type. You knew that, Dr. Wish, we all knew that. I think she just got nervous when I showed her those clippings about Mad Dog. Maybe she was scared he would pop *her* off too. Maybe—" He tugged at his beard.

"Mr. Demos," Dr. Wishnick said, "I'm very, *very* upset by what you've told me. For four days now we have all been beside ourselves with anxiety and yet you deliberately refused to give us any idea that you knew."

He grinned.

"How do the rest of you feel about this?" Dr. Wishnick said, "about Leroy's action or lack of action? Do you feel it was irresponsible?"

There was silence.

"If any of *you* had seen Ms. Zimmer leave, would you have let us know?"

No one spoke.

"I'm glad she's safe," Noah said, "that's all."

"Me too," Elton said.

"Me too," Tamara Grace said.

"Same here," said Leroy Demos. "Let's make a toast to her." He raised an imaginary glass. "To A.Z.—long may she wave."

They all, with the exception of Dr. Wishnick, raised imaginary glasses and pretended to drink from them.

The news that Alix was fine, not dead, safe, and would not be brought back to the hospital, affected Noah the same way as the news of her possible death. At night he could think of nothing else. She was free, she was out there. *Why didn't I run off with her? It could have been me they were talking about.* He thought of how every patient wished it was them, everyone had some kind of inner jubilation that it was possible. *They'll watch us more closely now. But it was clever. Just hailing a cab or calling one. So simple! Had her husband known?* He would tell Selma. Selma knew he felt close to Alix. Surely if she heard the story she would realize that in some cases you had to act against medical orders. She would help him.

Selma came to see him the evening before he was to go home for Leo's birthday celebration. Now that he had been in the hospital so long, she no longer came to see him every day, but tried to call. It seemed to him their conversations had become more stilted, as though neither of them knew what to say. He thought of the scenes in movies where wives or girlfriends visited their imprisoned husbands. That was how he felt, as though he were behind a grill, as though when their eyes met there was a hopeless deadness in them. He hated her because she was free. She pitied him because he was not. Those two facts, unalterable, poisoned the underlying sweetness of their relationship until at times he dreaded seeing her and would almost have preferred she stay away.

She sat beside him uneasily, looking around the room, clasping and unclasping her watch band. "It doesn't seem fair," she said, "the way your mother is going all out to celebrate Leo's birthday when she didn't even remember yours."

Noah sighed. "Who cares, really?"

"I do. I want to speak to her. I thought she should make it a joint celebration."

"To celebrate what?" Noah said bitterly.

Her eyes were frightened. "That—that soon you'll be well."

"Will I?"

She nodded, but it seemed to him a mechanical gesture.

"The longer I stay here, the sicker I feel," he said. "It's the way you're treated. It seeps into you. You're treated as a pariah, as someone repugnant, and so you come to regard yourself that way."

She touched his hands gently. "I don't think of you that way."

He wondered at times: Didn't she miss him sexually? Didn't the fact that part of their life had been removed so hideously and suddenly bother her? She never spoke of it. He hesitated mentioning it because his longings for her, although she was his wife, seemed somehow forbidden, tormenting. "Will we go straight to my mother's?" he asked.

"Well, yes," Selma said, frowning. "She wants us to be there at five."

Noah scarcely dared look at her. "Couldn't we go back to our place first, just so we'd have a little time together alone?"

Why did she look that way? Because the idea of being alone with him was scary, because it was "against doctor's orders"?

"I'm not sure," she said. "Dr. Stern—"

"It would mean so much to me," Noah said softly. "The other stuff will be a circus. All I want is to be alone with you, really alone." Somehow he didn't have the courage to say what he really meant.

She smiled at him. "Then I'll come at two."

From the look in her eyes he felt she did know what he was hinting at, and a warmth flooded through him that was more than sexual. The rest of the visit seemed more relaxed after that interchange. Even after she left, he allowed himself to fantasize about it, allowed himself to remember lovely moments between the two of them, her way of undressing, the light in her eyes as though her pupils were enlarged by passion, the way she touched him. If he could explain it to her properly, he knew she would let him stay home. Or perhaps he could get Alix to explain, to make Selma see. Otherwise she would be intimidated by Dr. Stern, the way she was by most men in positions of authority. He was too, at times, but beneath his fears was a feeling of contempt at their incompetence and self-righteousness. Selma simply saw them as authorities, people possessed of superior knowledge. He thought of calling Alix, partly to see how she was, partly to ask her details of exactly how she had escaped, but there was no place he could call from that was safe, where he would not be overheard. He would call her from his own home, he decided.

That night, the night before he was to leave the hospital, Noah dreamed he was on his honeymoon with Selma. In the dream they were both young, as they had been, and at the same time their present age. They cavorted in the water, snorkeled, lay in the sun, drank cocktails with rum, encased in coconut shells. The dream seemed to have no plot, it was like a lyrical montage from a forties movie. He was surprised, therefore, that when he woke up the first thought that entered his head was a newspaper item he had once seen which asked the question: Do sharks ever sleep? The answer had been that, though they never stopped moving, they might be sleeping while they moved. So what, he thought, almost angrily. The sharks had not been in his dream. Why did they intrude now? Who cared if they slept or not?

Alix is safe, I will be safe. They had entered the hospital at approximately the same time. He saw their fates as intertwined. She had shown him the way. But it was hard to preserve a light-hearted feeling in the hospital. The moment his eyes opened and he saw the bars on the windows, saw the other patients, a cloud passed over him. Think of it as the last time, he told himself. With that in mind he felt almost a tenderness for all of them. Even Leroy, who usually upset or disgusted him, he joked with over breakfast. "I'm leaving today," he said, "going home for my brother's birthday."

"Making a break, huh?" Leroy said, showing his gold teeth at the back of his mouth.

Noah wondered if he was psychic or whether Alix's escape had simply planted that idea in everyone's head. He just smiled.

"Oh man, I must have spring fever. What I'd give to get out."
He shook his head. "You're lucky. If they let you out, they must
think you're getting better."

Noah shrugged. "They haven't said anything one way or the
other."

"I figure I could be here forever," Leroy said. "Hell, it seems
longer than forever already."

Selma showed up in her beige silk dress with the gold dolphin
pin at the neck, a pin he had given her for her last birthday. The fact
that she had remembered it touched Noah. Outside it was hot, but
still beautiful. *I'm going to be free. I'll never come back here again. Never.
So I'll lose my teaching job. Maybe the jewelry store idea won't work either.
But something will. I know it.*

"I'm glad you're feeling better," Selma said as they entered the
apartment. "You *look* so much better."

"I feel better," Noah said. He decided to wait until after they'd
made love to talk to her. He put his arms around her and held her
tightly. "Darling . . . I miss you every moment. Have you missed me
too?"

"Of course," Selma said. Feeling his hands caressing her, she
added nervously, "Is this all right? Are we allowed to?"

"We can do anything we want," Noah said. "Anything." And
it all went perfectly, as though by pretending to have some "permission" for the act, he had bought her acquiescence. Her body seemed
known, but also thrillingly new. His wife. He had a wife, he would
make up for everything that had happened. He held back until he
felt her make that unconscious convulsive movement that indicated
she was about to come. Then he let himself go, kissing her neck and
face as he dissolved into her. "Sweetheart," he murmured, "darling
Selma."

They dozed in each other's arms and he felt such peacefulness
and joy, it hardly seemed possible. All that had happened was a
nightmare, something invented. From now on his true life would
begin. Finally Selma stirred, her eyelids fluttered. "We should get
ready," she whispered.

"You shower first," he whispered.

While she did, he went to the phone and asked the operator for
the number of Alix Zimmer. "A. Zimmer." He dialed from the
phone in the kitchen, wearing his bathrobe.

"Alix?"

"Yes?"

"It's Noah . . . Noah Epstein, from the hospital."

"Oh, Noah. I'm so glad to hear from you. Where *are* you?"

"I'm at home. They let me out for the day. It's my brother's birthday. Look, partly I just wanted to say how happy I was to hear you had escaped."

She laughed. "Yes, yes, it feels so good to be out. You can't imagine."

"I can. In fact, I want to do the same thing . . . Can you tell me how you did it? Did you tell your husband ahead of time? Did he know?"

"No, of course not," she said. "He would have brought me back."

Noah's mood darkened. "I thought of just asking Selma—"

"She'll bring you back," Alix cried. "Noah, don't you see? They convince them it's for our own good, they brainwash them in a sense. Your only hope is to find somewhere to stay for three days, for seventy-two hours. After that they don't bother to go after you. I'm not sure they even bother until then, but I felt I had to be on the safe side."

"They did bother," Noah said. "They were asking everyone about you. They had me in for an interrogation, whether I knew anything, whether you'd given any hints about where you might have gone. It was horrible."

She sucked in her breath. "Christ. I'm sorry that you had to go through that. But do be careful, Noah. Promise me."

He heard Selma moving in the bathroom. "Will you be in later, around six or seven?"

"Sure, why?"

"I thought . . . maybe Selma could speak to you. I think she'll listen to you, if not to me. Would you be willing to do that?"

"Of course, if you think it'll help."

"I can't face going back," Noah said. "It's too terrible. I just can't." His voice broke.

He hung up and hurried back to the bedroom. Selma was still in the bathroom, retouching her makeup, naked. He kissed her shoulder, and then got into the shower. It was strange how different it was, talking to Alix on the outside. Suddenly he resented her because she was no longer connected to him, no longer a prisoner. *But she'll help you, she wants to.* And once they were both out, it would be different. They could be friends, they could have Alix and her husband over for dinner.

"I got Leo some tapes for his birthday," Selma said as Noah emerged from the shower. "He loves show tunes and I found the original cast recordings of *Pal Joey* and *South Pacific*. Do you think he'll like that?"

" 'Some Enchanted Evening,' " Noah sang. He remembered Leo listening to those songs, trying to deepen his voice so he would sound like Ezio Pinza's heavy Italian bass. He remembered their laughing over the way Pinza pronounced "stranger." What was a 'strawhnger'? they wondered.

His mother lived in the Bronx. It was a long drive. Selma drove and Noah allowed himself to doze in the car. He felt peaceful, mildly uneasy, but no more so than he would have on any similar occasion in the past. His mother had always made a fuss over Leo. He was her favorite. They all knew that. *So? I can live with it.*

When he and Selma arrived, everyone was already assembled. Eloise had the same boyishly short hair style and was in a snow white dress with a large encrusted amber cross around her neck. Perfume whooshed at him as she lightly kissed his cheek. His mother was in bright red, her hair newly set, Horace at her elbow. Horace was the only one, it seemed to Noah, who greeted him normally. With everyone else, he sensed a tension, something odd. He wished they all, especially Leo, knew he and Selma were late because they had made love.

Leo opened his tapes. "Hey, terrific!" he said. He hugged Selma, although he had already hugged her when they arrived. "You always know my taste, Sel. Perfect! You know when we were dating, they had a revival of 'Pal Joey' at City Center. 'Bewitched, bothered, and bewildered am I' . . ." he sang to Selma.

Noah felt irritated, especially since Selma blushed. "I liked the other song, I can't remember how it went—"

"If they asked me, I could write a book," Leo sang.

What was Leo doing? He was singing, looking directly at Selma, who looked confused and touched. Had Leo been fucking Selma while he was in the hospital? Was that why she had seemed uninterested in sex? *No, don't be a fool, don't be paranoid. He had his choice of dozens, hundreds, much better looking, younger. Why should he pick Selma?*

They sat down at the long table. His mother had roasted a large capon which was surrounded by roast potatoes, onions, and carrots. "I didn't know it would be so hot," she said, touching her sweaty brow.

"Well, we have big news," Eloise said. "Gretchen was accepted at Harvard and . . . Leo's book is being strongly considered by CBS."

Leo winked, raising his glass. "I'll be played by Mel Gibson," he joked.

"That's wonderful!" Selma exclaimed. "Goodness. What *wonderful* news." She turned to Noah as though he hadn't heard.

Everyone lifted their wine glasses and toasted.

"Okay," Horace said, "Roz and I got a secret too. We did it. We got married."

Eloise looked startled. "Why did you do that?" she asked.

"Love," Horace said. "What else?"

Noah's mother was beaming. "I told him it didn't make sense at our age, but he convinced me. And you want to know something? I feel better. I'm the married type. I'm too old to change. All that fooling around, it made me feel funny, somehow."

"Fooling around?" Horace said, patting her arm. "I'm a gentleman, I don't fool around with anyone's wife but my own."

Noah stared at Leo. It seemed to him Leo was looking at Selma who was gazing down at the tablecloth. Eloise was chattering brightly. "Of course, the TV deal isn't *set* yet," she said. "So many things can happen, but their idea is Leo could be the host, sort of like Dr. Ruth, but on a more intellectual level, answer questions about sexuality, fit them into a societal context."

"Will people call in questions?" Selma asked.

Leo leaned forward and, in Groucho Marx style, said, "Ask me anything you want to know, baby."

He's a joker. He's been like this since he was nine years old. He has a girlfriend, a mistress, a wife. Suddenly Noah raised his glass. "I want to make a toast," he said.

There was a silence. Again he felt everyone looking at him strangely. "To what?" Leo asked.

"To Selma," Noah said. "To my wonderful wife and our wonderful marriage and the love we share and will always share." He held up his glass, but no one else did. Finally Selma raised her glass and gently clinked it against his.

"Thank you," she whispered, embarrassed.

"I've made mistakes in my life," Noah said, "but that's all behind me. And through it all Selma has stood by me. No man can ask for more than that."

"Some enchanted evening," Leo sang suddenly, "you will meet a strawhnger . . . " He grinned at Noah. "I never did meet a 'strawhnger,' that's a fact. I've met a lot of funny dames, but no 'strawhngers.' Hey, Noah, guess who I ran into the other day?"

"Who?" Noah asked, uninterested. His mother's cooking was overly rich. He shoved the oil encrusted potatoes to one side of his plate.

"Remember that woman poet you sat next to at the Literary Lions party—Ava? She asked after you, said she'd sent you her new book and you never responded. I told her you loved it, is that okay?"

Why was he doing this? He knew what had happened between them. Why, at a family party, would he refer to it? Noah felt that familiar burst of rage at his brother's teasing. "I don't remember her," he said curtly.

"You remember the party, don't you?" Leo said.

"Of course I remember the party."

"We have the book," Selma intervened. "It was such a nice gesture, considering she only met Noah one time."

"I think he made a big impression on her," Leo said with a broad smile. "You've got a touch with the ladies, kiddo."

"Shut up," Noah said violently.

Leo looked taken aback.

"I love my wife," Noah said. "You have a wife . . . leave mine alone."

Selma tugged at his sleeve. "Noah . . ."

"Hey," Leo said, flustered. "I was just horsing around. No offense. You have a great wife. I introduced you to her, remember?"

Suddenly Noah exploded with anger. "Look, if you wanted her, you could have had her. We all know that. We all know you could have married anyone. But you dumped her, right? And I got the leftovers. Well, I don't care. Who says she would have been happier with you even with all your literary lions shit and miniseries. Who says your wife is any happier than mine?"

"Christ, pipe down," Leo said. "I didn't dump Sel." He looked at Selma ingratiatingly. "Did I? You don't see it that way, do you?"

"No," Selma whispered tearfully. "We just—"

"She's a wonderful person," Leo said. "Have I ever said otherwise? I love her. I think you're a lucky son of a bitch."

"Lucky?" Noah said bitterly. "Lucky because I'm locked up in a nuthouse where they put handcuffs on me because they're afraid

I'll jump someone? Lucky to be a guinea pig for any drug they want to hand out? Is that what you call lucky?"

"Hey, hey," Leo said, "calm down. What is this? It's my birthday. Can't we just—"

But Noah couldn't stop. "No, we can't. You started it. Going on about Ava Bernier. So I sat next to her at your party? Does that make me a philanderer, a cheat, like you?"

Suddenly Noah's mother leapt to her feet and clamped her hand over Noah's mouth. "Stop," she said. "Shame on you."

Noah wriggled out of her grasp. "It was *my* birthday that night," he said. "The night of the Literary Lions thing. You didn't even remember. Did you?" He looked at his mother accusingly.

She flushed. "God, no, Noah, I'm sorry . . . I forgot. That's terrible."

Horace stood up. He was holding a glass of wine in one hand. "I want to make a toast," he said. "First to my wonderful wife who looks twenty years younger than she really is, who's the best cook any guy will ever meet and a real sweetheart. And then to her two sons, who are both swell guys, and their beautiful wives. I want to say I'm happy to be a part of this family."

There was silence. Everyone looked at him, bewildered, not knowing if he was joking or sincere. "Horace is right," Noah's mother said, sitting down. "We should count our blessings. We're healthy, we're well. Your troubles will pass, Noah. We all love you. Horace too. You should know that. As for forgetting your birthday, that was inexcusable. Will you forgive me?"

Noah felt abashed. "Sure . . . it doesn't matter."

They resumed their eating. Eloise, who had hardly touched her food, said in a strained voice, "I think you should apologize to Leo, Noah."

"For what?"

"He isn't what you said. I won't even repeat those words. How can you know anything about our marriage? Every marriage is different." Her voice was trembling.

All Noah could think of was Leo's harangue in the hospital about Eloise being like a boiled onion in bed, how she supposedly accepted his infidelities and didn't care. "You're right," he said. "I take it back."

"It's Eloise you should apologize to," Leo added. "*I* don't give a shit. Say whatever you want about me. But to drag her into it—"

"I didn't say anything about her," Noah said.

"By implication you did. Apologize!" Leo's face was sweaty, his hair falling into his face.

Noah felt weary, deflated. He looked at Eloise. Why was he apologizing? "I'm sorry if I hurt you," he said softly.

"I accept your apology," Eloise said, head held high. Then she looked with a bright smile at Noah's mother. "This chicken is delicious, Roz! How do you get the skin so crisp?"

"A paper bag!" Noah's mother exclaimed. "Any bag will do. Keep it on for an hour, then off for the crispness. That's my secret."

Horace squeezed her arm. "My first wife, bless her, couldn't boil an egg."

Noah's mother smiled impishly. "Neither could my first husband. But they had other virtues. They were good people."

She started to clear. Eloise and Selma got up to help her. Horace disappeared into another room. Noah found himself facing Leo across the littered table. They stared at each other. "I don't get it," Leo said quietly. "Why do you do it? Hurting Sel, hurting El. What did they ever do to you? Selma visits you every day, calls you, is worried sick over you. Any other wife would have called it quits years ago."

"She's loyal," Noah said. "She loves me. Is that so hard for you to believe?"

"You're such a baby," Leo said. "Grow up."

"Meaning what?"

" 'You forgot my birthday,' " he mimicked. "Who cares? Who cares about any of it?"

"I care that you're going after my wife now that I'm not there, that you sing songs to her and God knows what else. Of course I care!" Noah was breathless.

"Are you crazy?" Leo picked up a chicken bone and set it down again. "You think I'm making it with Selma? You really think that?"

"Why not? What would stop you? You've done it with half the female population of New York."

"You're my brother, for Christ's sake. You're a blood relation. What do you take me for?"

Noah's anger had faded. He felt a crippling sadness like a fog descend, veiling him in. "Our marriage," he said. "It's so hard . . . I miss her. I can't make love to her. You don't know what it's like."

Leo looked at him for a long moment. "No," he admitted, "I don't."

Suddenly the kitchen door was flung open and the three women came in, carrying an enormous cake with dozens of candles. There was a flat piece of marzipan on it saying "Happy Birthday." They set it down in between Leo and Noah, singing "Happy Birthday to you . . ."

"Now blow it out together," Noah's mother said. "Both of you together. Come on."

Leo and Noah stood up and, leaning over, together managed to blow out all the candles. Their eyes met over the cake and signaled forgiveness to each other. "You take the first piece," Leo said gallantly.

Noah's mother always bought cakes at a horrible bakery in her neighborhood. They were layered with sugary cream frosting. Noah took his piece and then sat down. He looked at Selma, who was quietly eating her cake. She looked sad, out of it. He hoped it wasn't his fault. The time they had spent together alone had left such a magical warmth and now, barely an hour or two later, it had dissolved as though it had never been, as though it were another of his fantasies. He thought of the hospital, of Dr. Stern, of the inedible meals with Leroy Demos breathing his fetid breath at him. *What have I done to deserve that?*

When the meal was over, Noah touched Selma on the shoulder. "Could you come in here a minute?" he asked.

She followed him quietly. He led her into his mother's bedroom. Her face still had that sunken, crushed look. "Sel, look, I'm sorry if whatever I said at dinner upset you. I didn't mean to. It's just—"

"Then why *did* you?" she burst out. "It was so cruel, so uncalled for—"

"I was jealous, I guess, the way Leo comes on to you, singing."

"But that's his way," Selma said. *"You* know that. He's like that with everyone. And he *didn't* dump me. Why did you say that? I fell in love with you. Don't you realize that?"

His heart flipped. "Did you?"

"Of course I did. I didn't want the marriage Eloise has. Any woman with two eyes in her head could have seen that's what Leo would be like. I wanted a man I could respect and admire, as a human being, not someone who writes books and grabs women at parties."

Noah felt this was the happiest moment of his life. *"A man I could respect and admire . . ."* He took her in his arms. "I love you so much," he said. "Let's put all this behind us. I don't need to go back to the hospital. Maybe my plan about the jewelry store was out of hand, but I'll think of something. I have skills. I have determination. Give me a chance."

Selma pulled away from him. "It's not up to me," she said. "It's up to the doctors."

"It *is* up to you. Just let me stay here for three days. That's all it takes. Seventy-two hours. If they catch you within that time, they can bring you back. But if they don't, they can't. Don't you see?"

"No," Selma said, frowning. "I don't understand."

He took her hands, squeezing them. "Remember Alix Zimmer? You met her and her husband one day? A couple of times actually."

"The dark-haired one who was so thin?"

"Right. Well, a few days ago she escaped from the hospital."

"Escaped? How?"

"It was simple," Noah said. "She hailed a cab and then spent the next seventy-two hours somewhere where the hospital couldn't track her down. They questioned me about her whereabouts, but I didn't know. Now she's home she's fine, she—"

Selma was still looking anxious and puzzled. "Did her husband know?"

"No. She was afraid if he knew he'd make her return. The point is, Sel, she's fine. In fact, I spoke to her and she said she'd love to talk to you about it. Will you? Please? It's so important to me."

Selma took the slip of paper he removed from his pocket which had Alix's number written on it. "What should I ask her?"

"Just about how she got out, how she is now, whatever . . ."

Selma looked around the room. "I want to speak to her alone, though."

"Sure, anything. I'll go back inside." Noah closed the door behind him. He waited a few minutes outside the door until he heard Selma say, "Hello? Is this Alix Zimmer?"

He was about to go back inside when it occurred to him that there was an extension in the den. He walked down the hall. Entering the den, he closed the door behind him. Then, with utmost care he picked up the receiver. He heard Alix say, "Yes, I'm feeling fine. You see, the doctor told me it might be months, even years before they would let me out. I just couldn't bear it anymore. I felt I had to take action."

"Isn't it against the law, though?" Selma asked.

"But the law is unjust!" Alix cried. "It's a violation of the most basic civil liberties. Mrs. Epstein, I'm a lawyer myself, and this is a bad law, if one can even call it that. Patients like myself enter the hospital, assuming they're voluntary and can leave at any time, only to discover they can't. They're prisoners."

"But Noah isn't voluntary," Selma said. "I had to have him committed."

"Don't you see?" Alix said. "It doesn't make any difference. Voluntary, not voluntary. If anyone could leave the hospital who realized they were being given horrendous medical care, the place would be empty in an hour."

"But the drugs," Selma said, "didn't they help you?"

"Not at all."

Selma hesitated. "Dr. Stern said he felt Noah would benefit from a series of shock treatments. He said they would calm him, make him less agitated."

Noah almost dropped the phone. The room swirled. "Don't let them do that to him," Alix said. "They can damage the brain permanently. It's a terrifying experience. My mother had treatments like that."

"But he had them once before," Selma said. "It seemed to help."

"Mrs. Epstein, please, don't let them do that to him! They can't unless you sign a release form. Refuse to sign it."

"I signed it already," Selma said.

"Then don't take him back to the hospital," Alix said. "Care for him at home. Look, your husband is a wonderful person. He's kind, he's gentle. Don't let them destroy him."

"I only want what's best for him," Selma said.

"Promise me you won't make him go back," Alix said.

"I have to think about it," Selma said. "But thank you, Mrs. Zimmer. It was good for Noah to have a friend like you in the hospital."

"Let me know what happens," Alix said. "You have my number. Call me. Okay?"

The moment Selma hung up the phone, Noah did also. He raced back to the bedroom. "Selma!" he cried. "How could you?"

She looked terrified. "You were listening?"

"You signed a release form so they could give me shock treatments and you didn't tell me? That's horrible!"

Selma was almost crying. "It will help you, Noah. They promised me it would. You'll be your old self again."

"I won't," Noah said. "It'll kill me. I'd rather you killed me, right here and now."

She stared at him. Noah ran excitedly from the room. He felt terrified, almost unbelieving. There was a fire escape from his mother's kitchen. He rushed in and ran out on it. locking the window from the bottom. Selma ran after him. "Noah," she screamed. "What are you doing? Help, Leo, everyone! Help!"

The entire family crowded into the kitchen. Noah looked down at the ten-story drop into the courtyard below. "He's going to jump," Selma said, crying, yanking on Leo's sleeve. "Stop him!"

"Noah," Leo yelled. "What're you doing? What's wrong?"

"She signed a form saying they could give me shock treatments," Noah said. "I'd rather die."

"Did you?" Leo asked Selma.

"Yes, but I—Noah, I'll take it back. I'll tell them not to."

"That's not good enough," Noah said. "You have to swear not to take me back to the hospital."

"I have to," Selma said. "It's against the law." She pulled at Leo again. "Tell him, Leo."

Leo moved so that his body was pressed against the glass. "Noah, Sel will just take you back in order to explain that she feels you can manage fine on the outside. I'll go with her. We'll talk to them."

"That won't work," Noah said. "You'll be killing me. Is that what you want? Do you want to kill me?"

At that, Noah's mother began to sob and clutch at Horace, who was standing, cigar in hand, an expression of total bewilderment on his face. "Make him come in," Noah's mother said. "He's going to jump. Please! Someone stop him."

Horace shoved Leo out of the way. "Listen, Noah," he said, "I don't get all this stuff. I don't know what the fuss is about, but why don't you come in and we can all talk about it like civilized human beings? Your wife here, she's hysterical. She loves you. It would kill her to lose you. It would kill all of us."

Noah looked down at the courtyard again. There was something so tantalizing about it, the thought that in one second it would all be over, all his torments and anxieties, his constant sense of having failed everyone. But then he turned and saw Selma's horrified face, tears streaming down her cheeks. Slowly, he crouched and unlocked the window. He stepped back into the kitchen.

"Oh my God," Noah's mother said, sitting down, "I'm going to faint."

Even though he was back inside, Noah still saw the courtyard below, the dizzying plunge. It was as though part of him had jumped, was, at that very moment, whirling down inexorably. Spots started jumping in front of his eyes, obscuring the faces of everyone in the room. "I'm going to pass out," he murmured.

"Quick, get him into the bedroom," Leo said.

Noah felt Horace and Leo dragging him into the bedroom. He didn't remember what happened after that. He seemed to sink into a black dream of swirling shapes and images, no plot, no people. The next face he saw was Nurse Kefaldis bending over him.

"So, you went off the deep end," she said with her grim smile. "Don't worry. We'll take care of that. Don't worry about a thing."

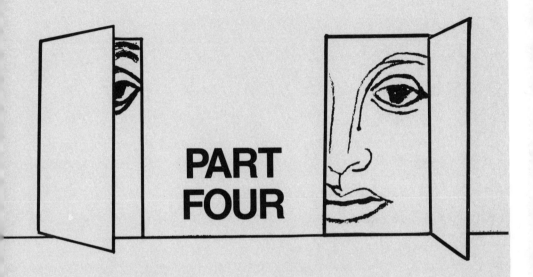

PART
FOUR

TYING
THE KNOT

The wedding was the following day. Both Darryl and Stern had rooms at the Barclay on the same floor. They were to appear together, an hour before the ceremony. Stern had already checked in, prior to the family dinner Saturday night. He had thought he might feel anxious, ill at ease, now that the great event which he had so long postponed, about which he had had such mixed feelings, had arrived, but it was not so. He managed to go through the motions mechanically.

Just before the family dinner Winifred disappeared, in tears, rushing from the room. Stern had been in the bathroom. As he reentered the living room, he saw everyone's startled faces: Tilden Sutton glowering; Maida Sutton looking frightened; Sydney, her face flushed, her eyes bright; Darryl, his back to all of them. For a moment Stern wondered if it had anything to do with him, but Sydney, leaping from her seat, pulled him into the dining room. "I can't believe it," she whispered. "How could he *do* this?"

"Darryl?" Stern guessed.

She closed the doors to the dining room. "You know Stanford, who's going to be best man? It turns out he and Darryl once—they once were . . . oh, I know it happened ages ago, but it *happened.* And he waited until now to tell us." She looked at Stern imploringly, certain he would have either a solution or a soothing comment.

"They were lovers in college?" he surmised.

"Not just once, many times."

"Isn't he married now?" Stern tried to remember the wedding rehearsal. His impression of Stanford had been of a hearty, beefy, prematurely bald young man with a jutting chin.

"Yes, but so what?" Sydney's voice rose shrilly. "Maybe they're just planning—oh, don't you see, Stu? You *must.* "

"I think you're all wrong," Stern said, attempting to play the role she wanted him to. "He would never have told everyone, especially now, if it wasn't the opposite, something in the past, something over."

Sydney was still frowning. "But is anything *ever* over?" she asked. "What if you wanted to invite that nurse, the one you . . . to the wedding? It would be terrible. I'd be so jealous I could hardly bear it." He had never told Sydney of Roxanne's death. There had been a police investigation but, mercifully, it had stayed out of the newspapers. No one knew at Nash. The police had concluded from the way she had fallen, as well as from her recent release from a psychiatric hospital, that it had been a suicide. "That's totally different," he said brusquely.

"How?" Sydney demanded.

"She's dead."

"What do you mean?"

"What I said. She killed herself." A surge of anger rose up in him. *Stupid, stupid, why mention it now, or ever?*

"Because of us?"

"No. Nothing to do with that. She just, she had problems, I told you. She was a—" His voice broke.

Sydney stared at the wall. "How could she do it? She did it to get at you. I hate her for that. Now you'll remember her always."

"I'm telling you she didn't," Stern shouted. "What do *you* know? Did you know her? Did you know anything about her?"

"I know she loved you."

"Sydney, I forbid you to speak of her. I mean it. It's a part of my past, it's finished, it's over. It would have been, even if she'd lived . . . Just as this business with whatever his name is, is Darryl's past. People can go from love, even from passionate love, to friendship. It happens every day."

"I don't believe that," Sydney said, chin held high. "I don't think it's possible."

"How would you know?" he said. "How many passionate loves have you had?"

She flushed. "That's cruel . . . Just because I saved myself, because I didn't fling myself at men. I wanted our marriage to be different, to be special."

The tension in the air was giving Stern a violent headache. He took Sydney's cold white hands in his. "Darling, our marriage will be special. We love each other in a special way. No one can change that. And I think, though I have no way of knowing for certain, that that's exactly how Darryl feels, that it took him a long time to find someone he wanted to share his life with, but now he has."

The expression on her face as she looked at him was transformed into the little girl who would believe anything she was told. "You think he really loves Win?"

"Of course. He's told me so a dozen times."

"And you think he'll be faithful?"

"Yes," he lied.

"You think men can be?"

"Of course they can. Look at your father."

Sydney sighed. "Oh, well, Daddy . . . but their generation was so different. Form was so important. We'll be in different cities, even."

"That's just a technicality," Stern said. "It's only for now. Let's rejoin them, shall we?"

"But Stu, I know this is an awful imposition, especially on the night of, the night before . . . but if you and Darryl happen to have a drink tonight, could you—"

"Of course."

Oddly, he had the feeling he had been married many times before, had had variants of this conversation, hurtling from tears over absurdities to coldness to anger to lies to comfort. Hearing himself say things he only half believed or even disbelieved seemed to come naturally. Only when Sydney had referred to Roxanne had some burst of feeling shot through the veneer and he wanted to fling her across the room, to hit her. But it had passed almost as rapidly as it came.

Some version of this reconciliation must have been going on between Winifred and Darryl because at dinner, everyone was calm, dignified, chatty. "You know, Syd, it's so funny," Winifred said. "I met *three* girls from our graduation class who are getting married this month! Can you imagine?"

"That's amazing," Sydney said.

Looking at Winifred, all Stern could think of were her very small pointed little teeth which she had worn in braces until a month ago. Now they were braceless, nipping into the salad like some ferrety small animal. He also recalled Sydney's saying that Darryl had sworn to always use condoms, even though Winifred had a diaphragm, "just to be on the safe side."

Since Roxanne's death three months ago, he had what could have been described as a sexual problem with Sydney. He never came. He had erections as easily as before, but somehow, no matter how long they labored, whether Sydney came or didn't, pretended to or didn't, the release never arrived. It was strange. But now it was almost a pattern. Was it the approaching marriage, some sense that he was locking himself in forever, throwing away his freedom, or was it Roxanne who continued to hover, like some demonic shadow, on the side of his consciousness? He tried not to think of her death as an actual death. She had simply gone away, somewhere he would never go. Instead of fading out of his life gradually, as would have happened in time, she had taken off. *The last thing we did was make love. That was the last interchange between us, not bitterness or hate.* And who knew what she was leaping to in that moment: safety, peace . . .

But at other times, he felt it had not been an impulse, that she had planned it all along, from the time he said he was coming over, that it had been done to him. If it was death she had wanted, whatever that meant to her, she could have done it quietly with no one there, or after he had gone. No, she wanted that heart-stopping hideous moment when he realized what had happened. She wanted to hurt him permanently in a way no other action could have. Or had she hoped he would join her, leap after her? In fact, he had rushed out of the building by the back entrance, unable to face seeing her body.

". . . don't you think, Stu?" Mrs. Sutton was saying.

He yanked himself back from his disturbing reveries. "I'm sorry, my mind was wandering. What was it?"

"I was saying that I think there *is* some point, after all, in the old ritual of the groom not seeing the bride on the actual day of the wedding. I'm glad you and Darryl understand that."

"Sure we do," Darryl said, grinning at Stern. "We could even slip in a game of squash tomorrow morning. The ceremony's not until one, is it?"

Winifred tapped him lightly on the wrist. "You know when it is," she said. "Don't be naughty."

" 'Get Me to the Church on Time,' " Darryl sang. The ceremony was to be at the Episcopal church which the Suttons attended.

"Do you remember our wedding?" Mrs. Sutton asked her husband. "I came down with a flu the night before. I had a fever of a hundred and one, but I was determined to go through with it. And that heavy silk dress, the veil—I almost passed out."

"Her skin was burning hot," Mr. Sutton said. "When I leaned over to kiss her, I felt like I was being scorched."

"How awful for your honeymoon!" Winifred said. "How long did it take till you felt better?"

Mrs. Sutton's blue eyes were cool, reflective. "I was sick as a dog the whole time. Tilden played golf and I slept in my room."

"Doesn't sound like much fun," Darryl said, smiling affectionately at his mother.

"Oh, honeymoons are overrated," Mrs. Sutton said. "It's just a vacation, after all. What does it have to do with what comes afterward? Wonderful honeymoons lead to disastrous marriages and vice versa. I've known *dozens* of cases of that."

"Darn," Darryl said. "I was counting on ours to be terrific." He beamed at Winifred, who blushed.

Mrs. Sutton looked wistful. "Well, everything in life is what you make it," she said. "Don't you think so, dear?" She turned to her husband.

"What?"

"Marriage, honeymoons," she said, raising her voice slightly, since he'd become a bit deaf.

"What about them?" He looked startled.

"They're what you make them," Mrs. Sutton said. "What I mean is, ecstasy, all that women's magazine nonsense . . . you can't go *planning* ecstasy. It happens or it doesn't. I hate all those articles that build up women's expectations so. I think men are so much more realistic."

Sydney looked downcast. "Oh, Mommy, that's so unromantic. I was *counting* on ecstasy."

Only Sydney, Stern thought, could have gotten away with a line like that: "I was counting on ecstasy." "Then you shall have it, dear," Mrs. Sutton said, giving a peremptory glance at Stern, which seemed to say: "Make it happen."

After dinner Stern and Sydney kissed good-bye and he joined Darryl in the cab which was to take them back to the hotel. Darryl closed his eyes. Stern wondered if he was tired or drunk. But when they arrived at the hotel, he said to Stern, "Want a nightcap? We could have one in my room."

"Great," Stern said. He suspected he would sleep badly, and was eager to postpone the moment of trying.

Darryl's room was a carbon copy of Stern's, with a small living room suite adjoining the bedroom. There was a bar in the room. Darryl poured himself some scotch. Stern asked for vodka. "There's no ice. Do you care?"

"No, that's fine." He wanted mainly to reach a point of near unconsciousness and then tumble into bed.

"God, what a farce," Darryl said. He slumped down in the easy chair, looking at Stern, who was sitting on the couch.

"Tonight? The whole thing?"

"Stanford is my fucking best friend," Darryl said. "Christ, if he hadn't made it, I wouldn't even have dared embark on this. But he says you get used to it. It's like anything."

Stern wondered what "it" referred to: monogamy, sex with a woman, day-to-day living with one person. "I imagine," he said.

"It's different for you," Darryl said. "You're in New York. Syd's here. Plus you're what, almost forty? I would think you've had a chance to get whatever out of your system by now."

"Right," Stern said. "I did."

Darryl had almost finished his drink. "Syd said you had some girlfriend in the city whom she thought you still saw."

"It's over," Stern said curtly.

"How'd she take it?"

"What do you mean?"

"When you told her—"

"She went away," Stern said. "She . . . wanted to start a new life somewhere."

Darryl shrugged. "That's easier, then."

"Right."

"So, you won't write or call or—"

"No."

Darryl was silent. "That's smart . . . I want to do that too."

"Is there anyone special you're referring to?"

"Can you keep a secret?"

"Sure."

"Yeah, there's someone . . . He's younger than me, kind of unstable, in fact. I think he expects . . . but I've told him I can't. I can't live like that."

"Won't he accept it?"

"He talks about suicide, he really scares the shit out of me sometimes. But I think it's just a bluff, don't you? Isn't that what they say? The people who really end up doing it don't talk about it, and the ones who talk are just that—talkers. Right?"

The vodka had smoothed away some of the urgency of the conversation. "Nobody knows," Stern said, pouring himself another drink.

"The trouble," Darryl said, "is I think I love him."

"Make a total break," Stern said. "Otherwise he'll never let go of you. He'll promise, but he never will, and neither will you. You'll think about him all the time. Then one day in a moment of weakness, you'll pick up the phone . . ."

"Is that what you think?" Darryl said, recoiling. "That I'm that weak?"

"We're all weak."

Suddenly Darryl leapt from the chair. "I don't want to live like that!" he said loudly. "I don't want that kind of . . . Oh, hell, I don't know *what* I want. I look at Mom and Dad and they seem dead from the toes up, but with my friend it's too—it's the other extreme. We'd eat each other alive. He's like—it's like he's inside me, he knows everything I think before I think it."

Stern felt claustrophobic, wildly anxious. It was as though Roxanne were in the room. He actually felt he saw her, sensed her presence, and turned quickly, but no one was there. He had seen a movie like that—a man had stolen another man's fiancée and for revenge, the fiancée had returned from the dead to spoil their honeymoon. Stern was sorry he'd had the vodka. It removed his ability to sever such thoughts at the root. "Look, I better go to bed," he said.

Darryl looked drunk too. He made no effort to get up from the couch. "You're a shrink and you don't know a fucking thing, do you?" he said.

"No," Stern admitted. "Not a thing."

"So, what's the point?" Darryl said. "Why're you doing it?"

"Getting married?"

"Yeah. Why not keep your freedom?"

Stern shrugged.

Darryl smiled sleepily. "We could just run off . . . not show tomorrow. Can you imagine the fuss? Mom and Dad, Win and Syd, all the guests?" His expression changed. "God, I feel sick. I think I'm going to throw up."

"Sleep well," Stern said, exiting.

He had drunk the vodka too quickly or perhaps just had too much. *Whatever.* Instead of easing, his thoughts seemed to loom uneasily. He dreaded returning to his room. *"Don't be stupid. It's just a room. Take a few Valium. Go to sleep."*

But his room was worse than being in Darryl's. All the objects in it were too bright and too three-dimensional. They looked half alive. What had happened to Roxanne's apartment? Who lived in it now? *Don't think of that.* He took the Valium and had another shot of vodka from the bar in his room. Had her phone number been given to someone else? What did they do with defunct phone numbers? Did they get rid of them or just pass them on? Impulsively, he reached for the phone and dialed Roxanne's number. It rang several times, and then a female voice answered. His heart stopped.

"Who is this?" the female voice said.

"My name is . . . I used to know someone who lived at this number. I've been away and I wondered if she was there. Her name is Roxanne Arlen."

There was a pause. "She's not here anymore."

"Do you have a number where I could reach her?"

"Look, mister, who are you? What's your name?"

"Stuart Stern. I worked at the Nash Institute for Mental Health where Ms. Arlen was employed."

"Are you someone who used to date her, or what?"

"No, I'm just a . . . friend."

"Well, listen, she died. I'm sorry if I'm the first to tell you. A couple of months ago, actually."

"Oh. Was she ill?"

"Yeah, she'd been ill."

"Why—why are you living there? Why do you have her phone number?"

"One of her friends told me about it. You know how it is, it's hard getting apartments in Manhattan. I lucked out. It's a great place."

"Yes," Stern said. "I know."

"So listen, I'm sorry to be the one to break the bad news to you."

"That's okay. Sorry to have troubled you."

Stern hung up. He felt worse. *You're crazy. Why'd you do that? Cut it out.* He hated the fact that her number had not been changed, that the apartment was still there. Maybe this young woman, whoever it was, had bought Roxanne's furniture too. "I lucked out": *You're getting married in the morning. These are demons.* The vodka was a mistake. He got into pajamas and clicked off the light. But the darkness was hideous, not a blanking soothing darkness, but something alive with unseen forms and voices. He heard the young woman's voice. *Had it sounded familiar? What if it had been Roxanne? What if she hadn't jumped, but simply gone away on a trip? Why are you doing this? Stop it. You wanted a new life, you wanted freedom. If she had lived, you would never have stood a chance.*

It seemed to Stern that he didn't sleep all night. The darkness in the room became so ominous that he finally turned on the light in the bathroom and kept the door ajar. At least that way he could see the objects in the room. He kept looking at the doors in the room, the door to the closet, the door to the hallway. Once, in the middle of the night, he got up and opened all the doors. The closet was empty except for the suit he had had made for the wedding. The hallway simply led down a long corridor with many other doors on each side. There was a deathly silence. Then someone peeked out of one of the rooms and set a pair of shoes out to be polished.

For some reason as he got back into bed, he thought of one of his former patients, Alix Zimmer, how she had reminded him of Roxanne, how she, too, had disappeared. But not to kill herself. She had simply escaped. He remembered seeing her that morning, pretending to go to her job at the counseling office. Was Sydney pretending too? Was anyone not? He saw Sydney's long white body, saw himself relentlessly trying to lose himself in her, her tiny muffled squeaks.

Tomorrow she would be a bride and he would be a groom. *Pretend, that's all.*

He and Darryl shared a cab to the chapel. Stern had asked the hotel to awaken him at nine, but when the call came, it seemed to come just after he had fallen asleep, after one moment of beautiful, blessed release. His eyes flew open as the computerized voice announced the weather, the time.

He shaved and dressed hurriedly, meeting Darryl in the lobby at ten.

"Well, no going back now," Darryl said.

"Right." Stern felt ashamed of the night before, of his fear of the closed doors. "I didn't sleep too well, did you?"

"Not a wink. I did something dumb."

"Yes?" Stern didn't feel like listening to a confession so early in the morning.

"I called my friend, the one I mentioned."

"You didn't have him come over?"

"No, but I—well, anyhow. Onward to the future!"

It was a brilliantly sunny day with a few wisps of white clouds, a perfect brightness, like color film that had been overprocessed. Roxanne had liked black and white film better, said the color was never natural, was always off, the skin tones not like real skin. In the cab, as he was exiting after Darryl, he realized she actually *was* there, that she was accompanying him to the wedding, would be there throughout the ceremony, would not leave his side, would whisper in his ear. He had a moment of convulsive horror at this, it seemed so unfair, so wrong. If she had wanted to disappear from his life, why not simply disappear?

The church was crowded. *We would have eloped,* Roxanne said. *I couldn't have faced all this. What a farce . . . I don't mind it,* he replied. *Ceremony is necessary. You never understood that . . . Yes, I did. I understood. Where's Sydney? . . . She'll be here in a moment . . . I can't wait. I wonder what she'll wear.*

Stern stood beside Darryl who looked deathly pale, but presentable, a tiny white flower in his lapel. Then the music began and Sydney, on her father's arm, began slowly walking down the aisle, followed by Winifred, on the arm of her father. Sydney looked delicate, soft, her hair drawn back. *She is beautiful . . . Really? Is that your taste?* Roxanne's smile curled contemptuously. *I always imagined her differently, more sexy, blonde, vivacious . . . She can be . . . Cold, wimpish, stiff . . . She's not, Roxanne, you don't know her. You know nothing about her. Go away!*

The minister recited the vows. Stern repeated them carefully, afraid his tongue might slip. Sydney's face was screened by the veil.

When she said, "I do," her voice trembled just slightly. Then she parted her veil and he leaned forward to kiss her.

Roxanne just watched, her eyes wary and alert and also dreamy. *Kiss me too. Now kiss me.* He did, hoping no one would notice, parted his lips slightly and let her move into his arms. Then she was gone, and he knew he would never see her again.

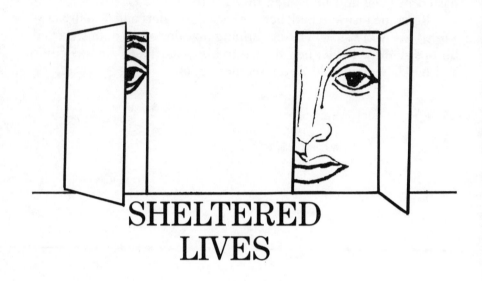

SHELTERED
LIVES

The school called to say that Pammy wasn't feeling well. Alix, at work, debated. It was past two. "Can you keep her in the office for an hour?" she said. "I'll pick her up in a cab."

The school was lenient, progressive, most of the parents worked or were single parents. But Pammy was rarely sick; she was in first grade, just past six years old. Laurel, who was a graduate student at NYU, lived with Alix and helped out with baby-sitting, but today was a day she had a late class. When Alix had decided she and Luke should separate, it had been Laurel who had suggested she get pregnant without letting him know. "You want a child. Won't it be easier that way than going through all the adoption agencies?" Probably it would have been, but Alix knew that she and Luke would be bound forever, their relationship living on in a child who would always be torn between them.

Pammy was Korean. It had taken two years to find her, to go through the necessary agencies, but she had never known a life other than with Alix. She seemed to accept it as natural, though who knew what she would feel later on. She was tiny for her age, with thin silky black hair that barely covered her ears and large black eyes that seemed to observe and take in everything. Her personality was merry, whimsical. She had imaginary friends, imaginary animals. When she started school, it had been hard for Alix to explain that possibly real friends could be just as entertaining and interesting. The real friends appeared, but the imaginary ones still flourished. Alix would hear Pammy talking to them in her room in her soft little voice, playing mother or sibling. Some of them had magic powers, could fly, could even go to school with her. But most of them waited for her to come home from school.

Luke had remarried three years after the divorce, a colleague whom he had known for years, a woman Alix's age with greying hair and an intense, scholarly look. She had never been married before. As divorces go, theirs had been amiable. They had divided possessions, not arguing about anything. It was as though they both felt that, if nothing else, they would preserve the good part of what was left of their relationship. It seemed to Alix they had gotten divorced when she had been in the hospital and that what happened afterwards was already set in place, preordained. If she had wanted the marriage to continue, she felt it could have, just as it had before. The feeling she got, running into Luke and his new wife at a concert at the Metropolitan Museum, was that he had moved into an identical marriage. Before going over to talk to them, she had watched them as they stood on line for the water fountain. They had that brother and sister quality, talking amiably, both looking a little distant, preoccupied.

She had been at the concert with a man she was seeing then, whom she no longer saw, a doctor who specialized in pediatric medicine. He was a little chubby man with greying hair, a few years her senior, who made her laugh and encouraged her all through the time she was trying to adopt a child. He had never married himself and said he loved children in the abstract, but the moment Pammy actually became a part of Alix's life, he had begun inventing excuses and had gradually ceased calling her. Single mothers Alix met in the park on weekends assured her that was common. "If it's not theirs, they don't want anything to do with it," one said. "They're jealous of whomever the father was, no matter what they say."

It was a world she wasn't familiar with, women who had dropped out of the work world because they could live on alimony, women with family money, women who were on welfare, even though they had college degrees. Before her divorce, all the women she had known were versions of herself, professionals either with or without children. She never had time to cultivate friendships outside work. Gerald had been her friend, Luke had been her friend. And now there was this world of women who partly accepted her simply because, in this one way at least, she was connected to them.

She still saw men, dated, even went on blind dates arranged by solicitous friends. But she saw that when she referred to Pammy, to having adopted a child on her own, the men's faces changed. They saw her as someone who could live without a man, who wasn't needy in the way they wanted. "It's admirable," some of them said. "But won't she need a father eventually?" Pammy seemed to view the men who came to pick up Alix at night with interest, but not as contenders for her mother's affection. Mainly, she was silent with them. She opened the presents they sometimes brought or listened to them describe their own children, but she always seemed relieved when Laurel came and took her off to have her bath or read her a bedtime story.

Before, living in the huge apartment with Luke, Alix had felt her life was almost excessively neat, defined, organized. Now she had two bedrooms; Laurel slept in the back in a tiny closet-sized room, occasionally bringing friends home at night. There was noise all the time: Laurel's stereo, Pammy singing or playing, and street noise, since they were on the ground floor of an apartment that faced the park. It was a different life. Alix's job was less prestigious, her salary a third smaller. She was no longer working on Wall Street, but at a firm that concerned itself with environmental matters; that part of the world seemed to have been cut off.

"Hi, sweetie," Alix said when she entered the nurse's office. "What's wrong?"

"I'm hot," Pammy said. She was not melodramatic, never had tantrums. When she was sick, she lay quietly, waiting for whatever it was to pass.

"How high is it?" Alix asked the nurse.

"One hundred and two," the nurse said. "I gave her some baby aspirin. Something seems to be going around. She'll probably have a sore throat by tomorrow. Keep her home till she's really better. Some of them come back too soon and have relapses."

"My throat's *not* sore," Pammy said clutching a bear made of corduroy that Laurel had sewn for her. It was the size of an apple and she liked to rub the small ears against the palm of her hand for comfort. Already one of the eyes had fallen off and the felt nose was ripped.

In the cab going home Alix said, "Should we fix your bear?" She noticed that even the ears were splitting.

"Fix?" Pammy leaned against Alix, her body warm and solid.

"He needs a new eye," Alix said, touching the spot where the button had fallen off.

"No, he doesn't," Pammy said. "He just needs one eye."

"How about a new nose?"

"No." She pressed the bear close to her. "He's perfect."

Sometimes she suddenly came up with new words like "perfect," which she used all the time, as though something about either the sound or the meaning appealed to her.

"*You're* perfect," Alix said, squeezing her.

But the little girl's eyes had closed; she was asleep.

When they arrived at the apartment house, Alix paid the driver and then scooped the child up in her arms. She seemed incredibly heavy, despite her diminutive size and, though still asleep, slung her arms around Alix's neck. Lately, she had begun talking about having a brother and a sister. Alix wondered if she could possibly manage that. She doubted it. She had never regretted her decision to adopt a child, but she felt as though her emotional life was as full as she could manage. When she looked ahead, she no longer saw a man appearing to "rescue" her. Nor was she filled with the embittered rage of some of the mothers she met in the playground who had horror stories about ex-husbands or ex-lovers. "You've had a sheltered life," one of them said contemptuously to Alix when she spoke of her life with Luke.

Had she? The time in the hospital was like a fiery inferno she had passed through. It had scarred her, but in ways that were invisible. She noticed things she hadn't before: not only ugly, violent stories in newspapers, but incidents at work or on the playground. And on the faces of some of the women who sat on benches, staring off into space, she saw herself at that time, trying to connect to a reality moving further away, becoming blurry. Once she tried to strike up a conversation with a woman like that who kept getting up and walking back and forth in a peculiar crooked line to the water fountain. "Are you okay?" she asked gently.

"What business is it of yours?" the woman demanded.

Closer up, Alix could see that the woman's arms were

scratched; Alix could imagine her dragging her nails along her skin at night, wanting to hurt herself, or maybe unable to connect to any emotion other than pain. "I just—" she began and then stopped. "I thought you might want someone to talk to." But the woman was already beginning her inexorable back and forth walk.

No matter what you were going through, was Laurel's contention, it seemed eighty percent, at least, of the people you met were going through the same thing. She said that when she realized she was gay, everyone she spoke to at college admitted they had come, within that very week or month, to the same realization, had spent the same years concealing it, felt the precise balance of pride and shame which seemed so peculiarly personal. Alix had seen that when she was trying to adopt Pammy. Even at work, half her clients confessed to long, arduous struggles to adopt babies, schemes tried and failed, hopes dashed when the birth mother changed her mind. Before her divorce, she knew only other married couples, both working: that was her world. Now most of the women she met were on their own, buoyant or defeated, but all seeing the world of the married as some peculiar little enclosed tribe.

No one has a sheltered life, Alix had realized. The very word was erroneous. Sheltered from what? Pain, the possibility of madness, death, disease, emotional breakdown? At best you were sheltered in one small way, by having sufficient economic resources or health or energy or a job you liked. But those things weren't shelters, just things you could cling to if everything else was on the verge of breaking down. She saw everyone, not only women and children, as more fragile.

By having lived through the time in the hospital, she had acquired both a knowledge of the horrors of the world and a knowledge of her own powers of survival. But through raising a child, feeling that kind of love, she saw herself as vulnerable all over again. Putting Pammy into bed, looking down at her feverish, pale face, she felt that aching twinge: *She must get better, promise me.*

By the next morning Pammy's fever was still high, though not hideous: one hundred and one. Laurel had no classes that day until evening. "I can handle it," she said. "She'll probably sleep most of the time. I'll call you if anything comes up."

"Would you?" Alix felt as though Laurel slid back and forth in her consciousness, becoming different people. At times she was like the older daughter Alix might have had, had she and Luke had children early in their marriage; at times, despite her being fifteen years younger, she was like a mother, solid and reassuring and unflappable. Mostly it seemed she was just there as a friend of a different generation, but occasionally a certain smile or way of talking would remind Alix of Pam. And she knew that to Laurel she was all of those same things: sometimes a mother, sometimes a friend, sometimes just someone to whom a blood connection existed through a person who was lost to them both. They talked about Pam occasionally. At first Alix hadn't wanted to. It was too painful, and she didn't want to hear any critical remarks Laurel might make about Pam as a mother. If Laurel started to criticize her, Alix became angry. Then, finally, that ceased, probably because Alix became a mother herself and saw the built-in imperfections of the role. At first both of them had nothing to do with Michael, wanting to punish him for remarrying. And then one evening he was in New York with his wife and they had him to dinner.

"She's so much like Mom, in the way she acts with him," Laurel said afterwards. "I can't get over it." "Do you think they're happy?" Alix asked. "As happy as Mom and Dad were, sure," Laurel said with a mixture of contemptuousness and acceptance.

At work that day Alix was preoccupied with thoughts of Pammy, but she had to conduct an interview in the morning. A position was open as secretary for the entire firm. Several of the lawyers had private secretaries, but someone was needed who could supervise the whole office. The week before she had seen four women, none of whom were spectacular, one of whom looked like she could do the job.

The woman who entered her office had grey-blonde hair parted in the middle. She looked Scandinavian and had a high-cheekboned face which had been ravaged by time, pale, uncertain looking blue eyes. Daphne Sonnenberg.

"You had been working at a law office?" Alix asked.

"Yes," Ms. Sonnenberg said. Her hands were woven together, reddened, the nails painted with colorless polish, a wedding ring on her left hand.

"I used to work in that building," Alix said.

The woman's face brightened. "So did my husband . . . Perhaps you knew him. Gerald Lehman?"

Alix started. "Why yes," she said. "Yes, we were in the same firm." A flash memory went through her head of the many times she used to pass Daphne Lehman's apartment house, almost pressing the bell. "He was very important to me at one time, like a mentor."

Daphne Lehman beamed. "Yes, he helped a great many people. I still wear my wedding ring because I feel, well, it's a way of keeping his memory alive . . . Did you know he was no longer living?"

"I had heard," Alix murmured.

They looked at each other and Alix wondered what the other woman was thinking. Gerald had been certain that Daphne had only suspected his affair with Giselle. She, Alix, was a nonexistent person in Daphne's life, perhaps. And yet Alix had spent so much time thinking about her, envying her for the early years, of knowing Gerald when he was young, when his health had been good, when he had been less cynical about the world, envying her for the children they had raised together.

"My children are grown now," Daphne said. "They're both out of college. Jon is in law school and Fiona is with the World Bank in Geneva. I have a grandchild, a little girl."

Normally if an interview had taken this direction, Alix would have cut it off at the pass, but instead she listened, fascinated. "You're lucky," she said. "Do you see her often?"

"Once a week. I adore her. She's the love of my life."

Impulsively Alix pulled out a photo of Pammy. "This is my daughter. I adopted her a few years ago."

"She's beautiful . . . I'm glad you had a child, after all."

What did that mean? "You mean that I waited?"

"Yes, well, you seem older than a mother of such a young child, that's all I meant," Daphne said.

"Right. I am. I was married a long time, but we never—" For some reason Alix broke off.

"Yes," Daphne said, though what she was agreeing to was unclear. "I know."

What did she know? About long marriages that seem like one thing and are really another? About sudden love late in life, for a small girl child? "Have you remarried?" Alix asked.

Daphne laughed self-deprecatingly. "Oh, no. At my age? Oh, I do have a man friend. He's fifteen years younger than me, and a lovely person. We go to plays, movies. I felt it wasn't fair, given the male-female ratio, to keep him all to myself so I introduced him to my best friend. We share him."

Her life seemed less blighted than Alix had imagined. "With this job," she said, "do you realize you'd be responsible for the entire office? So it requires certain management skills as well as secretarial ones. Do you feel you could manage that?"

"I could try," Daphne said. "I'm not that bossy a person. Do you need someone bossy?"

"No, not really, but someone who could make decisions, who wouldn't have to ask every time something new came up."

"I suppose you want someone with more experience," Daphne mused. "I've only been in the work world five years. After Gerald's death I became a bit of a recluse. The world scared me." Suddenly her expression changed, becoming almost hostile. "You probably wouldn't know about that."

"Yes, I do know about it," Alix said.

"You've always had a terrific job, you've been married, you've had it all. Not all of us are so fortunate."

Alix's heart was thumping. "No, that's true," she said. She was relieved Daphne Lehman was bolixing up the interview so totally. Clearly she hadn't the foggiest notion of how to apply for a job. Probably she'd gotten her first job because a friend of Gerald's had taken pity on her. *And I wouldn't want her around all the time anyway.* In whichever guise she adopted—the downtrodden ex-housewife or widow of the great man or ex-rival for a dead lover's affections. No, it was a relief to put her to one side. "Well," she said, "we still have quite a few applicants to see, but we'll get back to you." She stood up and shook Daphne Lehman's hand. "I'm glad to have finally gotten the chance to meet you. Gerald spoke of you often."

"I imagine," Daphne said wryly, or was it bitterly? It was hard for Alix to judge.

She had a quick break before the next interview and called home. For a long time there was no answer and she became alarmed. Did Laurel have to take Pammy to the doctor? Finally Laurel, breathless, got to the phone. "Where *were* you?" Alix cried.

"Giving her a bath," Laurel said.

"A bath! She has a fever!"

"A cool bath. Mom used to do that with us. It helps bring the fever down."

"But you—"

"I just splashed her off. Cool it, kid. You sound rattled. Anything wrong?"

"Oh no, yes. I'll tell you later." Alix hung up and tried to gather herself together for the next interview.

Taking a cab home at the end of the day she thought back on the interview with Daphne Lehman. Was she different from what I had expected? Gerald had said her beauty had faded, as it would with anyone in middle age. There was something more chunky and solid about her than Alix had expected. But what reminded her of herself, as she had been then, was that self-deprecating quality, undermining herself. *No, you were never that bad. You got over it . . .* And then the way she still wore the wedding ring. Here Pam had been dead less than a decade and Michael had not only remarried, but never referred to her, even when he was with Laurel and Alix. Her memory seemed to have been expunged. Alix thought of something Luke once said, after their divorce: "Neither death nor divorce ends a relationship."

At home she found Laurel asleep on the living room couch and Pammy playing in the corner, carrying on a quiet but animated conversation with her imaginary friends. They, too, died and reappeared. "Hi, Mommy," she said, not getting up. "Laurel's asleep. I got her worn out."

"I thought you were sick, hon," Alix said, rushing over, hugging her, holding her.

Pammy let herself be held, but then pulled away. "Laurel gave me a horrible cold bath. It was icy!"

"She wanted to bring your fever down, sweetie. You do feel a bit cooler."

"She never had a child," Pammy said. "Not even one." She looked at the sleeping Laurel whose arm hung over the sofa.

"Well, she's young," Alix said. "She's as much younger than me as you are younger than her, practically."

Pammy frowned. One ear peeked out from behind her hair. "She's younger than you?"

"Yes, she was my sister's daughter. I told you that once."

Pammy looked vague. "But where's your sister?"

"She died."

"Why?"

"She got hit by a tree. She was riding a horse."

"Oh." That seemed to satisfy Pammy. She only added, "Horses are too big," and returned to her playing.

When Laurel awoke it was almost seven. Alix had fed Pammy, who would only eat a bowl of strawberry ice cream, determined that her fever was down to one hundred, and read her one chapter of a book on moles. "God, I totally sacked out," Laurel said stretching. "I'm sorry. Is Pammy okay?"

"Fine. But I know how you feel."

"How do mothers survive whole days, whole weeks like this?" Laurel demanded.

"Search me," Alix said. "I never did it. But if you look at most of the ones at the playground, I'd say they barely do."

Laurel started setting the table. "I don't want kids ever, *ever*. I know this gay couple from college and they've gone the whole sperm bank, house in the country, picket fence route. I came back from visiting them and thought, shit, this is worse than marriage!"

"People like structure," Alix said, tossing the salad.

"Is that what kept you and Luke together so long?"

"Oh, not just that. We were in love. We loved each other. We could still be together."

"You always seemed—excuse me if this sounds rude—but kind of mousey and still when you were married to him. Both of you. I used to think of you like two mice. You were so neat and quiet."

"And now?" Alix said wryly.

"I don't know." Laurel yawned. "You're more scattered, I guess. You seem more like everyone else, like you don't really know what you want."

Alix carried the chicken casserole to the table, then returned for the rice. "What do *you* want?"

"To finish my master's first, I guess. And then a major passion." She grinned. "I know it sounds dopey, but yeah, I do. Is that allowed? I'm just twenty-two. I don't want some neat, creepy little paired off thing. I want all that messy gorgeous stuff you read about . . . Did you ever have that? Or don't you even want it?"

Alix sipped her wine. "I think I had it, as much as I ever will. I'm not sure you get it more than once, though."

At that remark Pammy came out of her bedroom. "You're eating," she said accusingly.

"Well, sweetie, you said you didn't want a real dinner. You only wanted ice cream before."

"Now I want some."

Though Alix suspected it was a ruse to stay up and be included in their conversation, she set her daughter a place.

"What do you not get more than once?" Pammy said, putting her head to one side.

Laurel stared at her. "Were you listening to our whole conversation?"

"Roger was listening. I was looking at my book on moles," Pammy said.

Alix looked over at her delicate face with the all-knowing soft eyes. "Perfect love," she said gently. "I'm not sure you get that more than once." But looking at Pammy, she felt she had gotten it again, as perfect a love as could exist in the real world, anyway. For the moment, it seemed all she would ever need or want.

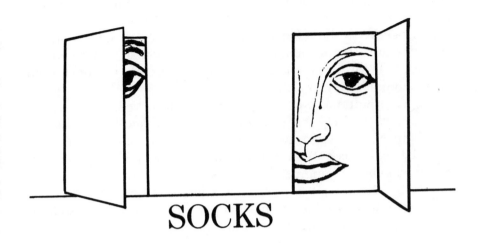

SOCKS

It was one of those days, when there were lulls of no business and then a flurry of customers who pushed impatiently forward, demanding attention. Noah had been working in the men's sock department at Bloomingdale's for almost five years; he was the senior salesman there, but still, at the times when bunches of officious customers gathered, clutching at his sleeve, he felt a kind of horror at being physically assaulted. What was their impatience about? Why was it so necessary that they buy socks that very instant, as though the socks were blood and their lives would go under without them?

"I was here first," one young woman insisted, pushing aside an older man who had a pile of socks in his hand.

"I'm terribly sorry," the man said in a slight English accent, "but I was standing off to one side. I've been standing there for ten minutes."

The young woman had spiky purple hair and heavily accented

eyes. "I was here before and came back. I went away to get my boyfriend a sweater. Doesn't the time I was here before count?" she asked Noah.

"I believe this gentleman was here first," Noah said, trying to be diplomatic. He looked around for the young man they had hired the month before who was always disappearing into the stockroom to smoke pot. "Harry?"

Harry sauntered out, looking glazed and bored.

"Could you help this young lady?" Noah asked him. "She was here before . . . " Then, turning to the man, he said, "Is this all?"

The man was still gazing with irritation at the purple-haired young woman. "Young people!" he said.

"Yes," Noah said vaguely. For a moment he thought of the young people he used to teach. That part of his life seemed so long ago, longer in time than his childhood or his early married years with Selma. In fact, most of it seemed to have been eradicated, perhaps by the series of shock treatments he had had in the hospital. He remembered only isolated moments, faces—the young student who named her child after him, the overweight, angry principal, the counseling director who used to put clippings on his desk. But the details of what he had taught, how he had taught, what it had been like to be a teacher were vague. Once a week he and Selma watched a sit-com called "Head of the Class" in which a sensitive humorous high school teacher became involved in varying ways with his students. Usually they just watched it, laughed at the jokes, then they would watch something else. But once Selma had said wistfully, "You were like that. You were that kind of teacher."

Noah had looked at her. "Was I?" He truly couldn't remember. He remembered feelings, that he had been idealistic, had convictions he had wanted to get across, but he couldn't remember about what. Another time there had been a commercial for condoms on TV and Selma had said, "Thank God they're finally doing that. Remember how many of your students used to get pregnant? It was terrible!"

Because he trusted Selma he knew the things she referred to had happened, that he probably had been a good teacher, probably had had pregnant young women in his class. But if she had said something totally different, it, too, would have seemed equally plausible: that he had been a terrible teacher, had been fired in disgrace, had made scenes, shouted. Once he had awoken from a terrible dream and asked Selma urgently if he had ever had experiences like those in the dream, of being held down, imprisoned. She had looked frightened and said no, it must have been a nightmare. In the beginning, after getting out of the hospital, the nightmares were so frequent he dreaded going to sleep at night. He would wake in the blackness of the bedroom, his heart beating so fast he was sure he was going to have a heart attack. He would stagger into the bathroom and sit there in the cold white light, just wanting to be able to see objects clearly. When he returned to bed, he would keep the bathroom light on and the door ajar so that the room would not be pitched into that terrifying darkness again. Eventually, he kept the light on every night, even now that the nightmares were less frequent.

When Selma was afraid he would forget something, she wrote it down on the small pocket calendar he always carried with him. He knew today was their anniversary, their twenty-fifth, and that they were meeting Leo and Eloise for lunch. When the customers had thinned, he asked Harry if he knew anything about the proper gift to get someone on a twenty-fifth wedding anniversary.

"Yeah, silver," Harry said. "Mom and Pop had a big shindig for their twenty-fifth. You know what I got them? An armadillo, spray-painted silver! You should have seen Pop's face." He loathed his father, a wealthy importer of sporting goods.

"It's my twenty-fifth anniversary," Noah said. He lifted up one of the socks that lay in front of him, a Gold Toe calf-length. "I'd like to get something for my wife, maybe jewelry."

Harry whistled. "Twenty-five years! Wow. God, I never had a relationship that lasted longer than twenty-five *days.*"

"You're young," Noah said. "Some day you'll meet the right girl."

"Yeah?" Harry shrugged. "I don't know if I want to especially, that's the thing. Doesn't it get on your nerves sometimes?"

"Doesn't what get on my nerves?" Noah asked.

"Well, you know, like making it with the same woman. No offense to your wife or anything, but I, like, need variety. Like that girl that was in here before?"

"The one with the purple hair?"

"Right. There was something really sexy about her. I know she'd drive me crazy after a week or two, but, boy, I'd love, like, a week. She wants to be a fashion designer. I told her I knew someone, gave her my card. I guess she's living with someone, but I can handle that."

Noah stared at the customers rushing from booth to booth. "My wife is the only person I've ever loved," he said. "I've been very lucky."

Harry raised his eyebrows. "Well, that's the way it is. Some guys like the same thing every day, even for breakfast, or, like, they wear the same underwear every day. But I need change. If I thought I'd work in *this* place all my life, I'd blow my fucking brains out."

"I didn't used to work here," Noah said.

"Where'd you work?"

"I was a high school teacher." He hoped it didn't sound boastful.

But Harry didn't seem to see it as very different from this job. "I slept through high school," he said.

"So did most of my students."

Half an hour before Selma was to come and pick him up, he slipped away to look at jewelry. There was a small lovely pin of a leaping dolphin. It was a little expensive, but he knew she liked animal pins. "I work here," he said, "I get a discount."

"Where's your card?" the salesgirl asked suspiciously.

"I don't have it with me. It's back in the sock department where I work."

"Well, go get it," she said.

"Can't you trust me?" Noah said. "I'm in a hurry."

She looked at him as if he was crazy. "Why should I trust you? I've never seen you before."

He rushed back to the sock department, found the card, hurried back and bought the pin. On his way back again, he ran into the store supervisor, Ms. August. "Where have you been, Mr. Epstein?" she asked. "It isn't your lunch break yet."

Noah tried to smile ingratiatingly. "It's my wife's—it's our twenty-fifth wedding anniversary. I was—I had to buy her a present."

Ms. August had thick, fuzzy eyebrows that seemed to run together into one irregular line across the middle of her face. "Do that on your own time!" she barked. "This is your *work* time."

"I will in the future," Noah said. She was right. He should have made a note of it, have thought of it the week before.

Selma showed up promptly at twelve, wearing a dark brown coat with a hood; her face had the sweetly anxious expression it almost always wore. They were meeting Leo and Eloise at La Caravelle at twelve-thirty. "Harry, this is my wife, Selma," Noah explained, feeling proud.

"Glad to meet you," Harry said. "Hear you guys are celebrating."

"Yes," Selma said softly. "Twenty-five years."

"Way to go," Harry said, raising his fist in a cheer.

They walked outside. It was November, a bitingly cold day. Selma looked at Noah anxiously. "You didn't wear your hat . . . or your gloves."

"I forgot."

She touched his coat. "I wish you'd get a warmer coat."

"This is fine." He hurried beside her, conscious that they would eat at an overly expensive restaurant, that he would look at the prices even though Leo would pay and could easily afford it. Restaurants like that made him nervous. He felt as though Leo, by taking them there, was flaunting the fact that he could afford such an occasion without giving it a moment's thought. In the years since Noah had come out of the hospital, Leo and Eloise had had their crises. Leo, after all his random fucking around, had fallen in love with the research assistant for one of his talk shows, a young woman who nurtured a desire to go to medical school. Leo had paid for her studies, planning, he told Noah, to leave Eloise the minute Janet finished her training. But when Janet met and fell in love with a fellow medical student, the whole plan dissolved. Noah had expected Leo to take it with his usual aplomb, but in fact, for over a year he went into a funk, said he thought life was meaningless, went from doctor to doctor hoping to find a "cure." When he emerged finally, he seemed chastened, quiet, almost humble, if that word had not seemed so incongruous in reference to Leo. "I came through," he would say, shrugging.

They were already at the restaurant. Eloise had dyed her hair coal black, though she still wore it in the same spiky helmet style. Recently she and a friend had expanded their design business; she traveled frequently to the Orient, buying materials. "Hi," she called. "The champagne is chilling. We're all set."

"I don't drink champagne," Noah said regretfully.

"Oh, have a glass, what the hell," Leo said, beckoning to the waiter.

"I can't . . . it wrecks my digestion."

Despite that, the waiter poured glasses for all of them and Leo proposed a toast. "To the two of you. To another twenty-five years together."

Selma's eyes were moist. "Thank you, Leo."

They ordered and in the time before their main course arrived Noah remembered the pin he had purchased. He took the tiny box out and placed it on Selma's plate. "For you," he said gently.

Carefully Selma unwrapped the box and opened it. "Oh," was all she said, frowning.

"Let's see," Leo said. "Show us."

Selma held up the pin.

"But you have one just like that," Eloise said. "Don't you? Or am I getting it mixed up?"

Selma hesitated. "Sort of like it, yes. But this is lovely, Noah."

"You have a pin of a dolphin?" he asked, crushed.

"Yes, I . . . but it doesn't matter. Really."

"You can wear them together," Eloise suggested. "Leaping in different directions."

"They're smarter than people, you know that?" Leo said, slathering butter on a chunk of bread. "That's what I heard, anyway."

How could I have done that? Bought the exact same pin? "Did *I* give you the other one?" Noah persisted.

"Yes," Selma said. She reached for his hand. "It doesn't matter, though. Really. I love it. I love animal pins."

"Yes," Noah said. "I thought you did." He watched as she took the pin out of the box and attached it to her suit.

As they were eating, a man passed by their table and clapped Leo on the back. "Hey, how's it going?" he said. "What's in the works?"

Leo introduced him. "This is Lester Morgan, my agent. Lester, you know my wife, and this is my brother, Noah, and his wife, Selma. We're celebrating their twenty-fifth wedding anniversary."

Like Harry at the store, Lester looked amazed. "Twenty-five? Two-five? That's something. I didn't know anyone our age had the stick-to-it-iveness to last that long. So, you're the professor, right?" he said to Noah.

"No," Noah said. He had ordered lamb and it lay on his plate looking too rare and bloody.

"I thought you had a brother who taught somewhere," Lester said looking down at Leo. "I guess I got it mixed up."

"I used to teach," Noah said. "In Brooklyn."

"Oh, where are you now?"

"Now I work in the sock department at Bloomingdale's."

Lester looked as though he wasn't sure if this was a joke or not. "Socks," he repeated. Then he grinned and said, "Nice to meet all you fine people. Call me, Leo."

When he had moved out of sight, Leo said to Noah, "Why did you say that?"

"Say what?"

"When he asked—" Leo began, but Eloise interrupted.

"This veal is really marvelous! So tender. I heard they changed chefs, but I must say I think this is up to their old standard."

Noah knew what Leo meant. He meant: Why did you humiliate me in front of someone I know by revealing you have such a nothing job? But he felt a certain perverse pleasure in doing that. It was no more nor less than the truth. Should he invent a job just to impress Leo's agent? The lamb looked more and more inedible as he gazed at it; he only picked at the vegetable. He was relieved when Eloise said she was going to the ladies room. "I'll go too," Selma said, getting up to follow her.

After they left, Leo's face sank into a brooding, vacant expression. Noah looked at him. "Anything wrong?"

"Christ, Janet sent me an invitation to her wedding today!" Leo said. "Can you *believe* that? She expects me to go to her wedding!"

"I guess she wanted to show there were no hard feelings," Noah said.

Leo broke apart a bread stick. "No hard feelings? I'd blow that guy she's marrying to kingdom come in one second. She was *my* girl, he *stole* her."

"Leo, you're *married*," Noah said softly. "He didn't *steal* her. She was available and he—"

Suddenly Leo turned on him savagely. "What the fuck do you know? I loved her, for Christ's sake. I was madly in love with her! I sunk a hundred thou into sending her to medical school. You don't even remember, I bet. Do you remember? Do you even remember who she was?"

"Of course I do," Noah said. "I'm not a nitwit."

Leo's face changed. He reached over and patted Noah. "I'm sorry. That was out of hand. I'm just—you're right. It's over. Other fish in the sea. Besides, with my heart condition, I should thank my lucky stars." But his eyes still had a black, hooded look.

The whole atmosphere of the supposed celebratory lunch seemed poisoned to Noah. He hated sitting there, eating overly rich food he didn't enjoy, raising a glass of champagne he had no desire to drink. *At least Leo's lived. He's done something with his life. He has a wife who's proud of him, kids.* Noah felt like a fool, actually buying Selma the same pin twice! A nut case, selling socks.

On the way back to the store, Selma noticed his change of mood. "It was too much," she said. "I hate those places. I always feel I'm eating with the wrong fork."

"I'm such a jerk," Noah said bitterly. "Giving you the same pin twice!"

"No," Selma said. "Not the same. It was just another pin of a dolphin. I love it, Noah, really."

"It's pure silver," he said, allowing himself to be won over. "Everything else seemed so heavy."

She was holding his arm. "You know my taste," she said. "So many men—they just give their wives a check. 'Buy whatever you want.' They don't even care."

He had never told Selma about Janet and so now couldn't tell her about the wedding invitation, Leo's violent reaction, when she said, "I hope Leo's taking care of his health. Toward the end of the meal he looked so strange, somehow."

"I think he was angry when I told his agent I sold socks at Bloomingdale's," Noah said. "Humiliated to have such a washout as a brother."

Selma's face tightened. "That's so stupid," she cried, "judging people by outward things! It's who you are that counts, not what you do."

Only she could say banal things like that and make them sound totally genuine, as though she believed them from the depths of her heart. "I do miss teaching sometimes," Noah admitted. Already it was growing dark, though it was just early afternoon.

"You were a wonderful teacher," she said.

After he had emerged from the hospital, the doctors advised them that teaching would be too stressful, that if he went back to a job that had highs as well as lows, Noah could be in danger again. "Let him do something that isn't taxing, something simple. Otherwise we can't take responsibility for what may happen." Noah had found this note about his "condition" among Selma's papers once. It had referred to him as someone with "paranoid schizophrenic tendencies" which were incurable. Reading the jargon-filled letter, he had felt both horrified, to see himself labeled, dismissed, and spoken of so harshly, and saddened for Selma who, despite all his experiences at the hospital, still maintained a kind of faith in the doctors. "They did their best," she would say. Noah felt that he had been chewed up like a piece of meat and then spewed forth, pulpy, tissueless. *I let it happen.* He had never blamed Selma for forcing him to return to the hospital. Only sometimes he recalled that moment of standing on the fire escape with his whole family in the kitchen, screaming. *I could have jumped, maybe I should have.*

But more days than not he was glad he had not jumped. Selma's life was interwoven with his. Her love for him might be neither sensible nor reasonable, but had he jumped, he would have taken part of her with him. What her life could have been with another man, the children she might have had, the anxieties she might have been spared, seemed not to concern her, or if they did, she never spoke of them. When she received a questionnaire from her college about how her life had turned out, compared to what she had expected, she had written, "I had no fantasies. My life is what I want it to be."

He wished he could have said the same for himself. Selma seemed able to live in the present, to accept it, while he was always adrift in the past, in the chances he had let go by, the mistakes he had made, the person he might have been. His envy for Leo had lessened. His life no longer seemed so gleaming, so brilliant. Remembering the black, vacant stare in Leo's eyes at the restaurant Noah knew he, too, had a sense of things he had desperately wanted that had, mysteriously, eluded him, despite fame, money, successful children.

Hurrying into Bloomingdale's, Noah caught Ms. August glancing his way. He was ten minutes late. He could see her torn between a desire to go over and reprimand him and some other thought. Then someone tapped her on the shoulder and she was forced to step away.

Several customers were lined up. Harry was taking care of one of them, a businessman in a fur hat who was trying to conceal a cigarette. An elderly woman stood to one side, next to a younger woman with dark hair who was busy with her child. The child was small, she looked to be only five or six and was playing a kind of game with the socks on display. She had moved them into piles, according to color, and was singing quietly to herself, "Red toe, blue toe, pink, purple toe, yellow toe, all in the sink."

Noah sighed. He knew it would take a long time to put all the socks back in the right size groups. The mother said, "These are pretty, aren't they?" and the little girl said, "Yes! Buy these!"

Few people wanted the brightly colored socks. Most men bought brown or grey or black. Occasionally women came in and bought the brighter colors for their boyfriends and then were back the following week to exchange them. Noah turned to the two women. "Who was first?"

"I think she was," the younger woman said.

The elderly woman took a long time trying to decide what color would go with her husband's suit. "It's sort of grey," she mumbled, "but with a touch of green . . . Do you have anything like that? More grey than these, but more green than these."

After he brought out box after box, she finally bought one pair of socks. Then Noah turned to the younger woman whose daughter was still singing to herself. "Can I help you?"

The woman looked at him. She had pale skin, cheeks flushed from the cold, and dark eyes that seemed familiar. Something inside him shrank and was excited simultaneously. "Noah?" she said softly.

"Yes?"

"It's me, Alix Zimmer. Do you remember? From the hospital."

He could have pretended he didn't remember, but a flood of memories rushed at him: Alix sitting with him while the other patients bowled, their going to the coffee shop and her saying suddenly, "Let's run off together," her placing her hand on his shoulder: "Take care." "Yes," he said, almost in a whisper. "I remember."

This was something he had been frightened of for years, that he would run into someone from the hospital. At times he saw men walking down the street who reminded him of Dr. Stern, short, stocky, bearded men with grim, relentless expressions. When Bloomingdale's had asked if he had had any health problems he had said no because Leo and Selma had assured him he would never get a job with it on his record. No one knew; he never spoke of it here. "This is wonderful to see you," Alix said in that bright, intense way she had. "I've thought of you so often. How are you? How is your life?"

"Everything's fine," Noah said guardedly.

"I was so terrified that they might give you shock treatment," Alix went on. "Did they?"

Noah felt his knees were about to buckle under him. "No, no, they didn't," he said.

"You know, since I've been out I've joined an organization that's investigating a lot of the awful things that go on at mental hospitals. Did you know that in California they're trying to pass a law saying it's illegal to give people shock treatment against their will? If it's passed, it will be such a triumph."

It seemed to Noah her voice was rising in excitement as she spoke of this. He thought he saw Harry turn and stare curiously at her. "Is this your daughter?" he said, to change the subject.

"Yes, isn't she wonderful?" Alix's face lit up. "I adopted her. She's the love of my life." After a moment she added, "My husband and I are no longer together. He's remarried, in fact."

"I'm sorry," Noah said.

"No, no, don't be," Alix said. "Our marriage ended, really, in the hospital, perhaps long before that. It was moribund. How about you?"

"Selma and I are still together," Noah said proudly. "Today's our twenty-fifth wedding anniversary."

"I'm so glad," Alix said. She gazed at him just as she used to in the hospital, with that gleam of sympathy and pleasure in his company. "Look, I really only need five pairs of these grey socks."

"Buy *these!*" her daughter said, holding up a bright orange pair.

Alix laughed. "Okay, what the heck, I'll take these too. A bit gaudy. But listen, would you like to come to this group I mentioned, the one for former mental patients? I'll give you the address and phone."

Panicked, Noah murmured, "Let me check to see if we have any of these in the stockroom." He rushed away. Surely Ms. August would come over or perhaps had overheard already. He would lose his job, he would have nothing. *No, don't be silly.* He tried to calm himself, but none of it worked. Standing in the dark stockroom, he was overwhelmed by hideous memories of the hospital, feelings that he had repressed in the years since he had left. The memories came at him, one after the other, until he was afraid he might let out a scream. Then Harry came up to him. "Hey," he said, "there's a lady out there who says you were going to get some socks for her. Can't you find them?"

Noah couldn't speak; he was sure he was going to faint.

"Are you okay?" Harry said. "What's wrong?"

Breathing heavily, Noah said, "I feel a little . . . Harry, could you do me a tremendous favor? Could you wait on her? I'll be out in a few minutes."

"Sure thing," Harry said. "Go get a glass of water. That'll help."

Noah went to the small bathroom in the back and remained there for exactly five minutes. Then he moved close to the door leading to the counter. He listened to see if he could hear either Alix's voice or the singsong chanting of her child. He heard neither. Timorously, he emerged. As he did, he saw her red coat disappearing out the door. She was holding her child by the hand, carrying a bag.

"Can I help you?" he said, turning to the group of faces in front of him.